"SINFU

Unlike her two sisters who followed their dreams to the altar, Kathryn Bright Goodale doesn't want to be a bride.

What she *needs* is to win the Grand Centennial Race now that her late husband has left her penniless. So Kate reluctantly turns to the famous adventurer Lord James Bennett for help. But once, long ago, James stole from her a lingering, forbidden, and unforgettable kiss. And now the lady wants the incorrigible rogue to stick strictly to business—and is troubled that she may not be able to resist him if he does not.

James, too, can never forget that wild, passionate moment in Kate's garden, and he's certain the rigors of a far-reaching adventure will be too much for her. But the fetching young widow surprises him with her bold determination and a courage that compliments her breathtaking sensuality. Might Lord James be competing for a more elusive, yet far more valuable, prize: the hand and heart of Kathryn Bright Goodale?

"Law writes about love with joy and passion."
Tanya Anne Crosby

Other Avon Romantic Treasures by
Susan Kay Law

If You've Enjoyed This Book,
Be Sure to Read These Other
AVON ROMANTIC TREASURES

Coming Soon

ATTENTION: ORGANIZATIONS AND CORPORATIONS
Most Avon Books paperbacks are available at special quantity
discounts for bulk purchases for sales promotions, premiums, or
fund-raising. For information, please call or write:

Special Markets Department, HarperCollins Publishers, Inc.,
10 East 53rd Street, New York, N.Y. 10022–5299.
Telephone: (212) 207–7528. Fax: (212) 207-7222.

SUSAN KAY LAW

A WEDDING STORY

An Avon Romantic Treasure

AVON BOOKS
An Imprint of HarperCollinsPublishers

This is a work of fiction. Names, characters, places, and incidents are products of the author's imagination or are used fictitiously and are not to be construed as real. Any resemblance to actual events, locales, organizations, or persons, living or dead, is entirely coincidental.

AVON BOOKS
An Imprint of HarperCollins*Publishers*
10 East 53rd Street
New York, New York 10022-5299

Copyright © 2003 by Susan Kay Law
ISBN: 0-06-052518-5
www.avonromance.com

All rights reserved. No part of this book may be used or reproduced in any manner whatsoever without written permission, except in the case of brief quotations embodied in critical articles and reviews. For information address Avon Books, an Imprint of HarperCollins Publishers.

First Avon Books paperback printing: October 2003

Avon Trademark Reg. U.S. Pat. Off. and in Other Countries, Marca Registrada, Hecho en U.S.A.
HarperCollins® is a registered trademark of HarperCollins Publishers Inc.

Printed in the U.S.A.

10 9 8 7 6 5 4 3 2 1

If you purchased this book without a cover, you should be aware that this book is stolen property. It was reported as "unsold and destroyed" to the publisher, and neither the author nor the publisher has received any payment for this "stripped book."

*My deepest thanks to the ladies of
Camp Wannabeawriter, Minnesota edition:*

*Connie Brockway
Geralyn Dawson
Christina Dodd
Susan Sizemore*

*I can't remember who made which suggestions,
but the book wouldn't have been
nearly as good without you.
Not to mention a lot less fun.*

Chapter 1

August 28, 1899

*B*attle preparations . . .

Were she a man, she might have checked the loading of her pistol one more time, held it out with one eye narrowed along the barrel. Or she'd have drawn her sword from its sheath and watched the light shear down the keen edge of the blade before swishing it through the air to reacquaint herself with its weight. Perhaps bounced on her toes once or twice like a boxing champion finding his balance.

But she was Kathryn Virginia Bright Goodale, and so, in the silent, lush hallway of the Waldorf-Astoria, she leaned closer to a mirror framed in elaborate gold and inspected herself with ruthless precision. She pinched fresh color into her cheeks and bit red into her lips.

Will it do? she wondered. Twelve years . . . She'd held up well, she judged. Kate didn't believe in false modesty, particularly when one could not afford it. Would he look at her and see a mature and blossoming woman or immediately note the fading of that glowing girl that had perhaps only existed for one brief moment, for him?

But delaying never solved anything. She'd little enough time as it was. And so she made one final adjustment—this, to the neckline from which she'd shaved a full inch for just this occasion—and turned her smile up to full brightness.

The door was a thick gleaming slab of rosewood; the sharp report of her knuckles against it, satisfyingly authoritative. She must not give the impression that she came in supplication . . . even though that veered uncomfortably close to the truth.

"Come on in." The voice was muffled through the door, low and hoarse, and her heart pounded harder than the echo of her knock. *Nothing ventured* . . .

"You coming in or not? Because I'd rather not get up."

Well, she hadn't sought him out for his manners, had she? Though he'd certainly owned them once; she recalled a handsome bow, an elegantly correct kiss of her foolishly trembling fingers.

She pushed open the door, stepped through in a hiss of expensive silk, and forgot how to breathe.

She'd been so busy worrying about how he'd view the changes in her that she'd never considered that he'd have changed, too. He'd remained constant in her memory, handsome and brash and so vibrantly alive the air had seemed to hum around him. A perfect reminiscence, one she'd no right to claim but had cherished just the same.

His skin had darkened. His hair, too, from light, sun-streaked brown to something richer and darker and far more interesting. His shoulders, clad in the thin silk of a burgundy robe, were broader. He sat sprawled in a chair, contemplating the half-filled glass in his hand, the gaping front of the robe exposing a long length of hairy, muscular leg and far too much chest for any healthy woman's composure.

"Put the towels down anywhere." Years of travel had roughened the edges of his aristocratic British accent but never eliminated it entirely, an odd contrast with the informality of his grammar.

"I—" She'd practiced her speeches, all the arguments she'd suspected she'd need. And they'd all fled the instant she stepped into the room.

"Huh." Eyes that were more than a shade blurry focused on the hem of her skirt. "Guess you're not the maid."

That put genuine warmth into her careful smile. "I most certainly am not."

He made no move to get up, just traced his gaze slowly up her until he paused at her chest. He grinned, lazy, seductive. "Heard this place had the best service in the city, but I certainly underestimated it."

And then he looked up, into her face at last, and every trace of boozy warmth disappeared from his expression. Hooded eyes, set mouth, all emotions carefully blanked away, the expression he'd worn the last time she'd seen him. Just before she'd walked away.

He set his drink aside, taking more care than the task required to place it square in the center of the tiny carved table at his elbow. Was he that soused? She hadn't considered him a drinker but a lot could change in twelve years. A lot *had* changed.

"Starting early this morning, aren't you?" she asked. She meant her comment to be light, nothing more than conversational—and winced when it came out sounding like an accusation.

"It's never too early," he said, in a tone that implied he'd have started a whole lot sooner if he'd suspected who would show up at his door. He pushed himself out of his chair with far less concern for the gap in his robe than Kate would have preferred.

His steps were slow, a bare saunter, yet they ate up the space between them with disconcerting speed until he towered over her, her nose level with his— *bare!*—breastbone.

She couldn't look up at him, so she studied the room instead. It was as lush and rich as the hotel lobby had promised, gleaming in shades of blue and gold and cream. It was an awful mess, three mismatched socks strewn over the Aubusson carpet, a crumpled khaki jacket tossed over the back of a chair, a clutter of glinting rock specimens and poor, stuffed creatures strewn across a fine tabletop. The bed was in worse shape, a riotous twist of sheets and blankets that gave testament to one sort of wild night or another.

"Mrs. Goodale," he said, so formal and stiff and suddenly British that he could have been another man than the warmly tipsy, casual one who'd spoken before he'd realized her identity, "I am sorry about your husband."

"I know that."

He was perhaps more sorry about her husband's death than anyone else on earth. "I would not have missed the . . ." He paused, cleared his throat. "I was in Greenland. I did not receive word until long after—"

"I understand"—then, because it was the truth—"and so would he."

"Good."

She'd have to look at him sooner or later, finally worked up the courage only to find that he was apparently no more eager to meet her eyes: His gaze focused over the top of her head. All Kate could see was the bold jut of his jaw bristling with at least a day's growth of dense beard.

"Then, with the formalities done, you can go away."

Well, she hadn't thought it would be easy, had she? "Lord Bennett—"

"Lord? Oh, please. You can do better than that."

She tamped down a spurt of irritation. "I was attempting to be polite."

"And when have you ever known me to appreciate politeness?"

"People change."

"Do they?" he murmured, and then he looked fully at her at last.

It made her suddenly realize just how close they stood; so near, a half step would bring their bodies together. She would have jumped back if that movement wouldn't have taken her out of the room—for she suspected that the instant she did so he'd slam the door in her face.

"Not that I've noticed," he finished.

"Now, why doesn't that sound like a compliment?" replied Kate.

"I can't imagine."

She could leave at any time, she reminded herself. Walk away and do . . . something. The fact that she'd no idea *what* didn't have to be a deterrent. But she'd never been one to wander off a path once she'd set her feet upon it. "May I come in?"

It hovered in the air between them—the *no* she knew he wanted to snap out. "Please, Jim?" She used the name deliberately, reminding him that she was not a stranger.

He sighed and stepped aside, a gesture to allow entrance. Her skirt brushed his bare leg and hissed as she passed, soft as surrender.

"May I sit?"

"I'd rather you didn't."

She swept aside a long striped scarf and crushed black bowler from an armchair upholstered in royal blue plush, and fluffed her skirts as she settled into it.

"Why did you bother to ask?"

"I always attempt the easy way first," she told him.

Not bothering to remove a pair of black leather gloves on the seat, he dropped into the nearest chair.

Kate had been married for nearly fifteen years; she was not an innocent young woman, terrified and fascinated by a man's body.

It took every ounce of determination she'd ever owned not to flee the room in embarrassment. "If you'd like to get dressed—"

"My less-than-correct attire isn't disturbing me if it's not disturbing you."

Pride left her no other answer. "Of course not."

"Glad to hear it." He sprawled back, by all appearances completely at ease, so big and male she could scarcely breathe. How could she have forgotten? How could she have believed that somehow in all these years he might have . . . aged, muted, diminished? Instead he'd become even more overwhelming.

But she was no longer young, foolish and easily impressed, she reminded herself. And if she'd failed utterly to handle him years ago, well, this time would be very different.

If only she could dredge up the right words.

"Wandering around the halls of a hotel unescorted, Mrs. Goodale? Not to mention slipping into the hotel room of a notorious adventurer." He shook his head. "Quite a risk to your reputation, isn't it?"

"I was supremely careful."

"You always are, aren't you?"

Except once. Once, which had been both the biggest and sweetest mistake she'd ever made. The memory bloomed over her, a memory she allowed herself to pull out and savor so very rarely, in case she'd become too tempted by it. A memory she indulged in only at the most difficult moments of her life, when she needed its consolation the most.

The scent of roses, the heavy, sultry air of late summer. The silver radiance of moonlight frothing through the intricate gingerbread of the gazebo. That hollow, empty ache for all she'd surrendered, an ache she'd almost always managed to subdue but which had seized her viciously that night, driving her out of her husband's party. And the young man who stepped out of the garden like he'd been conjured from her dreams, everything she'd never known, could never hope to know, and that brief moment of surrender to fantasy.

* * *

Enough! Only a fool did not learn from her mistakes. "I need to speak to you."

"You've been here five minutes and haven't said anything worth hearing yet."

"After the doctor's death, I—"

"The lawyers found me. You don't have to do this. I know he left me his maps, the books." She kept looking for a flicker of emotion in him, finding none. Had he always been so dispassionate? Had she imagined, then, the empathy and warmth she'd once seen in his eyes?

"There was a letter—"

"Oh, for God's sake!" He sprang up, coming back to his feet in a flash of bare legs, as if the chair couldn't contain him any longer. But he'd never been one to settle in one place; every time the doctor heard from him, he was in another country, embroiled in another quest. Kate would never admit it to anyone, but she used to pull out the atlas every time a letter arrived— driven by a curiosity she found both embarrassing and surprising— to find the exact spot on the map where he'd last reported himself. "Don't do this, Kate. I got the letter, the lawyers will hold the papers for me, so don't pretend you've anything from the Doc to give me." His mouth thinned into a sneer. "What is it? Or is it simply that you've come to conclude unfinished business?" His gaze, blatantly sexual, slid down. "I suppose I should be flattered, after all this time."

"Don't be." She snapped to her feet, jerking her skirts into place. "Believe me, you've *nothing* to be flattered about in that regard."

"Oh, really?"

"Yes, really." She wished she could climb on the chair to meet him nose to nose. "You know, you really don't wear this constant anger well. For some reason I thought you'd have outgrown it by now. Most young men do when they mature." He was not the only one who could sweep someone with a contemptuous gaze, she thought with some satisfaction.

"This is absurd," she went on. This . . . *this* was what she'd cherished all these years? How disappointing. She had no idea there was so much of the sentimental fool in her. "I've no idea why I ever considered for so much as an instant that this might work."

He was quicker than she, stepping in front of the door and facing her before she could sweep through it, denying her the grand exit.

"Move aside, please."

"That *what* might work?"

"Oh, *now* you're interested?"

"Interested? No." He inclined his head. "Call it curious, maybe."

"Yes, I do believe you are quite . . . curious."

Stalemate. Kate, ready to spring out the door should he give her the slightest opening. Jim, as impenetrable and implacable as a palace guard, thoroughly blocking her way.

Let her go. Even as his brain commanded his body, Jim couldn't seem to step aside. Letting her walk out that door for another twelve years would be the wisest move he could make. But he'd spent more years than he liked to remember with questions nagging him. This time, he'd have enough answers to finally put her to rest. And that was the only reason he kept her here, he told himself. And thought that maybe it was even true.

He reached behind and shut the door. "Wouldn't want anyone to wander by and see you here," he told her. "And I *am* curious. How did you find me?"

She relaxed a little. The set of her shoulders softened in their sheath of periwinkle silk; the line of her mouth curved up. Good. Perhaps if she were not so rigidly on guard he'd even pry the truth from her this time.

"Oh, that was hardly difficult. 'The famous Lord James Bennett, discoverer, adventurer, Arctic survivor.'" She quoted directly from the hotel's flyer. They'd sent it out before he'd had a chance to stop them, and he'd damn near gagged at it. He was everlastingly glad he missed ninety percent of what was written about him.

"'Scintillating stories of bravery, daring, and conquest from the most dashing explorer of our generation.'" She tucked her tongue firmly in her cheek, mischief lighting her eyes in a thoroughly attractive way. "Have they not heard of Sir Stanley, do you suppose?"

And then the attraction hit him like a sucker punch, sending his breath out, making him take a quick step aside in hopes of escaping the reach of her allure.

"'Lord Bennett, the famed explorer—'"

He snorted. *Lord* Bennett. He was not a Lord, merely an Honorable, a distinction that seemed lost on Americans, and a title he'd abandoned when he quit England, in any case. But he'd given up protesting a dozen years ago. The Americans, for all their egalitarian ideals, did love a title; and as long as that upgrade in status kept them flocking to his lectures and snatching up his books, why should he care?

"Don't you want to know what they write about you?" she asked. "Oh, I should have realized. You've memorized every word already?"

He would not smile at her, and felt the pull of it. The corner of his mouth twitched. She was dangerous enough when he was furious at her—and the mere fact that some anger still simmered when it should have faded to cinders long ago warned him how much—but there was no accounting what he might do if she could get him to smile at her. Didn't he know by now how she worked? A little softening was merely the first step on the way to surrender.

"How'd you find my room?"

She didn't even have the grace to look embarrassed. "That nice young desk clerk is most accommodating."

"Of course." He doubted there was a man in the place who could hold out against her charms if she was determined to wield them. Well, he'd just have to be the exception. "What do you want, Kate?"

It stopped her cold. The serene confidence she wore like a tiara gave way to a flutter of panic, quickly masked.

"Now there's a question," she murmured. "I wish I knew."

She could be doing it on purpose. The faint, plaintive note in her voice, the shadow of uncertainty in her brilliant eyes, could be as calculated an effect as the flirtatious smile she'd undoubtedly bent on that poor desk clerk.

And then that moment ended. She collected herself in a wink, her shoulders square and firm, chin set at a sharp angle, as if that instant of vulnerability had never existed.

"I beg your apologies for disturbing you. I thought

that—well, it does not matter what I thought, does it? I was wrong. If you'll step aside, we can both forget that this ever happened."

Forget? Where she was concerned, he'd never managed that nearly as well as he'd wanted.

So he stayed where he was, his eyes level on hers. Hers were brilliant blue and utterly cool, and he looked into them to remind himself of the truth. A man could scarcely look at her, all lush curves and gleaming hair and inviting smiles, without his brain getting all snarled up with baser urges. But her eyes betrayed her essential unavailability. She was not a woman there for the taking, or the giving. Not for him, and not for anyone.

"It was a foolish idea," she said. "Born of grief, if you will. But since you clearly will not let me go until you hear of my fancy, I'll confess it and be done. You have heard of the Great Centennial Race?"

His hesitation was brief. "Yes." But not brief enough.

"Oh." She smiled, wryly amused at her own foolishness. "Of course you have. You must have received an invitation as well."

"No," he said, wondering at the stray impulse that caused him to mouth the slight lie to protect her feelings. She was as unlikely to truly have them as he was prone to shield them. "Doc got one, did he? Surprised. He hasn't been out in the field for ages."

"They'd hoped to lure him back. Wrote an immensely flattering letter about how the slate of contestants would be incomplete without his presence." A bit of color had come back to her pale cheeks, a hint of life into her guarded expression.

"He would have liked that."

"Yes," she said softly. "He would have. But the letter came after he passed. It seemed a pity to let the opportunity go to waste, though."

"You intend to take his place?" he said, incredulity leaking through before he thought to stop it.

Her chin came up, a small, gallant gesture that somehow made her look vulnerable instead of brave. He wondered if she knew that, if she'd sought that effect. "There is no requirement that the invitation be used solely by the one for whom it was originally issued."

He laughed. He couldn't help it. And if that chin climbed any higher it was going to approach vertical. "Forgive me. I just . . . unless you've had some extraordinary transformation since the last time we met—and I must say you've shown no signs of it so far—I just can't quite picture you dashing madly around the world, scaling mountains, or creeping through caverns or whatever else they come up with, besting experienced adventures in search of . . . what the hell are they in search of, anyway?"

"Fifty thousand dollars," she said briskly, "for the first person who can finish before New Year's, or the prize will be forfeited."

"And you figured you'd win?"

"That," she said, "was where you come in."

Chapter 2

"**I** am not so unwise," she went on when he hadn't managed to dredge up a worthy answer—shock did that to a fellow, "as to think that I could do this alone. While I do have certain contacts, a number of useful skills"—she ignored his snort of disbelief—"and I have full confidence in my abilities to decipher the clues along the way, they are most mysterious about exactly where we might be headed. If it is to more exotic climes, well, I would be somewhat at a disadvantage without . . ."

She trailed off delicately. He had no such compunctions.

"Without me."

Color bloomed, a pale blush along the fine curve of her cheekbones, pretty as a just-budded rose. It was almost unfair, he thought, for her to have been so blessed. Unfair to women less favored, unfair to the men who had to look at her and not tumble into a dazed stupor.

"Why in God's name would you want to attempt this?"

He had to give her credit; he expected a clever prevarication, a lighthearted deflection. "I need the money," she stated baldly. "Or rather, I'd like the money a great deal. I would not oversell it. But I'd make a terrible governess, an unlikely companion, and going into trade requires more resources than I currently own." And then, more heated, "and I will *not* impose upon my sisters. The unmarried aunt, back and forth between the two, dependent and tolerated and forever just slightly in the way, however fond of me they might be." She shuddered. "I will *not*."

He did not want to find any common ground with her. It was there just the same; he could not stand dependency any more than she could. It was one of the reasons he'd fled England just past his sixteenth birthday.

"Surely the doctor left you better off than that." *Please, Lord, be merciful.* Doc *had* to have left her something. "If nothing else, your clothes and jewels would keep you for years."

"The jewels went to Norine," she said, in a tone that brooked no pity. "As we'd agreed from the very start. And everything else went to his children as well. The clothes are mine, but those would bring enough for a few years at most." She waved her hand as if to dismiss the problem. "Please, it is hardly a disaster. I am yet young enough and strong enough to work as seamstress or shopgirl if it comes to that. I would prefer that it did not."

"Christ." And damn, and damn. A promise barely remembered raised its dragon head, eager to bite. "I know that . . . he mentioned to me that he'd promised Elaine before she died that if he remarried all he owned would be protected for their children. But I figured after all these years . . ."

"All those years changed nothing. We had an agreement. Neither the doctor nor I am one to alter such," she said briskly. "If you agree to join the venture, you can be certain of that much at least—that I will adhere resolutely and minutely to whatever terms we lay down."

He had to think. And his brain didn't function properly when she was a mere foot from him. He turned away. Away from the sight of her, from the sweet feminine scent that he just now recognized had been clouding his brain since the start, and paced, until he came up against a chair, the room suffocatingly close. He'd considered the accommodations more than large enough until now.

"Why would you ever think that I'd be interested in throwing in with *you*?"

She blanched, her face betraying a discomfort it rarely exposed. "The adventure of it?"

He felt the trap closing in and tried one last time to squeeze out. If he wasn't expert at getting out of tight spots, he wouldn't have lived this long. "Not to burst any bubbles, Mrs. Goodale, but I don't need *you* for an adventure."

"All right, then," she snapped. "I assumed your reasons would be no different than mine."

"Really?" He glanced around at the luxury of his suite. "Does this look like I need the money?"

"Did you think I'd do no research? This room comes with the lecture engagement."

"I see." He frowned. "The desk clerk again?"

Her silence gave him his answer. "Resourceful, aren't you?"

"Resourceful enough to partner with?"

But he couldn't make it that easy. "Try again," he advised.

"All right, then," she said, with enough heat behind it to remind him that, behind her detached manner, the woman carried a lot more emotion than one would have thought. Either that, or she faked it really, really well. He'd never decided exactly which, and it'd be dangerous to set himself to solving the mystery. Dangerous, and dangerously tempting.

"I admitted my circumstances easily enough. But God forbid honesty should slap up against male pride. It loses every time. But really, haven't you read the papers? It's common knowledge that after your misadventure in the Arctic—" She caught a glimpse of his expression and bit off the words immediately. "I didn't mean—"

"Yes, you did," he said, stepping close enough that she backed away, toward the hard, flat door, until her backbone pressed against it. She wished the wood had some give—anything that would allow one more precious inch of space between them. He took up more than his share of room, more than his share of air.

She'd remembered him as a charming young man, handsome and laughing and vibrant with life. Irresistible. Had this prickly man with the bitter and dangerous edge always been there, only she'd been too

young and dazzled to recognize it? Or was it something that had taken him over in the years since, a
malevolent rot that putrefied all the joy in him into
something darker?

"Just let me go. I've obviously made a misjudgment
in coming here. I thought this could be simpler than is
obviously possible for you, and so I—"

"Possible for me?" His gaze drifted down, fasten-
ing somewhere at the base of her neck, and she felt
her pulsebeat flutter there, panicked and wild. He
seemed as likely to wring her neck as kiss it.

"I've been thinking," he murmured lightly, as if
merely musing over a menu choice, "that, in coming
here and asking for my help, you have perhaps swallowed some of that pride you wore so well. But
you've retained every shred, and gained more if you
believe that the mere presence of *you* in this proposition complicates things for me."

She eyed him warily. His head remained bent, as if
he counted each heartbeat, and she wished to blazes
she'd thought to bring a shawl. His lids shielded his
eyes from her view. She saw only the dense semicircle
of his lashes, shades darker than his hair, near-mink,
and the severe jut of his cheekbone. The angles had
grown sharper; any soft and friendly handsomeness
he'd worn as a young man had been worn away in
jungles and glaciers, scoured down by wind and sun
and hardship.

"You're not wearing mourning," he said, flicking a
flutter of lace at the top of her sleeve.

"No," she answered on a thready breath. "You know
the doctor had limited patience for what he considered
the artificial constructs of society. I thought that he
would rather I not . . ."

"Pretend?"

She flushed. "Yes."

"I wonder," he said, "just how badly you want this venture to proceed. You've no chance without me." He looked up then, and she felt his gaze like a physical thing, piercing sharp, sinking deep. "You know that, don't you?"

"Alone, perhaps not. But without you doesn't necessarily mean alone."

"Ah, but you want to win. What's the point otherwise? You need me."

"You're making too much of this," she said, too flat, not nearly convincing enough.

"Am I?" He exhaled, and she could feel the hot wash of his breath. "I wonder."

"Don't."

"Don't wonder? Ah, but I do. It is my curse, you see, curiosity. And now I find myself wondering . . . just what would you do to secure my agreement?"

Her throat was tight. "We could . . . discuss the terms."

"Could we?" His voice was low, the mesmerizing tone of a hypnotist. And then he lifted his hand and drew one finger over the wide expanse of flesh exposed by her aggressive neckline—it had seemed such a good idea when she'd first put it on, she thought in rising panic. He took his time, finger sweeping slowly, over a swell, dipping into the valley between her breasts, a bare inch from the satin edge of her bodice.

She froze. Blood, breath, heart, soul, as trapped as a rabbit in a wolf's jaw. Oh, she'd underestimated this so terribly—had never once considered that a glimmer of the passion he'd once roused in her remained. More than remained, had somehow, deep inside where she never knew it existed, been waiting and strengthening as the years passed, awaiting release.

"I'm certain we can negotiate an agreement," he murmured, his slow, wicked smile full of sensual promise.

She opened her mouth to object. She was sure she did. But at that moment his finger wandered farther, insinuated itself just under the edge of the fabric, stealing into thoroughly forbidden territory, and all that came out was a gasp.

And then, in an awful flicker of an instant, he changed. He dropped his hand, his smile twisted into bitter mockery, and he stepped away, freeing her to leave as she would. "Thought so," he said, as if she'd just confirmed every bad opinion he'd ever had of her. He turned away, dismissing her completely, and strode over to his cluttered desk.

He grabbed a random handful of papers, sifting through them as if he were alone in the room.

"Now wait a minute," she began, and he looked up in surprise.

"You can go now. It begins the first of September, right? Pack light."

"Oh, no you don't." A few moments ago, all she thought of was escape. Now all she wanted was battle. She whipped across the room after him, debated grabbing his arm and yanking him around so he had to face her.

No, better not.

"Though I know you cherish the conclusions to which you jump so enthusiastically I was *not* acquiescing to your suggestion."

"Of course not." Pursing his lips, he studied a random sheet of paper with too-obviously serious intent. "There. Are your feathers soothed? I never for an instant assumed that the glazed look in your eyes and utter lack of protest indicated agreement."

"It was not compliance," she said through her teeth. "It was complete shock at your extreme lack of manners and astonishing forwardness."

"Mmm-hmm." He tossed aside the paper, snatched up another sheet, and still didn't so much as honor her with a glance. "The first, then, isn't it? Where does this fiasco begin?"

"Oh, no. You're not coming with me."

"Rescinding your offer?" he chided. "We both know that you're fond of exercising your right to change your mind, but in this case it's too late."

She never thought that someone could actually strangle on anger, but she was a hairsbreadth away from doing so. "You have no choice. You are not in this. You could fall on your knees right now and *beg* and I wouldn't let you come with me."

"Keep dreaming, my dear. About me keeping out of this now and about me on my knees. Because neither one is happening in your lifetime."

"I'm going to that race. And I'm going to win it, too. *Without you.* Truthfully, I should thank you, for I'm now a hundred times more committed to success than I was when I walked in that door." Time for a grand exit, Kate decided. There, at least, she was on familiar and accomplished ground. "And you—you can live off the stale stories of ten-year-old adventures until there's not an audience in America who hasn't heard every tale. Twice."

She swept out in a furious swish of silk, a huff of frustration. Jim winced at the crash—not a bit too ladylike to slam the door, was she? He waited a beat, half expecting a bell boy to come running to see what had caused such a commotion. And then he frowned, disturbed because he'd found himself smiling. He would not be amused by her, not by her temper or her quick tongue or her ridiculous plan. *Amused* could slide too easily into *charmed*.

He tossed his handful of papers, from which he hadn't read a single word, in the direction of the table and shrugged when half of them skated off and fluttered down to the deep, patterned rug.

Kathryn Goodale. *Hell.*

Unbidden, unwanted, the memory rolled up in him, way down deep from where he'd buried it, where he'd tried to exterminate it completely. Sometimes months had passed and he didn't think of her, not once. But then, on a soft night when his guard was down, she'd slip back into his dreams and he'd wake up, sweating, wanting, hurting.

Heaven. He was drowning in heaven, in the glory of warm, seeking lips beneath his, in the wonder of a lithe, heated female form in his arms. Scents filled his nose, clouds of cultivated summer flowers, the softer, beguiling smells of a clean woman. Hair slid through his fingers, finer than any silk he'd touched in Xinjiang, softer than any fleece he'd bought in Kashmir. He was bedazzled, had been since the instant he'd stepped into the gazebo, weary from nine months of beating through jungles looking for a fabled temple and finding nothing, and seen her. *Her.* So lovely he'd almost thought he'd imagined her, a legendary beauty as ephemeral as the ancient myths he sought.

Then she'd turned, and smiled, and spoken to him. Simple words, polite mannerisms, and each one seemed to portend a thousand things more than their minimal syllables should have, as if each bare word that passed between them was one of cupid's arrows, sinking in deep, binding them together. As if he'd spent all those years searching, looking, hunting in far corners of the world, and all along what he sought above all was in a Philadelphia garden, waiting for him to find her.

Peace had flooded him. And a lighthearted joy like he'd never known. He'd kissed her—he hadn't thought, hadn't considered. Just kissed her, because he couldn't do anything else, because every step he'd ever taken in his life had brought him to this moment. And, miracle of miracles, she'd kissed him back.

He'd been lost. And found, a hundred times more so than he'd ever been on top of a mountain, more exhilarated than when he laid eyes on a treasure no man had seen for a thousand years. So much so that it hadn't registered at first that she was struggling in his arms, fists pushing ineffectually at his chest, squeaks of protest barely escaping his kiss.

It took him longer than it should have to let her go. Moonlight fell through the elaborate fretwork of the gazebo, throwing lacy patterns across her perfect face. Her eyes were wide, wild; her lips, kiss-bruised, parted with her staggered exhalation. Where the moonlight illuminated her skin, it gleamed pale as marble.

Damn. He'd been away from society too long, forgotten that something as innocent—though, it had hardly been innocent, he admitted to himself—as a kiss could send a young maid into palpitations.

"My apologies," he murmured, slipping more easily into the conventions than he would have thought. "It's not such a terrible thing, I—"

"God help me, but it is." She backed away from him, until the handrail against her rump halted her flight. "Oh, God."

Damn, he thought again. She looked right on the edge of panic. This was a different world than he'd grown accustomed to—still not the one he'd grown up in, thank God, where he'd known men married off for far more minor trespasses. Still, if he didn't get her to calm down, no telling what she might do. "Really, no one needs to know, I—"

"Hush!" With frantic, jerky motions, she yanked at the neckline of her dress, silk the color of Ceylon sapphires. A bit of one nipple showed above the edge and his mouth went desert-dry. It had been only the briefest instant, but he knew with perfect and knee-weakening clarity how her flesh had felt in his palm.

"Miss—" He fumbled for what to call her. How could he not have learned her name?

"Oh, please." Her voice broke as she whirled, presenting him with the fine, tense line of her back. "He's almost here. Can't you hear him?"

And then the bellow, above the sprightly dip and sway of the orchestra. "Where the hell are you?"

Jim smiled in automatic nostalgia. "The doc, he never did mince words—" And then he stopped, all the lingering heat in his veins suddenly frozen.

Doc's daughter. Nora . . . Nel . . . Oh, no matter. How old *was* she?

It couldn't be. How such an exquisite creature could

have sprung from someone with doc's . . . unique . . .
features—it was impossible. Still . . . "Ahh . . ."

She glanced over her shoulder at him, three silver
blond curls that had been tucked delicately among
the rest drooping over her left eye, her lips still soft,
blushing deep. If a father—even one less than dot-
ing—saw his daughter in such a condition, there'd be
only two choices: an altar, or Jim would have to disappear into the jungles forever.

"I'll go delay him. You"—he waved vaguely—
"repair. We'll say that—"

"Goddammit!" The exclamation was so close Jim
started.

"Just go," she begged.

"But—"

"Go!"

Jim leaped off the steps and met Doctor Goodale a
mere three feet from the gazebo, charging down the
stone path with the same determined alacrity with
which he'd once clambered up the slopes of Mount
Kilimanjaro.

"You there, have you seen my—" He frowned,
squinted into Jim's face. "That you, Bennett?"

"Didn't think your eyes failed you that much,
Doc."

"Hoo-hoo!" The doctor whacked him on the arm,
then frowned and pinched him through his shirtsleeve.

"Ouch!"

"Hold still." He probed urgently beneath Jim's
ears, lifted an eyelid and peered into his pupil. "Got
the Amazonian fever, did you?" He tsked unhappily.
"Couldn't you at least gotten yourself here in time for
there to be some symptoms left? I've an idea it might

be treated with the extract of an orchid I brought back from that trip up the Branco."

"I suppose experimental subjects are in somewhat short supply here."

Doctor Goodale sighed. "That is only too unfortunately true." Arms clasped behind him, he rocked back on his heels, thin mouth pursed. "Gads, but I miss the field!"

"Come back, then," Jim said, hoping the hearty good cheer he'd affected masked his doubts. The field was often hard on a man, aging him years for the months he spent in the wild. Doctor Goodale, however, had always seemed immune to its ravages, striding hearty and ruddy-cheeked through dense savannah or high desert. But now every year he'd escaped seemed to have returned to him a hundredfold. He appeared to have shrunk inches even as his waistline bulged in tandem. His skin had thinned, sagging from his bones as if it no longer fit him just right.

"Can't. Promised Elaine before she died that I'd stay here with the young ones. For all the good I do them; they're not much interested in my interference. And now"—he stamped the cane Jim hadn't noticed until then against the slate path and shook his head, as if refusing to finish the thought—"thought you'd never come. Must have invited you a dozen times." The lines that bracketed his thin mouth deepened. "Time used to be when you'd jump if I hinted."

"I'd still jump." Guilt tugged at him. From the looks of it he'd nearly delayed this visit too long. But who'd suspect three years in Philadelphia would take such a toll?

Doctor Goodale chuckled. "So why the hell are you lurking out here in the garden?"

"Ah—" Images assailed him, a sweet vital woman against him, and his head reeled. He cleared his throat and took a couple of deep breaths to steady himself. Next time he headed into the jungle for months on end, he was hauling a woman with him, he promised himself. For clearly he'd been far too long without a woman.

He indicated his sorry clothes, which had already given their best for the cause. "Seems like you've got the entire top slice of Philadelphia society in there. And I'm not exactly party fare at the moment."

"Oh, hell, why would I care about that? Besides, the ladies always did like it best when you were roughed up a bit. A little excitement for them. God knows, we could use some around here. I—"

"Excuse me. I apologize for the interruption, but Summers said that you were looking for me?"

She came from the direction of the house—how she'd slipped through the gardens and come the other way so quickly, Jim couldn't guess. Particularly as no evidence of her rush—nor, he realized with a twinge of dismay, of his kiss—remained on her. Her hair swept back, not a strand out of place, the severe style leaving nothing to compete with the pure, perfect lines of her face. Her bodice was in place, low but not extreme, the flurry of lace artfully arranged. She looked as if her maid had just spent hours fussing over her. And Jim had never wanted anything so much as, at that moment, to muss her up again. This woman, cool and perfect, was too far from the warm and vibrant one he'd held moments ago.

"Where the hell have you been?" Doctor Goodale growled.

She held out a fistful of delicate white lilies. "A few

of the arrangements in the entry were drooping a bit
and I thought that I—"

"Never mind," he broke in. "Who the hell cares
about the flowers? Norine is whimpering in the
ladies' retiring room again."

She hadn't looked at Jim. Still didn't, her attention
was fixed on the doctor in a way too careful to be accidental. Embarrassed, concerned, insulted? He
couldn't tell. It bothered him. He thought he should
have been able to read her. And then that made him
chuckle, to think that just because he knew her taste,
knew the soft pressure of her breasts against his
chest, knew the way her breath staggered in passion,
that he would *know* her.

He knew nothing about her.

"Oh, dear. Was it that young Meriwether boy,
then?"

The doctor shrugged in complete unconcern. "Just
go fix it. I'm not going to have her moods spoil my
party."

"Of course," she murmured, eyes downcast, shoulders pulled in.

Norine, the doc had said. Go in and look after
Norine. Which meant that this was not his daughter.
Jim released a sigh of relief and then harrumphed
loudly, wondering if three years in civilization had
improved the doctor's manners enough so that he'd
pick up on the hint.

"Something in your throat? Let me get my bag—"

"No," Jim put in quickly. The woman was a full step
away by now. "I was hoping for an introduction."

"Well, why didn't you say so?" By then the woman
was nearly fleeing down the path, rich blue silk drift-

ing behind her. "Hold up!" Doctor Goodale shouted after her.

She froze but didn't turn, the line of her body as tense as a hunting cat preparing to spring.

She spoke directly to Dr. Goodale as he approached. "I'd assumed you wanted me to address the issue as quickly as possible, so I—"

He waved aside her protest. "This won't take long."

Annoyance spiked into Jim's stunned intrigue. He could understand her being disconcerted by what had passed between them—hell, he was unsettled more than a bit—but couldn't she at least *look* at him?

"Jim, Kate. Kate, Jim."

Jim looked at him blankly.

"What, didn't I tell you?"

"Tell me what?"

"About my wife."

"Wife." Jim shook his head, dug a finger into his ear to improve his hearing. "What did you say?"

"My wife, of course."

It hadn't helped. His gaze swung to her, her face paper white, skin drawn and tense. Panic? Guilt? Both, he hoped on a surge of anger that had his hands shaking against his side. *Wife*.

"There." Doctor Goodale made a shooing motion. "You're introduced. Run along now and plug up Norine's wailing before she curdles the milk punch."

And then she looked at him—in one brief instant when the moonlight caught her eyes and glimmered wetly—before she turned and dashed off down the path. Ready to drag her back and demand answers, he took a half step after her before he caught himself. Ready to . . . God, he scarcely knew what he was ready to do. Blood pumped through him, scalding hot.

"She's a lovely thing, isn't she?" Doctor Goodale said. "Not much else, a pity. Thought at least she'd manage the children for me, but she's not much good at that."

Then he shrugged, dismissing the topic as easily as he'd shrug off a soiled waistcoat.

Jim studied his old . . . not a friend, exactly. He doubted Doctor Goodale claimed any of those, nor cared to. But a mentor, yes, one who'd opened the world to him. What did he owe him?

Where did his duty lie? How did you tell a man his wife had nearly cuckolded him in his gazebo . . . most likely had already cuckolded him a hundred times over, given how easily she'd yielded herself to a stranger.

Fury clouded his brain, making it impossible to think clearly. Anger for Doctor Goodale, anger for himself. Was it kinder to spare the doctor, or better to hear it now? Doctor Goodale was ever unpredictable; his reaction to such messy things as human emotions never easy to gauge. The doctor might already know of his wife's peccadilloes and not care. Jim would only do him a disservice by laying it out where his pride could no longer ignore it.

"Enough of this." Doctor Goodale rapped his cane to gain Jim's attention. "Tell me about Brazil. You found a new river, did you not?"

Forget it, Jim had told himself then. Forget every single sigh, every square inch of skin he'd savored, every trembling moment.

* * *

Now, a dozen years later, rigid, breathing hard, standing in the middle of his hotel room, he knew he never had.

He shuffled through the litter of papers on the table, snatched up his invitation to the race, and tore it into a thousand pieces.

Chapter 3

There were those who said the ballroom at the Rose Springs Grand Hotel had been inspired by the great hall at Versailles. Some even said it put Versailles to shame, with gilded ceilings that seemed to soar to the sky. The walls of mirrors, perfect and polished, reflected so accurately that a party rarely passed without some unfortunate guest, unable to discern the difference between reality and a mere likeness of it, walked straight into the wall. And, always, the air seethed with the inevitable, heady scent of thousands of roses.

Today, however, it seemed as if a circus, a Bedouin camp, a country fair had all been wedged into the space. Kate was perched on the small trunk she'd wrestled in two hours ago. She clutched her precious invitation in stiff fingers as she sat square in the middle of the chaos and watched the world swirl around her.

She'd never felt so out of place in her entire life. Not as a young girl who'd ended up a proper wife before she'd ever been a bride, not out in that desolate wasteland her youngest sister now called home.

From her left came a burst of incomprehensible language. Some Asian ruler, she thought, with an entourage that took up a full corner and spilled out into the room, all circling around the small, dark man in saffron robes. At his shout, three other men scurried out of the room as if in fear for their lives. There were at least a half dozen women in the group, young, exotic, and silent. Kate couldn't even hazard a guess as to whether they were wives, daughters, servants . . . or something else entirely.

A tall, raw-boned woman in trousers—*trousers!*—strode by. She nodded in Kate's direction, acknowledging another female, and kept right on, her cheeks wind-burned, her floppy brown hat pulled low, her bearing utterly confident.

There was only one other competitor completely alone. A young man, Kate judged, although it was hard to tell. So many yards of white fabric swathed him that only a slice of his face showed, his deep, dark eyes scanning the room with intense interest. He hadn't spoken to a soul.

She'd lived with the stares of men since she was no more than thirteen. They rarely bothered her. Why should they? Only a silly girl couldn't use a man's interest to her advantage. But now, under this one's steady regard, she shifted uncomfortably. Too hard to gauge what he thought underneath the shield of his costume.

Shouts exploded from the far corner. There was a flash of movement, flailing limbs. Two burly men muscled out of the scuffle, dragging a round balding figure by his arms.

"Look at that," said a man who appeared at her elbow, dressed in dapper tweed. "From the *Journal* or the *World,* I'd wager." He chuckled. "Caused them quite a dilemma when we announced the contest. Do they ignore it completely and get scooped or report on it and give the *Sentinel* more publicity?" He inclined his head toward the man, now being towed out the door. "Joseph Kane clinched it when he declared no reporter from another newspaper would be allowed in here. They *had* to try, then."

"Excuse me, sir, but I don't believe we've been introduced."

He touched a finger to the brim of his hat. "Charlie Hobson, ma'am. The *Daily Sentinel.*" He checked the watch that dangled from his vest pocket. "Only fifteen minutes to go. I'll be collecting credentials." He stared pointedly at her invitation. "And you are . . . ?"

"Not willing to hand this over until I'm able to ascertain whether you are precisely who you claim to be."

That made him grin, a flash of straight white teeth beneath the deep black swoop of a luxurious handlebar mustache. "You're only the second to ask, do you know that? You and him." He pointed to the still figure of the man swaddled in white robes. "Son of the Amir, I'm told. Couldn't get another word out of him." He bent his smile toward her again. "Now . . . I helped put the list of competitors together, and I'm pretty certain I would have remembered you. Just where did you get that invitation?"

"Does it matter?" she clipped. "I read the rules quite carefully, and it was quite specific that the holder of the letter should be allowed to enter."

"Huh." He rummaged in an inside pocket and pulled out a pad and a stubby pencil. "I'd be interested to hear how you got it. I'm sure my readers would, too."

"I hope you're not telling stories again, Katie my girl." Kate's back stiffened even before Jim's hand came down, heavy and possessive, on her shoulder. "And I hope you're not planning on writing a story based on anything she tells you." Jim leaned forward, lowering his voice conspiratorially. "Fond of pretending she's a society woman, she is. Can you imagine?"

"Really," the reporter said, flatly neutral. "I'm sorry, I don't believe I—" he narrowed his gaze thoughtfully—"Lord Bennett?"

Jim nodded as regally as any prince accepting his due. "The same."

"I hadn't heard you'd be attending."

"There's something you didn't hear? Hard to imagine. Too much time at the desk, not enough out and about reporting, eh?"

"I doubt it." Hobson tucked the notepad into his suit pocket. "I was having a most delightful conversation with your . . ."

"I'm sure you were," Jim said smoothly. "My Katie's nothing if not . . . entertaining."

"I can imagine. Still, we do need to know who's participating."

"Katie Riley. My . . . assistant."

Kate opened her mouth to protest, but Jim squeezed her shoulder hard enough to make her wince.

"Almost noon. Time to get this show on the road, isn't it?" he prompted the reporter.

"I guess it is." Hobson pondered for a moment. "I'll be following the competitors, writing a daily column. I imagine you'll be seeing me around."

"How pleasant."

He sauntered away, winding toward the platform that had been set up on the far side of the room, pausing on the way to speak to a man the size of a mountain.

"See that fellow the reporter's talking to? That's Baron von Hussman. First man to reach the summit of Chimborazo." Jim sighed in deep regret. "One less unconquered peak."

Kate knocked away his hand, which he'd apparently forgotten was still resting on her shoulder. "Katie *Riley*? What was that?"

"You really want him printing in that paper that Kathryn Goodale is wandering around the world completely unchaperoned with me? Ruin your reputation completely," he said cheerfully. "You'll never be able to go back to Philadelphia if this gets out. Who'd marry you then?"

Her molars ground together. "I'm not looking for someone to marry me."

"Maybe not right this very moment," he admitted. "But if we end up in, oh, the Gobi . . . well, let's just say I won't hold it against you if you decide to go running home. Perfectly natural."

"Oh, it is, is it?" She just barely resisted the temptation to march up to the platform and announce her presence to everyone there. She *hated* that he was most probably right. Oh, not that she'd ever want someone to marry her. She'd had quite enough of marriage for one lifetime, thank you very much. But there was no real reason to sabotage her reputation. And she didn't relish the idea of having her unchaperoned, completely scandalous trip with Jim splattered across a front page for the world to gossip over.

"I told you not to come," she said in her most severe tone, ignoring the tiny, idiotic corner of her that was relieved to see him.

"You've told me lots of things," he said. "I'm not inclined to start believing them now."

"I can't do this with you."

"And you can't do it without me."

"We'll soon see, won't we? But I'm not going with you."

"Fine. Stay here. I'll split the prize with you anyway. No, no—" He put a finger over her mouth for an instant to shut her up and her heart skipped a painful beat. His finger was hot, rough-textured, astoundingly male. "No thanks necessary. I know it's generous of me. Least I can do for the doc's widow."

"I'm not staying here," she finally managed.

"Then we go together," he said, and she thought: *Well, we'll see about that.*

"That what you consider adventure garb?" Jim asked, slowly circling her. It was all Jim could do not to laugh. He figured she'd dressed down almost to the point of pain for the occasion. A severely cut khaki skirt, a blouse of shiny white with only two rows of lace, a clever little hat that made it almost impossible to look away from her face. It'd all last about two seconds in that condition, but he had to admit she looked fetching. Silly, completely out of place, but fetching.

No wonder the reporter had been hanging around.

She glowered at him. "I suppose you'd rather I dress like *that*." She flung a disdainful hand toward the tall trouser-clad woman deep in conversation with a Chinese man who came up to her nose.

"Mrs. Latimore?"

Her head whipped around for another look. "Is that who she is?"

"You could do worse than emulate her. Survived two weeks alone in the Amazon jungle after her canoe capsized. Only one of her party who did."

"I remember the story."

"Can you imagine?" Jim went on. "Guides dying on her right and left. Insects the size of your fist, snakes thicker than your arm. Heard she had three different parasites when she escaped the jungle. Why—"

"Enough!" Kate shuddered, maybe even looking a little green around the gills.

She couldn't last long, Jim thought hopefully. How hard would it be to talk her into parking her pretty butt at the nearest decent inn and waiting for him to bring home the prize?

Despite himself, he felt the hum of anticipation. After the tragedy in the Arctic, he'd delayed undertaking another expedition. The price was too high, the memories too hard. He'd lost his partner, Matt, there, and the breezy self-assurance that he could control everything and everyone he considered under his protection.

But this wasn't exactly an expedition. And to be lodged head to head against every other explorer he'd every tried to beat to a prize . . .

"Only one trunk. I'm impressed, Kate." He bumped the trunk with his toe. "It's too big, of course, but you shouldn't have much trouble paring your things down to a reasonable load."

"The rest are in the stables."

"Then I hope you didn't leave anything important in them, because that's where they're staying."

"They are not! I—"

"Well, well. A lover's spat, is it?" Count Nobile's oily Italian accent hadn't softened a bit, Jim thought sourly as he turned to find Nobile already bending gracefully over Kate's hand. Kate smiled beautifully at him, full of expectation and promise, an expression that could not be more different from the one she usually bent on Jim. "Bennett, my old friend, aren't you going to introduce me to your lovely . . ."

"Assistant."

"Assistant?" The count raised a dark eyebrow. "You must pay your assistant well." He hadn't yet released Kate's hand, and lightly traced a finger along the edge of lace spilling over the back of her hand. "Worth?"

"You have an excellent eye, Mr.—"

"Count," he supplied. "Count Basilio Nobile, at your service." He made a formal bow. "And my service is certainly excellent," he went on with clear implication.

Jim felt himself scowling, tried to hide it, knew he failed. Shouldn't she be taking her hand back before he drooled all over it? "Kind of you to say hello. Don't feel you need to linger on our account. I'm sure you've much to prepare."

"Oh, my preparations were completed long ago," he murmured, never taking his warm gaze from Kate's face. "I never was one to leave things until the last minute."

"I'm pretty sure I saw some reporter poking in your supplies."

Count Nobile sighed. "I suppose," he said directly to Kate, in tones that included no one else, "that I must move on before our friend here forgets his breeding."

"Lord Bennett?" Kate slanted him a sly glance. "I can't imagine."

He gave her hand one last pat and released it with clear reluctance. "I'm certain we shall run into each other along the trail. If, at some point, you find you would prefer to . . . switch employers, I do hope you will give me an opportunity to make you an offer."

"I'll keep that in mind," she said.

Jim just managed to keep his mouth shut until Nobile was out of earshot. "If I'd made a proposition like that, you'd have slapped me."

Her smile was far too pleased. "Quite probably."

"You do know what he was suggesting."

"Suggestions are easy," Kate said. "If I'd taken offense at every veiled suggestion I've received over the years, my hand would never stop burning."

And how many had she not bothered to stop? The thought came on a surge of acid, a searing burn of anger that hazed his vision and scalded beneath his skin.

After all, she hadn't slapped him yet, had she? He was not so vain to believe that he was so different than the rest. That in all the years since they'd met, and likely several before, she hadn't welcomed the attentions of others as easily as she'd seemed to welcome that blasted count's.

"If you catch him unawares," he said, "I'd swear his accent isn't half so deep."

"It is quite charming, isn't it? No wonder he'd want to maintain it."

"Almost got himself slaughtered in Persia once. The Shah's not fond of sharing his wives." He leaned closer. "Of course, some say it was the wives who'd ordered his execution." He tsked. "Disappointed women. They're dangerous creatures."

"As I'm sure you know well," she said smoothly.

"Bennett! Fancy seeing you here."

Christ, Jim thought. Not another one. He turned reluctantly.

"Major."

Major Huddleston-Snell looked as if he'd just stepped out of the army he'd quit a decade ago. His carriage was rigidly correct, his face ruddily healthy, his jacket pressed into complete submission.

"How long has it been?"

Not long enough. "Haven't kept track."

"No?" The major tapped a finger along his ruddy cheek, appeared deep in thought. "Oh yes, looking for the source of the Zambezi, wasn't it? Sorry about that. I wouldn't have set out if I'd known you were headed that way. No reason for both of us to flounder around out there."

"Of course not." Jim was pretty damn sure the man had paid one of Jim's native guides a hefty sum to reveal Jim's next objective, but he'd never been able to prove it.

"And who would have thought I'd stumble across that diamond mine out there? Not that financial gain is ever my primary goal. Driven by scholarly pursuits, as you well know. Still, it's a great luxury to know your expeditions are well funded for the immediate future, isn't it?" He blinked in mock horror, as if realizing what he'd just said. "Sorry, old chap. I didn't mean—"

"I'm sure you didn't." No more than he'd meant it any of the other times he'd stolen a prize that Jim had damn near killed himself to discover. Or even the time he'd—*didn't mean it, sorry old chap*—led a warring tribe right into the middle of Jim's camp.

"So? Are you going to introduce me to your lovely companion?"

"No."

"I can well see why you'd prefer to keep her to yourself, but I didn't realize you were so shy about competition."

"Live and learn."

"Very well." Major Huddleston-Snell tipped his hat to Kate, who'd watched the entire episode with cool interest. "I'm sure we'll have other opportunities to become acquainted."

Back regiment-straight, the major marched into the crowd.

"Well," Kate said. "You've just collected friends all over the world, haven't you? I'm a bit surprised you ever come out of the jungle."

"They keep finding me out there, too." He jammed his arms over his chest. "Things will go much smoother if we set down a few rules up front. Every expedition needs one clear leader, and I—"

"I quite agree." She rose from her throne at last, gave her skirts a shake and they settled smoothly over her lovely curves. The porter lugging three suitcases by them nearly fell over ogling. Jim was simply going to *have* to get her some clothes that did a better job of covering her up. "And in this case, it's clearly me."

"What? You couldn't find a barn in a one-acre field."

"I am well aware of the advantages of hiring an expert in certain circumstances," she said, so composed he wanted to shake that calm right out of her. "And that is what I consider this venture. I'm providing the initial invitation, as well as the financing. You are simply the hired—"

The cacophonous clanging of a gong drowned out the rest of her statement, preempting Jim's response.

As one, the crowd turned toward the platform erected near the far end, backed by soaring windows. The stage held five men in suits, all trying too hard to look impressive.

Charlie Hobson came forward, thumbs tucked in the pocket of his vest. "Welcome," he boomed. "I trust you all know why you're here." He waited for the laughter that never came. "While the pope, the president, and the queen have all decreed the centennial doesn't begin until next year, *we* all know when the calendar turns to one-nine-zero-zero, don't we?" This earned him a cheer. He smiled, smugly gratified, before continuing. "The rules are simple. You will be given one clue now, which will lead you to the next, and the third, and so on. The first competitor to reach the final destination will claim the entire fifty thousand dollars." Excitement murmured through the room. Hobson held up his hand for silence. "However, if no one achieves the objective by midnight New Year's Eve, the prize is forfeited." He paused to allow the impact to sink in. "That's local time. Whatever local time is at your final destination."

To her surprise, Kate found herself caught up in the rising tide of enthusiasm that swept through the room.

The sensation was so foreign to her that it took her a moment to identify it. Anticipation, exhilaration . . . her heart pounded in a most uncomfortable way.

"Give us the clue!" someone shouted from near the stage.

Hobson chuckled, clearly relishing his moment in the spotlight. "One more rule. Anyone—and I do mean anyone—caught interfering with another team's progress or tampering with a clue will be immediately disqualified."

"Spoilsport," Jim murmured, and yelped when Kate's elbow found his ribs.

"And now . . ." The reporter held out his hand. A fresh-faced young girl scurried forward and posed prettily before placing a scroll in the reporter's hand. He took his time untying a scarlet ribbon and unrolling the scroll.

"Oh, just read it!" came another shout, followed by a rumble of agreement.

"All right, here you go. Good luck to you all." And then, reciting in singsong rhythm,

> "The wind blows East,
> The wind blows West,
> The wind blows over the Cuckoo's Nest;
> Shall he go East?
> Shall he go West?
> Shall he go under the Cuckoo's Nest?"

There was a heartbeat of silence as everyone held their breath. And then a wild flurry of motion erupted, a tumble of humans shouting, shoving, as if someone had yelled *fire!* in an overcrowded theater. It seemed only a moment before Jim and Kate stood alone in the room. A fringed blue scarf, handfuls of torn paper, spilled popcorn, a forgotten nosegay cluttered the parquet floor. A streamer drooped from a wall sconce.

Jim's deep green canvas bag which had been slung on his shoulder dropped to the floor, then he did too. He stretched out, linking his hands comfortably behind his head.

"So, boss," he said cheerfully, "what do we do now?"

Chapter 4

By Charlie Hobson
Daily Sentinel **Staff Writer**

And they're off!

Never before has such a collection of experience, will, and determination been gathered in one place, focused on one single goal. Over the next three months, this reporter shall endeavor to give you the inside story of the greatest contest ever devised by man.

There was a last-minute addition to the list of competitors in the form of the noted explorer Lord Jim Bennett and his very lovely "assistant," Miss Katie Riley. You can count on more in that regard in subsequent issues of The *Daily Sentinel* . . .

Kate paced.

She'd scribbled down the rhyme and now had it

spread out on top of her trunk, along with two maps, one of the United States and one of the world, that she was very proud she'd thought to bring along. She stared at them until her eyes crossed and still nothing came to her.

She tried, as she had periodically in the hours since the ballroom emptied out, to settle and ponder, only to jump back up a moment later. It was as if she'd been storing up energy for weeks in preparation for this moment and now it couldn't be contained. She wanted to *go*, to get on with it, but there was nothing to expend the energy on. It was making her crazy.

Jim, however, seemed to have no such problem. He'd rested his head on his pack like it was one of the Rose Springs' excellent pillows, told her to "wake me when you figure out where we're going," then dropped off to sleep as easily as a milk-sotted baby. Just one more thing to add to the list of his "annoying" qualities.

She paused in her pacing at his—clearly over-sized—feet. Glaring down at him with enough heat, it should have scalded him awake instantly. His "con" list was long enough to fill up a reporter's notebook and then some. Too bad there were a lot fewer entries on the "pro" side.

Except that she needed him if she wanted to win. And, relaxed in sleep, long limbs sprawled out over the floor as if it was his own bed, mouth—*lovely* mouth—a little open, a scrape of warm brown beard over his jaw, he was just so . . . so darn pretty.

Silly word to apply to a man, she thought. Never considered that she would. But he was, pretty as a mountain, the ocean, a sunset. Something elemental, soul-deep, that you could look on for a lifetime and never get your fill of.

"Ma'am?"

She swiveled around. Yet another employee, mop in one hand, bucket in the other, waited correctly in the doorway to begin swabbing away the debris of the night's send-off. She'd shooed three others away before midnight with so little tact it embarrassed her to think of it now. But they'd been an unwelcome reminder of just how long ago all the others had gotten underway.

"Feel free to begin," she said, sweeping the room with a wide gesture.

"Oh, no," the young woman said, wide-eyed at the very suggestion. "Can't be working if the guests are still here. I was just wondering if there was anything I could get you."

Kate sighed. "Not unless you just happen to have the solution to the first clue handy."

"No, ma'am, I'm afraid that I don't," the maid said regretfully. "But I suppose I could try . . ."

"That won't be necessary." The staff might as well have *whatever the guest wants* engraved on their foreheads. "Just give us ten minutes and we'll be out of your way."

It had to be only an hour or two from dawn. They'd extinguished the gaslights hours ago but the room still glowed, moonlight flooding through the high arched windows, gleaming over the glittering, gilded walls and spangling the spotless mirrors that hung between each window. Shadows and moonlight; she'd always thought of Jim that way, and to see him now, even more handsome than she'd remembered, made her stomach lift and press in her chest until her breath came hard.

She took two steps forward.

"Ouch!" Jim sat up fast, blurry-eyed, rubbing the crown of his head.

"Oops. Did I bump you?" she asked sweetly. "I'm so sorry. It's just so dark in here, I—"

"Dark." He scowled. "Yeah, it's darn near the 'Black Hole' of Calcutta in here."

"Now that you're up, though, we should get started. The staff's anxious to clean the place."

He blinked twice, then looked her up and down. "And you're going to start scrambling up those walls if we sit around here any longer, aren't you?"

"I—" She started to deny it, then shrugged. What was the point? "I *hate* everyone getting ahead of us."

"Hmm." Yawning, he rubbed his bristly chin. "Just because they're stumbling around out there doesn't mean they're getting anywhere. Why waste the energy?"

"Because we're falling behind!"

"Or we're thinking first, instead of jumping in without looking. Jumping in can get you killed in some of the places I've been, Kate. I don't recommend it."

"But we don't know anything!"

He shrugged, completely unconcerned. "We're not going north or south. We know that much."

"Oh, thank you. That's ever so much help."

There was agitation in every line of her body, a jerkiness in each movement. She was just annoyed enough to be graceless, he thought, finding the contrast fascinating. He'd assumed her fluidity was natural, her grace born in her bones. Its absence now hinted that perhaps it was studied and practiced, a skill deliberately honed as surely as he'd earned his expertise on a horse. He was alternately intrigued by the thought that she could control her motion to such a degree, and vaguely irritated that she was such a calculated construct. Was there nothing about her that was real? Perhaps she was nothing more than a lure, carefully designed to draw hapless men, efficient as an expertly tied fly tossed in front of a ravenous trout.

"We're falling miles behind with every second. I can feel it."

He resigned himself to the fact that he'd obviously be getting no more sleep. His bones creaked as he rolled to his feet. Nasty sound; he used to sleep on solid stone without a single protest from his body, he thought sourly. At this rate he'd become one of those prissy aristocrats he used to laugh at, one who traveled with a tea service and a tester bed and every other comfort they could cram onto a raft of servants.

"Floor a bit hard for you, hmm?"

The kind of man Kate would no doubt prefer to travel with. "Not a bit," he said, and bounced energetically on the balls of his feet to prove it. "Good for the posture, you know. And the character. Wouldn't want to go all soft." He surrendered to a yawn. "Now, then. Permit me to share a bit of hard-earned knowledge"

"By all means." Perfectly sweet words, but a sharp enough edge of sarcasm in her tone that he checked himself for blood.

"First off, it's absolute foolishness to wear yourself out running off in all directions without being absolutely sure of where you're going. A complete waste of energy and resources."

Her mouth pinched, as if she wanted to argue but recognized the futility.

"Exhaustion is equally stupid. Perhaps even fatal."

"Fatal." She blanched, cheeks going pale as perfect linen.

Good. People who went on expeditions as a lark, without a proper understanding of the seriousness of the undertaking, were dangers not only to themselves but to those who tried to save them. He had a damn strong suspicion what role he was fated to play in this partnership.

"Yes, fatal. For all the circus of last night, this isn't likely to be play. One makes much better decisions when one is well rested. Even more, it's sometimes difficult to predict when you'll be able to sleep again. One of the first things I learned from the doc was how to rest fast and hard when you can."

"You're hinting I should go to sleep."

"It wasn't a hint." Not now that he got a good look at her. Her eyes were red, the circles under them purple-gray. Not her best colors, and he'd have no compunction about pointing it out if the situation called for it.

"I couldn't sleep," she told him and ran an agitated hand through the tumble of hair that had come undone.

Did it fall into that luxurious, touchable disarray all on its own or did she coax it into place? "Consider it beauty sleep," he suggested.

"I couldn't," she said, her mouth curling in disdain as she inspected the snarl of blankets he'd used as a bed.

"If you're too much of a princess to sleep on the floor of the Grand Ballroom I can't wait to see how you handle the jungle."

She sniffed. "I've slept on the floor before."

"Uh-huh."

"I have!" she insisted.

"With how many thousands of dollars of carpets beneath you?"

"Not a one."

He tucked his tongue in his cheek and inspected her skeptically. "When?"

She froze a second before her mouth curved into a smile, one so flirty and sensual it took a moment before his brain started up again and reminded him that it didn't mean a thing.

"Maybe, someday, if you're lucky, I'll tell you all about it," Kate said with as much innuendo as she could muster. No reason for him to ever know, she thought, that the lone occurrence had been at her sister's. She'd much rather hint at a past as adventurous as his.

"Can't think of one, hmm?"

"I don't know why you think you know me so well. We've been in each others' company perhaps an hour in our entire lives."

"Sometimes that's all it takes."

"Implying there aren't a lot of depths to plumb?"

"I never said that."

"You didn't have to." If she murdered him on the spot, she'd never win. Not to mention his suffering would be over too quickly for her taste. There'd be lots of opportunities in the coming weeks. And so she tamped down the anger that he seemed to provoke so easily and let her smile soften. "You know, I've changed my mind. You're right, of course."

"I'm *right*?"

If she'd known that was all it took to put that expression of dumb shock on his face she would have agreed with him a long time ago. "Of course. I really should gather my rest while I can," she purred in a tone that would have had her sisters gagging.

He looked smug enough to choke on it. He really didn't think much of her, did he, to believe that his transparent challenge had prodded her into bed against her will? Ah, well. She'd been underestimated all her life, an oversight she often found convenient.

She slipped between the blankets. They still held something of him, scent and temperature, and everything inside her went soft. "They're still warm," she murmured. "I really don't know why I fought it." She stretched, arching her back.

Jim recognized her motion was a deliberate punishment, payback for his comments. It worked just the same. His mouth went dry, his heart sped up, and his eyes fastened on that lush curve, as she'd no doubt intended.

It was a blow to discover that despite his best intentions he was as predictable as any man. If he allowed her to see his weakness, the next three months were going to be about as much fun as crawling across a desert.

"It doesn't have to be a traditional bed, does it?" she asked softly.

She was sensual as hell, thoroughly in control, and he was right on the edge of losing it. He stared at her, knowing she couldn't miss the heat in his eyes, his struggle for control.

And then she blushed, sweet as a virgin, as if she finally realized her blatant innuendo.

Words had been on the tip of his tongue, just this side of crude, ready to toss suggestions back to see how she'd react. But her blush blunted his words and the sharp edge of his anger. She couldn't summon up that color at will. No one could be *that* good.

"Get some sleep. Or at least some rest," he added when he could see she meant to protest. "You'll need your energy soon enough. I'll frown over the map and the clues for a while. I'm as capable of being stumped by them as you."

Surprisingly, she closed her mouth, nodding a simple agreement.

He turned his back quickly—he had enough of seeing her on his blankets, and figured it was best not to test himself quite yet. Her allure was still new to him after all, born of only a few hours in her presence. That, and a young man's memories, dwelled on too often in lost places when he'd needed something to hold on to. It would undoubtedly get better over the course of the competition. Even the prettiest view paled with familiarity. No doubt her incompetence and complaints would overwhelm her appeal in no time. It'd likely be only a day or two before he could look at her and feel nothing but annoyance.

He pondered the map for only a moment before deciding it was pointless. The answer to that silly clue— did they have no one at that paper who could come up with something more interesting than a child's rhyme?—was not going to jump out from the map and announce itself. And he was at a distinct disadvantage. Simply for practical reasons, the first clue was probably within a few days travel. He was far less familiar with the terrain of the northeastern United States than he was with central Africa.

But his partner was not. "Kate, I—" As he spoke, he forgot his good intentions and automatically twisted

around to face her. She was fast asleep, head resting
on his wadded-up jacket, the blankets and her skirts
so tangled around her legs that it would take her a
good five minutes upon waking to free herself.

Surely she was safer now, more like other women,
stripped of her wiles and seductive smiles and smooth
charm.

He walked over to her, crossed his arms, and stared
down at her. She slept like a child, fist tucked beneath
her chin, hair loose and swooping around her ear, her
neck. But older, too; without her studied smile, her
determinedly smooth brow, he could see the marks
the years had left on her: a few fine lines at the corners
of her eyes, hugging her mouth, accenting between
her brows. Though he knew she wouldn't agree, it
didn't detract from her appeal a whit. Who wanted a
girl who hadn't lived when there was a woman full of
life and experience instead, one with ideas and opinions of her own to share and explore? Like the difference between a pristine canvas full of potential and
one splashed with color and life.

Her mouth fell open and sound rumbled, a snore
that would never be described as delicate, and he
couldn't help but smile.

"Sleep well, Kate," he murmured, and went to
work.

He'd left her.

It took her a full three minutes, and several blinks of
her sleep-clogged eyes, before it registered completely.
It was late, much later than she was accustomed to
sleeping—the sunlight that pierced, painfully bright,
through the tall windows proved that. The room
echoed hollowly, all the magic of evening scoured

clean. The debris of the night before was still scattered over the floor, like the remnants of a circus once the tent had been struck, and the strong morning light showed the beating the parquet floors had taken. They'd have to buff the entire place.

For a moment she'd thought he'd simply stepped out for a bit. With the random clutter, it wasn't immediately obvious what was missing.

But his things were gone. Fury knocked quickly behind panic. His pack, his jacket weren't there. He'd left the blanket beneath her but stripped off the one that had been spread over her shoulders. If chivalry had ever been drummed in his English head, he'd obviously abandoned it before now.

And he'd taken *her* maps. Left everything else she laid claim to—not to mention Kate herself—as if the maps were the only things of hers that could possibly be of any use.

"Why that . . ." She scrambled to her feet and kicked aside his blanket with the kind of force she longed to aim at his ungrateful head.

But he'd always taken her too lightly, hadn't he? Thought her frivolous and easy and loose. More than one man paid for that mistake, often without even realizing it.

He'd learn. She wouldn't give him any choice in the matter.

Chapter 5

H e would not feel guilty about it.
Damn it, he would not.

He slung the saddle off the back of the horse he'd bought within a quarter hour of bolting from that overwrought, overgilded, overheated ballroom. He gave Chief a pat for his efforts. He'd been lucky; the gray gelding was a very fine animal, one of a string of two dozen or so riding horses the hotel kept for its guests' use. It had been much simpler than he'd expected to convince the stable master to sell him one. Apparently the hotel's manager, or whomever the man had dashed off to wangle permission from, had decided selling him one might garner a favorable mention in the *Sentinel*. Fame, he reflected, did occasionally have its uses.

He really was doing her an enormous favor by

leaving her behind. He'd move a hundred times quicker without her . . . and her luggage. And just look at the miserable shack where he intended to spend the night. Not her style at all.

The sun was sinking low, behind the thick grove of oaks that stood behind the . . . he couldn't even tell what it had been. A stable, a gardening shed? Maybe a chicken coop. It was here, it was free, and he'd slept in far worse places.

And there wasn't much choice. He'd made good time, pushed Chief hard in an effort to catch up with the rest of the competitors. Gotten twice as far as he would have with her "help."

He led the horse around the back of the hut and tethered it near a stand of thick grass. "I know it looks like you should be inside," he whispered, "but this will have to do. Can you imagine what she would have said if she'd have to stay here?" The horse snorted, blowing air out its nostrils, and Jim chuckled. "Yes, I think so, too."

He rounded the corner of the shack and stopped dead in his tracks. "Damn."

Kate descended gracefully from a neat black buggy, beaming at Charlie Hobson as he assisted her down. She wore a deep blue traveling suit, a tiny, feather-topped confection perched on her upswept swirl of gold hair, as elegant as if she were arriving at a garden party.

She had to tug on her hand until Hobson blinked, roused from his stupor like a hypnotist's dupe. He released her, then Kate turned toward Jim, her smile perfectly in place, but her eyes . . . he didn't know whether to flinch or laugh.

"Lord Bennett! I thought that was you," she said brightly. "How lucky we stumbled across you so quickly."

"Oh, yes. Lucky."

"And wasn't it completely kind of Charlie to offer me a lift?"

"I'm sure he is kindness itself."

"Hello there, Lord Bennett," Hobson said, casual tone belied by the way his eyes scanned back and forth between the two of them. "You seem to have left a few things behind."

"Kate knows I like to travel light."

"Come now, Jim." She closed the silk parasol that sheltered her complexion and used it to give him a playful poke in the arm, which nearly sent him reeling. "No need to pretend. It was such a long ride out here, I'm afraid I told Mr. Hobson all about us."

"You did?"

"But of course." He got the tip in his ribs this time. Before she could pull it back he snagged the end and yanked, sending her wheeling before she released the umbrella. Her back to the reporter, she glared at Jim. He just grinned and tucked his new prize under his arm.

But the woman did recover quickly. In a blink, her mask was back on. "He asked so politely, how could I refuse to explain our little game?"

"Game?"

"Yes," With her free hand, she patted Hobson on the arm. "How, when we first met—"

"In Peru, right?" The reporter pulled out his pad and flipped it open, pen hovering above it like a waiting vulture.

It was a clumsy gambit, but Kate sidestepped with ease. "No, I said Brazil." Her laughter was low, a seductive lure, and Jim saw Hobson swallow hard. The sap was trying hard to hang on to his professional detachment. He'd give Kate three minutes to destroy it completely. "I'd journeyed there to join my father. He was a botanist. Sadly"—her mouth trembled prettily—"he was dead by the time I arrived. I needed a job, and your expedition sounded so interesting. You said I was hired . . . if I could find you. Honestly, Lord Bennett," she said, voice light with chiding disappointment, "it really would be more fun if you posed more of a challenge."

"I'll try to do better next time," he muttered, watching in disbelief as Hobson yanked crate after box after trunk of *stuff* out of the back of his buggy. Jim had taken less with him to the Arctic.

"There you go," Charlie said, sweating, red-faced. "Now, if you don't mind—"

"It was so very kind of you to give me a ride," Kate interjected, so smoothly it barely registered as an interruption.

Hobson's brow furrowed. "My pleasure. But now, Lord Bennett, if you don't mind a few additional questions." He yanked out his notepad again and flipped through the pages. "If I could just find my notes . . . ah yes, here we are. Now, when you and poor Matt Wheeler were planning your ill-fated expedition, did you—"

"I don't talk about that."

"I'm aware that you *haven't*, which is all the more reason that you should. As I'm sure you're well aware, in the absence of facts people are apt to fill in the spaces in the most imaginative ways. In fact, rumor has it . . ."

Kate adroitly slipped her hand through Hobson's arm and leaned against him. Ever so slightly, scarcely enough to be improper, but it was enough to send every thought from his head.

"Mr. Hobson, I am so very grateful for your assistance. I don't know how to thank you."

"I . . ."

Jim would be willing to bet ol' Charlie had more than a few ideas in that regard. It bothered him, though he knew it shouldn't. What did he care what she promised, or did, with another man? He was only annoyed she'd managed to track him down, he told himself.

"Charl . . . Mr. Hobson, you did say you wanted to reach the next inn before full dark, didn't you? And that you must begin to write shortly if you are to wire your story on time?" He was moving slowly but surely toward his buggy, blinking around him when he reached it as if he didn't quite know how he'd arrived there. "I simply couldn't impose on you any longer."

"It was no imposition." She looked up at him and somehow he found his foot on the running board.

"We will be seeing you again along the way, won't we?"

The slightest pressure of her fingertips on Hobson's elbow seemed to lift him up to the seat. "You can count on it."

He turned around a half dozen times as the buggy rolled away, his expression half-bewildered, half-suspicious. Each time Kate waved brightly after him, encouraging him on his way. The instant he rolled over a slight rise out of sight, she whirled on Jim with all the fury of an uncaged badger.

"You left me," she said bluntly.

"And you damn well should have stayed left."

"We had an agreement."

"Which I altered to what it should have been in the first place, if you'd been willing to be reasonable."

"Reasonable?" Her voice pitched higher. "It's reasonable to let you go off, grab all the glory and the money, and leave me wallowing behind, hoping you'll be charitable enough to pitch a few pennies my way when it's all over? No, thank you. I'll earn my way."

"And how do you plan to do that?" He'd no time for this, no energy. He was a half day behind the bulk of the competitors as it was. She would only slow him down. And so he raked her head-to-toe with as offensively insolent a gaze as he could manage. His brother had worn this expression more often than not. Though he'd tried to forget that, and every other thing about his vicious and brutally self-centered sibling and sire, he'd never quite been able to do so. First time it had ever come in useful, though.

"Truly, your skills are not . . . well, not to be insulting, but I'd just as soon conserve my energy."

He'd expected anger. Hoped she would go flouncing off in an offended huff, ridding himself of the problem. Instead, she betrayed no umbrage at all, as if crudities no longer had the power to shock her. "Yes, and *your* skills have been *such* an advantage up till this point." She waved her hand dismissively. "For all you know, we're headed for Newport. And I'd wager I'll be far more effective there than you."

"Newport? Yes, I'm sure that'll be a challenge."

"Oh, you have no idea, to so underestimate the treacherous and complicated waters of society."

He drew himself up, falling back on the role he'd spurned so long ago. "So much more difficult than English society, then?"

"As if you'd know."

"Excuse me?" After years of being accorded higher rank than he'd deserved, hearing that rank dismissed brought him up short.

"I've been considering."

"God save us."

She paid him no mind. "I've met a few lords in my time, a baron or two. Philadelphia is hardly the frontier, as you know."

"I know."

"Each and every one of them owned a refinement of manner, a courtesy that seemed as native to them as their accents. Not to mention an air of inherent nobility, all of which are remarkably absent in you."

"They are?" He could sketch a bow as well as anyone, dance attendance as if she were the queen herself if the situation required.

She didn't quite roll her eyes. "Well, *obviously*. So I've come to the conclusion that you've overstated your lineage."

"And why would I do that?"

Her expression bordered on pity, as if only a fool would need something so obvious explained. "Why does anyone? Pursuit of gain. Would all those books, all your lectures be quite as well received if you were, say, the son of a mere gamekeeper? Or a footman?"

A footman? Somewhere, his father's rotting carcass was rolling like a log downhill. He almost wished the old bastard were still alive, just so he could hear that insult. "I don't suppose they would."

"There. You see?" she said, satisfied at having proved her point.

He decided—quite generously, he thought—to allow her her fun. "So how did you find me?" he asked, then lifted a hand to gainsay her answer. "No, no, let me guess. Someone in the stables—someone male. A stableboy, or the stablemaster himself?"

She smiled, the first one since Hobson had trundled off into the sunset. "The stablemaster, of course. He was quite proud of the horse he sold you. He simply pointed me down the road. . . . If you're trying to avoid discovery, Bennett, following a straight path without ever turning off is not terribly effective."

"I'll keep that in mind." He hadn't bothered because he'd figured she'd wake up, realize he'd abandoned her, and commence to howling. And give up. In the future he'd take what was obviously her ridiculously cursed stubbornness into consideration. For the moment it appeared that dragging her along until she gave up might be less trouble than trying to shake her. "And Hobson giving you a ride?"

"I believe that Mr. Hobson considered the contest, and thus his future articles, more interesting with me in it than me out of it. He positively *scrambled* to assist me."

"No doubt. Having a neophyte die a spectacular death always makes for good copy."

She didn't even blanch. "Unless you don't want all those readers to think you too inept to keep me alive, you'd best help me stay that way." She squinted down the road. "Do you know where we're going?

Or are you simply following the trail the others left behind?"

"I know where we're going." He grabbed his dirty green pack from the ground, slung it over his shoulder, and started for the shack.

She waited for him to continue. When he didn't, she scurried forward to place herself between him and the sagging door. "Well?"

He glared at her for a moment, then sighed. "There's a place on the coast of Massachusetts, a day's ride north of Boston. Eighty years ago or so a shipping magnate brought an old castle from England stone by stone and rebuilt it on the highest point in a hundred miles. Cost him a good chunk of his fortune. Most people thought he was crazy." He shrugged, figuring it was no crazier than trying to search out a mythic temple or climb a glacier-sheathed mountain. "Locals call it the Cuckoo's Nest."

"Hmmm." She narrowed her eyes at him. "Amazingly versed in American history, aren't you? Considering I've never heard of it."

"I'm sorry your education is so inadequate." He tsked sadly. "Actually, the most fascinating young woman is employed at the Rose Springs. Well acquainted with nearly all points of interest in the entire northeastern United States. Very fond of rising early for energetic strolls. A highly intriguing woman."

She glared at him with decided heat—enough to be flattering if he were susceptible to being flattered by her jealousy.

"You didn't offer her part of the prize in exchange for her information, did you?"

"I most certainly did not. You're not the only one

whose charms are occasionally appreciated by the opposite sex."

"Hmm." She rocked back on her heels, sending her skirts swaying. "I thought you objected to my using my . . . charms for personal gain."

"I don't care one bit how you use your *charms*." There was too much of an edge to the words, enough bite that she had to suspect the lie beneath them. And right up until he uttered them, he'd no idea just how much of a lie they were. "I object to your attempting to use them on *me*."

"Oh, don't worry," she assured him, a flash in her eyes that a wiser man would have taken for warning. God save him, he couldn't help but view it as a challenge. "I've no intention of wasting my wiles on you."

"See that you don't. Not that they'd work anyway, but it's very . . ."—he paused just long enough for her temper to flare—"time-consuming."

"Time-consuming," she repeated.

"Of course. Think of all I could have accomplished if I hadn't wasted the last half hour listening to you babble."

"And clearly I was the only one talking."

"Yup," he said cheerfully. Too cheerfully. He should have been running in the other direction. He should have been ignoring her completely, making plans to leave her behind—for good this time. Or working out some sort of practicable agreement for the remainder of the trip, one that allowed him to pretty much overlook her existence ninety-nine percent of the time.

Instead he stood in the gathering gloom, trading barbs with the woman who'd betrayed both him and the doc, and likely destroyed dozens of lesser men along the way. Because it made him feel alive, tingly and edgy, alert with the kind of anticipation he used to feel when he was right on the verge of discovering something extraordinary.

"What do we next, Jim?"

"We go to bed."

Chapter 6

He studied her expression as she entered the shack. He knew what she saw: a half dozen tools, rusted beyond recognition. A stack of splintery boards, a pile of moldy hay, gaps in the walls as broad as her wrist. Any one of her gowns was worth more than ten times the place.

She looked lovely in the shadows, every bit as bewitching as she did in sunshine. Her hair shimmered softly, her eyes growing darker, mysterious as twilight. Some women seemed made for moonlight, others for the clear, bright day. She seemed a dozen women in one, different in every light, every situation, multifaceted as a gem, each one as beguiling as the next.

Perhaps that was her essential allure. A changeling seductress, all colors flashing in one—one moment all tender innocence, heartrendingly pure; the next the blatant sexuality of a practiced temptress.

He kept searching for remnants of that girl he'd known. He knew she was gone. Knew she'd never really existed anywhere but in his starved imagination. Yet he couldn't help but look for her, as thirsty for a glimpse of the girl he'd thought he'd known as he'd been for water when he'd first left the desert.

Her lip curled, only a slight hint of revulsion, smoothing into a cool smile in an instant.

She looked up at him then, too quickly for him to glance away. Caught, he felt the crackle of electricity, the air so charged that he half expected the pile of hay to ignite.

Her mouth waited. Half open, ripe as a summer berry, a soft gleam of moisture and temptation. He could only guess at the number of lovers she'd had in the intervening years. A dozen? A hundred?

It should have repulsed him. She was a woman who had betrayed not only him but Doctor Goodale as well. But oh, the wicked things she must have learned to do with that mouth. There was powerful excitement in the knowledge that she knew how to use it.

She saved him. She looked away, as if unable to hold his gaze any longer. In profile, she was pretty. Lovely, even, jawline cleanly defined, nose a perfect slope. But resistable; without the animation of her face, the light in her eyes, she was only another beautiful woman.

"It's getting dark," she murmured, gesturing to the open window. Outside, evening was sliding toward night, the sky bruising to deep purple.

"Yes," he agreed.

"Cloudy."

"Yes," he said again, as irritation tightened the corners of her mouth. Was it so easy for her, then? A hint and men leaped to do her bidding? Well, if she wanted something from him, she'd have to ask.

And maybe not even then.

"Don't you think we should get my luggage in?"

He shrugged. "You want it in, you move it."

"Excuse me?" she said, with enough disbelief he laughed aloud.

"You heard what I said."

"But—"

"Do I look like a porter to you?"

She slowly eyed the width of his shoulders, and his breath staggered. Damn, shouldn't this be wearing off by now? He simply couldn't spend the next few months aroused to the point of pain every time she came within a few feet of him.

But her gaze skittered away like a scalded cat. She seemed as unsettled by his presence as he was by hers. Perhaps it was guilt that disturbed her, though he wouldn't have considered her the guilty type. Or simple annoyance—they seemed unable to pass a word together without sniping at each other, and she was obviously accustomed to bending men to her will with the snap of her fingers.

His pride wanted him to believe it was ardor, the same incendiary passion, unwelcome and ungovernable, that blew through him with the force of a hurricane. But in that way lay certain disaster; if he dared accept that the same desire simmered in her, they wouldn't make it through the night unscathed, much less through the entire contest.

Would that be so bad? The thought was insidious, a whisper of potent temptation. He indulged it for a moment until his vision blurred and blood pumped in his temples.

Of course it was bad. Not to mention downright stupid. One kiss from her had haunted him for years. God only knew what a whole night might do.

She shook her head slowly. "You're really not going to bring them in?"

"There's no point in it. We're going to have to leave them all behind anyway."

"Hmm." She wasn't a bit convinced. Her mouth was pursed, the smooth arches of her brows drawn together in concentration. "It can wait until morning, I suppose. It doesn't look much like rain, and it's not as if a thief's likely to stumble across us in the dark."

"True."

"I need a few things, though."

"Go ahead."

She returned dragging a trunk that had to weigh more than she did, and pulled up short when she saw him settled in his pallet on the lone stack of hay.

"Why do you get the bed?"

"It's hardly a bed," he replied, and turned over with as much rustling and crackling as he could manage.

"It's as close as we've got."

"*We've* got nothing." He tugged a blanket over his shoulders and snapped his eyes shut. "*I* found a reasonably comfortable place to spend the night. It is not my problem that you decided to come barging in."

He heard the swish of her skirts as she approached, followed by the impatient tapping of her feet near his own.

"Did your mother teach you *nothing*?"

"She taught me all kinds of things." Mustiness filled his nostrils and his nose twitched. The old straw prickled in all sorts of uncomfortable places. Had he been alone, he would have already surrendered to the floor. But now it had become the principle of the thing. "But the field taught me a fair amount, too. And your husband even more."

"Well, now, *that* explains a great deal."

He dared to crack open one eye. She had both fists on her hips—and lovely, curvy things they were—and blood in her eyes. And he'd have pulled her right down with him if it wasn't guaranteed she'd fight him every step of the way.

Then her posture eased. "I'll play you for it," she said, such suggestion in her voice that she might have been proposing something else entirely.

"Play me?" He pushed himself up to his elbows.

"Play you *for it.*"

"Play what?"

She shrugged, as if it meant little. "Whatever. Cards, dice . . . riddles?"

There was no way in hell he was going to get tangled up in word games with her.

"I don't gamble," he told her.

She arched a brow. "Ever?"

"No." He knew the night was warm. And yet he pulled the blanket closer around him. "My father and my brother did enough of that for a dozen families, thank you very much. And lost enough for ten dozen, for they'd been as rotten at the tables as they'd been good at taking out their losses on anyone within reach."

"Oh." Her head tilted as if she didn't know quite what to make of his admission. "So you've never tried it?"

"For twigs or stones, around a campfire now and then. Nothing that mattered." When he couldn't talk his way out of playing without the explanations becoming more painful than the game.

She smiled broadly, a flash of even white teeth, a seductive curve of mouth. "Well, this should be fine, then. A night's use of that pile of straw is scarcely worth more than a handful of twigs."

"Oh, I don't know," he said. "If you get me started . . . who knows where I might end up, once you nudge me down that slippery slope."

"Would I lead you astray?"

Their mood had been light, verging on playful. It darkened in an instant, pulsing with seduction.

"I imagine you've done your fair share of leading astray."

She swallowed hard and took a step back, putting a strip of packed earth between them, and focused her gaze on the battered wood of the wall above his head. The cords of her neck stood out tautly above a soft ruffle of lace.

She couldn't be hurt, not by such a simple remark. She was not a young, sheltered girl to be wounded by the merest slight. He reminded himself that she was as capable of playing on his sympathies as playing on his passions.

"I would be willing to bet," she said softly, "that you've done your own share of leading astray, too."

Damn.

"Fine." He could not lay at her feet a moment longer and surged to his feet. "I'll play you for the bed."

"No." She backed away farther, shaking her head. "It was a silly idea. You were here first. The floor will suit for tonight."

"I said I'd play you for it," he snapped, more sharply than he intended.

"You should enjoy it while you can," she said. "Because you won't be beating me to the prime spot from here on out, I promise you." Her smile was bare of its usual dazzle. Interesting; this smile did not make his heart go thump, his breath bellow in and out of its own accord.

"I couldn't sleep at the moment anyway. I wouldn't mind the distraction."

She nodded, sharp and short. "All right."

"What shall we play?"

"Poker."

"*Poker?*"

At his astonishment, the smile became genuine, and just like that, his knees almost gave out beneath him. She drew herself up, mock-offended. "You don't think I look like the poker type?"

"No."

"What type do I look like?"

Mine.

He cleared his throat. "I believe I'll reserve comment on that one."

"Coward," she said. "It's a bit late to retreat into tactful silence, isn't it?"

"I'm afraid I'm fresh out of playing cards."

"Oh, I have some."

"You do?"

"You don't think those are *all* clothes in those trunks, do you?" She flew to the first one and flipped open the top. It held neatly wrapped packages, as ruthlessly organized as hospital supplies.

She didn't hesitate. She moved two square boxes, pulled out a small rectangle, replaced the two, and lowered the lid in less time than it would've taken to snuff a candle. She waggled the small box at him. "See?"

"How'd you know which one it was in?"

"They're all color-coded, of course," she said, as if pointing out the obvious to the slowest dullard.

"Of course," he murmured.

Color-coded. Cripes. He'd considered himself well prepared, carefully controlling every aspect of an expedition, double and triple-checking until Matt threatened to murder him by choking him on his own lists, but color-coding?

She lifted her skirts as though to sit, giving him just a glimpse of white-clad ankle, and then apparently thought the better of it. She dashed back to his makeshift bed, inspected all the blankets briefly before selecting the flimsiest one, and snapped it into place beside the trunk. She lowered herself to the blanket and, after smoothing her skirts into perfect array and placing the deck square in the middle of the trunk, looked up at him expectantly. "Well?"

He didn't bother with a blanket, just plopped right down in the hard-packed earth, making sure the width of the trunk was between them, a small barrier but better than nothing.

"Is there enough light, do you think?" she asked. The simmering dusk muted his vision.

"Don't tell me you packed a kerosene lamp, too."

"No, but—"

"This shouldn't take long."

"No," she agreed quickly. "It shouldn't. Would you like to deal?"

"Certainly." The small box that held her cards was rosewood, inlaid with a two-toned star, polished to a gloss that approached the shine on her hair. He brushed his fingers across its surface. It was slick against his thumb, so perfectly smooth it seemed unreal. "Where did you learn to play?"

"Where do you think?"

"Doc?"

"You seem surprised." She reached across the table and tapped the top of the box, reminding him of his duties. "He loved to play. It wasn't something he just picked up after he could no longer go in the field, was it? I assumed he'd always been so fond of the game."

"Yes, he was."

He opened the box. The cards inside were well used, the edges soft, the colors muted. He dumped them out and began to shuffle.

"Exactly," she said. "What did you think we did all the time together?"

The cards spewed up. "I don't." *Please, Lord, be merciful and never let me think of what they did together.*

"Oh, let me," she said, reaching for the scattered rectangles.

"I can do it," he insisted, and dove for the cards and the meager distraction they offered.

Night had fallen an hour ago, spurring Kate to dash out to the yard and, over Jim's protests, dig two candles from one of her trunks. Jim had suggested that they could simply quit and go to sleep, but Kate maintained it would be most unsporting of him to take advantage in such a way. She was rusty and he must give her a fair opportunity to recoup her losses.

And so, eight hands later, he sat across from her in a puddle of soft candlelight, perhaps fifteen twigs piled in front of him like a miniature fire waiting for a torch. Kate had no more than a half dozen twigs before her, arrayed in military precision on top of the trunk. She kept adjusting them, nudging them further into alignment that was already perfect, as she inspected the cards she held in her other hand.

The motion kept drawing his attention to her hands. He couldn't recall noticing her hands before. No surprise, he thought wryly; there was plenty else to attract his attention. Now he couldn't seem to think of anything else. Her fingers were long, tapered, the nails softly shining. They moved like quicksilver, movements blurring into a suggestion of grace like a hummingbird's wings.

He could remember her mouth, the feel of her beneath his hands, but no matter how hard he tried he couldn't recall if she'd ever touched him. It seemed a horrible oversight if she hadn't, a gap in his knowledge and his memories that he wanted far too much to fill.

"I think that I . . ." she hesitated, inspecting her cards with as much fierce concentration as she'd studied the map at the Rose Springs. Her mouth pinched up and lines speared between her brows, so different from her usual smooth expression that he'd be willing to bet he was the only living man who'd ever witnessed it. "Hmm . . ." She flicked one twig out of alignment, rolled it back in. "I see, and raise." She nudged two sticks into the small pile between them.

"See and call," he snapped out in an instant.

Her gaze flew up to him, then back to her cards. Seconds eased by as she deliberated; the only sound in the old shed, the scrape of the twigs as she adjusted their position. Flickering, delicate motions, a dance over the pieces. His vision hazed, cleared again.

"Stop it!" He slapped his hand on top of hers, stopping it in mid-motion.

She startled, her hand jerking beneath his. "What?"

Mistake. Oh, mistake. He thought he couldn't take it one more second, those brisk, little movements spawning lewd images of her fingers drumming on his belly, lower still.

But touching her, even on the back of her hand, was a thousand times worse. Her skin was warm, impossibly fine, as tender as a new petal. Her knuckles bumped into his palm, a delicate impression that scalded him with possibilities.

"Wh—" She cleared her throat and tried again. "What?"

He had to force his hand to move, peeling each finger away one by one. "Sorry." The hand now; lifting it felt like it suddenly weighed a thousand pounds. "It's just . . . the drumming. It made me twitchy."

Her scowl was a brief flicker, there and gone. He wanted to grab her by the shoulder and shake the expression out of her. Did she really think that smooth and cool was better than animation and life? She wasn't Dr. Goodale's remote hostess anymore.

"It annoyed you, did it?"

"Yes."

Deliberately, she began drumming against the trunk, nails clicking, smile bordering on smug.

"I believe I called," he said through his teeth. It would serve her right, he thought, if he told her exactly why her fidgeting disturbed him.

"Oh. Of course." She fanned the cards on top of the trunk. "Two pair."

She was a fair poker player. Her composure allowed her to bluff with relative ease, and she certainly had no compunctions about lying.

But try as she might, there was one thing she couldn't overcome.

The cards liked Jim Bennett.

Always had. His father and brother hated that he'd always been lucky when they'd been the exact opposite. He'd been no more than twelve when they tried to draw him into the games, thinking that he could win back part of the fortune they'd squandered. But he understood even then that it was a trap . . . the moment one depended upon Luck was the moment she turned against you.

He tossed down his own hand. "Full house."

Blinking, Kate twisted around to inspect his cards.

"Ah . . ." The sound was very low, but could only be considered a snarl.

"Now, now, don't whine," he chided.

Color flooded her face, dusky in the low light.

"You cheated."

"I most certainly did not."

"But . . . but . . ."

"Come now, be a sport."

Heat flashed in her eyes. "Now whoever said I had to be a sport!" she snapped.

It was as much animation as he'd ever seen in her. He sat back and contemplated her for a moment. "You hate losing."

"Of course not, I merely . . ." She paused, then blew out a breath. "I *hate* it. Hate it, hate it, hate it. There. You know my secret. It's terribly unladylike and not at all kind but truly—when I was in school, all my friends refused to play games with me."

He leaned forward on his elbow, the candlelight casting a conspiratorial oval around them. "What's the worst thing you ever did to win?"

"I couldn't—"

"Tell me."

"I sawed halfway through my best friend's croquet mallet so it would break in the middle of our championship match."

He laughed, thoroughly and heartily, the sound swelling up in the small room.

"Oh!" She pressed her palms to her cheeks. "I can't believe I just told you that. What you must think of me."

And just like that, their companionable mood ended. They both knew what he thought of her.

"Well," he said. "We'd best get to sleep."

"Oh, no!" she said, dismayed. "Just one more. It's only sporting."

He should say no. The rising simmer of a desire that he neither wanted nor knew how to manage should tell him that much.

"Please?" She didn't wheedle. She was too sure of her wiles to wheedle. She merely smiled at him and waited, skin gleaming like pearls in the candlelight, looking up at him through her lashes so her eyes looked mysterious and promising, luring him in.

Say no. The wiser part of him was flimsy, growing weaker all the time. If there was a man on earth who could say no to sitting across from a beautiful woman in the soft light, watching her move and speak and smile, breathing in air that was replete with seductive potential—well, there was not a man on earth who could.

"All right." He bent to gather up the cards.

"Let me." She was quicker than he, sweeping them toward her in a wide arc. The cards flashed in her hands, a competence born of long practice. "Whew. It's getting warm in here, isn't it?" She reached up and flicked open the top button of her blouse. The collar released immediately, lace sagging loose and lush against the pale wedge of skin revealed. She fanned herself, blowing the lace aside, giving tantalizing glimpses of more.

So, that would be the approach now, would it? He was surprised that she hadn't tried it before now.

He'd no intention of falling for her attempts at distraction. That didn't mean he couldn't enjoy the show in the process.

She leaned forward on her elbows, squeezing in with her upper arms, and her breasts swelled into the slight opening. And just like that, his brain shut down.

"Are you ready?" she said brightly.

"Huh?" He blinked, coming back to the present as if swimming up through murky water. She'd dealt without him realizing it and had her cards fanned neatly in front of her, amused eyes peeking flirtatiously over the top. He snatched up his cards and thumbed them open.

He threw down a card. "I'll take one."

"Only one?" Somehow she'd opened another button. He was sure of it; there hadn't been that much lovely bosom exposed before. He started plotting ways to draw out the game, wondering just how far she'd go. "I would have thought you'd take more," she purred.

He swallowed hard. "You did?"

"Hmm." She delicately ran a fingertip down the

curving edge of her hand of cards. "You always struck me as the kind of man who'd take a risk. Who'd go for broke, as it were; who'd reach for all he could." She reached up with her free hand and plucked the pins from her hair. It tumbled free, a rich, glorious spill that captured the candlelight for its own. "I hope you don't mind," she said. "After a long day, the pins start to hurt."

"I don't mind," he said, and hoped he hadn't squeaked. He couldn't tell; blood roared in his ears.

"Good." He had to watch her mouth to make out all her words. Which only made it all the worse. Her mouth gleamed with moisture and her lips curved around the words as if they were a solid thing. "Just one? It's not too late to change your mind."

He shook his head, not so much a no as an attempt to clear out the fuzz. "Just one."

She put one card on the flat surface and pushed across to him with her forefinger—slowly, her hand inching over the surface, directly toward him. "There you go."

She didn't lift her hand. "Aren't you going to take your card?"

"Ah . . . of course." He pinched the card by the edge and managed to slide it from her grip without brushing her fingers.

Damn it.

She pouted over her cards, her mouth drawn up in a coquette's promise. "I think I'll take . . . three," she whispered. "One's never enough for me."

He'd memorized his cards in that half-second when he'd first glanced at them. Now he stared at them as if his life depended on the knowledge—not because he had any concern for his hand but just because he didn't dare look at her again. He'd vastly overestimated his resistance. It didn't matter that he knew very well she was simply trying to distract him, not attract him. That every move she made was calculated and there was nothing of true passion on her side. She was expert, thoroughly detached, as professional in her role as a Broadway actress.

It made no difference. It was impossible to remain immune. And so he studied the tiny printed hearts marching across his cards with the desperation of a drowning man latching onto one last, tenuous lifeline.

He bid quickly, jumping in after her declarations with a speed that bordered on rude, hoping only to get it all over with as quickly as possible. Though sleep was rapidly becoming unlikely, putting a little distance between them might—*might*—make it possible for him to keep his hands off her.

"Jim," she said softly, and waited. The little hearts swam before his eyes. The silence grew awkward, then obvious.

"Jim," she said again, and he knew there was no help for it.

Reluctantly, dreading, hopeful, he raised his gaze.

Lord. When had that happened? He could see her nipple. No, not quite, but almost . . . nearly . . . a shadow of it, at the edge of a loosened flutter of soft cotton. It was more arousing than her bare breast would have been, just that promise of it, making him suck in a breath and hold it, waiting for that cloth to slide down another fraction.

Well, no, not more arousing, he admitted ruefully. He'd still take the whole damn sight of her, gloriously naked, given the chance. Still, this was pretty darn—

"Four aces."

Her voice clipped through his heated dreams like a torrent of ice water. "What?"

"Four aces." She tapped her finger on the fan of cards she'd arranged across the trunk.

"Huh?" He knew she expected something of him right now; her head was tilted, her smile sweetly smug. He just couldn't quite fathom exactly what she wanted.

"Your cards," she reminded him. And then, when he only swallowed hard, she said more forcefully, "Your *cards*."

He threw his cards down, face down. One hit the edge and flipped over as it fell to the floor, revealing a ten of hearts. "You win. The bed's yours."

She was on her feet in an instant, as if she were afraid that he would change his mind and insist upon another game. "I'll just go outside and . . . I'll just go outside."

She backed toward the doorway, wagging a finger at him. "I'm not going to come back and find you've stolen the bed, am I?"

"Would I do that?" he asked.

She answered with insulting speed. "Yes."

"You're right, I would. But not tonight."

She studied him suspiciously for a moment, then shrugged. "All right, then."

He didn't get up, just pondered the empty, densely black rectangle where she'd been standing a moment ago. And then he reached down and, one by one, flipped over his four remaining cards. "Straight flush," he murmured before, in one wide sweep, obliterating his final hand.

What the hell, he thought. She'd earned it.

Chapter 7

Kate had gotten up long before Jim. Hours, by the look of her. She'd piled her hair up on top of her head in a complicated arrangement of swirls and dips that showed off her long neck, the smooth pink curve of her ears. Her skin glowed, delicate rose blooming on her cheeks, her mouth—he'd no idea if the color was natural or if she'd helped things along.

She had on a different white shirt; a more severe cut, a lot less lace, every bit as flattering. But if the rest of her was as flawless as if she'd just stepped out of her dressing room, here was the slightest hint of where she'd spent the night. One lone crease dared to slash across the bodice; one wrinkle marred the crisp navy blue of her narrowly cut skirt.

She stood over him, tapping her foot—sooner or later that was going to drive him insane.

"Oh, good, you're up. I was just about to wake you."

With a painfully aimed kick, he had no doubt.

"Don't you think we should get going?" she asked.

"Sure." He yawned, ears popping. "Sleep well?"

"No."

"I'm sorry to hear that." He stretched and rolled to his feet, hearing every joint protest along the way. At this rate he wouldn't be able to move by the time he was fifty.

"Are you always so slow?"

"Yes." As he bent to grab the limp pile of his blanket, he saw her scrub the palms of her hands briskly up and down her upper arms.

"Problem?"

"No." She dropped her arms and held them rigidly against her sides.

"If you say so." He turned away for an instant, whipped back to catch her in the act. A smile tugged at his mouth. "No problems, huh?"

"There was something in that hay," she admitted, thoroughly disgruntled. "I don't know what—" She stopped as his smile broke free. "You knew!" she accused him.

"Suspected," he corrected. "Just look at that stuff. Be more surprising if there weren't a few beasties crawling around in there."

"No wonder you surrendered it so easily." She gave up and scratched her forearm in earnest. She glowered at him, two seconds of fierceness before her expression smoothed again. "Why didn't you warn me?"

"I've always been of the opinion that cheating gets its own reward."

She froze in mid-scratch. "Cheating?" she asked, wary, composed. "I didn't cheat."

"Two aces tucked beneath your thighs?" He shook his head sadly. "Not subtle enough, Kate."

"You knew?"

"Your distraction was most entertaining, I'll admit." He grinned broadly. "You can practice on me anytime."

"Thank you ever so much for the offer."

"You underestimated me."

"Terribly easy to do, I'm afraid."

"And always a mistake."

She arched, twisting one arm behind her back in an attempt to get at a spot between her shoulder blades. "If you're waiting for me to apologize, we'll be here all day."

"I'd be disappointed if you did."

"Excuse me?"

"First hint I've had this whole time that you might be worth dragging along. If you're willing to cheat to win—not to mention exploit certain natural assets— well, you might present a tactical advantage after all."

"Darn it!" She spun, presenting him with her back. "Scratch. Please."

She stood still before him, waiting. The nape of her neck was bare. Fine tendrils of gold trailed down. He drew his nails slowly down her back and she arched into his touch.

"There's just one thing I must know." He leaned forward, closer than he should have, until the scent of her clouded his brain. "Just how far would you go?"

She sucked in a quick breath. "I imagine you'll just have to wait and see, won't you?"

"Oh, I'll see."

The scratch veered dangerously close to a caress. Her back was firm, lithe, a sinuous line. And if he didn't stop touching her right that second, he never would.

"Shouldn't we be going?" she asked.

"Going?" he murmured. "Oh yes. Going." He dropped his hand and started for the door. "I'll just go clean up while you pack, and then we'll get on our way."

"I am packed."

He wheeled around to face her. "Uh-uh. One bag. I don't care what you put in it, but you'd better choose carefully, because that's all you're getting."

It wasn't fair, Kate thought. Not one bit. There he was, just rolled out of bed, his eyes still foggy with sleep, his posture relaxed. His hair was rumpled, standing up in all directions. A thick, prickly growth of beard studded his chin. His clothes were in worse shape than his hair. And yet he looked better than she'd ever seen him, completely male, totally appealing— and he'd looked awfully good before.

If he'd seen her the instant she'd woken up, he would have burst out laughing—if he hadn't run shrieking from the shed. It had taken her a good half hour of repair before she'd dared to rouse him, and it was a barely passable effort at that. She hadn't done badly, considering the limited conditions, but it would have been immensely satisfying to see him stunned into silence.

"Don't be ridiculous," she said.

"One bag."

"There you go again." She shook her head. "I couldn't possibly—"

"One." He crossed his arms over his chest, as implacable as a palace guard.

"I realize your rudeness is deeply ingrained, but I really will not tolerate interruptions," she snapped. "You seem to be overly fond of the roles you've cast us in. That is all well and good in front of Hobson, but I am most certainly not your assistant and I have no reservations about reminding you of that fact."

"I am well aware you're not my assistant. Any assistant I hired would have enough sense to know that she couldn't drag half of Wannamaker's along."

She continued as if he hadn't said a thing. If he could interrupt, she could ignore. "I have compromised in this instance already. I will consider you, in light of your experience in such matters, an equal partner despite it being *my* money and *my* invitation. You simply must listen when I say one bag is simply and utterly insufficient for my needs."

"Then change your needs."

"Oh, come now. You cannot convince me that you would ever undertake an adventure with inadequate supplies. I have brought only the necessities, I assure you."

He flicked a glance toward the trunk she had brought in the previous night and the two packs stacked neatly on top of it. "It is as foolish to be weighed down with frivolities as it is to be undersupplied, and we are hardly entering the Sahara tomorrow. If the time comes that we need to buy more, so be it. We can choose specifically for the environment and terrain we encounter."

"Why buy again what we might already have?"

"Kate." He sauntered toward her, deliberate steps, as though they had all the time in the world. She would not shrink, darn it, would not step back, even though he stood altogether too close.

He pointed at her then himself before he held up two fingers. "Two people," he said, slowly and clearly. "One horse. Just how many bags do you think we can bring along?"

"You do not need to address me as if I were mentally deficient."

He grinned widely and let the implication rest.

"We'll get another horse," she suggested. "One can't carry us both for long in any case. Perhaps even a wagon."

"Can you afford that?"

She considered her small hoard, pondering all the myriad of expenses likely to arise along the way. Certainly Count Nobile and the baron would not be constrained by their budget.

Ridiculously, horrifyingly, she felt the burn of tears and the thought of abandoning all her trunks.

They were only *things*. But she'd lost so many things already.

"Perhaps," she said, carefully keeping her eyes turned away from him.

"All right," he ground out. But just as she thought he might be giving in, he stomped over to her trunk and yanked open the lid. "Let's see what you consider so essential that you'll jeopardize the whole damn venture for it, all right?"

"Now wait a minute!" She scurried over, half offended, half grateful. He was ever so much easier to deal with when he was acting the simple, blockheaded male. And she functioned much better angry than sad. "That's private!"

"Private." He tossed her one quick, heated glance

that implied so many things she could only be grateful it lasted a bare second. Any longer would have had her knees giving out beneath her. "Privacy is going to be darn hard to come by when we're traveling, Kate, and you'd best get used to that right now."

Oh, now there was something to think about. Too much to think about, guaranteed to disturb her sleep even more than whatever little creatures had lurked in that nasty pile of hay.

He reached into the trunk, grabbed a purple silken bag, and held it aloft like a gladiator displaying his opponent's head. Glass clinked.

"Would you be careful!"

"Why?" He lowered it and tugged open the gold cord. "What is this stuff?" He spilled a handful out into his palm, tiny glass pots that glittered like gems. He poked at them suspiciously. "There must be dozens."

"Don't be ridiculous. There are no more than fifteen or sixteen." *In this particular bag.*

He lifted one to his nose and sniffed as if he suspected ammonia. His brows went up and he inhaled more deeply this time. "No wonder you always smell so good."

She tried very hard to ignore his comment, pushing it back behind more pressing concerns. But it was there just the same, a warm, slow glow—*he noticed my scent and he liked it.*

"And the rest?" He peered into the depths of the bag.

She sighed, crossed over to him, and began to lecture like a reluctant teacher addressing a hopeless pupil. "That one, there, that's eye cream." She nudged a silver-washed pot. "That's excellent in a dry climate for your elbows and your heels. And that one, there, that's simply a colored powder."

"This one?" He prodded a midnight lacquered one with his thumb.

"Eye cream."

"Thought the other one was eye cream."

"That's for daytime use. This one's for night."

"Dear Lord, Kate, it's more complicated than 'change futures.'" He dumped the whole mess back into the bag. "What good is any of it?"

"What do you mean, what good is any of it?" she asked, hands on her hips, thoroughly offended

"Don't look at me like that, Kate. You cannot for one instant believe I implied you were anything less than the loveliest creature I've ever seen."

She'd received thousands of compliments in her day. Maybe more, trussed up in pretty words and poetry worthy of the bard. None had ever left her openmouthed, unable to summon a polite reply.

"I simply meant that, well, there is such a thing as gilding a lily. And truly, who exactly are you trying to impress? Nobody knows who you really are. That leaves only me."

"Don't hold your breath," she said darkly. "But a woman never knows . . ."

He shook his head. "You can't possibly need *all* of them."

She didn't even bother to try and charm him into it, merely pressed her lips together in a mutinous line. After a moment, he shrugged and let the bag drop, leaving her to dive for it, snagging the cord the instant before it hit ground.

She straightened, ready for battle, to find him already head down, burrowing in the trunk again.

"Shawls." He came up bearing four, beautifully wrapped in thin, crinkly paper, the top two peaking out—gossamer silk, the color of fine pearls; and the other, fuzzy blue wool that nearly matched her eyes. "All right, then. Why four?"

"Unpredictable weather?" she suggested helpfully.

He snorted and tossed them away.

Things flew from her trunk faster than she could protest, catalogued and dismissed in an instant. Four pairs of fine leather gloves, beautiful spangled handbags, slippers worked with silver threads.

"Stop!"

He paid her no mind but just unearthed a hatbox wrapped in lavender-flowered paper.

"Wait!"

He ripped off the cover. Violet feathers sprang free, a froth of ostrich feathers as thick as a hedge. "Good God, Kate, just how many birds were sacrificed for this monstrosity?"

"It was their honor to serve," she snapped at him.

He snorted and threw it over his shoulder, the hat flying out of its box, feathers fluttering behind like a tail. She dashed for it too late and watched mournfully as the hat, acclaimed last spring as the most fashionable ever created by Philadelphia's best milliner, flopped to the ground like a slaughtered pheasant.

She whirled on Jim, ready for battle, to find him standing, stock still, big rough hands holding a fistful of gauzy, ice blue silk.

He pinched a corner between his forefinger and thumb, as delicately as if it were a glass snowflake. He released his other fist and the entire garment spilled out, a slide of filmy silk and fine lace. She felt her cheeks heat. It was as wanton a thing as Kate owned, created by a French dressmaker the last time she'd replenished her wardrobe but never worn. As if she'd wear such a thing to bed with the doctor! The thought had been absurd, but she'd been unable to explain when the couturier had pressed the negligee on her.

She should have gotten rid of it a long time ago. It meant nothing to her, was utterly useless to anyone but a bride bent on encouragement or a courtesan intent on conquest. Yet it was so pretty. The one time she'd tried it on, the silk had whispered over her skin like a fantasy, then she burrowed it away in her drawer, one more wicked secret to add to the only other one she owned.

And now the other one stood right in front of her.

The fabric was thin as smoke. Kate could see the outline of Jim's hand behind the fabric nearly as clearly as if there were no cloth at all. She saw him brush one hand down the length of it, slowly as if he savored each inch, as if it were a woman's skin he touched instead of merely fabric meant to enhance it. He swallowed hard.

Then he looked up and met her gaze. He flushed, cheeks going bright as a schoolboy caught lurking around the girls' privy, his fist wadding up the fabric as if to hide how carefully he'd held it before.

"I—" He cleared his throat and tried again. "Here." He thrust the negligee at her as if he couldn't wait to rid himself of it. She snatched it away and tucked her hands behind her back—foolishly late, but she couldn't help herself.

"One pack," he told her, turning abruptly. "As long as you keep it down to one, I'll let you decide what goes in it."

"How magnanimous of you."

"Don't you forget it," he said, an automatic rejoinder but without his usual relish for the byplay. He strode toward the door, head bent, intent upon escape.

The fabric floated over her hands, a gossamer touch, and she shivered, remembering the look on his face. Her only solace was that he was clearly as affected as she.

"Jim?" she called after him.

He paused, one hand on the doorframe.

She waited for him to turn, and when he didn't, tried again: "Jim?"

He flinched, lifted his head so he could—just barely—be said to be looking at her.

Casually, she made a gesture, waving the flutter of shameless fabric in the air like a red flag before a bull. "Two bags," she said.

His eyes flashed, then darkened with heat. For good measure she lifted the gown and rubbed the fabric against her cheek. "I'm going to miss this." His jaw dropped a full inch lower. "Two bags," she repeated.

"Two bags," he agreed, and lunged through the door.

Chapter 8

MY FORMERLY FAVORITE SISTERS. STOP. I'M HAV-
ING AN ADVENTURE, JUST AS YOU SUGGESTED.
STOP. HOPE YOU'RE HAPPY NOW. STOP. I'M NOT.
STOP. LOVE, KATE. STOP.

Two and a half days later, Kate's horse trudged
along a road hugging the north coast of Massachusetts while Kate did the same thing she'd done every
minute of the day since they'd quit that little shack:
marveling that she had ever, for one single second,
considered this foolishness a good idea.

Only a mile or so down the road that first morning
they'd stopped at a small farmhouse. Jim left her
stewing in the yard—having given in on the "two
bags" issue, he'd made it clear in no uncertain terms

that he wasn't surrendering on this one—while he went in to negotiate.

He'd refused to tell her what he'd said. But somehow, without ever dipping into her purse, he'd managed to procure not only a healthy chunk of good yellow cheese and a nice loaf of bread for their breakfast but also a plodding little mare. She wasn't half the horse that Chief was, but it was far better than having him walking while she rode. And having him ride *with* her—well, that wouldn't bear thinking about. Except she did, too often, and in far too lurid detail.

And so they rode, until Kate's legs cramped and her bum complained. They caught meals where they could and slept in places that made that decrepit shed of the first night seem like the Rose Springs Hotel. And Kate cursed the damn fool idea that had prodded her into this in the first place.

Okay, so she'd had no place to go, nothing to do. The sisters she'd spent most of her life raising were settled, her husband dead. She'd negotiated the squabbles between her stepchildren over the estate to the best of her abilities, given that, despite her hopes and persistent efforts, they'd never regarded her as more than an interloper.

Nobody needed her anymore. Her sisters had told her to do something for herself, to take the risk she'd never taken, but it was hard to do something for oneself if one didn't have the means to pay for it. The doctor's invitation to this fiasco had fallen into her lap at what she now considered a despicably weak moment.

They'd pushed harder today, past the time they would have normally stopped. The fading sun sent deep shadows snaking across the road. The air held the briny tang of the ocean—they'd glimpsed it twice in the last hour, when the road dipped tight to the coast before pushing back into the woods—and she could hear the crash of the waves muffled through trees. Sometimes louder, sometimes softer, ever present.

They rounded a curve and there it was, a massive, horror-tale castle awkwardly perched on a rocky bluff as if it knew it had never been intended for this place. The warm, buff stone clashed with the cooler tones of the gray granite beneath. The walls were bare, sharp-cornered, as if no native vines could find purchase there.

Though it had stood empty only ten years, after the shipping magnate had been finally carted away to the sanitarium for good, it looked like it had been abandoned a century ago. Most of the windows were gone; someone had bothered to board up only a few. One pane of diamond-shaped glass remained intact, high on the lone tower, glinting gold in the lowering sun.

Brush choked the lawn, hawthorn and brambles creeping in from the surrounding forest. It soon became easier to dismount, tie their horses, and pick their way across on foot.

"A moat." He chuckled without amusement. "Why do Americans think there always has to be a moat?"

"Because we never do anything halfway, of course."

They smelled it before they reached it, the fetid, rank odor of unmoving water and the things that had died in it. It had to be a good thirty feet wide. The depth was harder to judge. A good ten feet of slick, algae-clotted wall sheered down from the edge until it met the green surface, so thick with scum that it looked as if one might walk right across.

And since what had once been the draw bridge

now lay beneath them, a pile of grayed lumber, splinters spearing up like spikes on a mace, they may very well have to.

Jim stood so close to the edge of the moat the scuffed toes of his boots extended a full inch over the brink. "Jim, get back."

He didn't move, just kept staring up at the ridiculous structure, his eyes hooded, jaw set. He lifted his head, looking up at the crooked heights of the tower, and swayed a little.

"Would you just get back, you stupid man!"

His head jerked back before he turned her way. "I'm not going to fall," he told her. "But it's nice to know you worry about me."

As if she were fool enough to worry about him. A woman who worried about a man like him, a man who spent half his life in dangerous places, clinging to the side of a mountain, rafting down rivers that had swallowed dozens of men whole, would forfeit countless nights' sleep staring at the ceiling and imagining the worst.

She simply wasn't that dumb. And all those nights during which she'd memorized every fold in the silk canopy over her bed, learned exactly where the moonlight fell on her wall every hour between midnight and sunrise—it was only ridiculous coincidence that so many of them happened shortly after one of his letters arrived.

"I wasn't worried about you," she snapped. "But having my partner die in the first week doesn't bode well for my chances of winning."

Pain streaked through his sherry wine eyes, causing her to realize the implications of her words. "Oh, Jim, I'm so sorry. I didn't mean . . . I didn't think . . . darn it!" Unthinkingly, she placed her hand on the tense muscle of his forearm. "I never for an instant meant to stir up bad memories. Nor ever, ever believed the papers had the right of it and the tragedy was your fault."

"It doesn't matter." He contemplated her hand on his arm for a moment. His shirt was rolled up, his skin dark beneath her fingers, encased in thin cotton not quite as white as it had been two days ago. She felt the flex of muscle beneath her fingers, perceptible even through the cloth, too interested to move her hand away even though she knew she should. Without realizing what she'd intended, she squeezed, marveling that his flesh had no give to it at all.

"It doesn't matter what I think?"

"It doesn't matter what anybody thinks," he said, voice utterly without expression, and shook off her hand.

Doesn't it? she wondered. Then why did he look like that, hollow-eyed, pale?

"We're already behind." He stepped over the edge of the moat, skidding down two feet as he dug in his heels. He dislodged a clump of mud that tumbled down and plopped into the green water, punching a dark hole in the scum that was quickly swallowed up by the backwash. "Time to get moving."

"Where are you going?"

The look he tossed her was all too familiar. The *you're pretty, but you're not too quick on the uptake, are you?* look. "Where do you think?"

"Through *that*?"

"How else?"

"How else do you suppose everybody else got there?" Somehow she could not imagine the prince of . . . whatever he was the prince of . . . trailing his beautiful silk robes through that. But then, he probably sent his minions into the muck while he relaxed in a tent with one of those poor women.

Jim hooked a thumb in the direction of the remnants of the drawbridge. "Over that, I imagine. But I don't think it's an option for us."

"But—"

"See how gray most of the wood is, how pale the sharp edges are? It hasn't been down long."

"Oh." She hadn't noticed the details, but it was perfectly obvious now that he pointed it out. "Wonderful. That bridge has stood for decades and it falls down just when we need it."

There was that look again, so dismissive that she was half tempted to give him an assist down that slope—with her foot.

"Somebody smashed it after they'd gotten their clue?"

He inched halfway down. "You can bet on it."

"But that's not fair!"

That made him laugh, so much so he had to grab for a protruding root to steady himself. "So says the queen of fair play. Or should I say the ace."

"Point taken," she admitted. "But the rules . . ."

"You'll find the rules pretty darn flexible when fifty thousand dollars, not to mention a lot of pride, is at stake. We'll be lucky if someone didn't booby-trap this damned moat."

"Booby traps?" She eyed the slick water with open suspicion, half expecting spears to pierce the undulating green. Jim was only one short slide from the edge. "Wait!"

"For what?" He probed the edge with his toe. Muck rippled sluggishly away from the contact.

"How deep do you think that is, anyway?" Nerves jittered in a stomach already offended by the stench.

"What do you care? No one's asking you to come along."

He said it so easily, as if it had never even occurred to him that she might try. If she didn't go now, she'd be sitting in the shade with a fan the entire trip, waiting for him to do all the work. Tempting, but she'd committed to doing this and she was damn well going to *do* it. "Of course I'm coming!"

"I wouldn't really recommend it."

"I want to come," she said, with enough fake enthusiasm to choke a bull.

He snorted, then waved her nearer. "Come on, then."

"How deep?"

"What does it matter? I can swim."

"I can't," she lied.

Frowning in exasperation, Jim glanced up and down the wall of mud. "Hand me that stick."

"This one?" The branch, six feet long and no thicker than her thumb, decorated with a few shriveled oak leaves, balanced on the edge of the ledge. She held on by the very tip and extended it to him, though her nose didn't appreciate bending so close to the moat.

"Thanks." He yanked it from her grasp. Unprepared, she wavered on her perch as her stomach lodged in her throat.

Jim jabbed the stick into the muck. It sunk in two feet and stuck there, vibrating like a tuning fork. "Two feet. Good enough?"

"Wonderful." Just wonderful. She'd been hoping it was deep enough to swallow up that stupid stick. Two feet gave her no excuse at all.

Jim waded in, water lapping at his shins.

"How's the water?" she asked, as sprightly as if they were in Newport and he'd just dipped a toe into the frothy ocean.

"Slimy." He surged forward.

"Wait!"

"What *now*?" he asked, irritation finally getting the better of him.

She dredged up the most winning smile she could manage. Odd, how the encouraging expressions, always so easy for her to wield, were becoming so hard for her to aim convincingly his way. "There's no reason for both of us to ruin our shoes."

"I already said you didn't have to come."

"There are . . . other options."

Hands on his hips, shin deep in muck, he stared at her in disbelief. "You want a *ride*?"

"Oh, it's not like you allowed me to bring along so many shoes that I can afford to waste a pair for no good reason." She caught herself halfway to a pout. Petulance might have worked when she was seventeen, but she could do much better now. "And it's not as if you'd have any trouble carrying me," she purred, her lashes fluttering, casting a provocative look down his strong frame.

"Oh, no you don't." He surged toward her. "*Don't* try that on me." He pitched his voice high, the annoying whine of a mosquito, and mimicked: "Oooh, you big strong man. You simply *must* rescue little ol' me."

"I wouldn't do that," she said, trying to look offended, knowing a smile was on the verge of betraying her.

"Of course not." He turned around, presenting her with a broad, cotton-clad back. "Climb on."

"But I thought you said . . ."

"Not because you simpered at me." He glanced over his shoulder at her. "But because you're right. It would be stupid for both of us to ruin our shoes."

You're right. Lord, but those words from him could keep her going a while. She began to gather her skirts but felt the heat of his steady regard. "Do you mind?"

"Not a bit. Go right ahead."

After ten seconds it became clear that he wouldn't be shamed into politely turning his back. Kate bent to her skirts again, feeling heat climb her cheeks no matter how many times she told herself not to be girlish. It was not as if she hadn't flashed her cleavage at him that first night with ruthless abandon. But that had been so calculated and detached there had seemed nothing whatsoever sexual about it. But now, as he watched her with open appreciation, she felt anything but detached.

She hadn't been shy about such a silly thing since she was barely into her teens. And so she yanked up her skirts in one abrupt motion, drawing them nearly to her knees, giving him a full view of stocking-clad ankles, a long length of shin. "You're going to have to turn around now," she told him.

"Huh?"

"So I can get on."

He shook his head. "Of course." He spun around, stirring up a small whirlpool around his ankles.

His head was bent. The thick, rich waves of his hair had been clipped short midway down his strong, dark neck, a faint V arrowing down until it disappeared into his collar. His shoulders were broad, a lovely width of muscle beneath limp cotton.

She swallowed. Saving herself from wallowing

through that nasty water had seemed like such a good idea at the time. But lately all her good ideas seemed to have unintended consequences. "Umm . . ."

"You've got two seconds before I start walking. If you want to cross after that, it's going to be under your own steam."

Gingerly, she stepped as close to the edge of the water as she could manage without actually touching the slop. Then she reached out, put one hand on his shoulder, and jumped. Skirts billowed around her, around him, as she latched on, arms around his neck, legs hugging his side.

"Jesus!" He staggered back. "You're not as light as you look." He leaned forward, trying to find his balance, then tugged at her arms clenched around his neck. "You're strangling me."

"I'm so very sorry," she said, and squeezed tighter.

"I meant you're light as a bird. A little bird. A feather, even. You just jump with, um, purpose, that's all. And I was unprepared."

"That's better." She loosened her hold. But only a bit—why risk tumbling off?

He moved through the water, his body shifting against hers. It was an intimate posture, her breasts pressed hard against his back, her thighs snug along his sides. His hair, sun-warmed, silky, was just beneath her nose. He'd dunked his head nearly every time they passed a stream. Every time they made camp, he'd disappear for a quarter hour and return dripping. And now his scent came to her, blotting out the stench of the moat. He smelled of clean water, warmth, man—*oh, what was it about a man that smelled so good?* She dropped her head, allowing her nose to just brush the top of one wave, as soft as it looked.

With each step he took, the muscles of his sides flexed against the inside of her thighs, the motion steadily rhythmic. Sometimes she bumped against his back, sending a jolt of pure sensation spearing through her.

"Stop that." His words barely penetrated her lovely haze.

"Stop what?" she murmured.

"Stop wiggling, I'm going to drop—" At that, his arm whipped around, his hand coming up hard beneath her rump, and she yelped. "Sorry," he said quickly. "I wasn't aiming—I mean, I just wanted to keep you from falling, and . . . oh, hell." He released her abruptly, forcing her to cling like a monkey, and charged across the moat. Water lapped behind them, dampening her trailing hem, but she paid it no mind. Speed now took on primary importance, for if she stayed plastered against his back for much longer, their little indiscretion in the gazebo was going to be the least of what they had to regret.

The instant he gained semidry land she let go, sliding down like a jelly released from its mold. Jim was puffing as if he'd run five miles instead of a mere thirty feet, his chest bellowing in and out—a chest that she was now far more familiar with than her peace of mind allowed. Her palms still held the feel of him, slab-hard, completely male. And she'd always been one to appreciate a well-made man, even if she'd never had the right to touch.

But why not now? Foolish, treacherous thought; it whispered along the edge of her mind like a poisonous serpent, lurking, waiting, every bit as lethal. She was no longer a married woman, no longer a girl.

Neither vow nor convention prohibited her from touching a man who appealed to her.

But if she did, the least she could do was choose a man who actually *liked* her. And no matter how attractive Jim was, no matter how sturdy and utterly lovely his muscles, that was an insurmountable flaw.

"Thank you," she murmured, unwilling to meet his eyes. Good intentions, she'd learned long ago and to her everlasting regret, often failed beneath the power of Jim Bennett's eyes.

"Forget it."

She nearly laughed aloud. As if that were ever going to happen.

"We'd best get going," he continued, and held out his hand, palm up.

"I—" She hesitated. She didn't need any more evidence that touching him, having him touch her, was a very bad idea. But the bank above her was steep and slick, and she didn't relish the thought of slipping back into the muck. She took a deep breath, trying to steel herself against the feel of him, and knew the instant that she placed her hand upon his that she'd failed utterly. There was no way to armor herself against him. His hand was warm, hard and rough and entirely gentle, his fingers wrapping around hers with firm possession.

"It's all right," he promised. "Do you think I'd let you fall in, now that I've gone to the trouble of getting you this far?"

He was as good as his word. They clambered up with little incident. Kate nearly forgot the treacherous slope beneath her—every sense she had, every thought, was too thoroughly occupied with the feel of her hand in his. His strength was so obvious, the skin callused from the work he'd done—not the hands of a pampered aristocrat at all. These were competent hands, hands that had done their share of work and done it well. Hands that could drag a man his size up the side of a mountain surely wouldn't let her slip away.

"Here we are." He gave one last pull, lifting her over the rim and setting her down in one movement. "Are you feeling all right?"

"Of course I'm fine. Why wouldn't I be?"

"You're a little flushed."

She snatched her hand away, hoping he hadn't noticed that she'd left it in his too long. "I'm fine," she snapped.

His mouth flattened into a harsh line. "Whatever you say." He turned toward the doorway.

The big arched door that must have once filled the massive opening was long gone. They stepped inside and instantly the temperature dropped a good ten degrees, the light blotted away as if the sun had just dropped below the horizon.

"Well, isn't this cozy?" Jim asked. The walls were dark and stained with damp, hung with the shredded remains of fake ancient tapestries. Two rusted crossed swords hung above a soot-blackened hearth flanked by the moldering heads of two unfortunate stags.

"Remind you too much of home?"

"More than you know." And then he visibly shook off the gloom. "Ready to start? We've only got an hour or so of daylight left."

"What are we looking for?"

"Anything that doesn't belong." He nudged a rotting carpet with his toe and it shredded at the first bump. "Something that's not falling apart, maybe."

"There can't be much of that." Kate wandered farther into the room, looking up at the swags of thick
cobwebs that swung from every beam.

"Well, if we're not in the right place, everybody else
came here, too." Trails ran through the thick layer of
dust over the slate floor. A flurry of muddy footprints
clustered in front of the hearth. "Seems like most of
the action was this way," he said, heading for the
opening that led off to the left, a dark tunnel beneath
the curve of the stairway to the second-floor gallery.

He paused in the shadow of the archway and
waited for her. He hadn't waited for her since they'd
begun. Usually he just strode off with an impatience
that implied he hoped she wouldn't follow. But now
he stood expectantly, hands on those narrow hips
with an expression on his face that, while not exactly
welcoming, no longer said: "The sooner you get away
from me, and the farther, the better."

She'd always thought she preferred polished men.
Men with carefully combed hair and crisp white
shirts and manicured nails.

And there he was, green and damp to his knees,
hair badly cut, sporting whiskers that should have
been shaved two days ago. A man who might have—
and she had more than a few suspicions about that—
been born to drawing rooms but who'd quit them a
long time ago and thrown himself into the wildest,
most uncivilized places he could find. And yet . . . he
drew her now, even more than he had that evening
he'd wandered into her gazebo and burned himself
into her memories. There were twin gathers on the
front of his shirt, the wrinkles where her fists had
clutched him to hang on, and it all rushed at her at

once, sensation, the smell of him, the feel of his body beneath her, however innocent it had been at the time. But there was nothing, ever, the least bit innocent about touching him.

"I think I'll go this way." She gestured awkwardly behind her and fumbled for the explanation. "There's no sense in us going together, is there?"

No longer forbidding? The glower returned in an instant, brows drawn down, shadowing his eyes to the point that no expression could light them. "Meet back here in half an hour. If you're not back, I'll come looking for you."

For the space of a heartbeat, she allowed herself to believe it, to sink into the promise contained in that one sentence. *I'll come looking for you.* But his next words brought her back to reality with a nasty thump.

"Don't do anything stupid."

Chapter 9

He beat her back to that ridiculous great hall. She hurried in, out of breath, from the far depths of the house's kitchen—and what a smelly wreck of a place that was—to find him posed *en guard* in front of a rust-coated, one-armed suit of armor.

"I'm pretty sure you could take him."

He spun. For one second she surprised a moment of boyish happiness on his face and it froze her in place. "I'm really good with opponents that can't move," he said. "Find anything interesting?"

"Three mouse carcasses, an entire library of chewed up books, and a whole lot of bat droppings. You?"

"How did you get all the interesting stuff on your side?"

"Nothing useful at all?"

"Only the torture chamber. A complete collection of

111

chains, manacles, and rotting leather. Interested?"

"I think I'll pass."

"You're no fun at all."

"Maybe when we get to know each other better," she said. "So what next?"

"Nothing left but the tower."

"The tower?" She hoped he didn't notice the way her voice pitched up; one's throat closing had that effect.

He shrugged. "We should probably have gone there first. The clue did mention 'nest.' "

"But . . . the whole place is the nest, isn't it?"

"If they're sending us to a nest, I'm guessing they're sending us as high as they can."

She'd suspected at the very start of this venture that she'd be forced to do things that were out of her area of expertise. That was the whole point, wasn't it? But really, shouldn't one have an opportunity to work up to such things?

"It's getting dark," she pointed out. "Shouldn't we wait until morning?"

"I found a couple of torches in the hall. Should give off plenty of light." He grinned. "And atmosphere."

"How clever of you." *Darn.* "Won't it be dangerous?"

He smiled wider, more cheerful than she'd seen him since they'd begun. In his element at last, she thought unhappily.

"Let's just go take a look, shall we?"

He's obviously scouted the tower already.

Jim, unhesitant, moved through a series of narrow tunnels that were completely confusing Kate's unreliable sense of direction. Once she accidentally brushed up against a wall, shuddering when her hand came away wet.

"What?" he asked after she surreptitiously swept her hand down his back.

"Excuse me," she said quickly. "Did I get you? There was a bug—most annoying—and I was simply trying to shoo it away. It didn't bite you, did it?"

"A bug? What kind?"

"Does it matter?"

"I . . . no." He continued down the narrow hall, a wide, dark smear marring the back of his shirt. Kate suppressed a twinge of guilt. It was not as if his clothes were perfectly clean to begin with, not after all the abuse they'd taken already. Why not protect her own?

The passageways grew darker. The narrow slits that served as windows, allowing brief glimpses of the crashing waves below, grew farther apart. Finally Jim lit one of the pitch torches, throwing flashes of inconsistent light around them, making the rest of the tunnel-like hallway look even darker in comparison. Only a few minutes later they ended up in a small round room at the base of a narrow stairway that clung to the wall and spiraled up into nothingness.

"It's about damn time." He stamped on the bottom stair, the sound echoing hollowly above them. "Seems solid enough."

Kate tipped back her head. The torchlight gave her a view of only the first few turns of the narrow staircase. The rest disappeared into blackness until far, far above there was a narrow pinprick of starlight. Her head went light.

"Looks like the roof's gone," Jim went on, completely matter-of-fact, a businesslike catalogue of the situation. "And there's not much of a railing left, so it'd be best to hug the outside wall. Keep your hand on the wall and you should stay away from the edge."

"I really think it'd be wise to wait for morning."

Holding the torch high in one hand, he turned to her. Shadows and light danced across his face, making the angles sharper, the hollows deeper. The torchlight was harsh, orange-red, reflecting an unholy glow in his eyes. It made him look dangerous, unpredictable, a devastatingly handsome creature of the night.

She hated danger. A heart that was already beating too hard knocked even more furiously, and yet her growing fear was edged with a sharp excitement that tingled in her fingertips, her toes, other places. She was *alive,* in a way that her safe and carefully comfortable world had never allowed.

"There's not much point in it," he told her. "The torch gives enough light to see at least the next couple of steps. If they become unstable we'll have to reassess, but the danger's pretty much the same either way."

"Hmm." It was easier, she discovered, not to think about it—the narrow walls and thick darkness that pressed too close, the empty space that spired overhead—if she thought about him instead. And, with that excuse, she watched him, the way she wanted to anyway. Light flickered in his eyes, turning the rich brown to gold, burnished his hair to fire. His mouth—how beautiful it was, the way he formed the words, a gleam of even white teeth that she found herself awaiting, breathless and fascinated.

"Stay close behind me," he said. "I mean it, Kate. This is no time to ignore me as you're wont to. And keep up against the wall."

She could do this, she told herself, even as panic fluttered high in her chest. She had to do this.

"You don't have to go," he said, his voice soft, almost kind, and it nearly undid her. If he'd challenged her, insulted her, the affront of it would have prodded her up at least a half dozen stairs. This only made it harder.

"Yes I do," she whispered. A year ago, she would have remained on firm ground and used all her wiles to prod him into doing as much of the work as she could. But her life was different now. It, and she, *had* to be different now.

"Kate—"

"I should go first," she said, spewing the words so there was no time to change her mind mid-sentence. She focused her attention on the tiny triangle of light that illuminated his neck, the wedge of skin exposed by his open top button. No chance of looking at the stairs that way. "I'm lighter, so if a step breaks, it probably won't do so quite as abruptly. And you could catch me." She swallowed hard. "Probably."

"I've never let someone in my party go into an unknown situation first."

"Jim." She lifted her gaze higher, looking directly into his eyes. "If you go down, you're going to go down hard and fast. There's no way I'm going to be able to stop it. And then I'm going to be stuck on that damn staircase until someone finds my dusty bones because I'm going to be too scared to move."

There. She'd admitted it. And he didn't sneer, didn't tease, didn't leave her behind. Just nodded and stepped aside for her to mount the stairs.

She took a deep breath and moved forward. And couldn't help but stop, just at the base, as her foot refused to lift.

Then he was behind her, close enough for her to feel

the warm wash of his breath against her neck as he spoke. He took her hand and placed it against the cool, rough stone of the wall. "Keep your hand against the wall," he said softly. "It'll keep you from getting too close to the other edge."

She nodded, struggling to draw another breath. She gathered up her skirts in her free hand, told herself to concentrate on the fact that Jim was behind her, not that there were dozens of stairs shearing sharply up ahead of her, and took one slow step. She flinched, half expecting the wood to crack beneath her.

"There you go," he said. "The first one's always the hardest."

"Hmm." She was pretty sure the farther the floor got beneath her, the harder they were going to get, but she appreciated the attempt.

At the rate she ascended the stairs, they'd be lucky to reach the top by midnight. A step, a quick seizure of panic before she waited for it to collapse, a sigh of relief, and then a few moments to gather herself for the next one. And the next. Jim didn't say a word, his warmth and even breathing a reassurance behind her. She concentrated on that, and on the solid cold bulk of the stones against her right palm—who cared if they were slimy now? They were stable. But the stairs seemed to narrow as they ascended, the walls coming closer, darker, until her breath began to labor. She wasn't sure which bothered her more—the dark, the close quarters, the yawning emptiness she knew fell only a foot or two to her left—and she reminded herself by the second not to look that way.

"Oh!" She forgot herself for an instant, yanking her hand away from the wall to wave it wildly in front of her face, clawing at the thick drape of spider web she'd just walked into.

"Kate." He was tight behind her in an instant, right arm around her waist, the solid reassurance of his bulk firm against her back. She felt the flare of heat from the torch and realized an instant later that neither one of them was touching the outer wall. She slapped her hand against it.

"Don't let go, you fool!"

"You let go first," he reminded her, calm, reasonable. "Are you all right?"

All right? *All right* was not her first choice, no. But she was no longer in immediate danger of pitching into hysteria, either. "I'm sorry," she said. "There was a spider web, and—"

"Spiders?" He shuddered, body vibrating against hers. "I'm glad you're in front."

"You're afraid of spiders?" She dared to twist slightly, peering at him over her shoulder.

"Afraid of spiders? No." He frowned. "More like terrified. Of spiders and beetles and flies and every other of those damn, creepy little things."

"Really?" She narrowed her eyes, trying to read him. "But there had to have been a lot of insects in the jungle."

"No kidding. Big crunchy black things with veiny wings; crawly little ones with a thousand legs that kept wiggling into my shoes." His arm jerked in reflex, tightening around her. And she realized they were very, very close, wrapped in the darkness, bound by their precarious position, his mouth mere inches from hers. "Why do you think my last expedition was to the Arctic?"

"I—" She was no longer sure exactly what was the cause of her breathing difficulty. Wasn't sure whether it was worse to blame it on the tower or his nearness, and which weakness promised more danger. "That's not true."

"You think you're the only one with fears, Kate?" His mouth was sober, serious. "Or that fears are always reasonable, or amenable to explanation, or easily willed away?" He shook his head. "They are what they are. You can face them or not. That's really the only choice."

She still couldn't decide if he was telling her the truth. There were no outward signs of panic; his voice was even, his arm around her steady. And if perhaps his breath was a bit labored, she thought that maybe, just maybe, it had as much to do with her as a few fragile strands of web.

But it didn't really matter if he'd confessed his phobia merely to soothe hers. It worked. She hesitated longer than sanity dictated in telling him that, because she wasn't quite ready to surrender the feel of him close to her yet.

"I don't want to hurry you," he finally said. "But are you ready?"

"I'm ready," she said reluctantly. An instant later his arm dropped, he moved back down a step, and she was once more facing forward.

Thirty more steps. Enough so that Kate began to feel the strain of it, short of breath from the exertion instead. Darkness pressed in from all directions. She'd lost track of how far they'd come, had no idea how much farther they'd yet to go.

"Are we nearly there, do you think?"

"Not yet."

Automatically she looked up, searching for that sliver of sky that might give her a clue. At the same time, her right foot came down and hit air.

She screamed, pitching forward. The tiny blur of star she'd just located streaked across her vision and disappeared as she fell. But she plunged only inches before Jim caught her, hauling her back to safety. Back, once again, against him.

"Kate. Kate?"

Dimly, she heard him call her name, but it seemed far away. Her breath caught in her throat; she couldn't pull it in, push it out, and her heart raced like a cornered rabbit's.

"Kate?" His mouth was right against her ear. She made a slight motion with her head, all she could manage. The ocean roared in her ears, taking her down. *Down. Oh, God.*

"Kate." He spoke sharply now, breaking through the heavy darkness enveloping her. "Kate, you're safe. I've got you."

Her limbs were stiff, frozen into position.

"Kate, do you know where you are?"

"Jim," she managed. It sounded hollow, distant, as if someone else had said his name.

"Good. I'm sorry, I should have been watching more carefully. The stairs have been so solid that—"

"No. I wasn't watching." She couldn't let him blame himself.

"But—"

"No!"

The sea pounded, sounding nearer than it was, the rhythm vaguely soothing, blending with the more labored sound of their breathing.

"We're closer to the top than the bottom," he finally

said. "It's only one step—the next one's fine, can you see? We might as well keep going."

"No!" The hysteria that had been seeping away boiled back.

"It's all right," he said, soothing as a stablehand calming a rattled horse.

"If that one broke, what makes you think the next one won't, too?"

"It didn't just break." He held the torch out, casting flickering light before them, and the sight of the gaping hole had her swallowing hard to keep her bile down. "See? Nobody's foot just went through that. Somebody smashed it away, just like the drawbridge. Just a little deterrent. The rest of the steps are fine."

"Just a little deterrent?" If she could have brought herself to move she would have slugged him.

"Yes. If they'd wanted to hurt someone, they would merely have weakened the step, so someone would actually fall through, instead of completely removing it so anyone going up would notice it was gone. They just want you worried, discouraged, and slowed down."

"It worked."

He gave her a quick, warm squeeze. "Did I ever tell you about the time the Doc and I nearly got cooked for dinner along the Maranon?"

"You've never told me *anything*, Jim, and truthfully, at any other time I'm sure I'd be fascinated, but at the moment I just don't care."

He chuckled warmly. "We can't stay here all night, Kate—"

"Why not? I'm rather fond of this step. Perfectly

comfortable. Don't see any reason why I should move."

"The treads aren't very wide. You can step over easily, as long as you keep your skirts out of the way."

"No."

"Here, I'll help you—"

"No!"

"Okay. Not going up. I understand."

He started to loosen his hold and she clutched at his arm, pressing it against her waist. "Don't let go!"

"I bet you never had to say that to a man before." He sighed. For a moment, he rested his chin on the top of her head, a layer of warmth spreading over the panic.

"Jim?"

"Hmm?"

"Thanks for being nice about this."

He lifted his head and Kate wondered why she'd said anything. "I learned a long time ago that yelling at someone had a troublesome tendency to make things a whole lot worse."

"Oh." There was no kindness in it then, merely expediency. She straightened, taking some of her weight off him. Her knees wobbled but held. "You can release me now."

"Really?"

Her bravery lasted about half a second. "No."

"Can you turn around?"

"That's going to be a problem, too. And before you ask, moving in general is going to cause some difficulty, so you might want to take that into consideration."

"If we move *down* you'll get closer to the ground with every step."

"Closer to the ground. I like the sound of that."

"Thought you might. All right, here's the plan. I'm going down a step—"

"Jim!"

"Just one, I promise. Only a few inches. I won't even have to let go of you. Then, when I'm there, my feet firmly planted, I'll guide you back. Ready?"

No, she wanted to say, but she could not admit to him that she could not do something so simple. She'd humiliated herself already.

She held her breath the whole time. But Jim was as good as his word, his support unwavering, his calm presence utterly comforting.

"There," he said when she'd eased down to the next step, "that wasn't so hard, was it?"

Yes, it was. "It was pitifully slow and you know it."

"Ready for one more?"

This time she almost meant it. "Ready."

It seemed quicker going down than it had coming up, and it did, indeed, get easier each step of the way. So much so that she was almost—*almost*—sorry when they reached the bottom.

They'd barely hit ground before Jim let go and stepped away, as if he couldn't stand to touch her a moment longer than he had to.

He turned half away from her, the torch he still held lighting the tense line of his jaw, his set mouth. "Better get started back," he said.

"No." She'd already forced them to waste half the night. That was enough. "You go on up. I'll wait here."

He half-turned toward the stairs, then stopped. "No, let's get you out of here."

"You're not really going to make me face that moat again, are you?" She forced a smile, blessing the amount of practice she'd had. He came closer, peering at her a bit too closely, and she felt her smile start to wobble. "What's the matter? Afraid of all those nasty spiders without me to clear the way for you?"

"You caught me." His brow smoothed, the severe lines easing. No doubt anticipating getting on his way, unencumbered by her.

"Stand there much longer, Jim, and I'll start thinking you can't tear yourself away from me."

"You tried." Awkwardly, he chucked her beneath the chin as if she were a child. "Never feel bad that you tried." He spun so fast the torchlight danced in a circle, and started up the stairs at a pace at least five times what they'd been able to take when she led the way.

Kate held on until the sound of his sure footsteps began to fade. Then she backed up until she came up hard against the wall and sank down into a miserable little ball.

It only matters that you try your best. The platitude mocked her. She distinctly remembered spouting it more than once when she was raising her sisters.

What an utter crock.

Chapter 10

His torch finally sputtered out about two-thirds of the way back down. Thankfully, it was after he'd passed that missing step, which was about the only thing he had to be grateful for in the whole damned mess.

Without the glare of harsh light in his eyes, he realized there was light below. Carefully he peered over the edge but could only see the descending coil of stairs, a bright orange glow seeping up from the center.

"Kate?" he called.

"Yes!" Her voice was clear and steady, as welcoming as the light.

She was all right, then. Poor thing. It was hard to think of her as a calculating, grasping woman when she'd shuddered with fear in his arms. Still, it wasn't as if one had much to do with the other, did it? he reminded himself. And if her terror had been real, and he was convinced that it was, that didn't mean she wouldn't play the card again if she suspected he were vulnerable to it.

When he reached bottom she was waiting for him, posture as beautifully erect and proud as a duchess anticipating her guests' arrival. There was no hint of the woman who'd shivered on the stairs, who'd quivered so deliciously against him that he'd nearly forgotten the reason for it, nearly forgotten the *who* and the *where* and simply lost himself in the feel of her. She was very easy to lose oneself in; he'd done it years ago, in a heartbeat, and wasn't entirely sure he'd ever found himself again.

"You lit the torch," he said. "I should have done it before I left."

She shrugged and smiled. "It chases the spiders." The torchlight loved her, turning her hair to bronze, her skin to amber. "So? What's the next clue?"

He lifted one hand and opened it, pouring out a river of crushed rock, the granite chips glittering when the mica caught the light.

"Dust?" She stepped forward and poked at the flakes remaining in his palm. He wanted to tell her to back off, that she'd no idea what she risked when she came so near.

But then she'd back off.

"I know you're good, Jim, but that's not much of a clue. Do they really want us all stumbling around stupidly, not knowing where we're going?"

"It's a newspaper. I wouldn't put it past them." He dusted his palms together, whisking away the remaining bits clinging there. "But I don't think that was the plan this time. There was obviously some sort of rock or tablet there, but somebody crushed it before I got there."

"Well, there's just fair play all around, isn't there?" She bent down, tilting the torch to illuminate the small pile of crushed rock, and poked through the remains. She picked up a large chip and peered closely at it. "There's something carved on it." She straightened and dropped the shard into his palm.

"I noticed that." He tossed the stone away.

"Hey! Why'd you do that?"

"Because it's worthless."

"It's all we've got." She hurried to where it had bounced off the wall. Head down, she searched the floor intently.

"Kate, come on. I saw what was up there. We're not putting the damn thing together like a jigsaw puzzle. You'd have a better chance of swimming the length of the Amazon alone than we do of finding something useful in that pile of gravel."

"But there was something on it."

"I saw it. A vee, the tip of an arrow, a goddamn clown hat. It could be a hundred things. And I can remember well enough what the stupid thing looked like without wandering around with it in my pocket." He hadn't really meant to yell at her. But the frustration gnawed at him.

His greatest strength in the field was his preparation. He left nothing to chance, anticipating every possibility, and so when the unexpected happened—and it always did—the problems were usually small, simply solved. At least they always had been until the last time.

But this—he was constantly scrambling, running

behind, bumping up against walls and bouncing off like a windup soldier. He hated it.

Kate, however, for all the fussy fragility of her appearance, was not the type to wither just because a man yelled at her. Hands on her hips, she matched his glare. "So what, exactly, are you suggesting we do next?"

He had a very clear and lurid image of what he'd like them to do next, but he didn't think she'd appreciate the suggestion. "I could beat the next clue out of Hobson."

"I imagine you could," she said. "But I also expect they'd disqualify us a minute later."

"Spoilsport." He gave up the idea with some reluctance, though he knew full well she was right. But it would have made him feel immensely better. "Most of the other competitors aren't exactly working to cover their tracks as far as I can tell. We'll just pick up somebody's trail and follow it," he said sourly. "Lord knows, it isn't as if the major hasn't ridden my draft more than once."

"But—"

He lunged toward her, snatched the torch from her hand, spun, and put her behind him.

"Jim!"

"Hush," he said, brandishing the torch before him, fleeting, eerie, glowing figures flaring on the walls for an instant before merging into shadow. "I heard something."

"Really?" Her hand settled on his shoulder as she peered over it. "I didn't hear anything."

"You haven't spent half your life wondering if there's a tiger just beyond your tent, waiting to pounce, have you?" he whispered back. "Now *hush*."

Her breath remained steady, as if she had no worry at all about his ability—or willingness—to protect her. Her hand remained on his shoulder, resting casually. It was as if all the contact of the day had removed that barrier between them, so that it was no longer unthinkable for her to touch him when and where she chose. Yet she seemed to barely notice the contact. But it seared him, the heat of her skin burning through his shirt, daring him to grab her hand and drag it down to places far more daring than his shoulder.

He'd almost decided that his nerves and his imagination had gotten the better of him when he caught the flutter of pale fabric in the black arch of the doorway.

"Jim," Kate whispered, her fingers digging into his shoulder.

"I see it."

The white figure floated into the room. For an instant Jim thought that one of the other fools in the contest had decided to try and dissuade them with a little mock haunting. He couldn't help but be insulted; did one of them really think he would buy such a thing? But then the specter slid farther toward them, barely into the edge of the glow cast by the torch.

It was the robe-wrapped young man from the ballroom on the first day. He was as completely covered as before, head, body, toes, making it impossible to guess at his expression or intent. Only his eyes showed, a dark reflection when he moved into the light.

He stood motionless in the center of the room, watching them.

"What do you think he wants?" Kate whispered in Jim's ear.

"How the hell should I know?" The muscles of his back and shoulders tensed in preparation.

"I thought you knew his father."

"*If* that *is* the son of the Amir—which we don't know—and *if* the Amir hasn't been overthrown since I was there, and *if* the Amir even cares or remembers meeting me ten years ago, yes, I know his father."

"That's not very much help."

"It almost never is."

A good thirty more seconds passed in silence, which felt more like thirty minutes. Kate had apparently had enough of waiting.

"Hmm." Before he realized what she was about, she'd stepped from behind him, waggling her fingers at the white-clad man. "Yoo-hoo. Hello there. Do you speak any English?"

"For God's sake, Kate, what do you think you're doing?" He snagged her wrist and hauled her back behind him where she belonged. "Stay behind me."

"Heavens, Jake, if he intended to hurt us, he would have by now. He certainly seems to be alone. What could he do?"

"I know it's your automatic reaction to any man and you probably can't help yourself, but *don't flirt with him.*"

"Oh, why not?" She tried to inch out from behind the shield of his body. He stuck out his arm to hold her in place.

"Kate, do you know how many wives the Amir has?"

"What difference does it make?"

"Do you have *any* idea how many of them had any choice whatsoever in the matter?"

"Oh." That shut her up. For all of about five seconds. "Oh, just look at him, Jake. He's only a boy."

"I believe the Amir took his first wife when he was eleven."

She waited a bit, and then: "He's older than eleven."

"I would say so, yes."

Head tilted, he'd watched them the entire time, without so much as a flick of a finger. Suddenly he bent down, his hand emerging from the deep folds of his sleeve, and dropped a roll of paper on the floor. He straightened, nodded to them, and melted into the darkness.

"Well, would you look at that." Kate made a beeline for it, brought up short when Jim grabbed her hand. "Would you *stop* doing that!"

"That's not what you said when I caught you before you fell through the stairs."

She stopped trying to tug away. "Point taken." At least the woman knew enough to recognize when she was wrong. "But I hardly think it could be dangerous. Maybe he left me a present. He seemed to like me."

"I'm sure he did," Jim growled.

"His family must have extraordinary jewels," she said. "Just think . . . one nice necklace, and I can go home right now."

"I don't think that . . ." he began. But then he saw the teasing glint in her eyes, the smile that flirted with the corners of her mouth. "You're teasing me."

"You need it, don't you think?"

He realized his fingers were still looped around her wrist and abruptly released her.

"I really don't think quite *that* much of my charms, you know, she said." Her eyes flashed a warning. "Don't say it."

He swallowed his quick rejoinder, and his smile.
He did not want to be so drawn by her. Kate, in a
playful mood, was irresistible. But if she had not
been charming, lovely, and skilled in attracting a
man, she wouldn't have snagged poor Doc so easily,
would she?

She'd moved closer to the paper the young man
had placed on the floor.

"Kate—"

"All right, I won't go any closer. Not until you've
thoroughly satisfied yourself as to its benign nature."
But she bent at the waist, bringing the torch closer to
the paper. "What is it, do you suppose?"

He joined her, squatting down to inspect it from a
closer angle.

"It looks innocuous enough," she said.

"So does a jellyfish. Until it floats into you." His
thigh throbbed at the memory. "Give me your shoe."

"My shoe? Why *my* shoe? Why don't you—oh, all
right." She shoved the torch at him, put her hand on
his shoulder to steady herself, pushed aside an entire
snowstorm of ruffles and lace and petticoats, and
tugged off a black leather pump.

"Hey, that's better. You're learning. I didn't have to
threaten you once."

As she straightened, Kate smoothed her skirts back
into place and thrust the shoe at him. "You weren't
just trying to catch another glimpse of my stockings,
were you?"

"Of course not." But it was a very nice bonus.

"What are you—" She broke off as he hammered
the small scroll, very thoroughly, with the heel of her
shoe. "Okay, I now know what you were going to do
with my shoe, but I still don't know why."

He tossed her shoe back at her and she caught it easily. "There's only so much trouble one can tuck into something that small. I figure most of the possibilities are alive—scorpions, small vipers, maybe a poisonous spider." He nodded to the now crushed roll of paper. "None of those will be a problem now."

"Eewww." She inspected the sole of her shoe with open suspicion. Finding nothing, she shrugged, set it down, and wriggled her foot back into place.

He carefully pinched the edge of the paper between his thumb and forefinger. He'd smashed it enough that it didn't unroll easily when he lifted it. A couple of quick flicks of his wrist solved that problem, and he held it at arms length.

"Has anyone ever told you that you're overly careful?"

"Yes," he said, snapping the paper a couple of times in the air. "I just don't believe there's any such thing."

"What are you doing now?"

"There is such a thing as contact poison."

"Really?" She stepped closer, peering curiously at the paper, and the smell of her overwhelmed him. It was no longer novel to him, and he thought that it should have lost some of its power by now. But familiarity had its lure as well; there was some pleasure to be found in trying to sort out the notes, decide which scent came from all those pots and creams and whether the sweetness that underlay it all was purely Kate or yet another artifice.

But it was terribly distracting at the moment. He eased away until the dank odor of damp stone and seawater overwhelmed the scent of her.

He took firmer hold of the paper and drew it closer, tilting it into the torchlight.

"What about the contact poison?"

"There comes a point, Kate, when you've taken all the precautions you can and, if you want to accomplish anything, you simply have to take your chances."

She was a complicated woman, far more so than her superficial façade suggested. But for the first time he had not the slightest clue what she was thinking. She tilted her head, drawing her brows together, puzzled, thoughtful. "Yes," she finally said, "I suppose there is, at that." And then her meditative mien was gone, her mannerism briskly businesslike. "So what is it?"

"I'd say it's a map." He angled it her way. "Though a rather amateurish one, at that. And even worse, a pretty poor copy of it."

"Not exactly a work of art, is it?" She studied it, focused, intent.

"What do you expect from the *Sentinel*? Probably their idea of a treasure map."

"Is it the real clue, do you suppose? Or is someone trying to lead us astray?"

"*Now* you're getting into a properly suspicious mindset."

"So happy you approve." She reached for the map, stopping when her fingers hovered a bare inch from it. "Is it all right if I touch it?"

"I—" The risk was minimal to nonexistent. She'd been in more danger taking a bite of the apple she'd had with supper. He'd spewed out that stuff about poisons and vipers just to tweak her—well, mostly he had. But for one absurd second, he nearly said no.

Doc had ordered him to take care of her. That did not mean he had to shield her from every single danger that existed. It was not even possible.

But he wanted to, which did not bode well for the rest of their travels, unless he went back to his original plan and locked her up, safe and sound and heavily guarded.

"Sure," he said quickly. "Here you go." He handed the handdrawn map. She smoothed it out against her thigh—*lucky paper*—and held it up where they both could study it together.

"It would have been somewhat easier to read if you hadn't beaten it to a pulp first."

"And here I thought you liked a challenge."

A jagged line bisected the paper. The right side was dense with figures—triangles, squares, swirls, squiggles. The left was nearly bare, sprinkled with a few wavy lines.

"A few letters would have been helpful, wouldn't it?" Kate asked.

"Now you're the expert on treasure maps, are you?"

"I'm just full of hidden talents." She bent her head, giving him a clean view of the pure line of her cheek, a small, soft slope of neck that seemed the loveliest thing he'd ever seen.

He forced his gaze back to the suddenly uninteresting map. "Try turning it around."

"Hmm?"

"It's upside down."

"How do you know?" He took the map, spun it, and placed it back in her hands. He pointed at a small geometric figure that now resided in the upper right corner. "See? A compass dial."

"Hmm." She leaned closer, squinting. She dug into her skirt pocket. "Look." She held the stone shard next to the map. The tiny triangular carving perfectly matched one of the compass arrows.

"Well, that's one point in the map's favor."

She looked up at him, eyes alight with interest, mouth soft. For a moment he could think of nothing else; it would be so easy to kiss her, to drop his mouth to hers and drink her in. And it was the very ease of it that warned him off; *easy* was so often a trap, a seemingly simple step that started one down a treacherous slope that was almost impossible to crawl back up.

"Do you think it's a fake?" she asked him.

"Oh, hell, I don't know." He was tired of thinking about it. Tired of remembering all the reasons he couldn't just kiss her. "We didn't *have* one to start out with, so there doesn't seem a whole lot of advantage to giving us a fake one. And the arrow does match. Nobody's shown much attention to fine detail thus far."

"Including us."

He nodded. "Including us."

"But why would that boy bother to bring us a map? There's no advantage in it. We're his competition."

"Maybe he *really* likes you." He shrugged. "Hey, it could be a good move for you. You said you've limited skills, and you're accustomed to luxury." He wiggled his hips. "Kate Goodale, harem girl."

She tried to scowl at him but ended up smiling. There was no way to remain angry at the man, Kate realized, when he looked so ridiculous swiveling his hips like a drunken dancing girl. The rare, light moments like this were the only reason she hadn't retreated to Philadelphia in failure already. But where was the line between failure and good sense, between admirable determination and throwing good energy after bad?

"Unless, now that you've gotten a taste of the simpler life," he went on, "you've decided to forswear luxury."

"Not in a million years. And the next time I get an idea, *any* idea, that requires me sleeping anywhere other than the biggest featherbed in existence, I don't care where you are. It's going to be your solemn duty to come and lock me up rather than allow such insanity."

"I promise," he said, sober as a knight taking his vow. But his eyes were lit with mischief and pleasure.

No wonder the foolish, lonesome girl she'd been had succumbed to his charms the instant she'd met him. She should consider herself lucky it hadn't gone any further than it had; the man, when he forgot he was supposed to be angry and suspicious of her, was pretty darn irresistible. And she'd lived with enough shame about that incident as it was, spending much of her marriage attempting to atone for the indiscretion the doctor had never known existed.

"So it's likely a fake, then." She didn't want to believe it, which surprised her. Her hips hurt from sleeping on the ground and her skin was already withering from all this fresh air. Her hair needed a trim, and her wardrobe would never be the same. She would have thought she'd have lunged on any excuse to call the whole thing off.

But she didn't want to give up.

"Oh, there could be reasons. There could be a thousand things going on beneath the surface that we have no idea about." He ran a finger down the wavering line that zagged through the center of the page. "He's the only one of the competitors who's acting

entirely alone. He might have just decided it'd be useful to have us owe him a favor."

"Hmm." The bottom of the stairway was only a few
feet away. She looked up at the spiral, grew dizzy just
at the memory. If she went home right now, she'd
never have to worry about getting more than a floor's
height above ground again.

But the truth was, there was no home for her to go to
anymore. Philadelphia was empty for her. The house
had never been hers, and her sisters were settled—and
if not as well-settled as she would have liked, her interference would only make them less so.

"So are we using it?" she asked, and didn't even
know what answer she hoped for.

The torchlight was starting to fade, making the
small, indistinct drawings on the map nearly impossible to read. Jim carefully rolled it back up and
tucked it under his elbow. "You wanted to be the boss.
What do you think?"

"I say we give it a try."

Chapter 11

By Charlie Hobson
Daily Sentinel **Staff Writer**

Residents of Hollingport, Massachusetts, have always known Marston House as the Cuckoo's Nest, the monstrosity of a faux castle built upon a bluff high over the churning Atlantic by shipping magnate David Marston, whose eccentricities long ago degenerated into madness. The castle, fallen to ruin years ago, has been avoided nearly as long, deemed haunted by local lore. But this week it was the center of the world's attention as the contestants in the Great Centennial Race scoured each dusty cranny for their next clue.

All the competitors were successful in achieving this first milestone. However, their speed varied widely. Two clear leaders emerged, Baron von Huss-

man and Count Nobile, who careened into the yard beneath a full moon only two nights after the first clue
was revealed. Undeterred by the spooky atmosphere,
they raced each other up the stairs to discover a mysterious map carved into a stone tablet . . .

Fitz Rafferty, managing editor of the *Daily Sentinel*,
who had not achieved his position by mincing words,
hurled today's copy of his newspaper on his cluttered
desk, clamped down on his ever-present cigar, and
snarled at his city editor. "It's boring as hell!"

Irvin Webb waved a hand in front of his face and
choked back the cough that plagued him whenever
he entered his superior's office. Rafferty spewed out
as much smoke as the Trenton Iron Works. "I thought
it was an excellent summary. Vivid, succinct—"

"And nothing happened!" The tip of his cigar
glowed red as he sucked in, matching the furious
gleam in Rafferty's eyes. "What's that damned Hobson doing out there? I didn't assign him to write a
travelogue."

"He's our best reporter," Irvin said soothingly. Half
his job was editing; the other half was keeping Rafferty from killing one of his reporters during one of
his rampages. "Give him time."

"Do you know how much we're spending on this
stupid contest?" Rumor had it Fitz Rafferty was approaching fifty. From the neck up, he looked twenty
years older, jowels and bags drooping like a basset
hound's. From the neck down, he'd somehow held on
to the powerful build that had made him the best
rower Yale ever had.

Of course Webb did, to the precise penny. He also
knew exactly how many papers they'd sold every sin-

gle day since it began. "It's not a stupid contest," he said, because sooner or later Rafferty would remember it was his own idea. "And I also know circulation is up nearly seventy percent. Pulitzer and Hearst must be on the verge of hurling themselves in the East River."

Rafferty chuckled, partly mollified. "Now, there's something I'd pay to see."

"If this keeps up, maybe you will."

Unfortunately, *mollified* and *Fitz Rafferty* never went together for long. He jammed the tip of his cigar into a glazed brown bowl overflowing with butts—hadn't been a good morning, Webb judged. "Not if we don't come up with a better story than this. Gawd almighty, all they're doing is stumbling around in the woods! You'd think somebody would have fallen off a cliff by now."

"What a shame they're all still alive," Irvin said dryly.

"Yeah, I—" He stopped and jabbed his finger at Webb's chest. "Now, don't go all soft-hearted on me. We don't make people do stupid things, we just report it. We've got a newspaper to keep running, for Christ's sake. You know how many people'd be on the streets if we went out of business?"

Webb wondered how many things Fitz had rationalized over the years with that particular line of reasoning. But as he would be one of the first on the street, and he'd been there once and didn't like it much, he kept his mouth shut.

As he did at least three dozen times a day, Rafferty stalked over to the door to his office, which he kept open at all times unless he was closeted with someone who'd come directly from the mysterious, powerful owner of the *Sentinel*, Joseph Kane. Fitz liked to stand there and look out over his domain, a dozen reporters hunched over typewriters and cigarettes, the racket of clattering keys increasing to a furious level every time he appeared in the doorway.

"Make the clues easier," he ordered.

"Easier? Wouldn't it be better to make it harder, have people dropping out?"

"No." He tucked his thumbs in his waistband and rocked back onto his heels. "The more people out there, the more potential stories for Hobson to dig up. I want them all there, and in the same place. Tripping over each other, getting in each other's way, talking to Charlie about whoever pissed 'em off the most."

"Got it. Easier." Of course they were going to throw out all the rest of the clues that he, Irvin, had sweated over for a full month. He'd been so pleased with his own cleverness. Now no one would ever get to admire it. Wasn't that always how it went?

"Yeah. Oh, and Webb?" Rafferty glowered over his substantial shoulder, spearing Irvin with the glare that could still, after ten years of working together, freeze him in place.

"Yes, Mr. Rafferty?"

"You tell that overpaid ass Hobson that he'd better start coming up with something better, or he's not going to be overpaid much longer."

According to the map that Jim bought the morning they left the Cuckoo's Nest, there were five formations on the coast of the Atlantic between Massachusetts and Nova Scotia that closely matched their hand-drawn map. They spent the next two weeks checking out the first three, each a perfect set of three tiny islands about a hundred yards from the shoreline, a thin spear of a peninsula that jutted toward the rocky islands like an arrow pointing the way.

After the second day, Kate had stopped bothering to ask where Jim dug up the tiny rowboats he'd used to ferry them to the islands, any more than she asked where he'd come up with the provisions for their daily meals and the extra blankets they'd needed once they crossed into New Hampshire. She was pretty sure she didn't really want to know. And truly, the handsome bulge of his arms as he pulled on the oars was the only bright spot in the entire sorry trip.

Her hopes had soared at the third stop, where the most seaward island held a crumbling redbrick lighthouse. There wasn't much left to the stairs, and Kate felt only a twinge of embarrassment at staying safely on the ground while Jim fashioned a complicated rope system to drag himself to the top, a twinge that couldn't compete with her utter relief at keeping her feet safely on the damp rock floor. But it turned out to be nearly—but just *nearly*—as hard to wait, worrying over Jim's safety, wondering what he'd found. When he'd come back down empty-handed, her disappointment had been overwhelmed by her relief at seeing him safe and sound.

They'd occasionally run into the other competitors. The son of the Amir appeared regularly, often enough that if she didn't see him for two days she'd begin to worry, something that annoyed Jim to no end—but Jim was pretty easily annoyed these days. The boy never said anything, never even came closer than twenty feet or so, just regarded them with those dark eyes for five or ten silent minutes before lifting his hand in salute and melting into the forest.

They'd run into Count Nobile twice—not at all by accident, Jim had maintained. The count had invited them to dinner—all right, he'd invited *her*, tagging Jim on the end of the invitation only after Kate had signaled it with her eyes as emphatically as she could. He'd promised some lovely Italian specialties that she couldn't decipher but just the sound of had her mouth watering. Jim had turned down the invitation before Kate had a chance to accept.

Major Huddleston-Snell they'd seen only once. They'd passed on the road, the major and Jim swinging wide on either side so as not to pass any closer to one another than absolutely necessary. And then as soon as the major and his party disappeared, Jim dove for the map, poring over it for a good hour to try and discern why the major could possibly be going in the opposite direction.

Baron von Hussman, it was rumored—Kate had lured this tidbit from the count, before Jim dragged her away with some ridiculous excuse about needing her advice on the next day's route—was so far ahead of the rest of the competitors that they could ride all night and never stumble into him.

On two days it had been so cold that Kate had been reduced to wrapping a blanket around her shoulders since, as she reminded Jim at every opportunity, he had not allowed her enough room to pack her thick woolen cape, a complaint which eventually caused him to throw two of his own shirts at her and tell her she could either wear them or stuff them in her trap. She chose to wear them.

They'd had heat. They'd had rain. On one memorable morning they'd been pelted with hail as large as crabapples. Kate had been closer to shelter and had reached the overhanging ledge first, enjoying, in a way that was probably unkind but nevertheless undeniably satisfying, the ice balls careening off Jim's hard, dreadfully grouchy head.

And it was a grouchy head. Extremely so, and getting more so by the day. Kate could only marvel at how wrong she'd been about him, that the wistful, heroic image of him she'd built on one enchanted evening, a few stray letters, and every word he'd ever published, could be so utterly mistaken.

He was not charming. Perhaps he could be, if he set himself to it, but he was certainly not trying it out on her. He was not kind and thoughtful. He might have been articulate, but who could tell? He hardly ever spoke to her anymore, except to bark orders.

Oh yes, he was big and handsome and competent. Fascinating to watch as he pitched a makeshift tent or dressed a rabbit in the blink of an eye. He made excellent coffee, quick fires, and she could happily occupy the better part of a day admiring his seat on a horse.

Or off one, she admitted in honest moments.

At the very beginning of this trip, she'd had some concerns about the two of them on the road together. She'd considered that perhaps her memories, her newly unmarried state, and her sisters' ridiculous urgings, not to mention his admittedly splendid physical presence, might overwhelm her good sense. But Jim's true nasty nature was proving a rather effective deterrent. Not to her fantasies—that couldn't be helped—but at least she was seldom tempted to act on them.

Today, it was raining. They slogged along on a narrow, pebbled road about fifty miles into Maine. The sky was gray, the sea pewter. It wasn't raining particularly hard; if it had been, even Jim would have had to call a halt and start looking for shelter. No, it sputtered and spurted and spit at her, sometimes pausing just long enough to give her hope, but never long enough to let her drawers dry out.

The wind gusted higher, blowing a spray of mist into her face, and she bent her head, trusting her horse to find its way. Considering how much time they'd spent plodding along behind Jim and Chief, Kate figured her mare could manage without much guidance. She shifted her hands on the reins, frowning at the condition of her broken nails.

It was utterly amazing how quickly, after a lifetime of diligently taking good care of oneself, a woman could go to hell. After so much time in the open air, she couldn't seem to slather on enough cream to keep her complexion smooth, and her mother would have worn a mask rather than appear in public with this much color in her skin. The humidity of the seacoast had expanded her hair to the volume and texture of a small bush, and her clothes . . . she absolutely refused even to think about her clothes. She'd settled on ruining one set completely, preserving the rest, but that strategy was going to fail in the near future when her current blouse and skirt shredded the next time she washed them, for Kate was fairly certain it was only the layer of grime that was holding them together right now.

Because conversation was out of the question—Jim ignored her a good portion of the day, which was a novel experience for her—Kate occupied herself with mentally composing her next letter to her sisters. No more telegrams; her current mood required more than a bare minimum of words.

She could not believe they'd prodded her into this foolishness with all their mumblings about "freedom" and "adventure." Lord only knew what disasters would ensue if she gave serious consideration to Emily's instruction that Kate undertake one grand, passionate affair.

And it was much easier to be angry with her sisters than miss them.

Dear Emily,

All right, my dear, I know that you are completely convinced of the value of spontaneity and optimism, but I have to say you have oversold their utility. This adventuring is a most uncomfortable business. Oh, not that I am in any danger; nothing could be further from the truth. Quite honestly, aside from such matters as lumpy, hard beds and terrible food, a great deal of this venture is downright boring! Why did you not warn me? You both seemed so charmed by your escapades, and met such lovely men in the process, I was lured to undertake one myself. Either I am going about this entirely the wrong way or your accounts of such matters were distinctly edited.

Have you guessed where I am? No, I shall not tell you. You shall suffer and wonder, as I am suffering . . .

"What did you say?"

Kate looked up. "I didn't say anything."

"You were muttering under your breath. Damn near hissing, from the sound of it." He pulled his horse to a stop, waiting until she came up alongside him before urging Chief forward. "Cursing me, were you?"

"I was not." It really was most ridiculously unfair. She knew she must look like a drowned rat, hair snarled, nose dripping. He, on the other hand, had never looked better. He'd run his hands through his hair, slicking it back from his forehead, throwing the clean lines of his face into sharp relief. The light rain glistened on the high rise of his cheekbones, glittered in his thick dark eyelashes. His dampened shirt clung to every plane and swell of his body and gave her overactive imagination far too much to dwell on. If he looked like that in clothes, he had to be downright spectacular naked. "Not that you don't deserve it," she said.

"Who, then?" His gaze settled on her, a bit too sharply to be casual. "The doc, maybe? That he left you in such difficult circumstances?"

She didn't want to talk about Doctor Goodale. That part of her life was over. She did not precisely regret it, but she certainly didn't cherish it. And she did not want to be reminded that while the doctor had scrupulously lived up to his part of the bargain, she once failed in hers. And her lapse was all the worse for it having been with Jim. "If you must know, it was my sisters."

"Fond of them, are you?" he asked, sarcasm heavy in his voice.

She blinked away the raindrops that smarted in her eyes. "Enormously so."

"Oh, yes, I pegged that right off. All the kindness in your voice, and all that."

"This is all their fault." The rain picked up, droplets stinging cold when they hit her cheeks. "If they hadn't gone and grown up so that they no longer needed me, not to mention run off to get married to prove it, I would not be here. In fact, I—"

They'd rounded a corner as they talked, passing a thick stand of oaks to their left. In the shelter of the trees someone had made camp, a neat little compound with two brown tents and a fire that glowed cheerily beneath the protection of a canopy mounted on poles. A tall figure in a yellow slicker, back to them, stirred a pot on the fire, the smell good enough to make Kate's mouth water even from a hundred yards away.

The figure looked up as they approached and Kate recognized Mrs. Latimore, as composed and comfortable in the rain as she'd been in the ballroom. She was motionless for a moment, studying them, her face a mask. And then she waved them over.

Kate, thinking only of two things—warmth, and food—had her horse pointed that way before Mrs. Latimore completed the first gesture.

"Wait," Jim said beside her.

"For what?"

"I'm not so sure that's a good idea."

"Oh, for heaven's sake." She whirled on him, furious when he reached down and caught her mount's reins, stopping her in place. "We can't just ignore her. That's so rude. You may not care, but I do."

"I'm not saying ignore her. I'm saying let's discuss this before we go charging over there."

"Let me go." She was cold. Her nose was dripping and no doubt red. It would take an hour to work the snarls out of her hair and longer to warm up her bum. A fire was mere steps away, and she could not believe he was delaying her from it for a second longer. "*Now.*"

"No. Kate, I—"

"I don't care!" She yanked hard on the reins, hoping he'd be forced to release her, but though her mare danced beneath her, his grip remained firm. "You've been doing nothing but telling me what to do for two weeks. Why did you even bother to ask me back at the Cuckoo's Nest if we should go on if . . ." Guilt flashed across his features. "Oh. You thought I would say no, didn't you?"

Chief—reliable, unflappable Chief—shied beneath him, as if Jim's legs had suddenly clamped down, and Jim finally had to release her reins to calm his own horse. "I thought that was a strong possibility, yes," he admitted.

"You were hoping to quit?" Try as she might, she couldn't quite reconcile that with him. He seemed more the type to hang on to the bloody, bitter end.

He answered her with silence, a bulldog-stubborn look on his face.

"Hmm. You meant to go on without me? *Hoped* to go on without me?"

He sighed heavily. "It would have saved me this discussion now."

She shouldn't have been surprised. He'd tried to be rid of her from the start, hadn't he? But when he'd stopped trying to sneak off without her she'd assumed he'd accepted, if not welcomed, her presence.

They'd—she'd thought—settled into an uneasy truce. It was not vanity but honesty, she considered, that made her understand that few men sought to free themselves from her presence. Though she'd known from the start that what she had to offer was of less value to him than most, she'd thought they'd moved beyond it. It pricked, maybe a little more than it should have, to discover nothing had changed.

She wheeled her horse around and headed for camp.

"I would have shared the prize!" he hollered behind her.

He really didn't know or understand her at all. The fact that no man really ever had, that she'd never *allowed* any man to, didn't seem to matter a bit.

She vaulted from her mount the instant she gained the small, orderly camp. Though she knew Mrs. Latimore and her party couldn't have been there long, there was an efficiency and spare comfort about the enclave that appealed to Kate. She was willing to bet that not a single *man* competing had so cozy a home each night.

Mrs. Latimore, after setting down her spoon, folded her hands and waited patiently for their arrival. She wore a broad-brimmed hat draped with yellow oilcloth. Little showed of her features but that assertive nose and sharp-boned chin.

Jim gained Kate's side before she took two steps. He gripped her elbow—not painfully, but decidedly commanding—to hold her up, then bent to her ear.

"Be careful," he whispered. "She has a reputation for ruthlessness and a history of survival in the most difficult of circumstances. It is a dangerous combination when one is not used to dealing with such qualities."

Kate faced him squarely. "I lived, quite successfully, with Doctor Goodale for over fourteen years. Do not speak to me about dealing with difficult qualities."

She turned, briskly dismissing him, her steps quick until she ducked under the dripping edge of the tarp.

"I'm Kate . . ." Jim arrived just in time to jab her, less gently than he could have, in her ribs. Now, what name had he given her? Oh, yes. "Katie Riley."

"Mrs. Latimore." Her handshake was strong and brief. "I saw you in the ballroom. Thought you were a—" she shot a quick, accusing glance at Jim—"Well, it no longer matters what I thought. That annoying reporter says that you are Lord Bennett's assistant."

"After this experience I shall never believe the papers fully again. They simply cannot seem to get the details correct, can they?" Kate said smoothly. "To be precise, Jim and I are partners."

"Really? Equal partners?"

"Hmm." Ignoring Jim—and wouldn't her life be so much easier if she could always ignore him?—she leaned slightly toward Mrs. Latimore. "Well, some of us are more equal than others, aren't we?"

Mrs. Latimore laughed, an unselfconscious bray. "Would you like to stay for dinner?"

Behind her, Jim cleared his throat loudly. As far as Kate was concerned, he could loosen phlegm until he choked on it; she wasn't paying any attention. "That is very kind of you. I would love to."

"Am I invited, too?" Jim asked.

Mrs. Latimore's mouth pinched in disapproval. "I suppose so."

"It smells wonderful," Kate put in.

"Yes, doesn't it?" Mrs. Latimore smiled broadly. "I'm afraid I can't take credit. Miss Dooley is camp cook and a finer one you'll not find." She indicated two folding chairs that hugged the far side of the fire. "Please, make yourself comfortable." She addressed Kate alone, as if Jim was not hovering so near behind her that Kate could feel the warm brush of his breath against her neck each time he exhaled.

Mrs. Latimore strode off to the farthest tent and ducked inside.

Jim flopped into a chair, extending his big, booted feet toward the fire. "Well, isn't she just charming?"

Kate pointedly dragged her own chair to the other side of the fire before settling into it herself. *Heaven.* "I liked her."

It was the most pleasant evening they'd spent since they set foot in the Grand Ballroom. A warm, savory stew and golden biscuits filled bellies that had grown used to quick meals of crackers and jerky. The mellow glow of the fire dried out damp clothes and the rain clouds drifted away on a warmer wind.

Mrs. Latimore proved to be an interesting, if acerbic, raconteur. She and Jim spent much of the evening trying to top each other with outlandish tales of narrow escapes and harrowing triumphs, stories which had Kate praying fervently that their next clue would not send them hieing off to places that humans were clearly never meant to set foot in. They even found an uneasy truce when Jim admitted that he, as had Mrs. Latimore, had failed to fully conquer the summit of Cotopaxi.

Miss Dooley was quietly friendly, offering food and coffee, smiling and interested in the conversation, offering few comments even though she'd accompanied Mrs. Latimore on most of her journeys. Through it all the houseboy—man—Mrs. Latimore called Ming Ho served with silent, polished efficiency, filling glasses and whisking away soiled dishes.

"Well." Jim patted his stomach in appreciation and stood. "Mrs. Latimore, I don't know how you manage it, but your hospitality has managed to make me nostalgic for home and Africa at the same time. Truly a marvel. But we'd best be going, as we hope to get an early start tomorrow morning."

"Do you?" Unsmiling, Mrs. Latimore stood as well, as if reminding him that she was nearly as tall as he. "Miss Riley, there is no reason to set up your own camp at this late hour. Wouldn't you prefer to stay here? Ming Ho would not mind surrendering his cot for one night, and there is room for it in our tent."

Kate hesitated and glanced at Jim, waiting for him to object. But he said nothing, his expression shuttered.

"I—"

"The mosquitoes promise to be quite fierce tonight," Mrs. Latimore said.

A cot. A tent. It sounded like heaven to Kate, who had once slept in a bed that had belonged to a duchess. Amazing how quickly one's standards changed.

"Well?"

"Jim—"

"Can surely find himself somewhere to plop his bedroll." She flicked him a dismissive glance. "He looks like a resourceful fellow."

Oh, why was she worrying about what Jim would say, anyway? "That is very kind of you. Thank you."

Mrs. Latimore nodded. "This way."

"Katie." Jim moved to her side and touched her elbow briefly. "A moment, please."

Mrs. Latimore glared at him. "Miss Riley, you do not have to—"

"It's fine." When Mrs. Latimore raised one eyebrow, Kate went on, "No, really, it's fine. We have a few details to settle, that's all. I'll be along in a moment."

For a moment it seemed as if Mrs. Latimore would object. Then she nodded crisply, shooting one last warning glare at Jim, then disappeared into her tent.

"For some reason I don't think that woman likes me."

"A novelty for you, I'm sure." Kate braced herself before turning to face him. "Jim, tomorrow you can rail at me about accepting her invitation all you wish. At least I'll have had a good night's sleep."

"That's not it." He looked at her, and away; shifted once, twice, before shoving his hands deep in his pockets. "I did not mean . . ." He frowned into the distance. "I know it is my habit to issue orders. It is simply safer in the field for all parties to follow certain procedures exactly. On the few occasions I have lost that control . . ."

She knew there was nothing in that wavering edge where the firelight surrendered to the night that held his attention so fiercely. She had read and heard only fragmented details of his last, doomed expedition to the Arctic; it had happened during the doctor's final illness, and her attention had been occupied. But it took very little empathy to see the lines that tightened around his fine mouth, the stark hunch of his shoulders, and know that his partner's death haunted him.

"Yes," she said softly. "I admit that I, too, have sometimes been accused of being overly controlling in certain situations. Though my sisters have been quite annoyingly successful at ignoring my very wise orders."

The corners of his mouth lifted and he turned her

way. The remnant of the day's rain misted the stars behind him, a softness at odds with the clean, severely defined lines of his face. It was hard to believe that he'd sprung from the background attributed to him, from soft, pampered English aristocrats and luxurious, rose-entwined manors. He was so much a creature of the wild and brutal places, sure and strong, stripped of all the trappings of frivolous society, pared down to the vital and powerful; nothing else would have allowed him to survive.

"Did you just accept my apology before I made it?"

"I'm exceptionally accommodating that way," she said with a grin.

"Accommodating. Yes, that's always the first adjective that comes to mind when I think of you."

"Well." He was nearly smiling. She counted it one of her better victories.

"Good night, then. Sleep well." His grin widened. "You're going to need it."

"Back to the taskmaster already, are you?"

"Did you expect anything else?"

"Hoped, perhaps. Expected? Never."

He turned. The fading glow of the firelight clearly illuminated a large, green-tinged stain on the back of his shirt, vaguely hand-shaped.

"Oh, for heaven's sake." Life would be *so* much easier without the inconvenience of a conscience. "Give me your shirt."

"What?" He swung around, more surprised than she'd ever seen him.

"Your shirt." She held out her hand. "I know your standards are somewhat . . . flexible, but truly, its condition is ridiculous. Ming Ho promised me some warm water in the morning. I might as well rinse that out when I'm doing a few of my own things."

Surprise spun into open suspicion. "Why?"

"What do you mean, why?" Was it so unbelievable that she would offer? "If you'd prefer to wear that shirt until it can stand on its own, far be it from me to interfere."

"Hey, now, that's not what I said." He held up his hands, palms out. "You're just the farthest thing from a washerwoman I've ever met, that's all."

"All right, then." Slightly mollified, she gestured for him to hand it over. "Your shirt."

"Right now?"

"Modest?"

"No, not really." Jim had not been away from civilization so long that he'd forgotten ladies were prone to vapors when someone mentioned "legs." Yet Kate seemed fully prepared to stand there and watch him strip.

Well, he thought with more than a touch of intrigue, might as well see if she meant it.

He had to give her credit. She didn't flinch, simply stood there with one hand extended, the other on her hip, eyes level on him.

He didn't expect to fumble with his buttons. He'd once danced stark naked in front of an entire tribe. But with Kate only a few feet away, watching him steadily, his fingers grew clumsy.

He yanked the shirt off his shoulders the instant the last button parted. "Here you are."

"Thank you." She crushed the fabric between her hands. "I'll get this back to you tomorrow."

"No rush. I do own another."

"You do?" she asked lightly. "I never would have guessed."

She turned as if to go and suddenly he didn't want her to leave. Considering that he'd wished her gone a hundred times in the last two weeks, the urge might have caught him by surprise. But what man would not want to stand there with her, awash in firelight. And he knew, although he didn't want to, that the reason he'd wanted to leave so badly was because, try as he might, he simply could not make himself immune to her.

It was impossible. A hundred men, a thousand men, had no doubt had the same problem before him. But now it was *his* blood that roared in his veins, *his* heart that threatened to beat right out of his chest in demand.

"I must give you credit," he said. "Nary a blush. I didn't think you could do it."

"I am no longer a girl," she reminded him.

Who wanted a girl? Only young boys yearned for innocence. Perhaps fools who were afraid they would not measure up. Only those who had not learned the allure of boldness, of passion that met your own and heightened it. Of the wicked temptation of a woman who could stand in the misty evening and watch with open admiration, without a whiff of demure offense.

A man couldn't help but wonder if she were completely without inhibition.

"I wonder," he said, before he could think better of it, "what it would take to shock you."

Kate was very nearly shocked now. Not by him taking his shirt off—oh, not that, though his shoulders were very fine, the swell and planes of his chest clearly delineated beneath the tight, thin knit of his undershirt. But by the intensity of her reaction to him. It thrummed through her, strong and clear and demanding.

His shirt was still warm from his body. Her fingers caressed it of their own volition, as if he still wore it and it was the flesh beneath that she explored.

Oh, why did it have to be him? They had a past, of a sort, a painful and embarrassing one. A prickly and ever-shifting present. Certainly no future. It would be so much easier if it were someone else, someone with no complications. It was as if something in her had fixated on him—more honestly, on some shining image of him that had very little to do with the real man—all those years ago and refused to let go.

"You might be surprised."

Chapter 12

The third cot crowded Mrs. Latimore's tent but not unduly so. A lantern swung from the ridgepole, casting soft and comforting light through the small space. On a trunk turned on its side as a night table, there were soft cloths, beside a pitcher of warm water brought by the silent, smiling, and ever-capable Ming Ho. The sheets were so fine Kate nearly sobbed when she touched them for the first time and she hurried through her evening routine in order to slide in between them as quickly as possible.

"Before you turn in—" Mrs. Latimore and Miss Dooley were ready for bed long before Kate finished, and were sitting upright on their cots, swathed in twin, voluminous cotton gowns, when Kate ducked beneath the tent flap and dropped it behind her. "We'd like to speak to you a moment, if we might."

"Of course." She lowered herself to the cot, sighing as it gave gently beneath her, and restrained herself from toppling right into it. "I really cannot thank you enough for allowing me to stay here tonight."

Mrs. Latimore waved her hand. "It's the least we can do. Women embarking on ventures such as this face challenges that males do not. It is therefore incumbent upon us to assist where we might," she said meaningfully.

But whatever she was hinting at was too subtle for Kate to discern. "Of course," she murmured.

Mrs. Latimore frowned. Her features were brutally sharp in the dim lamplight, the angles clean as a fresh-stropped razor. The years she'd spent in the sun had left their mark; lines scored deeply along the tight seam of her mouth, around her intense eyes. Yet she was a striking woman still. "If there is anything we might do to assist you . . ."

"I am most grateful for your offer, but it is too much to ask for you to assist us on your quest merely as a gesture to another female—"

"No!" Mrs. Latimore surged forward and clutched at Kate's forearm, her grip strong. "You do not understand."

"Apparently I don't." She twisted her arm away as subtly as she could.

"Let me try." Miss Dooley joined Kate on the cot, a whiff of powder and violet soap accompanying her arrival. "We realize that Lord Bennett has some rather . . . obvious charms. We also understand sometimes women find themselves in . . ." she paused delicately before plunging on. "Situations from which it is difficult to extricate oneself. Believe me, I know." Mrs. Latimore and Miss Dooley exchanged glances. "Only too well."

Kate searched for an appropriately noncommittal answer and settled for "Hmm."

"Would you like our assistance?" Miss Dooley asked gently.

"With what?"

"With getting away from that man!" Mrs. Latimore snapped.

"Jim?"

"Of course, Lord Bennett."

"Oh." Understanding dawned. "I do appreciate, so very much, your concern. But I am fine. Truly."

"Come now, there is no need to lie for him. We've seen how he treats you." Agitation simmered in Mrs. Latimore's voice. "He did not want you to come over when I first invited you, did he? And I saw him grab your elbow to stop you."

Kate bit back a most inappropriate smile. The women's concern was admirable, but having Jim cast as the worst sort of cad was too entertaining. "I can only assure you that I am not mistreated."

"After what we witnessed in such a brief period of time, we can only wonder what else goes on in more private moments," Mrs. Latimore said.

"Mrs. Latimore, Miss Dooley, I am touched and grateful. But Jim . . . I grant you he is sometimes— often—ill-mannered, and is prone to issuing orders without due consideration. But he is not cruel."

"Miss Riley." Mrs. Latimore's tone was pure steel. "The holds men can wield over women are many. I do not know what weapon he uses to control you, whether financial, sexual, or simple fear, but I can help free you. I promise."

"I—" The suggestion that Jim held a sexual claim over her echoed persistently in her brain. Her cheeks heated. "I do not know what further I can say to convince you. Our arrangement is strictly business. A legal and moral one," she added hastily.

"Miss Riley—" Mrs. Latimore began with real heat until Miss Dooley's soft interjection stopped her.

"We cannot press her further, Anne, or we are no better than what we have accused him of."

Mrs. Latimore considered briefly then nodded. "We will drop the subject for now. But know, Miss Riley, that should you change your mind we stand ready to offer our assistance at any time. You may depend upon our word in this matter."

"I do." A rush of warm gratitude caught her by surprise. "And I *am* truly grateful. There was a time in my life when I might have welcomed your rescue, but I can handle Lord Bennett."

Handle Lord Bennett? Her conscience jeered at her presumption. She doubted there was a woman alive who had ever handled Jim Bennett.

Miss Dooley turned down the lantern wick and the three women slid beneath their bedclothes a moment later. Like Jim, the other two women had apparently learned the skill of falling asleep at the closing of an eyelid, for it seemed only a few seconds later gentle snores rumbled from the other cots.

But try as she might, though she might have given half her wardrobe to keep the pillow, though the feel of crisp linen against her limbs had her shivering with long-denied pleasure, Kate could not seem to fall asleep.

They simply did not breathe like Jim. She'd become accustomed to the rhythm, like a child who needed to hear the same lullaby each night before she could drift off. And while half the time he frustrated her to no end, while his presence in her life was neither simple nor easy, she could not deny that, whenever he slumbered near her, she had always felt utterly safe.

Handle Lord Bennett? Perhaps she could. But her own response to him? Now that was something she clearly could not handle.

But then, she never could.

Jim stumbled out of his tent and slammed his eyes shut against the bright sun that felt like it was going to gouge them right out of his head. He pressed his fingers against his temples, trying to massage away the stabbing pain.

Damn, he thought. That stuff Ming Ho had hauled out after the women had retreated into their tent— what had he called it, Maotai?—was potent. And who'd have thought the little fellow could drink him under the table?

It had brought back good memories. Slouching around a campfire with other men, passing around a bottle and outrageous stories of places most of the people on earth had never heard of much less slogged through.

That was his life. Straightforward, far away, wild. Resolutely male, except for an occasional night or two with exotic, dark-skinned women who considered an evening of passion a much less complicated transaction than a woman such as Kate viewed a waltz. There was no allowance in his future for any other kind of woman, and even less for a woman like Kate.

These few weeks were an aberration. He would do well to remember that. Then he'd get out of places with roads and houses ruining the landscape, away from women who wielded their beauty like a mercenary used his rifle, and back to somewhere he only had to worry about simple things like wild animals that considered him a snack and rivers that turned into rapids without warning.

Hell, he should have done it months ago. Stupid of him to think he'd need a little time to let Matt's death settle; that brief break had somehow ballooned into reluctance to head back out again. He should have known he needed to get right back on the horse. In retribution, fate had handed him Kate Goodale.

And of course, because the thing you wanted least always showed up right when you were thinking how much you wished it wouldn't, there she was now, hurrying up with her face flushed and her eyes bright.

Christ, it really wasn't fair. Despite his best intentions she almost always rose before he did. By the time he crawled out of his bedroll she was already primped and polished, looking more like a dressmaker's sample doll than a real woman. Like you might get your knuckles rapped if you dared to touch one glossy wave on her head.

She had on a fresh shirt, crisp and white as if some maid had handed it to her freshly ironed. He wondered how she kept coming up with them. This one was at least the third since they'd begun. Her skirt was perhaps worse for the wear, smudged along the hem, but it tugged smoothly over the lush curve of her hips before erupting in the back over the bustle she'd yet to surrender. The stiff geometry of civilized women's clothes never ceased to amaze him. Though he had to admit there was a certain fascination in trying to discern the true curves beneath. Maybe that was the point.

She was still so beautiful, nearly to the point of unreality. Slickly cool, almost artificial. He hated that she still affected him, even knowing all she was. She'd cuckolded the doctor and nearly lured him into it, too, however unwittingly.

But it wasn't that simple. It had been easier when he could label her the calculating bitch and nothing else. By now he had to admit that she was not nearly so basic as that. And those flashes of more beneath the surface, of humor and vulnerability, of shadows and intelligence, were far more devastating than her mere beauty had ever been. But maybe that was what had trapped the doctor so neatly.

It bothered him that, even now, he couldn't tell for sure. Couldn't neatly catalogue her, separating the truth from the lie. But reading people had never been one of his strong points. Currents, clouds, the plunge of a valley or the best line up a mountain, yes. But not people. It was why he'd always been much more comfortable in Brazil than in England.

Was it really so wrong of him to . . . enjoy her? As long as he kept in mind precisely who and what she was? And that, he thought, was where things got really tricky.

"Sleep well?" he asked.

"Oh." She stopped abruptly, skirts fluttering around her ankles, hands flickering at her waist. "Yes. I guess I did. I—" She darted a quick look over her shoulder, in the direction of where the clearing faded into the trees.

"Kate?"

"Hmm?" She shot another quick glance toward the woods. "Fine. Just fine. I—" She took a quick breath, trying to calm herself, and failed.

"What is it?" When she didn't answer he turned and headed for the stand of trees.

"No!" She grabbed his arm in both hands and hung on. "Don't go in there!"

A man couldn't be blamed for enjoying for a moment before he peeled her hands off his arm. "Tell me why I shouldn't or I'm going."

She bit down on her lip in indecision. When he took one more step she burst out: "Oh, all right! Really, though, it's nothing. And I'd really rather respect her privacy. It's nothing that'll matter to you in any way."

"Why don't you let me be the judge of that?"

"I got up early—you know I like to do that—and there's a stream, only a few yards in that direction. Ming Ho mentioned it last night, and I—"

"You shouldn't be wandering around alone."

The glance she shot him simmered with impatience. "Do you want to discuss that *now*?"

"Depends. Are you going to get to the point any time soon?"

Color flooded her cheeks. *"I saw them,"* she whispered.

He squinted into the thickening copse of trees.

"Who?"

"Mrs. Latimore and Ming Ho."

"So? You saw them last night, too, and . . . oh. You *saw* them."

"Yes." She gestured at her waist. "He didn't have a stitch on, and . . ." Her eyes fogged. "Who would have thought that's what he looked like underneath? He's not nearly as skinny as he looks. You know, I always imagined that—"

"Kate." Now that, he thought, was asking too

much of a man, expecting him to listen while she rhapsodized about another.

"What? Oh." She grinned cheekily at him. "I'm sorry. I can't help it. An artistic eye, you know."

"Is that what you call it?" She'd just handed him evidence of her wandering eye. He should have been furious, offended. But she was so damn good-natured about it, her eyes dancing with laughter, and it was just so much work to stay angry with her. What difference did it make now, anyway? "Huh. Mrs. Latimore and Ming Ho? And here I always sort of assumed it was Mrs. Latimore and Miss Dooley that—"

"Jim!" she gasped, truly shocked.

"Come now, Kate." He nudged her beneath the chin that had nearly dropped to her chest. "You really need to get out more often."

She struggled to overlay her astonishment with a mask of worldly sophistication. Jim wondered if she had any idea just how badly she failed. "But I . . . I . . ." She lapsed into stunned silence.

"So that's what it takes to make you speechless? Good to know."

She recovered quickly. "I'm not speechless. I'm just . . . too much of a lady to speak about such things."

"Oh, yes, too much of a lady to speak about such things, but not too much of a lady to ogle a naked man you just happened to stumble across, huh? Just how long did you watch?"

Now that got all her feathers ruffled. "I didn't watch! How can you . . ." In the face of his knowing grin, she stopped, shrugged. "Can I help it if it took a few seconds to recover my wits?"

"Perfectly understandable." He debated prodding her a bit more. But if her face got any redder, she might suffer a burn. "Did they know you were there?"

"No. They were . . . otherwise occupied. And, whatever you think, I really was there only a moment."

"Good."

"Can we go now?" He'd left his supplies beside the tent he'd shared with Ming Ho and now she bent down, snagged the strap of his pack, and heaved it at him. He caught it automatically, surprised at the momentum behind her throw. Three weeks ago she probably couldn't even have lifted it. "I'm already packed."

"Hoping to get out of here before they finish . . ."

"Simply anxious to be on our way," she said. "I've already expressed my appreciation and taken my leave."

"Kate."

"Oh, all right. I'm not sure I can look either of them in the eye without turning red as a tomato, and it's really not my color."

"I'm not sure I could, either," he admitted.

Her smile was warm, hinting at the intimacy of shared amusement, and he thumped his chest with his fist, just to remind his heart to keep beating.

"Shall we go, then?" she asked.

He nodded. "Gather your things. I'll fetch the horses and meet you by your tent." As she turned to do as he asked—not one single protest, he thought, would miracles never cease—he said, "And actually, I thought you looked very nice all blushing-red."

The color bloomed again, softer this time, along

with the shy, uncertain smile of a young girl who'd just received her first compliment from a stammering suitor. For that moment, as she stood in the strong morning light, even with the few lines that had etched themselves in her skin, even with the deeper curves of her body and the more sophisticated style to her hair, she reminded him so strongly of the girl he'd kissed that night long ago that he nearly reached for her now without thinking, because he had so many times in his dreams.

He abruptly bent to sort through his pack, and so he missed how her smile faded when he brusquely turned his back to her.

"Get going," he ordered her roughly.

It took Kate only a few moments to ready her things. She'd done most of it in advance, as she'd told Jim, but she was also impressed at just how efficient she'd become at packing. The last time she visited Emily, she thought, it had taken her nearly two weeks of dithering to decide what to pack in her trunks.

She tried, and nearly managed, to shrug off Jim's rudeness. It wasn't as if she shouldn't be used to it by now. If he wanted to keep her on her toes by being alternately friendly and downright hostile, well, she wouldn't give him the satisfaction of showing that it bothered her.

Though she wouldn't bet that it wasn't calculated and the man was merely horribly moody. No wonder he spent so much time stumbling around in the wild. No civilized human would put up with him for long.

She waited impatiently for him to bring the horses around. Why was it that the morning she was anxious to be gone, he was taking absolutely forever?

Finally she gave up. Perhaps he was having trouble with the horses. God knows he'd never ask for her help, even if he needed it, and she was becoming quite proficient at dealing with her mare if she did say so herself.

If they didn't hurry up, Mrs. Latimore and Ming Ho were going to be . . . finished. She sped around the corner, prepared to do whatever was necessary to get the man moving, and pulled up short when she saw him.

He wasn't ready, wasn't even near ready. Was further from ready than he'd been when she left him. He was kneeling on the ground beside the tent and he must have dumped nearly every single thing in his pack and his bag on the ground. Now he was pawing through them. As she watched, he tore through a pile of clothes, throwing each one over his shoulder after he examined it, punctuating each toss with words the likes of which would get him thrown out of every parlor in Philadelphia.

"What in heaven's name are you doing?"

He sat back on his heels and the potent snarl on his face had her taking an involuntary step backward. "Our map's gone."

"What?" She flew to his side and tore through a pile of blankets. "I'll help you look."

"There's no point in it. I've checked everywhere. It's gone."

"Where'd you keep it?"

"Pack. Side pocket."

She dragged his limp canvas pack near and burrowed into the pocket that tied with a thin leather strap. "It's empty."

"I told you that."

"Where'd you leave it last night?"

"Right there with the rest of my stuff."

"*Outside?*" She couldn't believe it.

"Yeah, well." He would not shift guiltily, damn it. "That's where it was this morning, so it figures that was where it was last night, doesn't it?"

"You don't remember?"

"Of course I remember." Barely. Foggily. "I left it right there."

"You *left* it?"

The woman sounded as if he'd abandoned a baby in the middle of a busy street. "Well, it would have been rude of me to insist on bringing all my stuff into Ming Ho's tent, wouldn't it? It was tight as it was. It's a little tent, and I'm a big guy."

"Oh, yes, I know that not being rude always takes complete precedence for you," she said dryly.

He tossed aside the small leather pouch he was pawing through, stood, and wheeled for the woods.

"Where are you going?"

"Going to find out who stole our map."

"Just a minute." She pressed her fingers to her temples. "I have to think."

"Thinking takes time."

"And how are you going to explain that you knew where they were? If you go in there, they'll guess that I saw them."

"So?"

"Jim, if they've stolen the map, they're hardly going to tell you just because you accuse them. They're not that weak."

He flexed his fingers, balled them up into a fist. "Oh, I think I can convince them."

"You are *not* going to beat it out of them, Jim," she ordered him.

"Why not?"

She stared at him, incredulous. "Even if you could—"

"Oh, I could."

"It'd likely get us disqualified."

He couldn't admit that she had a point.

"Besides which, I really don't believe Mrs. Latimore's the one who took the map."

"Know her so well, do you?" He kicked at a ball of rope in his way, sending it wheeling across the clearing, unraveling all the way. "I should have known there was something odd about their inviting us here last night. Mrs. Latimore was never known for her hospitality."

Despite everything, a smile flitted at the corners of her mouth. "Jim, they invited us to rescue me."

"From what?"

"From you, of course, the overbearing, vile, and violent cretin who was obviously taking wicked advantage of me."

"What?" His laugh was loud enough to startle a crow from a nearby tree; it winged away, squawking in complaint. "If there's anyone taking advantage here it's you."

"Yes, well, you just keep comforting yourself with that thought, all right?"

Arms crossed, foot tapping, she waited impatiently for him to finish whooping.

"It still could be them," he suggested. "Their kind concern could have been merely a clever diversion to throw you off the trail."

"I don't think so," she said darkly.

"Ming Ho could have been acting on his own. Obviously got more initiative than apparent at first glance." He'd been damn fine company, though. Jim was really rather reluctant to beat the truth out of him. Not to mention those little Asian fellows had a tendency to know all sorts of sneaky moves, as he'd once discovered, to his immense pain, in a saloon in Macao.

"That boy in the robes was lurking around near the edge of the road last night," Kate offered. "I saw him when I was returning from washing up. There's something odd about the way he keeps appearing and disappearing."

"That'd be an interesting tactic, considering he gave us the map in the first place."

"Maybe he changed his mind," she said defensively. "It makes as much sense as thinking it's Mrs. Latimore."

"It doesn't really matter." Much as he'd like to know whose neck to wrap his hands around, it wasn't terribly productive. "Might as well get packed up."

"Are you giving up?" He shot her a look that would have sent most men screaming. "All right, silly question," she said. "What are we doing next?"

"Figure the quickest and simplest thing would be to steal one back."

He bent to gather up the garments he'd scattered in his haste while she regarded him with open and hostile suspicion. "Not from Mrs. Latimore."

"It'd be expedient."

"No."

It might be fun to tangle with Kate over it, he thought. It was always a bad policy to give in to her about anything without a fight. Start giving her ideas that maybe she was in charge. But it'd take time they didn't have to argue with her. Unless he bound and gagged her to ensure she didn't go shrieking to Mrs. Latimore and give him away.

"Why are you looking at me like that?" she asked warily.

"No reason," he told her. "Actually, let's pinch it from Major Huddleston-Snell. He owes me anyway, and a lot more than a map at that."

"Do you know where he is?"

"I'll find him."

"I might have a quicker idea," she ventured, more unsure than he'd ever seen her, tentative enough to spark his interest. Kate was always so blithely confident. This was something else entirely.

"Do you . . ." She hesitated briefly, then squared her shoulders and plunged on. "Do you have any paper? And something to write with?"

"I did." He looked around at the mess he'd made, locating his notebook beneath his shaving kit. He unearthed it, tossed it at her, along with the stubby pencil he dug from the pocket of his jacket.

"Thank you." She caught them with the ease he'd come to take for granted. Then she glanced around before settling delicately into the folding chair that Jim had spent the better part of the previous night in, before he'd finally slipped to the ground. She frowned over the paper for a moment, then quickly drew the pencil down the length of the page.

"Kate—"

"Hush." She made two more quick strokes, then looked up at him, her eyebrows lifted in graceful arches. "You might as well begin packing up. This will take a moment."

It didn't take him long to stow everything away.

He'd had plenty of practice, and the mess he'd made was no worse than the time a band of apes had invaded his camp. But he couldn't help sneaking a peek at her now and then.

Her head remained bent, her neck an elegant curve. Sunshine flowed over her, as if the light had been made for her alone, gilding her hair and the line of her cheek as she tilted her head and studied the notebook thoughtfully.

She was frowning in fierce concentration, her mouth puckered, her brow furrowed. It was not a pretty expression. But it was fascinating, both more vibrant and far more powerful than one of her lovely, empty smiles.

The pen scratched over the paper, the movement of her hand quick and fluid. Then she stopped, tapping the pencil against the pad in agitation as she studied what she'd done.

"Finished?" he asked, unable to wait any longer.

"I think so," she said slowly. When she made no move, he went over to her. She lifted the notebook against her chest, blocking his view.

"May I?" He held out his hand. For a moment he thought she would refuse. And then, grimacing, she handed it over.

She'd reproduced the map. It was better drawn than the original, the lines flowing, a suggestion of movement in the representation of waves off the shore. She'd produced an exceptional amount of detail in a brief time, down to the spiky compass wheel in the upper right corner.

"Kate," he murmured, amazed.

"I know the detail of the interior is missing," she

said quickly, her hands fluttering in the air like a nervous moth. "I hadn't paid as much attention to that. But the coastline . . ."

"How close is it?"

"I don't know . . . it should be . . . close, I think." Then she paused, nodded briskly as if trying to convince herself. "It should be very close," she said firmly. "I should know it, as much time as I spent staring at the damn thing." He smiled at her language; it was the first time he'd heard her swear. Nice to know spending so much time together was having some effect on her. "I have an excellent visual memory."

"You certainly do," he murmured, his gaze tracing her sketch in admiration. "Ready to go?"

"Does that mean you're going to . . ."—she gulped, as if she wasn't quite sure what answer she wanted—"depend upon my sketch?"

He folded it up with all the care of jeweler wrapping up his most prized ware and tucked it safely away in the pocket of his shirt. "It mostly certainly does."

Chapter 13

"**W**ell, Webb, what do we do?"

In the fifteen years Irvin Webb had been the city editor for the *Sentinel*, he couldn't recall Fitz Rafferty ever asking him that question before. Which only goes to show what a mess this whole thing had turned into.

"What do you . . . want to do, Rafferty?"

"What do I *want*?" He dropped a sheaf of paper on his desk and leaned back in his chair, which shrieked as though it was going to collapse beneath him at any moment, a sound which it had been making for a good ten years. "I *want* Hobson to send me something other than crap, that's what I want. I want him to be the one digging up such good dirt on the competitors that I can print the damn story and be done with it." He slapped his hand on the top paper. "But I'm not

177

gettin' what I want, am I?" He tapped his finger, a death knell, and Irvin tugged at the tight band of his starched collar.

"You got any idea who sent you that article, Fitz?"

He scowled. "Not a one. I have the best reporters on earth in my employ, and not a one of 'em can figure out who dropped it on our lobby desk in the middle of the day." He made a sound of disgust that must have dislodged an egg-sized clump of phlegm. Fumes curled furiously from his cigar.

"The thing's well written, though."

"Wouldn't be having a crisis of conscience if it was a piece of crap, now would I?"

Irvin's own throat clogged. "Guess not."

Fitz shoved his chair back—there had to be grooves deep as a grave in the wood floor by now, Irvin thought, for all the times Rafferty had done just that—stood up, and started pacing. Irritation rolled off Fritz, and Irvin started plotting escape routes.

"It goes against my grain to print a piece that I don't know the author of. A newspaperman knows where every word in his paper comes from, Webb. I've always believed that."

"A newspaper doesn't generally start a contest just so's it's got somethin' to report, either," Irvin said without thinking, and then nearly bit his own tongue off because it had been dumb enough to spout that out loud.

Fitz turned one squinted eye in his direction and Irvin shrank down into his chair. Not that Rafferty ever did anything but yell, but at that he was world-class.

And then Fitz chuckled, surprising them both. "It's a different world, isn't it, Webb?"

"That it is," Irvin agreed.

"I wonder how long . . ." Rafferty sighed. "Guess we'll find out soon enough." He contemplated the papers on his desk. "How much confirmation *do* we have?"

"The priest wouldn't talk."

"They never do. How many stories we lost because of that, do you think?"

"Oh, hundreds. But I'm betting the police superintendent regrets it even more than we do."

Fitz stretched his mouth into something resembling a smile. "That he does."

"But we got two witnesses in Brazil. Lucky that Mac was down there already and we could put him on the story. He dug up some church records, too. They weren't in great condition—damn jungle—but he said the names looked right to him."

Fitz nodded. It was as much confirmation as they were likely to get, and he'd made calls on less. "Run it, then."

Irvin got up, wondering just when his knees had started creaking every time he moved. Too much time behind a desk. "Just how mad's Hobson going to be, do you think?"

Rafferty chuckled. " 'Bout as mad as he deserves to be. Mad enough to get off his ass and give me a good story."

From the churning gray ocean off the coast of Maine, three islands punched through, too small to shelter anything but a few nesting terns. All that remained of them after years of abuse by wind and sea were battered boulders nearly the color of the water and scraggly pines that clung to them with the determination of a true nor'easter.

Kate shivered on a rocky stretch of shore. Behind her stretched uncounted acres of forest, a riot of the blazing autumn color that had swept inland from the coast a week ago. The tide slapped at her feet, and the fifty yards or so that lay between her and her destination looked far wider than that, packed with waves that rose up toward the slate sky before falling back, defeated.

These were the last of the five possibilities they'd originally chosen. If the clue could not be found here, they'd be back to square one. And though Jim had not hinted at such a thing, Kate knew it would be her fault. She had not remembered the map well enough, or portrayed it accurately enough.

"Kate!" She glanced down the shore. Jim strode toward her, towing a small rowboat in his wake. The air had a distinct, salty chill, the kind that was only found within sight of an ocean, yet he was barefoot, his pants rolled up to his knees, strong legs pushing through the waves. The rope was looped over one broad shoulder and he leaned into the weight of it. The wind caught the long waves of his hair and tossed them back, cool, muted light glancing off it, and, once again, just the sight of him stole her breath and settled into her memories the way no one ever had.

It had taken her years to get over him the first time. Or, if not exactly over him, to put him into the nice, neatly labeled box in her memories where he belonged. *Sweet, romantic young foolishness.*

She was terribly afraid it was going to be a hundred times harder this time.

He gave her a brief, cocky wave, pleased with his prize. It wasn't unusual for him to disappear and return with something they needed, from the horses to boats, dinner, or nicely dried and split firewood. She'd stopped asking where he got them. He never told her anyway, and she decided she didn't really want to know. At least her funds were holding up, though she suspected, if they won, she was going to use half her winnings tramping up and down the coast paying people back.

He dragged the boat around, pointing the prow toward the tiny trio of islands, only a foot of the stern on shore. Dubious, Kate peered at the battered vessel. A few streaks of red paint remained on the graying wood and the crossbars looked like they'd snap in two if she leaned on one.

"There's water in the bottom," she said. "Is it leaking?"

"Maybe a little," he admitted with annoyingly good cheer.

"And you don't believe that's a problem?"

"I'll row fast." He gripped one side of the boat with both hands, holding it steady. "Are you coming?"

He'd offered her the same option every single time. Though she'd tried mightily to put on a good front, he had to know that she'd rather shave her head than get in another one of those creaky, scarcely-better-than-a-toy-raft things he kept digging up.

It would be immeasurably wiser to stay behind. A few hours apart might allow her to shake off the effects of his potent appeal.

But the simple truth was she'd much, much rather be tossed around in a rickety boat on the verge of sinking with him than remain on nice, safe dry ground without him. She gathered her skirts and climbed in.

They started on the farthest island out, on the assumption that the newspaper would want to allow the greatest opportunity for capsizing or blowing out to sea or whatever interesting story they might luck into. But despite combing every square foot of the first two islands they came up empty yet again.

The sun was threatening to go down before they began searching the third island.

"Cheer up," Jim told her as he looped the line around the twisted remains of a pine trunk after he'd handed her out of the boat. He gave the rope a jerk, tying it off with practiced ease. "We'll find it."

She scowled at him. It really was rather freeing, she thought, to be able to frown at him without worrying how unattractive the expression was. She'd avoided anything that even slightly resembled a reflective surface since they'd left the Rose Springs, but she could guess only too well how bedraggled and downright unkempt she looked. So she figured she could make any face she wanted at him; she couldn't possibly look any worse.

"My sister is a devoted optimist," she told him. "And she has survived thus far only by blind luck, and because I love her enough to overlook such an extreme flaw. You, however, have no such advantage."

He chuckled. "Shore or sea?"

"I'll take the shore side," she said. At least on that half of the island she could be in sight of the land. And maybe that clump of stunted trees that perched on top of the boulder passing for an island might blunt the wind that whipped in from the sea.

An hour later, Kate was so discouraged, so cold to the bone, that she nearly missed it. A dark smudge lurked beneath the sharp edge of a ledge of rock that jutted toward shore, nearly lost in the growing shadows that slid across the face of the island as the sun sank toward the horizon.

She squinted at the dark blotch, trying to make out the outlines. It was impossible to tell if it was a shallow depression, capable of providing shelter for nothing more than a baby gull, or something more promising.

What she could tell was that scrambling down there was going to be a pain in the bustle.

Kate briefly debated calling for Jim. What was the use of having a fellow like him around if he didn't handle the uncomfortable tasks? But the fact that he saw her as such a useless fribble—something he didn't even attempt to hide—was beginning to disturb her greatly. She was accustomed to such things; nearly every man she'd ever met, including her husband, viewed her exactly the same way. But she couldn't help feeling that, by now, he should know better. Even worse, this entire escapade was making her see herself that way. With the single exception of drawing the map, she'd contributed exactly nothing to their venture.

She made it, though not without earning two scraped palms, one large rip in her skirt, and a good smear of dirt across her shirt for her trouble. So she stood at the entrance to what proved to be a decent-sized cave and peered down at the water, perhaps six feet below, inordinately proud that she was only slightly dizzied by the perch.

She turned, inspecting the inside of the cave. It smelled of seawater and rot, the walls slick and dark. What remained of the daylight gave out only a few feet from the entrance and she allowed her eyes to adjust before venturing farther. The walls narrowed abruptly, folding into sweeps of darkness. She edged forward hesitantly—who knew what sorts of things could lurk in here? She didn't know enough about where snakes and bears lived to rule it out.

After two weeks of diligent searching and disappointment, it was almost anticlimactic. A neat, careful stack of books piled right in the center of the small cave, no more than ten feet inside.

"Jim!" The cave slapped the sound back at her, set her eardrums to vibrating. She snatched up one of slim volumes and dashed back to the entrance before screaming at the top of her lungs. "Jim!"

The wind carried her call toward shore. She'd give him a few minutes, she decided, before going to find him herself. She'd just earned the right to stay put and let him do the climbing.

"Kate?" His voice was muted, hard to locate.

"Down here!" she called.

She edged out to give herself a good view of the slope and narrow ledge she'd used to clamber down the face. And then jumped and shrieked when a body swung down no more than a foot in front of her.

Jim hung there for a moment, backlit by the setting sun and gleaming water, before he gave a kick that swung him into the cave and released the ledge above. He hit the ground hard, stumbling nearly to the ground before regaining his balance. He straightened, grimacing.

"For heaven's sake." Kate pressed a hand to her racing heart. "You scared me nearly half to death." She gestured to the path she'd taken. "Coming down the side's a lot easier."

"Not nearly as fast, though." He gave her a quick once-over. "You're fine?" he asked flatly.

"Of course I'm fine," she said. "Oh. You were worried about me?"

"The screaming's usually a hint, yes."

She tried not to be flattered. Likely he'd have come running for anyone who shouted. But for the first time that day, she felt warm.

"Look what I found," she said, and handed him the book.

"Well, well, look what we have here." He turned it over and ran his finger down the binding. "Open it yet?"

"Would I do that without you?"

"Here. You do the honors. You found it."

"I need more light." She moved into the lone wedge of light that remained in the cave, near the right front, and tilted the book toward the weak coppery glow. Jim followed her with a halting half step. "Are you limping?"

"No," he shot pack. She frowned at him. "Just a little. Twinged my ankle. I'm fine."

She gave him a skeptical look, then shrugged and turned her attention to the book.

"How many did you find?" he asked her.

"A whole pile of them." She turned it over and over in her hand, as if reluctant to open it. The volume was thin, the dye of the reddish leather so uneven that in places it appeared pink. The cover barely hung on at a cock-eyed angle. Someone had made a very half-hearted effort to brush metallic paint on the edges of the paper. "If they were going to go to the trouble of binding it, you'd think they might have put a little more effort into it than that."

"We're talking about a newspaper here. It doesn't matter what it really looks like, only how they can write it." He pitched his voice low and flat. " 'The competitors discovered a treasure trove of tomes'—don't look at me like that, alliteration is a respected literary technique—'secreted in the caves as if they'd been sheltered there a hundred years. Bound in rich red leather, edged in gold, they held for the intrepid adventurers the glittering promise of a brighter future.' "

"Oh, for heaven's sake." But a smile, pretty and warm, flirted with her mouth. "I wouldn't give up your day job."

"I don't intend to," he said. "Let's see what we've got."

Kate flipped it open. All the pages, so thin one could see right through them, were blank but for the very center sheet.

An emperor is subject to no one but God, the sea, and justice.

"Hmm." Kate methodically ticked off possibilities. "It could be a geological structure called the emperor, I suppose. What countries still have an emperor on the throne?" She traced the quote with one forefinger. "For some reason that doesn't sound quite right to me. 'No one but God and justice' . . . Jim?"

"Huh?" He'd come up behind her, leaning over her shoulder as she tilted the page toward what remained of the sun, so close his breath stirred fine hairs at the side of her neck.

"That new ship, the *Emperor.* When does it sail?"

"Damn." He went still, like a leopard waiting to pounce. "Twentieth? Twenty-first? Something like that."

"That gives us . . ." She turned to face him, only the

slim book wedged between them as a barrier. "Jim, I've lost track of the days. How long do we have?"

"Enough," he said flatly. "Barely. If we get moving." He grasped her wrist and took a step toward the ledge. His ankle had stiffened while he stood, and it almost gave out beneath him. Grimacing, he shifted his weight to his right leg.

"Jim!"

"Forget it," he said through gritted teeth.

"Don't be stupid," she told him. "I know it's difficult, but give it a good try, all right?"

"Kate, there's no *time*—"

"There's no time for you to be hobbling along a narrow ledge, either, and even less for me to fish you out of the ocean when you fall in," she snapped. *"Sit down."*

He sat down, stretching his injured leg before him. Kate knelt in front of him and lifted his foot to her lap.

Hell, he thought. I'm in worse shape than I thought, much, much worse.

Because the sight of his foot snuggled up right *there*, in the sweet curve formed between her belly and thighs, the look of the scarred and battered black leather of his favorite boots against the deep midnight blue of her skirt and the white of her shirtwaist with its narrow trace of pretty lace along the placket—just that simple sight damn near had him dizzy with want. He hadn't been so simply aroused, quick and hard, at something so innocent since he'd been seventeen or so, when the barest hint of anything female would have him salivating.

He was never going to survive the next few months. A man simply could not walk around with the blood perpetually draining from his brain and live.

Her finger crept up his ankle, disappearing under the ragged hem of his trousers, and a moan eased from his throat.

"Sorry," she said quickly. "I didn't mean to hurt you."

"Hurt?" he managed. Barely. "It's not that bad."

"Hmm," she said. "You're very pale, not to mention sweating. Are you sure you didn't hurt more than your ankle?"

She was probing his ankle now, gentle fingers gliding over swollen, tender flesh.

"Yeah," he said, once he collected enough air to form a word. "Just my ankle."

"Hmm." She frowned a little, tracing along the edge of his boot. "It's swelling up terribly."

"No kidding."

"Huh?" She took a firm grip on his calf, her hand stronger than he would have guessed, and slid her other hand down toward his heel. "We're going to have to get this off." She glanced up at him, face taut with concern and concentration. "It'd be easier, and far less painful, if you'd let me cut the leather off. Do you have a knife?"

"No," he said flatly.

"I take it you're not going to let me do this the easy way."

"Correct."

"It's going to hurt," she warned him.

"You could distract me so that I'd never notice," he suggested.

"Oh?"

"Sure. Just pop a few of those buttons—say, six or so—and I'm betting I won't feel a thing."

She shook her head even as she smiled at him.

"You're no fun."

Her smile turned instantly seductive, mysterious and promising. "Oh, yes I am," she purred, and yanked his boot off before his brain cleared.

"There," she said brightly. "That wasn't so bad, was it?"

Pain pulsed through his newly freed ankle.

"This really isn't my sort of thing," Kate murmured as she inspected it. "But I don't *think* it's broken."

"It's not," he put in.

"Had a medical college out there in the jungle, did they?" Having apparently completed her examination, she sat back, and regrettably took her hands away. Having them wrapped around his ankle wouldn't be his *first* choice, but hell, at this point he'd take what he could get. "But it's certainly badly sprained. We're going to need some support."

Jim shrugged. "I'll manage."

"Hmm."

It really was too bad, he thought, that she was who she was and he was who he was. The line between harmless appreciation of someone who was, after all, a riotously attractive woman and "appreciating" all too well a woman who'd betrayed his friend was getting thinner and thinner all the time.

"I've got an idea. I know, I know, it's a shock," she said, the words lighthearted, wry, but Jim thought he detected a bitter edge, "but let's give it the benefit of the doubt, shall we?"

He was terribly unhappy when she slid his foot out

of her lap but cheered considerably when her fingers went to work at the top button of her blouse. "I suggested this already, remember? I liked the idea then, too," he said, then cursed himself when his words stopped her with her top button halfway through its hole.

"I don't suppose I could trust you to close your eyes and keep them that way?"

"Oh, sure you could," he said heartily. "Trust away." To prove it, he slammed his eyelids shut.

By his calculations, he waited a full thirty seconds, a noble feat if ever he'd performed one. He cracked one eye open the barest fraction only to discover she'd turned her back to him.

She slid her shirt off her shoulders.

Lord. Oh, Lord. The line of her shift ran horizontally a third of the way down her back, cotton so thin it was nearly gauze, edged with a flutter of pretty lace. He could see where her neck flowed into her upper back, the intimate angle of her shoulder blades until they disappeared beneath her shift, and how the fabric bunched and gathered where it tucked into the edge of her buff-colored corset. The straps were just narrow strips of lace, a rainbow curve over her lovely round shoulders.

Her skin glowed in the dimness, a pearly sheen as if it held moonlight within. She bent her head and she folded her shirtwaist carefully and set it aside, exposing the nape of her neck, the fine line of hair that tapered there beneath the sophisticated twist of her hairstyle.

Her hands came around behind her, working quickly at the tight lacing of her corset. He'd have offered to help, but his hands were shaking and his tongue was paralyzed, and she was finished before he could get the words out.

She bent forward, her back curving, spreading the laces. She pulled off the corset and he would have died rather than move, waiting to see what she might do next. He longed to ask what she was planning, but he was afraid a single word might bring her to her senses. As long as there were pieces of clothing coming off her body he wasn't risking *anything* that might stop it.

But his luck didn't hold. She'd no more than stripped off her corset than she shrugged back into her blouse. He was still trying to recover from his disappointment when she turned around again. Her shirtwaist was loose, one button still undone at the top, two at the bottom, deep creases in the once-crisp cotton where it had been tucked into the tight waistband of her skirt. Not her usual flawless neatness, but dressed. Definitely, most regrettably, dressed.

She approached him with the corset in her hands, laces dangling nearly to the rock floor of the small cave as she sat down beside him.

"I thought," she said uncertainly, "that this might be better than merely binding it up with cloth. The stays are quite firm, the cloth sturdy, and it should supply excellent support."

If anyone at the Explorer's Club saw him wandering around with a woman's corset wrapped around his ankle, he'd be laughed out of the place. "Good idea," he said.

She beamed like a ten-year-old who'd just won the spelling bee.

She scooted over and—*bliss, bliss*—lifted his foot back into her lap. His brain fixed irrevocably on the fact that she had one less garment on. Her breasts moved as she did, unbound, swaying softly, potently sexual.

"There." She gave the laces a firm tug, finishing off a loopy bow. The corset cradled his ankle snugly, wrapping him in warmth that he imagined was a ghost of her skin's own heat. "How does it feel?"

"Let's find out." He got to his feet and bounced gingerly, testing it out. "Not bad," he admitted.

Her smile was blinding. As if she'd never received praise in her life, when she must have been showered with compliments.

He took a couple of limping steps. "Thanks for sacrificing your corset. It really does hold much better," he said, and the smile grew brighter still. He blinked underneath its power. She could have leveled an army, brought down a monarchy, began a religion with that smile.

It was far too much to waste on one battered and cynical man who couldn't surrender to it. For if he'd felt guilty before, for having kissed—having *wanted*—the doctor's wife, however unintentionally, he'd feel all the worse now if he allowed himself to get lost in her knowing exactly what she was: no longer the doctor's wife but still his betrayer.

She leaned toward him and whispered conspiratorially, "It was no sacrifice."

He cleared his throat. "We'd best get going." He turned away from her because if he looked at her for one second longer they'd never get out of that cave. Night had fallen fully, with a faint wash of lighter indigo behind the pines on shore the only remnant of the day. Beneath him the ocean glimmered, black rippled glass.

"*Shit.*"

She hurried to his side. "Oh, dear, you're hurting, aren't you? I should have known it wouldn't work, I—"

"No," he said, and inclined his head down the sheer front slope of the island. "The boat's gone."

Chapter 14

"What?" Kate lifted to her tiptoes, peering over Jim's sturdy shoulder. Gleaming rocks, wet from the rising tide, rose from the dark water. "I thought it was right in that shallow curve."

"It was," he said with flat assurance.

"Maybe it just drifted down the shore a bit," she suggested hopefully. "The knot came loose as it was bobbing around—"

"The knot did not come loose."

"We were in a hurry. You must not have—" He slanted her a look that simmered with anger and conviction. "All right, you tied it perfectly. I don't know what I was thinking. So what happened?"

"Our 'friend' showed up again." Tension vibrated in the set of his shoulders, the angry jut of his jaw. She could only hope that he was never that angry with her. If whoever was sabotaging them saw Jim right now, she had no doubt they would abandon the contest in an instant, fifty thousand dollars be damned, in favor of putting as much geography between themselves and Jim as possible.

"We're not going to find the boat conveniently around the corner, are we?"

"Nope."

"Oh, well." She attempted a light, philosophical tone but decided she'd failed miserably. So much for her sudden, inexplicable urge to at least attempt to be a good sport; she was clearly unsuited for it. "I'm cold. And hungry. And not terribly thrilled by the idea of sleeping on rock."

"Anything else?" he asked dryly.

"Many," she told him, "but I'll spare you for now."

"I'm so grateful."

"Good. I rather like the idea of you grateful." Clearly she'd been at this too long, she decided. For all her complaints, she really was not as upset as she should be. She wasn't certain if she trusted Jim to get them safely off the island—trust Jim, what a bad idea that had to be—or if she was simply becoming inured to setbacks, they'd had so many already. "What next?"

He'd yet to look away from the water, staring at the space between the island and shore as if he could will the distance to close. "A swim."

Her unconcern vanished abruptly. "Don't be ridiculous."

"You have a better idea?"

Anything would be a better idea. "Why chance it? There'll be someone along sooner or later. I doubt we're the last ones here. There were plenty of books left."

"Kate." He turned toward her. "It could take days. We've no food, no shelter, no water."

"How far could they be behind us? And I saw a few puddles in a depression in the rock. We'll be fine. It's better than drowning." Her stomach lurched. "Besides, we'll freeze."

"I'll swim fast," he said. "Why 'we'? Thought you couldn't swim?"

"I . . . uh . . ."

He merely shrugged. "Doesn't matter if you can or can't. I wasn't planning on us both going."

"I thought you were supposed to have a swimming buddy." It was all too easy to imagine herself helpless and too far away, on shore while he thrashed around in the water. "It's not safe."

"Kate, be reasonable. I'm not going to sit around here and hope to be found. I'm a very good swimmer, I'm strong, and I'm careful."

"You are not *that* careful," she said.

"Oh? Can you think of one time that I've acted recklessly on this entire trip?"

She tried. His seemingly casual attitude toward things that terrified her and his breezy confidence gave every appearance of a casual attitude toward his personal safety. But he triple-checked every line, every knot before he depended upon them; he tamped out every fire until not a spark remained, he cleaned his gun every night, and he never assisted her into a boat without making certain a life ring was within reach.

"That's just because you have to watch out for me."

"No," he said flatly. "It's not."

Careful. It was a word she would never have thought to apply to him. It bothered her that she'd so easily bought into the legend. It made no difference that every article she'd ever read about him portrayed him as a man who embraced risk like a lover. She, of all people, knew that the surface was a very brittle foundation upon which to build a judgment.

But there had been that death in the Arctic on his last expedition. Perhaps he'd learned something from that terrible experience.

"I suppose you've had to learn to be," she said.

"No. I've always been careful. *Somebody* in my family had to be."

Curiosity burst like fireworks. She'd never before considered what kind of family he might have had, what sort of forces might have formed him. To her, he'd sprung full-blown, walking out of a floral-scented darkness on a soft summer night, a one-dimensional, perfect construct. But he was a real man, one shaped by a thousand influences both small and large, a completely unique conflux.

"Your family?" she prodded, but that was all she was going to get. He shook his head, dismissing the subject as if it wasn't worth another second.

"I would never set one foot in that water," he told her, "unless I was absolutely sure I was going to come out the other side."

She nodded. "You'll wait until morning, at least."

"What? Can't stand to miss a chance to spend the night on cold stone?"

"You wouldn't want to spoil a lady's fun, would you? Why, I—"

"No need to convince me," he said. "I'll wait for low tide."

"You're ever reasonable, aren't you?"

"That just about sums me up, doesn't it?"

* * *

Kate huddled miserably against the curved stone wall only a few feet from Jim. The cave swallowed up light within yards of the entrance, so that the only reason she could locate Jim was the sound of his even respiration. She couldn't mark the time other than by the inching of the thin slice of moonlight across the floor at the opening of the cave. The air was thick with moisture, a cold mist that lifted from the ocean and sank through her clothes as if she wore nothing at all.

"You're cold." His voice was rich and low. The walls of the cave seemed to hold it in, concentrate it, the only warmth in the whole damn place.

"Whatever gave you that idea?"

"You get snippy when you're tired, do you know that?" She heard him shift—the scrape of his boots against stone, the slight creak of bones that reminded her that he was too old to be trying to sleep on uninsulated surfaces, too. "I can hear your teeth chattering."

"So sorry I'm keeping you up."

Waves slapped against rock. Wind whistled past the entrance, calling forth a low moan. Even the cave was complaining, she thought.

Finally he spoke again. "Come here," he said with all the reluctance of a man prodded into something for honor that he'd never suggest of his own accord.

"Come where?"

"You know where."

It stung. Even if dozens of men might have begged for the chance to warm her up in the dark, she'd never given any of them the opportunity to ask, much less do it. The one man that had ever slipped under her defenses, the only one she'd ever wanted to, was offering the comfort of his body but only because it was the polite thing to do.

"I'm fine," she forced out. Her teeth couldn't chatter as long as she clamped them together.

"I've no patience with hypothermia through stupidity or pride or whatever the hell's your problem," he said with enough anger under the words to remind her they skirted painful territory. His voice came nearer. "I'd rather knock you out to keep you warm than let you shiver over there alone."

She had no time to prepare herself. He scooped her up with ease, one quick motion, and yanked her into his lap. His body enveloped hers, her back firm against the plane of his chest, one arm wrapped around her waist, the other angled across her chest, his thighs pressed snugly along the side of her legs.

Heat bloomed. Inside, outside—whether it came from him, or deep within herself, she couldn't tell. Probably both. She could feel the warmth of his breath across the top of her head each time he exhaled, the thump of his heartbeat against her back. She went rigid, afraid that if she moved, if she *breathed*, she'd do something he'd take the wrong way.

Or the right way.

"Relax," he murmured.

Laughter burst out of her at the impossibility of his suggestion.

"All right, maybe relaxing's asking a lot," he admitted. "But are you warmer?"

She nodded, not trusting herself to speak. Her skirts were bunched uncomfortably at her hip, her blouse twisted around her waist.

"Comfortable?"

"Well, no, not exactly."

"So get comfortable."

"I'm not sure that's possible." She lifted her hips to adjust her skirts and carefully settled back down. Behind her Jim sucked in a hissing breath. "Jim?"

He chuckled ruefully. "Okay, I admit it. Comfortable and relaxed is beyond us."

"I'm sorry," she said, starting to get up.

"No." His arms tightened around her, bringing her more firmly against him. The inside of one forearm pressed against one breast, sparking a delicious throb. Oh, it had been so long since she had felt like this, balanced on the keen edge of want and anticipation, her body so alive she imagined she could feel the pulse of blood through her arteries, the swell of air in her lungs. "We should be practical. There's no reason for you not to stay, except . . ." He paused. "No etiquette my mother ever taught me covers this particular situation, does it? I'm not sure whether I should apologize if I . . . react, or apologize if I don't?"

Heat flooded her face. That he could say something so outrageous so calmly . . . it seemed a challenge, to see whether she would respond in kind, as the woman of the world he clearly expected her to be. "Heavens, luv, you should know that much about me by now. Apologize if you don't." But now that he'd planted the thought, she couldn't help but think about . . . *that*, and *that* was all too obvious, the solid length of him hard against her hip.

So what now? Did she pretend not to notice? Pull away in shock? Or turn into him, sink into him, fill her hands with him?

She was not a girl. Not an innocent. Not unaware of

the pleasures that could be found in the flesh. And she'd never thought that she would feel this driving surge of need, a pierce-point of vivid emotion in a life that had been very bland for a very long time.

"Then I won't apologize," he said.

It seemed terribly blatant to speak of it so baldly. Like the conversation of people who'd been lovers so long, there were no longer any *musn'ts* between them, nothing that remained unvoiced. The intimacy of it struck her as strongly as that of their position.

He did not move away. He still held her close. But there was no welcome in it, his touch as impersonal as it could be in such a situation.

Well, if he could be honest, so could she.

"You don't like me very much, do you?" she asked. "Oh, you probably like how I look just fine, but you don't like *me*."

Silence slid through the cave while he weighed convention, politeness, and truth. "No."

Kate had expected nothing else. And yet her breath gushed out of her in a disappointed rush. "Ah. Well, I asked, didn't I?"

"If it helps, it's not easy." One hand rested against her side, and his thumb was stroking her there, back and forth, as if he'd no idea he was doing so.

She'd not had on so few undergarments since she was twelve. She knew she should be worried about it—her waist was not nearly as narrow without her corset. But oh, that bare touch felt so good.

"You're not as . . . well, you are fair company when you choose to be."

"Thank you ever so much." Her eyes stung and she blinked hard. Oh, what did it matter? she asked herself. She could not allow it to matter.

Silence stretched. She counted the pounding of the waves, tried to sink into the mindless rhythm of them.

"You're still cold," he said. "Shivering."

"I'm not cold."

"Oh." He paused. "Kate, why did you marry him?"

Five waves slapped against the rock before she spoke: "You know why I married him."

"Tell me anyway." Kate was light in Jim's arms, warm and soft, with drifts of scent lifting up from her hair, blending sweetly with the smell of the ocean. Jim found himself balanced on a sword-thin edge, too painful to enjoy, too arousing to relinquish.

The young woman in the garden—the doctor's wife—had been hard enough to resist. This woman he could hardly recognize. She was not the submissive, simply ornamental girl the doctor had called his wife, the one who'd meekly followed her husband's commands and seemed to have nothing more to offer than a pretty face.

Her sharp wit honed his own. Her strong will intrigued him, a self-possession he never would have suspected. She carried a mature sensuality that seethed in every motion, every breath, so that he could not be within ten feet of her without thinking about . . . not attraction, not emotion, but sexuality in its rawest and basest form. She vibrated against him now, and he could not forget that she was a woman who had embraced the pleasures of the flesh. Who now accepted the presence of his erection against her with an equanimity that promised a complete lack of inhibition.

And yet, it was her own free sexuality that he hated. He could not rid himself of the corrosive truth of it. *The doctor's wife. The doctor's faithless wife.*

She sighed. "I married him for his money. There. Is that what you wanted to hear?"

"I want to hear . . ." What did he want? Explanations, excuses? Something that would make him want her less, or something that would allow him to want her cleanly?

"What difference does it make now?"

"I'm not sure. Maybe none. Maybe a lot." And maybe they could just stay right there, in that cave, a thousand miles away from the world, and none of it would matter except the way she felt in his arms.

"We were . . . my father was wealthy. I thought. We all thought. He probably was, once. But by the time he died, it was gone. Far enough gone that there was no way to even know how much there had been, or where it went."

He should have told her to stop right there. It was the last thing he needed, this thread of commonality with her. "It happens."

"Well, it wasn't supposed to happen to us!" He felt her relax against him—her spine softened against his chest, her legs went lax, as though she was too distracted by the tale to guard herself against him any longer. "We weren't prepared. We'd no way . . . I had sisters. Two of them, younger than me. One much younger. I was accustomed to caring for her anyway—my mother died within weeks of Emily's birth."

"So you did it for them," he said flatly.

"Well, no, that would perhaps be broadening the truth a bit." She refused to latch on to the excuse he'd so conveniently handed her. "I was concerned, no doubt about that. But we may well have made it. Anthea had a job. But . . . I am unsuited for struggle.

I'm sure that is no surprise to you. We'd no experience in it. There seemed no reason . . . why should one live like that if one didn't have to? It seemed an imminently practical solution at the time." Her voice hardened. "It *was* an imminently practical solution."

"Practical." It was no different than most of the marriages he'd known in his youth. No different than his own parents' had been, if it came right down to it. Which was probably why the mere suggestion of it made his blood run cold. "Poor Doc."

"Poor Doc!" She laughed. "Who do you think suggested it? And in precisely those terms, if I remember correctly. I thought you knew the man better than that, Jim. If there'd ever been one shred of warm feeling in his soul, it died with Elaine."

Stop! Stop right now, he told himself. But he'd never been able to hold firm against his curiosity; it was the one thing that kept him hacking through a jungle when it would have been so much easier to quit. "So he really didn't care?"

"Didn't care? I suppose you could say that. He liked looking at me. He liked his colleagues, his acquaintances, looking at me and knowing he could claim me. He liked me ordering his life and otherwise staying out of his way. That was what he cared about."

"And he didn't mind if you . . . explored other interests?"

"Explored other interests? Why should he?"

"Most men would."

"But . . . oh." She stiffened abruptly, sitting up, away from him. He should have known better.

He should have bit off his own tongue before going down this topic. Now she'd moved away, and he'd loved the feel of her against him even if he wasn't very fond of her.

"You thought that . . . you thought that because of what we did, you assumed that's how I am. That I did that with anyone. With everyone."

"Well." He paused, tried to think. For most women what he suggested would be a terrible insult. But for her . . . she was what she was. Maybe. "You were not . . . you were not the most, er, remote woman I've ever met."

She laughed. Not joyfully, but as if she couldn't help it, with the hopeless, bitter edge of one who knew it was no use to do anything *but* laugh. "You thought because I kissed you so easily, so shortly after we met, that I was . . . loose?"

"I . . ." His brother, his father, might have been slick enough to talk their way around it. He was not. "Yes."

She kept laughing. She was still sitting in the spread of his legs and she put her hand on his shin, bending over with the force of hollow amusement until the sound of it veered toward hysteria.

He placed a calming hand on her back. "Kate—"

She shook him off. "I should have known. I never thought—"

"What?" he asked gently.

"Guilt is an interesting thing, isn't it? That night, with you, that one lapse—it probably did more to turn me into the wife he wanted than his money ever did. From that day on, I don't think I disagreed with him once."

"So . . ." Careful, he reminded himself. He knew better than to assume when on expedition. And she must have been courted by half of the gentlemen in the eastern United States, men far more experienced in luring married women into betraying their vows than he. It would be absurd to let his pride—and his hope, he admitted—lead him into thinking that he was the lone exception to her rule. "It was just that time? With me?"

"Yes." He wished he could see her. Look into her eyes, see her expression. But perhaps it was better that he couldn't. Those eyes had been created expressly to lead men astray. "It was just you." She sounded inalterably tired. As if she'd just dragged the whole world behind her all the way up the seacoast.

"All right." He touched her shoulder. "It's late, and it's only going to get colder. Let's get some sleep."

She jerked. "What?"

"I'm tired. Talking's hard on a man, you know. Not much practice. Can't do it long without needing a nap to recuperate."

"That's . . . it?"

"What more do you want? You want to know that I've never been so damn flattered in my whole life? Better we go to sleep right now because, if I think about that much longer, I might get so puffed up I might not fit back out the cave entrance." And if they didn't go to sleep, right now, he might get too caught up in the knowledge that she was not the woman he'd hated, not the one he'd mistrusted. But this was no better. She was a woman to be courted and married, a woman who could demand a thousand things that he could never give her.

"Nothing to be proud of." She mouthed the words automatically. "Maybe it wasn't you. Maybe you were just there the exact moment I was at my weakest." She fell silent for a moment, and then, tentatively, "You believe me?"

"Yup," he said easily.

"But . . ." She couldn't seem to settle in to it. Couldn't believe it was that simple. She tried not to assume, to tamp down on the warmth and hope that sparked and swelled.

"Is there any reason I shouldn't believe you?"

"You've heard me . . . shade the truth before."

"But not to me. And only when you want something. Do you want something from me, Kate?"

She was tucked between his legs, her skirts frothing over his shins. They were insulated from the world by the sea, by the night, and she couldn't bring herself to answer.

"We should sleep now," he said and held out his arms to her.

Carefully, she eased back down, settling in. His chin rested on her head, his heart thumped against her back, and her rump snugged right up into the V of his legs.

Dear God, she thought. She was in a cold, damp, and smelly cave. They were stuck on a stupid little island in the middle of nowhere. And, right at that moment, there was no place on earth she would rather be. *Dear God, she was in trouble.*

Spending a night sitting upright, leaning against chilly stone, made the morning every bit as painful as Jim expected. His back screamed at him for his foolishness; his hips ached, and his knees protested even before he asked them to move.

He'd counted on waking up with Kate in his lap to distract him. Unfortunately, he woke up empty-handed.

Gray morning light washed through the cave, penetrating ten feet or so into the interior. Mist blurred the light, making it dim and soft and hazy. It had to be early, very early, and the chill seeped up from the floor and sank deeply into his bones.

She knelt a few feet away, frowning as she tugged her fingers through the snarled length of her hair. Her outlines were indistinct, as if she were a figure that came to him in a dream. Her blouse was untucked, thoroughly crushed, and beneath it her curves were soft and unstructured. She looked like a woman who'd spent an entire night in slow, hot lovemaking and had only just rolled out of bed, surrendering very reluctantly to the morning.

She must have felt his gaze upon her for suddenly she looked up, meeting his eyes only briefly before dipping her head again.

"Don't look at me like that!"

"Like what?"

"I'm such a mess," she said. "I wouldn't want you to . . . oh, just don't look at me right now. All right?"

He got up and went over to her and then knelt down in front of her, near enough for their knees to bump gently. She kept her head down, limp swaths of golden hair shielding her face.

"Do you want to know the truth?" he asked quietly.

"No. Whyever would I want the truth?"

He chuckled. "You're getting it anyway." Gently he brushed back her hair, exposing the side of her face, beautiful bones that stood out more sharply now than in her youth. "You've never looked more kissable in your whole damn life than you do right at this moment."

"What?" She whipped her head up, disbelief written on every feature.

"You heard me."

She searched his face, trying to see through to the truth of it. Then she shook her head. "You lie so prettily."

"No." He let his fingers trace down the curve of her cheek, the slope of her jaw before he placed them beneath her chin and tipped her head up. "Usually you look"—he hesitated, trying to form the thoughts clearly—"perfect. Like you wouldn't be warm to the touch. Like a man should be afraid to tumble you because he might disarrange your hair. Like a man might take his pleasure *looking* at you, but he could never hope to *share* any with you."

She was mute, her eyes wide and brilliant blue. "But right now you look real. Real and alive and wholly female, the sort who could get sweaty and wild in bed, one who'd give as well as take. A woman a man could *live* with, rather than just worship."

She stared at him for so long he was afraid he'd really mucked it up and insulted her horribly. He knew he was not the sort of man she was accustomed to, full of pretty phrases and empty compliments. But Christ, did she really think a few hairs out of place muted her appeal?

"Then, for God's sake," she said, low and urgent, "would you just please kiss me and get it over with?"

Chapter 15

H e shook his head, unable to believe what he'd just heard. "Excuse me?"

"When we . . . when first we met, the first time we . . ." She wrinkled her nose, as if she wasn't quite sure of what she was about to say. "I was very young, and very lonely, and missing what I'd given up. What I'd never had, if the truth be told. Very susceptible to handsome, dashing young men who wander out of the moonlight." She smiled with fond nostalgia. "I've been dreaming about that for all these years, which is no doubt why I've managed to build those few moments into something much larger and grander than they were."

"Grander?"

"But of course." Her uncertainty gone, she forged ahead as if laying out a business proposition. "It *couldn't* have been that good. No kiss could be."

"Is that right?" he asked flatly.

She continued blithely on. "Of course it is! I mean, it's ridiculous. A few kisses between two young and, well, clearly irrational people. My imagination built the moment into something outrageous over the years because it had so little else to work with."

"Undoubtedly," he said, carefully neutral.

"And that's why, after dwelling on such a minor thing for so long, I simply cannot seem to think about anything else now."

He knew full well pride was a dangerous sin but, hell, how was a man supposed to take that? He didn't trust himself to talk, to make one single move, because what she'd said was now lodged front and center in his brain, big as life, twice as tempting.

"So you see." She spread her hands, as if the truth had to be perfectly obvious.

He shook his head.

"Hmm." She pressed her lips together, impatient with his delay in comprehending the obvious. "Our trip would be much simpler and easier if . . . if I didn't *think* about this so much. And so the reasonable step is for you to just kiss me and get it over with."

"And you think that will help how, exactly?"

"Well, it certainly couldn't live up to my memories, could it? Nothing could. It's obviously only the *wondering* that's got me so fascinated. Once we've proven that it is, after all, only a kiss, like every other kiss, then we can put it in its proper place and move on." She beamed at him, securely pleased with her unassailable logic.

"Oh well, then. If you're sure it'll help." He gave his

shoulders a little shake, arching his neck side to side like a boxer preparing to enter the ring.

"I'm sure it will help enormously."

It was a lot more likely it was going to hurt. For about three days, which is how long he figured it would take him to get the blood to flow back to his head.

"Are you ready?" he asked.

"Just a moment." She started to smooth her skirt, then paused with her hands in mid-straighten. "Close your eyes."

"You like taking the initiative?"

"No, I—just close your eyes."

He complied. A moment later, he opened the lids the barest slit. He could see only a vague image, blurred and grayed, through his lashes. Her hands flew: tucking in her shirt, ruffling up her skirt and arranging it in perfect poufs along her thighs, fluffing out the mess of her hair into something resembling curls. She pinched color into her cheeks and gnawed on her lips, leaving them plump and gleaming.

"Okay. No, no wait!" She reached up and popped open the two top buttons of her blouse, a move of which he approved most heartily. Then she closed her own eyes, thrust her chin forward, and puckered up. "I'm ready."

"You're sure?"

"I—" She squeezed her eyes shut so tightly, fine lines scrunched at the corners. "Yes," she said, firmly enough to convince herself as well as him. "I'm ready."

He opened his own eyes completely. Kate held herself still, tension vibrating in the set of her shoulders and the rigid purse of her mouth. If he kissed her, he thought, she was just as likely to spring through the roof as kiss him back.

And so he looked at her instead. Took in the gleam of her skin, as if the mist had settled there, and the color that blushed along her cheekbone.

She is such a problem, he thought. For now he could no longer fit her into that neat, off-limits package: the doctor's deceitful wife. But as much as that revelation had released him, it now also chained him. For she was firmly placed back into the category of a "lady." No more could he contemplate a simple tumble, one that meant nothing the moment after it concluded except an erotic memory, where she could go back to her life and he could hie off to unknown lands without a worry. Now there were rules attached to her, ones that his mother had drilled in well enough that even all his years away from England hadn't drummed them out of him.

But she was not a complete innocent. And it wasn't as if they hadn't kissed before. She wouldn't make too much of this, would she?

And when it came right down to it there was no way in hell he could refuse her this. Not just out of curiosity, although there was a fair helping of that as well, the same curiosity that no doubt spurred her. Would it be as he remembered? Had she learned something over the years?

But mostly because, on her knees in front of him, waiting for his kiss, she was the most wildly tempting thing he'd seen since he'd walked into that damned gazebo and laid eyes on her the first time.

Kate got tired of waiting. Her eyes popped open, and she jammed her fists on her hips. "Well? What are you waiting for?"

"Maybe I'm not waiting. Maybe I'm just taking my time," he said slowly. And then he reached out and laid his hand along the side of her neck, his thumb stroking the cords of her throat and easing along the first ridge of her collarbone. "Lord, but your skin is soft."

Her pupils dilated, deepening the pure blue to midnight. "Atkinson's Honey Complexion Cream," she murmured automatically.

His lips twitched. Laughter right as this moment, he decided, would be a very bad idea. But who would have guessed she was so *sweet*? Exceptionally confident in one realm, heartbreakingly unsure in another. Alternately sharp and fiercely protective.

His thumb made soft little circles in the hollow of her neck. He breathed in the anticipation, the feminine scent that seemed bound to her skin. And waited for her to relax.

She'd so clearly braced herself. As if expecting a blow rather than a kiss. But sooner or later one had to breathe, muscles had to unkink. Finally her neck softened and her shoulders dropped. The tense line of her mouth eased and her forehead smoothed.

It lasted only until he bent nearer, bringing his mouth within inches of hers. She stiffened again, relentlessly apprehensive. He should give her one more chance, he thought, to back out. But it was too late for him; she'd given him the opening, and he could no more resist it than he'd ever been able to resist her.

"Easy," he murmured. He was close enough to feel the heat emanating from her skin, the moist wash of her breath touching his lips.

"Oh, please, just get it over with!"

"Now there's what a man wants to hear."

"But—"

He took advantage of the slight opening as she formed the words, lowering his mouth to hers at the first syllable. Softly, surely, a bare meeting where their breaths tangled more than their lips. He held his mouth still, though he felt the effort of it through his shoulders, in the tight coil of tension in his belly, and just breathed her in, smell and taste and feel.

"Oh," she sighed softly, and went lax. He felt the tension seep out of her, the easing of her muscles where he touched her, the softening of her lips against his.

And he lost all intent, all plan and control. It blurred into one great, shimmering haze of sensation, the physical experience overwhelming thought.

Her mouth trembled and opened for him. Her hands found his back and clutched there, crumpling his shirt, digging deeply into muscle.

Tenderness surrendered to greed. Too many places to touch, to much to explore, too many wonders to appreciate—he couldn't separate out any one of them, couldn't focus on her mouth or the feel of her back twisting beneath his hands. There was just one slick blur of her, a heated, shifting fantasy of all the dreams of her he'd ever had, all the visions he'd never allowed to star her face, and *now*, the woman he held, her vivid presence making all the rest, those memories that had tortured him for so long, suddenly go pale.

"Oh, God." She broke away, jerking herself from his grasp, stealing her wonderful mouth from his with such abruptness it left him dazed, grasping at empty air.

"Oh!" She flapped her hands before her face, as if

trying to dry away tears, and pressed her knuckles to her mouth.

She swayed on her knees, only a few tempting inches away. Her skin was flushed, her mouth tender-looking. Without thought, without intent, he reached for her again.

"No!" She shrank away. "Damn. Damn *you*."

"What?" All right, perhaps he'd been too lost, too taken with her, at last, in his arms, to take the care he should have. There were a thousand tricks, a hundred secrets he'd learned in mysterious corners of the world, and he'd been too absorbed in her to use any of them. "Here," he said. "I'll fix it. Come—"

"Damn you," she said again, the sweet, passionate haze in her eyes sharpening to open accusation.

He winced. "I—"

"I cherished that kiss in the gazebo for *years*," she went on. "Boxed it away in glass, perfect and fragile. I dreamed of it, longed for it. For all the things I'd never had, never *would* have, I'd had that. If I had nothing else, I'd had a kiss for the ages.

"And now you—" She jabbed a finger into his chest, the force of her rage pushing him back. "You had to go and ruin it."

"I'll make it up to you," he said, thinking frantically. What would she like best? He could—

"You *stole* that from me. To find out that my perfect memory was merely a girl's kiss after all, that it was merely *nice* compared to what a kiss could be— oh, what am I supposed to do now? If I longed for *that* for a dozen years, I can barely guess how long *this* is going to haunt me."

"I—" He shut up and let the words swirl around in his brain a bit until he was sure he was making sense of them. She . . . she wasn't disappointed. She worried that he'd marked her for life? *Damn*, but that went to his head, a peculiar mix of pride and worry. For she'd marked him every bit as strongly, and wasn't that a mess?

He had to say something that would make it okay. Preferably something that would make this nice and simple and clean for him, while ensuring she'd never forget one solitary instant. "Kate—" Hell. Words. What good were words? He gave in and reached for her.

"Oh, no." She scrambled to her feet and backed away, hair and skirts swirling around her like a vengeful siren. "I can't think straight when you're touching me."

"Trust me, darling, that's a good thing." He grinned and followed her up, smiling when she took a step back. Her skirt was damp at the knees and her mouth was still puffy from his kiss, and did she really think she could get away from him that easily? "A very good thing."

"No." She flung a hand out to put space between them and touched the other to her temple. "There's a reason we can't do this. I know there is. I can't come up with it right now, but I'm sure there is."

A very faint suspicion, the barest suggestion that she might be right, niggled at the back of his brain. He wouldn't listen to it. It was paying attention to just those sorts of qualms that robbed men of fun all the time.

"You can't come up with a reason because there isn't one," he said, and moved forward until the palm of her hand came up flat against his chest. Even that contact seared him, sent his heart into a wild rhythm as if it were trying to beat its way out of his chest to her.

Her eyes fell to where she touched him, her small hand pale and shaking and so erotic just laying there against his chest that if she touched him anywhere else it would surely destroy him. And in that moment he didn't give a damn. Her eyes went soft and unfocused, and her fingers swept in a gentle arc while he held his breath and felt every single increment of movement.

And then her gaze cleared. She snatched her hand back. "No," she said, with a ring of finality that sounded a death knell to his plans.

"Yes," he said, one last-ditch attempt even as he knew it was hopeless.

"No. If there's no reason not to, there won't be any reason tonight, or tomorrow."

But there'd be reasons. Doctor Goodale, big and real between them. The fact that Jim fit into her life no more neatly than she would fit into his, which was not at all. That they'd a competition to win, one that required more attention and thought than either one was expending on it at the moment.

But damn. Damn!

She rubbed her palms together, then smoothed them down the front of the ruin of her dress as if she didn't know what to do with them. "I'm not the sort who leaps without looking," she said. "I like to *decide*."

"Maybe that explains a lot, doesn't it?"

Her eyes darkened. "That's not fair."

He had the dim notion that someday—in a week or two—he'd know that it wasn't. But at the moment, caught in the vicious, painful grip of frustrated passion, he didn't much care about fair.

He turned away and strode over to the rim of the cave, staring out at the roiling gray sea. It seethed between him and the shore, waiting to slap at him with cold and power.

"Jim." She'd come up behind him—nearer than she would have if she had the slightest inkling of how thin his control had shredded—and spoke softly.

"I wouldn't," he warned her, his voice dangerously low.

"Jim—"

"*Not now.*" The icy churn of the water seemed the lesser evil. "Time to go swimming." He began to strip off his shirt.

"You're not going in there."

"Here." He tossed his shirt in her direction and began to pick his way down the slope toward the water.

"Hello!" Their heads swiveled in tandem toward the sound. Charlie Hobson wavered on the narrow ledge that led to the cave's entrance. He ventured a wave, bobbled, then flattened himself against the side.

"What the hell?" Jim clambered back up to her side.

"Well." Charlie pointed his thumb back up the slope. "Let's meet topside, shall we?"

Jim grabbed his shirt and shrugged into it. The trip back up seemed much easier than down. It felt like only a few moments had passed before they rounded the top to find Hobson waiting for them, red-faced and sweating in the cool morning mist.

"Well, well. You do show up in the most interesting places, don't you?" Jim said.

"Part of my job." He spoke to Jim, but he *looked* at Kate. "Rough night?"

Two words, and Kate was suddenly, unbearably

conscious of how she must appear. A glance at her skirt showed it to be hardly worthy of a rag basket. Her hand crept up to her hair and found it a snarl the size of a bird's nest near the back. She must look . . . *old. Ordinary.*

Jim edged between her and the reporter, blocking the man's gaze. For a second she was grateful. And then she thought, *no. No.*

She stepped out from his protective shadow. "Actually, it was surprisingly . . . comfortable." Beside her, she felt Jim's amazement and didn't dare glance his way. "No, it's his insistence on a morning swim that's disturbing me."

"Is that what you were arguing about?" Hobson asked.

"Arguing?"

"When I first saw the two of you, you looked a bit . . . intense." Was that the reporter's stock in trade, Kate wondered? A leading comment, a level gaze, then the pregnant waiting silence that encouraged one to blurt something, *anything*, to fill it?

"Facing a choice between swimming in *that* and starving to death on this rock tends to make me a bit serious," she said smoothly.

He smiled blandly. "I suppose it would."

"Convenient of you to show up," Jim put in. "Very timely. Seems to be a habit of yours."

"I try."

"How'd you know we were here?"

"Been following the competitors. Everybody has to show up here, sooner or later."

"Everybody?" Kate asked, all innocence. "Who's been here so far?"

"Oh, no." Charlie waggled a chiding finger. "I'm

not telling you how far along anybody else is."

"I was just curious."

"I'm sure you were. Anyway, I saw you two come over yesterday. When you didn't come back—"

"Yesterday? You saw us then and just *left* us here all night?"

"Hey, now, how was I supposed to know?" He spread his hands. "Thought maybe you two wanted to be alone. Deserted island and all that."

"That wasn't the plan, no. Our boat left without us."

He shrugged. "Sorry. This morning, I figured I'd row on over and see what was up. Just in case."

"How lucky for us," Jim said without inflection. "Much as I've enjoyed the chat, I'd as soon get going."

"Wouldn't do to get too far behind, would it?" said Hobson, his smugness almost perfectly disguised. He knew very well where everyone else was, Kate thought, and thoroughly enjoyed knowing something they didn't.

"Let's go."

Hobson had tied his boat behind a boulder out of sight of most of the island. No wonder they hadn't seen him coming. Jim's hand hovered at Kate's elbow as she clambered over the rough rocks, perfectly correct on the surface, but his thumb stroked inside her elbow with easy sensuality that had her stumbling along the way.

"Bet you're glad to see that boat," Hobson said.

"I most certainly am," Kate answered, and wondered why she wasn't nearly as happy as she should be.

Chapter 16

◦━━━━◦◯◯◦━━━━◦

*I*t'll *do*, Hobson thought. The handsome, shirt-
less adventurer with a wild reputation and the
beautiful woman, cloistered together on a romantic
island rising out of the mists and the sea. Yeah, it
will do.

He gave a hard pull on his oar, feeling the twinge
all across his shoulders, knowing he'd be feeling it tomorrow, too. Beside him, Lord Bennett was stroking
smoothly, barely putting any effort into it. But that
was his way, wasn't it? Born with position and looks
and money, he'd probably never had to put much effort into anything his entire life.

It would have been better, Hobson knew, if he'd
have found them in a more compromising position.
That was certainly what he'd hoped for, planned on.
Readers ate that kind of thing up. You could write the

best story in the world about a legislative committee, really important stuff, and they'd go for the lurid every time. He'd gotten two raises in six months once he'd finally figured that out.

But while he could selectively present the truth, had no problem nudging it along now and then, he couldn't outright make it up. He'd been in Havana Harbor when the *Maine* had been blown up, for Christ's sake. Teddy Roosevelt himself had said he'd written the very best account of the taking of San Juan Heights, so vivid he'd requested his own signed copy of the article. He was a real reporter, not a novelist. And he never forgot it.

But these two . . . they'd sell a few papers for him before he was done. And let that mystery reporter Fitz had dug up who'd gotten so damn lucky with his first story try and keep up with him this time.

Dear Emily,

I have only a moment to dash this off, but I trust you will make sure the important points find their way to Anthea as well. I'm sure I've had the wires humming and the cables flying between Montana and Colorado for the last few weeks already.

I know the news is abysmally slow to reach you two out in the hinterlands, but maybe you've heard of the Great Centennial Race? Sponsored by the Daily Sentinel? *I suggest you begin paying attention, for I've entered.*

All right, take your time. Finish laughing. I have. You won't read about me in the papers—I'm travel- ing under an assumed name. No reason to let that out if I don't have to. And I'm not going to tell you what it is. You can guess. Consider it fair compensation for all you put me through this year.

And here, my dear sister, is where you can say "I told you so." I know you love that. Perhaps there is something to be said for this adventuring thing after all. Not that I'd ever want to do it again, mind you— heaven forbid!—but it is rather educational to have experienced it once, if only to reinforce my previous opinions of such matters.

You cannot imagine all the places I've been sleeping! Some of them make me downright nostalgic for that horrible floor of your hut. Last night I stowed away on a railroad car! I am almost certain it was once used to transport cattle.

I must go. We're behind, and you know how I hate that. One last thing, however. You remember that other helpful suggestion you made? About having one wild affair in my life?

I confess I am seriously considering it.

Must go. I've got a boat to catch.

All my love,
Kate

"Are you sure they're going to be all right?" Kate asked.

"I promised, didn't I?" Jim replied with admirable patience, given that he'd answered that question at least three dozen times in the last thirty-six hours as they'd raced to reach New York before the *Emperor* sailed. "I made it worth the kid's while to make sure of it. He'll get both horses back to the stables at the Rose Springs. And if he doesn't, he'll be answering to me. I made that *very* clear, believe me."

"Now there's a terrifying thought, answering to you." She gave a mock shudder, her eyes sparkling with that teasing light that seemed to reduce him to stuttering faster than anything else on earth. Then she sobered. "I'm going to miss her, that's all."

"I know." Kate had grown almost absurdly fond of her little mare. Not that kindness to animals wasn't a truly commendable quality, but still—"After we win, you can go back and buy her, all right?"

"Promise?" she asked, and he would have done anything in the world she requested just to put that expression on her face.

"I swear," he said solemnly, and then turned his attention to the matter at hand. Around them bobbed the chaotic, colorful hubbub of the Hudson River piers; above them beamed a warm, benevolent autumn sun. "So what do you think?"

Kate contemplated the *Emperor*, moored snugly into her jetty. If the ships got any bigger, she thought, they were going to have to rebuild the docks to get them to fit. Out in the river, her attendants awaited her, a floating court of tugboats, lighters, fireboats, and what had to be the entire membership of the New York Yacht Club, decks packed with partiers.

The *Emperor* lived up to her name. France's attempt to finally wrest the prize for the fastest Atlantic crossing from England and Germany, who'd held the title for years, she'd done just that, winning the coveted "Blue Riband" on her maiden crossing from Le Havre. But she was a beautiful thing as well, majestic in her size, glorious in her formal tuxedo colors of black and white, punched with a few vibrant shots of red. She settled firmly into the water, commanding it easily, her four funnels—the first full four-funnel ship built in France, none of that three-funnels and a dummy business for her—tilted slightly back, making her look as if she were steaming quickly through the ocean even while at rest. Flags snapped from every pole, fluttering against the clear sky, as if she were dressed for a party. Which, in a manner of speaking, she was.

"Hmm. I might be able to . . ." She glanced down at herself and grimaced. "Not like this, I can't." She snatched up her bag and slung it over a shoulder, an easy gesture that looked as if she'd been packing it herself for years. "Will you wait?"

"Will I wait for what?"

"You'll see."

She glanced around, then clipped off across the docks toward a small office building, entering without knocking. For five minutes, perhaps more, he waited for her return before wandering over to the edge of the pier.

Water, a deep gray-green, threaded with dying seaweed, bobbing with refuse tossed from ships and shore, slapped at the pilings, the dark wood slick and green where the water slid over it, striking and retreating again, a relentless attack, and he started to plan.

"There you are," she said from behind him, her voice breathless, a bit perturbed. "I thought you were going to wait."

"I did. I'm still here, aren't I? I . . ." He turned and whatever he was about to say evaporated like alcohol held on the tongue.

Surrounded by the ragged, work-grimed men that toiled on the wharf, she stood as if alone in the sunlight, everything else gray and smudged. A queen's necklace in a pile of tin and dirty crystals, shining and true.

Silk shimmered and flowed over her elegant form, the fabric the color of the very heart of the orchids he'd found in the jungle where they bloomed in wild luxury. It was a perfectly proper dress, tight-necked, long sleeved, but with dozens of buttons like tiny pearls, winking at him in the sunlight as if they dared him to pop them off. A swath of filmy fabric encircled her waist, drawn through twin circles of hammered silver before fluttering to her hem, drawing his eyes to the narrow slope of her waist, the lush curve of her hip beneath the silk.

Her hair was almost completely uncovered, bits of lace and feather peeping flirtatiously from within the rich tumble of gold. She'd twisted and turned the strands, pinning them in a haphazard manner that looked as if a maid had labored over it for hours to achieve just that studied disarray.

"Where the hell did you get that?"

"Magic bag." She patted it fondly before dropping it to the ground. "Aren't you glad you let me pack it myself?"

"How—" He had to stop to breathe. He'd nearly forgotten she could look like this, every man's fantasy taken human form, just real enough to dream about but too far beyond any human's reach ever to think that she might actually be yours. To admire, but never touch. "But—"

"Oh, stop stuttering," she snapped. "You've seen me in my natural state—" She stopped, reddened prettily. "You've seen me in an unguarded state for weeks. You, of all people, should no longer be reduced to idiocy."

Interesting. She'd made no secret of her wish to be admired, nor of how accustomed she was to the appreciation of men. And here she didn't want his, at least not like this . . . *interesting*, he thought again.

"It's just shock. Not to mention annoyance that you've been wasting precious storage space hauling around useless fripperies like that. I could have used more rope."

"Oh, it's not useless," she said airily. "Just you wait and see."

Three men—two bearded dockworkers with shoulders the size of tugboats and a tall, thin gentleman in a charcoal gray suit, a gold-tipped cane swinging over his arm—stopped dead at the sight of her, spurring a logjam in the human traffic on the docks. She flashed them each a smile in turn, one that somehow managed to make them preen and blush but held them all at a safe distance.

"Somebody should have pressed you into the diplomatic core long ago," he mumbled under his breath. "The Americans might have avoided that whole business in the Philippines."

"What?"

"Nothing." He grabbed her elbow and tugged her a few feet away from her clutch of admirers, who had now expanded to five. "We've got to get you out of here before there's a riot."

Stunning as she was, Jim wasn't at all sure he liked this version. The woman who'd chased up and down the seacoast with him, that was *his* Kate. The one that only he had been allowed to see and appreciate. This Kate—this was the Kate that belonged to Dr. Goodale. Or rather, he decided, a woman who might have al-

lowed a few men along the way to believe that, but
who'd never given away a piece of herself that she
hadn't calculated to the precise quarter-inch.

His Kate, he thought, bemused and more than a little concerned. Just when had he started to consider
her that? Better he was reminded now, before it was
too late, that she was not his Kate and would never
be. She was her own Kate, and any man who believed
otherwise was a fool.

"Not to worry," she said. "I'm going." She turned
to face the harbor. "Will you wait again?"

"For what?"

"For me to take care of things."

"There're barely two hours before she sails," he reminded her.

She tossed her head and gold shimmered like a
king's treasure. "This won't take long."

Except that it did, much longer than Kate antici-
pated. Talking her way onto the ship proved to be
simple, but tracking down the captain was nearly impossible. Truly, shouldn't the man be at his helm this
close to sailing? There were people everywhere, rush-
ing here and there, the decks crowded with passengers, reporters, and dignitaries with temporary
passes, and workers still loading supplies. So by the
time she'd completed her business and dashed back
to the dock, Jim was gone.

There'd been no time to look for him. She'd hesitated only a moment before scurrying back aboard.

And so now she sat in her cabin, on the little
pseudo-Louis XIV settee which was no less pretty for
being pseudo—and tried to decide what to do next.

Unpack? Freshen up for the departure? Begin searching this monstrous behemoth of a ship for the next
clue?

She'd become so accustomed to Jim's ordering her
around—whether she followed his commands or
not—that his absence now was unsettling, as if she
were listening to an orchestra where one instrument
was perpetually a beat behind.

And then her door flew open and he was there,
soaked to the skin, clothes clinging to a form that
seemed much larger in the small space of the cabin
than he had in the open air.

"You're dripping seawater on the carpet," she told
him. "It'd be a shame to ruin it already."

"Toss me a towel, would you?" Unconcerned, he
dropped his pack, as sopping wet as he, to the floor
and shook himself like a dog, spraying droplets.

"Oh, for heaven's sake!" She raced over to the small
armoire bolted to the wall beside the porcelain sink,
grabbed a thick white towel off the stack, and tossed
it to him. "It's a very good thing you're usually in a
tent, if this is how you treat a decently decorated
place."

He scrubbed the towel briskly over his head and
then looped it around his neck, hanging on to both
ends as he contemplated her through the dark, damp
strands of his hair drooping over his eyes. "What
were you doing?"

"Right now?" At his nod, she continued, "Waiting
for you."

"Waiting for me?" he repeated with enough surprise to make her smile.

"Oh, I had a suspicion that a little detail like a ticket
wouldn't keep you off this ship," she said, then

looked pointedly at the puddle around his feet. "Though if you'd had a bit more trust in me and waited, I could have gotten you on without quite so much . . . trouble."

He shrugged. "Needed the exercise."

"How'd you find me so quickly?"

"Believe me, darling, all I had to do was eavesdrop on a couple of the sailors. Your arrival on board was not exactly unremarked upon."

"It's so nice to be noticed."

"Uh-huh," he said, carefully neutral, then quickly surveyed the cabin. "Nice place."

"Yes, it is."

One of the smallest of the first-class cabins—a fact for which Captain Dupree had apologized most profusely—it was nevertheless well appointed. The berth stowed neatly away, leaving a charming salon with furniture that looked as if it had been stolen from a lovely chateau. There were taps for both cold and hot water, subdued electric lighting, and a button which the captain had assured her would summon a steward in a matter of moments.

"So? What did you have to promise to get it?"

"Jim!" Pain stabbed, quick and sure. How *dare* he, after all this time—

"I'm sorry." He took a step toward her and lifted one hand, as if he meant to touch her. Water trailed off his cuff. He grimaced and stayed where he was. "Jesus, Kate, I'm sorry. *Sorry.* It was a reflex. An idiotic one, I'll admit. But there you were, looking like . . ." He trailed off.

"Like Dr. Goodale's wife?" she asked tightly.

"I—" He clamped his jaw together.

Sometime in the last few weeks, she noted, the man

had finally learned when to shut up. "Never mind," she said, wondering just why it bothered her so much. It wouldn't have before—when had she ever cared what others thought, except as necessary to further her own ends? But he'd seemed to believe her so easily in that cave, the kind of faith that no one but her sisters had ever shown in her. It had . . . touched her, tempted her.

Oh, grow up, Kate, she scolded herself. The man had a reflex reaction. And hadn't she had enough of building him up into something he wasn't by now? "Besides, I do owe this"—her gesture encompassed the entire cabin, and perhaps more—"to Doctor Goodale. Have you heard of Emile Marcil?"

"Who hasn't? Banking magnate, railroad magnate, shipping magnate. Not to mention owner of this fine vessel."

"That's the one. Also an old acquaintance of Dr. Goodale's. And mine."

"An admirer," he said.

"Well. Of a sort." She would have given a lot to know what was going on behind Jim's neutral expression. There were few men who could hide things from her, especially after she'd spent some time and effort into discovering their secrets. It was alternately frustrating and immensely intriguing that he continued to be able to do so. "Marcil came over on the maiden voyage, of course, and is staying for some time in New York. He's quite pleased at the publicity generated by having part of the competition take place on his ship, and more than delighted to allow me passage back."

"So there's no more Katie Riley, hmm?"

"Oh, no, he's more than happy to keep my little secret. And you, by the way, were to be my trusted manservant. He even offered you a third-class cabin. Not nearly as nice as this, of course, but I'm sure it would be far more comfortable than you're going to be as a stowaway, bedding down in some hidden corner of the cargo hold. Not to mention having to work off your passage as a stoker once you get caught."

"Lucky for me that won't be a problem, isn't it? Since I'll be staying in here with you."

Her blasé confidence evaporated. *A bed. A door. Jim. Trouble.* "What?"

"What's the problem? You've been sleeping with me all along—"

"I have not been *sleeping with* you."

"What would you call it, then?"

"I—" Mercifully, the long blast of the ship's horn split the air, saving her from having to explain something that she couldn't.

"Guess we're shipping out," Jim said. "Want to go?"

"I suppose we shouldn't miss it, should we?" And we shouldn't stay in here alone, skirting on the edge of things that were best approached cautiously, if at all, she thought.

"We shouldn't." He offered his elbow, which dripped steadily, and for a moment Kate wondered if it were only the launch he referred to.

"Aren't you going to change?"

"Into what?"

"Oh." She started to take his arm, then thought better of it. She tugged off her gloves and tossed them on a small, marble-topped table before linking her hand through his arm. His flesh was cold, the fabric so wet as to be no barrier at all. She swallowed hard.

"Ready?"

"Ready," she said. *Ready for what*, she wondered. *Ready for anything?*

They peeked at the port side of the ship, a wild, happy festival both on board and ashore, jam-packed with people, confetti, and streamers thickly showering the air and the excited crowds. And then, deciding that even in that carnival Jim's appearance might provoke one too many questions, they retreated to the starboard side.

In contrast, here it was nearly deserted. They chose a spot on the lowest promenade, near the stern, so they could look out at the water as the rest of the passengers contemplated the land.

Jim leaned on his elbows on the mahogany rail, his face unreadable as he stared out at the river.

"The beginning of another journey," she said. "You must feel right at home."

He took so long to answer she'd begun to think he wouldn't. "Yes."

One syllable, that did nothing but whet her curiosity. "Do you have a plan for the next trip? After this is over?"

"No."

Clearly the man was not in a mood to be forthcoming. But when had that ever stopped her? "You must have some idea, though? Someplace that you'd like to return to, or somewhere you've never been?" It would be helpful to fix it in her mind. Jim would be leaving when this venture was over, heading off to someplace that the mere mention of would give her shudders. It would keep her from letting her imagination run away with her again.

There was one final blast and a cheer went up from the other side of the ship. Powerful engines rumbled deep within the hull, and the ship inched from her berth.

"You should go back." Jim pointed over his shoulder with his chin. "No reason to miss all the fun."

Kate turned away from the water, and him, choosing instead to survey the ship. "She really is magnificent, isn't she? The next clue could be anywhere."

Jim made a noncommittal sound.

"I believe I'll begin the search," she said. There was clearly no point in talking to him right now. "Why wait?"

"Good."

"Are you coming?" Kate asked.

"You take half the ship, I'll take the rest," Jim said. "You pick."

Kate huffed and flounced down the deck. Jim tried not to watch but couldn't help sneaking a peek or two. Damn, but the woman flounced well. A jiggle here, a wiggle there. If the aim of a woman's flouncing was to get a man to come after her, he had to admit hers was world-class.

But he was sticking with staring at the water. She hadn't earned his rudeness and he knew it, but he just . . . he just had nothing to say about what happened when this contest ended. Why couldn't women comprehend that sometimes a man just had nothing to say? Best that she understood it right now. Of course he was going back out. That's what he did. And if heading out in search of the unknown now had a few terrible memories attached, well, he'd just have to get over it, wouldn't he?

It's what he was. Moving out, moving on. He knew nothing else, knew how to do nothing else. And if the truth was that he'd never quite found what he was looking for out there, that didn't mean a man should quit trying.

Boats clustered around the ship, carrying city officials, reporters, curiosity seekers, barely giving the ship enough clearance. The *Emperor* eased through the water; she'd be slow and careful until they cleared the river and the bay beyond.

Hands flat on the smooth railing, he leaned over to watch the water slip beneath, the movement barely perceptible. His chest smacked against the railing as someone hit him hard from behind, nearly sending him over the rail. He clutched at it, dipping his knees as he bent to bring the bulk of his weight safely below the rail's danger point. But then hands slammed beneath his back, pushing him up. Reflexively Jim dropped one shoulder into solid mass, and then heaved upward. His attacker, who'd thrown all of his weight behind his own upward thrust, had too much momentum and was catapulted over the railing.

"*Aahh!*"

The shout brought Kate running, dashing back with her skirts lifted, with more speed than he'd given her credit for. She leaned over the railing, then whirled on Jim. "You threw him overboard?"

"No. He was throwing *me* overboard. I just went with it." Lifesaving rings hung along the promenade wall. Jim grabbed the nearest, took firm hold of the rope, judged his target, and gave the ring a toss.

"But— but—" She bent over the side again, far

enough to give him a sweet view of the curve of her rump, as if she couldn't believe what she'd seen the first time. "That's the major . . . oh, hell, Major What's-his-name."

"Major Huddleston-Snell." The major bobbed in the water, arms flailing. His lips were flapping, too, and Jim had a perverse wish to know just exactly what the major was calling him. The lifesaving ring was just out of his reach and Jim took three quick steps down the promenade, trailing the ring into position. When the Major grabbed it, Jim let go of the rope. "Good thing the ship's not moving too fast yet, isn't it?"

"But—you—he could *drown*."

"Naw. One of those boats'll pick him up in no time. Good story some reporter'll get out of it, too." True to his word the nearest boat, a spiffy mahogany pleasure launch, spurted through the waves toward the major.

She gaped at him and Jim couldn't help but smile. She was so shocked. Imperturbable I-know-men-better-than-they-know-themselves Kate was completely stunned by what he'd done.

"But—"

"Somehow I think we'll have no more trouble with broken stairways and missing maps and stolen boats."

"Hmm. Really?"

"I'd bet on it. A bit of convenient sabotage now and then is the major's stock in trade. I've got more than one scar to prove it." *Oh, just give me a chance,* he thought. *I'd love to make you just that shocked again. In a much, much better way.*

But she wasn't going to give him a chance. Why

should she? She could marry someone like . . . well, someone like Emile Marcil. Why would she stoop to a fling with a broken-down adventurer with nothing to show for it but some good stories and a couple of trunks of dusty artifacts, a man who would disappear from her life as suddenly as he'd shown up in it?

He sighed and turned his attention to the one thing they had in common. "Did you say something about searching this boat?"

Chapter 17

~⌒OᴏⒸ⌒~

"Have you seen this?"

"Have I seen what?" Kate set aside her
hairbrush and took a couple of breaths—*easy, calm*—
before she turned to face Jim. Last she'd seen him, he
was headed for the gymnasium to search, while she'd
elected to start in the Moorish smoking lounge, which
was empty this early into the journey. She'd found
nothing of interest before one of the lounge's waiters,
dressed in flowing trousers and a gold-tasseled fez,
reported for work and told her in no uncertain terms
that women weren't allowed in the smoking lounge.

She'd returned to her cabin to freshen up for dinner, all the while eyeing Jim's pack, a stained and
fraying interloper slumped against one of the gilded
chairs, and the still-damp clothes he'd draped over
the back.

It made her . . . uneasy. She'd grown so accustomed to traveling with him, just the two of them, outside the normal bounds of society. This ship was so much more her usual world, and he was so far outside of it. It was almost unsettling to run into so many people when she stepped out of her cabin—curious, judging people. She didn't know where she fit anymore, how *they* fit.

As unsettled as she felt, however, he seemed perfectly comfortable. "This," he answered her and tossed a folded paper onto the table.

"Hmm?"

"It's a recent edition of the *Sentinel*. They've got quite a collection in the library. Read it."

She pinched the edge of the paper between her thumb and forefinger. It was folded carefully to reveal one article.

SECRETS

An Anonymous Reporter

The Great Centennial Race has spawned a hundred stories, tales of triumph and disappointment, determination and what man is willing to risk in the pursuit of glory and riches.

But what are even more fascinating are the stories of its participants. Here we have collected many of the world's most interesting people, men and women who have experienced and seen things few of us would dare to dream of. How many stories have they left in those jungles, on top of those mountains? We know of their experiences only what they wish to tell us, for there is no one to witness their triumphs and defeats so far from civilized lands.

But here is just one of those stories, about one of
the Race's most famous and respected participants.
It is, at its heart, a love story. But it is a forbidden
love, and therein lay the secrets.

Mrs. Anne Latimore has long been a shining ex-
ample of her kind, a brave and independent woman,
a widow since she tragically lost her husband in an
Amazonian jungle fifteen years ago. That story is
well known. She has admirably forged on, continuing his work, consistently supported only by her
bosom friend, Miss Camelia Dooley, and a stalwart
Chinese servant, Ming Ho.

But if Ming Ho began as her servant, he did not
remain so for long. For this reporter has learned
that, twelve years ago, in a tiny chapel in a mission
not all that far from that same, dangerous jungle,
Mrs. Latimore secretly married her servant and em-
barked on a life of lies . . .

"Oh, no." Kate raised worried eyes to meet Jim's serious ones.

"I know. Damn reporters. It's probably been
splashed up and down half the eastern seaboard by
now, laid out bald for the curious, and it's nobody's
business but theirs if they don't choose it to be."

"But *I* was interested," Kate said guiltily. "I
couldn't wait to tell you, I—"

"It's not the same."

"Isn't it?" she asked, troubled.

"No. You didn't go looking for it, you ran smack
into it, and you didn't tell anyone else."

"No, I didn't." Her brow creased. "Was that a
question?"

"No." When her frown deepened, he repeated,
"No, Kate, no. I never thought it was you."

She nodded, accepting. "But she's going to think it was me." She headed for the door and had the handle in her hand before she stopped and glanced back at him. "Jim?"

"Two decks down. Room 43."

Mrs. Latimore was exactly where he had promised, in a tiny but comfortable second-class cabin, although the only response to her initial knock was a firm "Go away" from Miss Dooley.

"It's us. Katie Riley and Lord Bennett."

"Go *away.*"

"No, please." She exchanged a worried glance with Jim. "Please, I really need to speak to Mrs. Latimore."

Miss Dooley pulled open the door and waved them inside. "Hurry up. Quickly."

Mrs. Latimore, wearing her usual khaki garb, sat perfectly upright on the narrow bunk. But this time, Ming Ho was beside her, his arm looped comfortably around her waist. Wearing a deep, flowing blue tunic and loose pants, he was at least three inches shorter than his wife. But there was something in his posture, in the way his body leaned toward hers and shielded her, that had turned him from servant to husband. They looked so at ease together that Kate wondered why she hadn't pegged it right off.

"So you've read the article," Mrs. Latimore said flatly.

"Yes."

"Everyone has." She nodded. "It goes against my grain to hide in here. But when we first tried to get on the ship—the reporters, they—"

"They were like vultures," Ming Ho said. His hand moved up from her waist, making soothing circles on her back. "We had to hide Anne and Miss Dooley in a crate and have them loaded as cargo."

"And you? How did you slip onboard?"

"Ming Ho is quite . . . creative when necessary," Mrs. Latimore said with warm pride. "Are they all still out there?"

"Most of the reporters were just let on board to report on the launch and are long gone. I saw Hobson, of course. Maybe two or three others. That's it," Jim said.

"Then they won't be a problem," Ming Ho said, and Kate didn't doubt him for a moment.

"The other passengers will, though," Miss Dooley said softly. "It's exactly what you've been trying to avoid all these years. People staring, judging, commenting, interfering in something that's none of their business." Her expression turned fierce.

Kate flinched. "I'm so sorry, Mrs. Latimore. It might have been my fault. I don't think so, but . . . I've been racking my brain on the way over here, wondering if I might have dropped a hint, if something in my expression might have given it away, but—"

Mrs. Latimore's head snapped up, her eyes narrowing on Kate. "You knew?"

"Well, yes," she admitted. "The night you took us in. The next morning . . . I saw you two"—her cheeks heated—"well, it was obvious there was more to the two of you than you were allowing the world to know. I didn't know you were *married*, of course, but . . ." She stopped. "This is getting worse, the longer I try to explain it."

"Yes, but you blush so prettily while you do so," Jim supplied helpfully.

"Yes, and thank you *so* much for jumping in to help me explain. In any case, Mrs. Latimore, if in any way I revealed your secret, truly it was not my intent."

"I'm sure it wasn't you," Mrs. Latimore said. "And I'm not sure it matters who, either."

"It matters to me," Miss Dooley said with more heat than Kate would have thought her capable of.

"And to me as well," Ming Ho said. "As for the one who wrote that piece of . . ."

"Darling." Mrs. Latimore put a calming hand on Ming Ho's knee. "It doesn't matter now. And perhaps it was time it came out."

"It should have been your choice," he said. "It was taken from you. From us."

"I'd put it off too long," she said. "It was unfair of me to ask you to pretend for so long just so that I could continue my career unfettered."

"I didn't mind," he said softly, and Kate thought, *Oh, there it is.* What she'd never had, never would, had sacrificed so many years ago without even truly understanding what she was surrendering: a love so pure and solid and shining that just the witnessing of it pierced her heart. She dared a glance at Jim to find him watching her, his eyes intense, dark, impossible to decipher, and the pain in her chest went deeper.

Oh, no, not him. She couldn't be that unwise. Quickly, she turned away.

"But I did," Mrs. Latimore replied.

"So what are your plans now?" Kate asked.

"We've land on a little island near Borneo. Nobody there cares much about our marriage; we're both outsiders anyway, and no threat to them. So we'll grow cinnamon and nutmeg and enjoy each other. It's time."

"You're retiring?" Kate asked in surprise. She'd always doubted that people with adventure in their system had it in them to quit; certainly it had run so deeply in her husband's blood that he'd never been able to live settled and civilized again without longing to return to the wild.

"Yes." Mrs. Latimore smiled broadly. "After we win this competition, of course."

Jim managed quite successfully to avoid Kate for the next two days. Oh, it had been tempting not to. Her clear consternation when he'd mentioned sharing the cabin had been both amusing and pride-deflating, and he was powerfully inclined to make it as uncomfortable for her as possible.

But the simple truth was he no longer trusted himself around her. He couldn't think with her around, couldn't plan or resist or *decide*. Or do anything else that required his brain, for that matter. It simply ceased to function when she was near—or, if it functioned, any commands it sent were quickly overcome by the demands the rest of him made. And then he'd forget that he could promise her nothing and give her even less.

So for two days, he'd worked. He'd dove to the bottom of the Pompeian-style swimming pool. He'd tugged on every piece of equipment in the gymnasium. He'd spent six sweaty, sooty hours crawling around behind every one of the twenty-five boilers. He'd talked his way into the cardroom and spent a good portion of the evening and a fair chunk of the night there, watching his competitors carefully to see if any of them looked too pleased with themselves or gave any other sign of having dug up a clue. He'd even swallowed his distaste and bought Charlie Hobson a whiskey, hoping to pry a hint from the weasel.

And when he returned to the cabin each night,

bone-tired, frustrated, he allowed himself one carefully measured minute to admire Kate curled up in her bunk, her hair streaming over her pillow, her mouth relaxed in sleep, before he plopped himself down on a makeshift pallet on the carpet—which wasn't nearly as plush as it looked—and tried to sleep.

They mumbled a few words at each other each morning, rushed and awkward, carefully circumspect. Kate had been busy as well. She'd poked in flower and vegetable pots in the greenhouse on the afterdeck. Prodded carved cherubs on the columns in the three-story, glass-topped grand dining room. Shook out gold, tasseled drapes in the ladies' salon.

Tonight Jim was taking a break, competition be damned. Nobody else had found anything, either; that much he was sure of.

The topmost deck of the ship had become his refuge. Nobody bothered to come up here much. The lower decks were warmer, sheltered from the wind, and stocked with deck chairs and blankets. Only the sturdiest souls braved the tennis court between the two foremost funnels for a chilly half hour of exercise. The lifeboats lashed to the railings spoiled the view of the water.

And so now, approaching seven o'clock, he had the place to himself. Or so he'd thought.

He'd propped his back against a ventilation pipe and watched the slate gray clouds shift and slide across a sky that was as restless as he felt. He wasn't fond of being confined on a boat, even a floating palace like this one. He sailed when he had to because he was on his way to the jumping-off point of an expedition, his time and head always fully occupied with the challenge ahead.

Though he had to admit that his current impatience likely had far less to do with the ship and the contest than it did with Kate.

Out of the corner of his eye he caught a flutter of fabric to his right. Damn, he thought, not inclined to share his hideout.

A slim figure leaned at the railing, braced into the wind. Robes, a deep magenta worked with glittering gold threads, draped her completely, the wind snapping them like the flags overhead. One of that eastern prince's brides, no doubt, though the women had been rarely seen since they, completely swathed, had been herded on board the day they sailed. Rumor had it the women took their meals in their quarters, the doors guarded by massive men with equally massive swords, only glimpsed when one of them was summoned to the prince's suite.

Suddenly she turned his way, as if something had caught her attention. The thin scarf of silk covering her head fell and dark hair streamed back. She was very young, far too young to be a wife, and she was smiling, her lovely face alight with anticipation as she looked toward the stairs from below decks.

And then her smile vanished as a man lumbered up the stairway and headed straight for her. One of her guards, undoubtedly; he was built like a bull, dark-skinned, bald-headed.

Uh-oh, Jim thought. *Trouble.*

Neither one of them seemed to notice he was there. The guard dwarfed the girl, his size and posture a clear threat. She said something to him; Jim saw her mouth move, though the wind carried the sound of her voice away. The giant shook his head. Then the girl swept by him, heading for the stairs, the guard falling into place right behind her.

She breezed right by Jim. For an instant her head turned his way. Her expression was serenely composed, her face a vision of lovely, unlined skin and soft, inexpressive mouth. But her eyes shimmered with moisture.

And then the guard stepped between them, giving Jim a clear view of his powerful back, before the two of them disappeared down the stairway.

Jim's muscles clenched. There was no point in going after them, Jim reminded himself. What was he going to do? The girl probably didn't speak a word of English. And even if she did, she wouldn't admit to a stranger what was wrong, if there was even something there to admit. It would be utterly pointless for Jim to hurl himself against that brick wall that was her guard. Although it would be a convenient outlet for all the frustration and restless energy that had gnawed at him.

Jim sprang to his feet. He'd love to go down to the gymnasium and take it out on the punching bag, but there'd probably be other people there, too. Right now he was in the mood to transfer his irritation from the bag to anyone who was handy. It was almost too bad he'd thrown the major off the ship. He would have done nicely.

He began an easy lope. A few laps around the upper deck should exhaust him enough so that he no longer felt as though he might burst at any moment. Perhaps he'd even manage a decent night's sleep despite being a few feet away from Kate.

Eighty or ninety times around the ship should do it.

The cold stung his cheeks and burned in his lungs. He welcomed the bite, the blood that pumped in his veins. This competition was too sedentary for his taste, too tame, apparently designed to allow the reporters access rather than provide a real challenge.

Coming around again, nearly back to his original position, a couple blocked his way near the railing. Damn, he thought again; the deck was getting nearly as popular as the grand salon. The two were standing very close together, heads bent, oblivious to his approach.

And then he realized who they were.

Feeling foolish, he ducked behind the ventilation pipe and peered around it, spying as blatantly as one of those nasty reporters.

Kate was in the orchid silk again, though she'd done something to the neckline that showed a hint of cleavage beneath a veil of lace. Count Nobile, only a few inches taller, wore relentless black, save for the brilliant white of his neck cloth.

Jim watched Kate throw back her head, laughing. The count lifted her hand, pressed a light, utterly correct kiss to the back of it that had Jim's fists curling until his fingers went numb.

Enough. He started forward, but he saw Kate shake her head. The Count bowed formally, then turned for the stairs. As soon as he'd gone, Kate turned toward the pipe.

"You can come out now," she shouted.

The wind slapped at him the instant he stepped out. Kate stood exposed, without so much as a shawl to protect her. He tugged off his jacket and slung it around her shoulders.

"Thank you," she said, though he had to bend close to hear her words.

"How long did you know I was there?"

"Does it matter?" Hell yes, it mattered. It mattered if the only reason she sent the count away was because she knew of Jim's presence. "The two of you looked . . . cozy."

She smiled slightly. "It's difficult to hear unless you're standing close, as you've no doubt noticed."

Oh, he'd noticed. Noticed that the wind had made a tangle of her hair, blowing it straight back, exposing the line of her jaw and the side of her neck. Noticed that his jacket covered her nearly to her thigh and wondered if it held the heat of his body and whether she felt it. Noticed that if he took but one more step, his body would come up against hers and reason be damned.

"Friendly, then."

Her head tilted, that secretive smile still playing at her mouth, as if she knew something he didn't. "Basilio has some interesting ideas about the possible final destination of the competition. It seemed wise to listen to them."

He made a noncommittal sound. "Let's get you someplace warmer."

"Oh, I'm fine." Her smile broadened. His stomach dropped with the dip of the ship through the waves. "Better than fine."

"Yeah?" His shoulders twitched. If that slick, falsely kind count had anything to do with *better*, well . . .

"Do you know," Kate mused, "that half the reason I began this venture was because my sisters so clearly thought that I couldn't? They said I needed an adventure."

She stepped nearer. A hint of her scent, sweetness and floral, tangled with the brine of the sea. His throat closed, raising his voice a half note. "They did?"

"Mmm-hmm." She brushed a strand of hair away from her cheek and he wanted to tell her to stop, that it was *his* job. "Right before I left, Emily said something else."

The wind stung roses into her cheeks. Her eyes were bright as moonlight, gleaming with secrets. "She did?"

"Yes. I came here in part to prove her wrong, to show her that this whole adventure thing was ridiculous. She insisted I needed the experience. That I needed to stretch myself to discover what I was meant to do with the rest of my life. I was certain she was utterly mistaken. But I have to admit that there was something to it."

He was losing the trail of the conversation. How was he supposed to listen and respond reasonably when she was so near?

"I've been giving it a great deal of consideration. And I've decided that her other suggestion merits my full and complete efforts as well."

"Oh?" His thoughts moved sluggishly, as if he'd sucked down a half bottle of whiskey, but he knew the only thing that intoxicated him was her. "And what's that?"

"She suggested," Kate said slowly, "that I should experience one grand affair."

Chapter 18

"An affair?" he choked out.

"Yes."

I'll kill him, Jim thought, automatic, simple.

"Jim?" she asked uneasily.

All right, so he couldn't kill him. But maiming . . . maiming sounded good. "So. You and the count, huh?"

"The count?" She shook her head. "No, not the count. You."

Still plotting in bloody detail how to ensure the count would be of little use to Kate, it took a moment for the word to burst into his brain. *You.*

Me. "Kate?"

"Oh, come now, you can't be that shocked."

The boat's running lights flared to life, pure white light that momentarily blinded them. Their sight returned in stages, each other first and then the rest of

252

the world, as if their eyes knew what mattered most.

"It would be much simpler if it were the count, I suppose. I'm certain he is very experienced in such matters. Uncomplicated, proficient, even routine. He would be the wise choice, wouldn't he?" She touched his jaw briefly, a searing contact. "It seems, however, that one's brain does not govern such matters. As much logic might dictate the count, the rest of me appears quite determined to select you."

"Me."

She'd been so sure, Kate thought. She'd considered so carefully. She did not think it had been vanity alone that allowed her to believe that he wanted her, too. But yet . . . he'd gone still and white, as if the lights had leached the color from his skin.

"You," she repeated, less certain.

His hand shot out, snagging her around the wrist. "Jim?"

"Come on." He towed her behind him, heading for the stairs, and then stopped. "No, no, that'll take too long."

"What?"

He tossed her an impatient glance. "Do you know how many decks it is down to your cabin?"

He glanced up and down the length of the deck, as if searching for something. And then he headed for the railing, hauling her behind him like a captive.

"Jim?"

Lifeboats, suspended from pulleys, lined the side of the ship. Jim untied the strap securing the tarp covering one of them and flipped back the canvas. He swung over the side and climbed in. "Get in."

"*What?*"

"Kate," he said, "I am going to touch you within

the next five seconds. If you don't want it to be right out on the open deck where anyone might see, you'd best get your lovely butt in this boat."

Smiling, she placed her hands on the rail. And caught a glimpse of water, very, very far below. "Jim?"

"It's all right. It has to be lashed very securely or it would bang against the boat every time we hit a wave." He held out a hand to her.

She started to climb over but her skirts got in the way.

"Three . . . four . . ."

"Wait!" She reached down and rucked up her skirts, exposing a length of lace-clad leg; she figured it was the lesser of two evils.

"Nice view."

Kate tried to scowl at him and failed utterly. She swung a leg up, hooking it over the railing, and could go no farther.

"Here." He reached around her waist, plucking her up as if she weighed nothing. The world spun and then she was upright, her back to him, trying to find her balance as the ship dipped and the wooden lifeboat creaked. Her stomach lifted—from the motion, a little fear. From *him*, and his arm around her waist, and the thought of what he might do to her in the next few moments.

There were no seats in the boat, just a planked bottom that curved up sharply on each side, oars secured near the edge.

"Now what?" she asked.

In answer Jim plopped down, lying flat on the bottom. He tugged her down on top of him in a froth of petticoats and laughter, then he reached up and flipped the canvas back, cocooning them in abrupt darkness. It was warm inside, the sounds of the wind and the waves, the throb of the ship's engines all muted to an urgent whisper.

"Jim—"

"Shhh." He didn't move. Seconds ticked by and she felt herself relax, sinking into him. She lay upon him all out, protected by his hard length beneath her. Her head rested against his shoulder and when she turned it toward him, her nose fit between his chin and neck. The smell of him filled her—warm, vibrant male, tinged with the sea. In the absence of movement, of sight, the physical became primary, each point of pressure where his body pressed against hers, each instant of contact acutely felt. His chest lifted and fell with each breath, pushing against her back, lifting her up until her own breathing fell in rhythm with his. His thighs were tight against hers, steel-hard even through the layers of her skirts.

And against her rump . . . she didn't know if it was her imagination or she could feel him in truth, hot and thick, and the wondering was itself exciting.

And still he didn't move, only the shift in pressure of his body as the ship swayed in the water, a constant rhythm beneath them, until she thought she might go mad with anticipation. "Jim?"

He brushed her hair away from her neck, his fingers icy cold, and she shivered. Then his mouth was there, open, hot, and the shiver became a tremble.

She had no way to judge the time. It was as black with her eyes open as closed. He feasted on her neck, his tongue coming to lick and stroke, his lips nibbling, tugging gently on soft skin.

His hands inched from her waist toward her

breasts while she held her breath until her head grew light. And then he cupped her breasts while a sigh slipped out of her, easy and slow. Warmth spread wherever he touched her.

He peeled away the lace she'd draped around her neck to disguise where she'd tucked the button plackets of her bodice. His hand slid inside the fabric, easing beneath her shift, gliding into her memories.

His fingers were warmer now, the skin just rough enough to burnish her skin to a fine, warm tingle. With the flat of his palm he made circles against her nipple, again and again, until she arched into his touch.

The motion brought her rear harder against him and his hips lifted in reflex. He brought his free hand flat against her belly, keeping her still.

She might have stayed there forever, caught in the hazy, heated border where desire ebbed and flowed like the ocean, relentless, threatening to drown her. She was awash in it, unable to guess if it would build to a peak or if Jim would hold her there until dawn, captive to his will and the pleasure of his hands.

Her hands were at her sides and she clamped them against his hips. Her fingers flexed. He was rigid beneath her, the muscles as hard as his hands were gentle, as if he used all his will to keep his touch tender.

His hand moved from her stomach, tracking down her thigh as far as he could reach. He inched up her skirts, a handful at a time as the lace hem of her petticoats brushed her ankles, her shins, her knees, until they bunched around her waist. And suddenly her clothes frustrated her; they were in her way, a barrier she hated, but she couldn't think clearly enough to figure out what to do about them.

"Kate," he murmured against her neck. Her thoughts thinned out and shifted like dissipating fog. Jake drew his hand up her thigh, the warmth of him burning through the thin cotton of her pantaloons.

And then he was there, his hand cupping her fully, and she bucked against him hard, causing pleasure to spear through her, a bright stab of sensation.

"Not yet," he said. He waited until she stilled, her body loose and pliant. Then he moved only his thumb, whisking an arch above her pubis, near enough to incite, never close enough to satisfy.

The world narrowed to a single point: his hand, stroking her.

And then—ah, at last—he began to caress her with his middle finger, gliding easily against her, her flesh plump and slick. She arched into him, a low moan slipping from her throat.

"Shh." His other hand moved from her breast to her mouth, smothering the sound. "There's someone."

Kate stilled, random sounds penetrating her haze—the clump of boots, the low rumble of men's voices. "Who?" she murmured against his hand, the hard callus of his palm rasping against her lips.

"I don't know," he whispered in her ear, the warm wash of his breath arousing in itself. It was as if anything that was *him*, the simplest touch, the barest suggestion, was a further spur to senses already stimulated to a knife edge.

There was a low rumble of laughter, a drift of smoke.

"Crew taking a break," he murmured.

They were frozen like that, his hand over her mouth, his finger laid firm against her most sensitive flesh.

And then his finger began to move again. She bucked against him once, hard, and a moan rose in her throat.

"Shhh," he said again. "They're still there." But his finger took up a steady rhythm, spiking sensation through her. Her hips began to circle in rhythm. "Shh."

She opened her mouth, touching his palm with her tongue, and air hissed out of him.

Quiet, she reminded herself. Quiet. And then his finger slid inside her deeply, bringing the heel of his palm hard against her most sensitive spot, and she nearly strangled on a shout.

She turned her head and took one of his fingers in her mouth. She felt him tense completely beneath her, every muscle going hard. She flicked his finger with her tongue, drawing it more deeply inside.

And then his other hand began to move, faster now, his finger stroking her deep within, his palm without.

Wait, she told herself, wait until the men were gone. But the rumble of voices only a few feet away, the threat of discovery—it was so *wicked*, so beyond anything she'd ever thought herself capable of.

Jim bit down on her earlobe, a tiny sprite of pain. And suddenly it was all too much: the feel of his finger in her mouth, in her, the bob and dip of the boat, the tug of his teeth, the strain to keep silent. And Jim, always Jim, only Jim, the past and now, the memories and the reality. It all burst in her, white-hot, every sense exploding at once.

She broke beneath his hands, shuddering against him, crying out into his palm. Too much, she thought wildly. It was too much. Perhaps she would stay here forever, spiraling with the stars.

She calmed slowly, tiny little aftershocks of pleasure twinging in each nerve ending. Jim's strokes grew soothing, his kiss against her ear gentle. She drifted in it, a sea of warmth, relaxing against him, replete. There was no choice in it, no control; she simply was where she was meant to be.

Her bed was hard. And terribly lumpy.

Reluctantly, Kate pried open her lids. She saw a haze of white only a few inches from her nose, diffuse light glowing through it, black smudging the white.

And then she came fully awake.

Lord. Oh, my Lord.

She was sprawled on top of Jim. One breast swelled free of her neckline, fully exposed to the air, which was cool enough to make her nipple pucker. Her skirts wadded around her waist and her legs sprawled, wide and wanton, and his hand—

His hand was still *there*, one finger against her full-length, touching flesh that tingled and burned as soon as she recognized it.

She sucked in a shocked breath.

"You're awake," Jim murmured.

Memories scalded her. She started to sit up, to escape, but the canvas got in her way. One of Jim's arms looped around her waist, pulling her firmly back on him. His other hand stayed right where it was, an intimate, blatant claiming, as if they'd been lovers for years and he owned free access to every corner of her body. Mortification flooded her, an uneasy, sensual twin with renewed passion.

Last night had been . . . she didn't know what to name it. Didn't know what they *were*—lovers or friends or something else entirely. He hadn't even kissed her. He'd dragged her into a boat and manipulated her to a blazing peak while people chatted a few feet away. And then she'd promptly fallen asleep, and he'd not even . . .

Gasping, she struggled to get up.

"Wait. It'll be easier if I help." He was most efficient, tucking her breast back into her bodice, smoothing the lace back into place, fluffing her skirts back down so that she was, at last, decently covered for all that she was still in a most compromising position.

"What time is it?" she whispered.

"Morning. But early. Very early." He pushed up one edge of the canvas. "Here. Take a peek, make sure there's nobody there."

She sat up as far as the space allowed, a position that pushed her rear more firmly against his pelvis. Having an affair sounded so terribly romantic. But she'd never considered this part, the awkward aftermath, messy hair and messy clothes, limbs in strange positions. And it was unaccountably arousing for all that it was unpretty.

Next time, she decided, she would only get carried away in a nice big comfortable bed.

"Seems clear," she said, and scrambled out of the boat as fast as she could. "Sorry," she tossed back when she heard an emphatic "oof." She didn't want to know what part of him she'd just connected with.

The sun was just coming up, a thin sliver of gold edging the gray-green waves before disappearing again into the dark gray clouds.

Kate took one look at her clothes, ran a hand over her hair, and moaned.

"I have to go," she said, and scuttled toward the stairs.

"Wait a minute." He snagged her elbow. "You don't want to run into anybody."

"Oh. Of course." He tugged, swinging her around to face him, but she couldn't do it. She kept her eyes firmly lowered. There were creases in her skirt and a bit of lace sagged below the hem.

"Don't do this," he said.

"Don't do what?" She managed to lift her eyes to his chest. Oh, he was rumpled, too, wrinkles crushed into his shirt, but she was sure it looked far better on him. Three buttons were open, exposing a wide triangle of muscular chest, and she couldn't decide whether to curl up against it and hide her face or put her mouth right there and . . .

"This." He lifted her chin, forcing her to look up. "Be embarrassed. Have regrets. There's no reason to, not this time."

His hair stuck out in random spikes. Whiskers darkened his chin. There were shadows under his eyes and his collar was bent.

He looked wonderful.

"Did you sleep at all?" she asked.

"A little."

"Oh, Lord." She closed her eyes.

"It was worth every second." His hand moved from her chin to her cheek, his thumb rubbing along her jaw. Only moments ago, that hand, those fingers . . . she thought she could smell herself on him and her knees went soft.

"I have to—"

"Kate." There was no avoiding him. "You look wonderful. Here"—he brushed the side of her neck—"a scrape from my beard. And here"—he touched the snarl of her hair—"all tangled up because you tossed your head back and forth at your peak. Here"—she shivered as he drew a slow line down her neck, down her upper chest, until her bodice stopped him—"disordered, a little rumpled, because you abandoned yourself to me." His voice went low, heated, the words pouring over her like warmed honey.

"But you didn't even . . ." She didn't have the vocabulary for this. What made her think she could smoothly slide into an affair, sophisticated, uncomplicated? This was hopelessly messy, in more ways than one.

"How do you know?"

"What?" Her head snapped up. While she wasn't exactly a professional, she would have sworn she wouldn't have missed something quite that . . . obvious.

He chuckled. "All right, I didn't." He drew his hand down farther, smoothing her blouse over her breast, his hand dark and obvious and male against her curves, and she forgot how to breathe. "I have every faith you'll make it up to me."

"Make it up to you?" she managed.

"It's only fair," he said solemnly.

The man looked extremely pleased with himself. Her anxiety eased a notch. "Did you do this on purpose?"

"Darlin', that doesn't happen by accident."

"No, no." Her cheeks heated, but she plunged on, determined to be as comfortable with this discussion as he. "You chose not to . . . so I would owe you. So I would have to . . ." Despite her good intentions, she couldn't seem to bring it off. Blasé sophistication was going to require a bit of practice.

"You mean, did I purposely, er, deny myself so that

you could not go skittering off this morning and pretend it never happened? So that you would feel a certain obligation to even the score, thus ensuring myself another night in the very near future?"

It sounded absurd. And yet . . . "Yes."

"Would I do that to you?"

It didn't sit well, the idea that he could predict her behavior so well that he might plan it out that way, all the while she could stare into his eyes right now and not discern whether he told the truth.

"Kate." He lowered his head, mouth drawing temptingly near. And she knew that as soon as he kissed her, her good intentions would evaporate and he'd have her back in that boat in an instant, no time to prepare herself, no time to plan.

She ducked from his embrace and walked over to the railing, still marveling that he'd actually taken her in that boat without her uttering a word of protest. It was so unlike her.

The boat appeared larger from the outside than it had seemed from within. The cover was flipped back, revealing the wooden planks of the bottom, and . . .

"Jim?" Kate leaned over, ripping at the remaining ties that held the canvas in place, peeling it back. The smudges she'd seen on the fabric became lines, thick and curving, curling into loosely recognizable shapes. "What do you think?"

He leaned over her shoulder, stretching to release the farthest corner. "I think there's no reason not to spend the rest of this cruise in bed."

Chapter 19

Jim had been all in favor of, after they made a quick but careful copy of the map, adjourning to Kate's cabin and seeing just how much he could play on her sympathy and guilt. Once they'd sneaked back down to her room, however, she'd squeezed in the door, told him she needed a few moments to repair and she'd meet him in the Palm Room for breakfast, and shoved him on his way before he'd framed a protest.

So Jim took a quick dunk in the swimming pool, threw on a fresh shirt, and went to the Palm to wait.

It was still early enough that the room was empty, awash in pale light through the leaded skylight over-head. Lush palm trees in golden pots rose nearly to the roof, dozens of small tables arranged beneath. Glowing pink silk draped the walls, parting here and there to reveal murals of tropical gardens framed in

gilded molding, as if one were looking out the windows of a grand villa. Creamy, gold-veined marble
gleamed on the floor.

Jim found a table in the far corner, dropped into one
chair, propped his feet in another, and settled back to
wait. Every bone in his body protested the abuse of
the night before, his temples pounded from the lack
of sleep, and he'd never felt better in his life.

Kate was going to be his lover. They'd stumbled
over—under—the next clue. With any luck he wasn't
going to have to set foot out of that cabin for at least
four more days. It wouldn't be enough to make up for
weeks of frustration—not to mention years—but it
was pretty damn good.

Maybe there'd even be a storm. Slow them down
enough to keep them from docking for another day,
which he fully intended to put to excellent use.

He linked his hands comfortably over his belly.
Breakfast wouldn't hurt, he thought. Beyond that—

"You're up early."

Damn. Should have known he couldn't be *that*
lucky.

Hobson stood pointedly beside the chair Jim had
appropriated as a footstool. When Jim merely raised
one brow, Hobson grabbed another chair from a
nearby table, dragged it over, and plopped down.

"So are you," Jim said.

"Oh, you know. The early bird, and all that." He
leaned back. "Christ, man, but you don't look too
well."

"Thank you very much. And how very kind of you
to offer your opinion."

"Any time." Jim started planning his escape. But if
he missed Kate on his way out, she'd be stuck here

with Charlie. "It's only natural that you are a bit worse for the wear, of course. It's a demanding competition."

"Oh yes, terribly taxing. Right up there with climbing Kilimanjaro."

"Well, that was some years ago, wasn't it?" Hobson smiled, that oily, calculated little smile that should have warned anyone who witnessed it to beware. "Perhaps it's good that you're retiring."

As if the little weasel was one day younger than Jim. "Who said I'm retiring?"

"But of course I—" His expression was sympathetic but his eyes gleamed. "I just assumed. Everyone did. The guilt you must live with after that poor Mr. Wheeler's death. Not to mention the difficulty of funding another expedition after that one went so horribly wrong, and of course it has been nearly a year since you . . ."

"Mr. Hobson!" Kate marched across the floor, arms swinging. "How dare you?"

"Ma'am. How dare I what?"

"Imply that Lord Bennett was in any way responsible for that terrible tragedy. Why, I can assure you—"

The reporter snapped to attention. "Excuse me, ma'am, were you there? I assumed that—"

"I was not."

"Well, then, with all due respect, you're not the one who can set the record straight, are you? And, interestingly, the other members of the expedition are impossible to contact or completely unwilling to discuss what really happened," he said mildly. "Of course, it's something I run up against frequently in my business. There are all sorts of things that keep witnesses from telling their side of the story. Although I'm certain—"

"Mr. Hobson," Kate interrupted, "are you in such

dire need of a story that you are *still* flogging such old news?" The men stood as she reached them, and Kate glared at Hobson with such heat that he took a step back, nearly tripping over his chair.

"I'm simply doing my job, Miss Riley."

"Really? I thought that perhaps you had decided upon a vacation, considering that some unnamed reporter has taken over the front page of the *Sentinel*?" She looked excellent in high dudgeon, Jim noted, her color vivid, eyes bright. Hobson looked as if he was torn between suffering insult and throwing himself at her feet. "There are back copies in the reading room, did you know that? I read every word. Whoever he is, he certainly can write, can't he?"

"Anyone can get lucky once," he said darkly. "Producing good copy again and again is the mark of a true reporter."

"Then I'm certain you have much to write," she said. "So if you'd excuse us, Mr. Hobson, I'd like to speak to Lord Bennett privately. I'm sure you understand."

"Yes." He inclined his head formally. "I rather think I do."

As soon as Hobson made his way across the polished floor and out the double doors, Kate turned to find Jim studying her, an odd half-smile on his face.

"Are you always like that?" he asked.

"Like what?"

"Like a lioness whose cubs are threatened. Is that how you were with your sisters?"

Her mouth twisted ruefully. "I suppose I am. A habit of long enough standing that's difficult to break."

"You said your sisters were married."

"They are."

"Really?" He grinned. "I'm surprised a man ever got within twenty feet of them."

"They're sneaky." She sighed. "And I must be losing my touch. A month ago, a few soft words, a smile, and Hobson would have gone on his way, scurrying to happily do what I wanted without ever knowing what hit him."

"Maybe you're not losing your touch. Maybe you just lost your patience."

"True. The man does have that effect on me."

"I don't believe you're alone in that." He cupped her cheek, tracing the line of her lips with his thumb, and her body came alive. He had the right to touch her like that, she reminded herself; she'd given him that. There was no longer any reason to resist, no reason not to sink right into it and enjoy. And oh, enjoy it she did. "While I do appreciate the thought, Kate, I don't need you to protect me."

"Don't you?" She tilted her head into his hand. "Don't we all, sometimes?"

And who'd protected her? Jim wondered. He doubted the Doc had ever bothered.

"People have been asking questions about Matt's death from the day I returned," he said. "It'd take more than Hobson poking around to make me spill it."

"He won't give up," she warned him. "He thinks there's a story there."

"There is. It's just not what he thinks it is."

"Really? What—" She stopped, pursing her lips together. "Sorry."

"You could make me spill it," he said, stepping closer, sliding one arm around her waist.

"I could?" It was so easy to slip into his arms. As if they'd been together every day of the past twelve years. Maybe it was simply that he'd been present in her life for that long. Not physically, of course, but he'd been there just the same.

"Care to try?" he asked, his voice roughly suggestive.

"Really?" The thought was terribly tempting, for more reasons than one. "It's none of my business."

"*I'm* none of your business?"

On the surface, it was all light, teasing, seductive. But there was an undercurrent of seriousness beneath, as though they both were probing, testing to find out just where they fit into each other's lives. "Are you?" she asked carefully.

Their gazes caught and held. His eyes were so intense, golden-brown, like the eyes of the lion she'd once seen in a zoo. Kate would have given a lot to know what churned behind them. But she didn't want to pry it out of him by seduction or trickery. Whatever he chose to share with her, she wanted it to be given freely. There were limits to their relationship. She'd understood that from the first. He was no more capable of settling down into comfortable, urban domesticity than she was of tramping around the world after him.

But now, when she looked back on it a decade down the road, she wanted to know that what they'd had, whatever they'd had, at least this time it was honest and true.

"I met Matt in Brazil only a few months after Doc had been called home. Fished him out of a river, though he always claimed that he'd had the upper hand wrestling that crocodile and I'd only interfered," Jim said with warm nostalgia. "I was on my way to Manaus. He'd nothing but a yen for adventure and a lot of enthusiasm. Doc had done me a favor once by taking me on. It seemed right to do the same for him."

He gazed blindly over her head. Looking into the past, Kate figured, back to a time when the two of them were young and daring and had the world at their feet. "What was he like?"

Jim smiled. "He was fun. It seems like such a simple thing to say, but when you're stuck together for months at a time, sometimes in quite uncomfortable circumstances, *fun* is a very valuable quality."

"I can imagine."

"I was . . . I was a very serious man then. Matt never took anything too seriously. Impulsive as hell. Thought risks were there for the taking and life was to be lived, not worried over."

Kate leaned back until the loop of his arm pressed against the back of her waist, keeping her from going any farther. She would have liked to have seen his expression, watched emotion chase through his eyes, flicker at his mouth. But he was too tall, too near; she could read only patchwork impressions, the slide of his Adam's apple as he swallowed hard, the tensing of his jaw before he spoke again.

"He was like that about everything. He married May two weeks after he met her, had her pregnant before the month was up, and promptly left for the Congo. Got back home, so he said, four hours before she went into labor."

"His wife didn't mind?" Kate couldn't credit it. She tried to picture herself newly married to Jim—oh, that part was far too easy—and waving him good-bye as he headed out for someplace exotic and dangerous.

She would have chained him to the bedpost before she let him set one foot out of the door.

"Oh, I imagine she minded. But what could she say? Matt had never promised her to be any other than he was. I suppose she thought Matt, some of the time, was better than Matt not at all. She knew what she was getting into."

Pain and sympathy twinged in her chest. "It's always good to know what you're getting into." Accepting it . . . that suddenly seemed much, much harder.

"They had ten years like that, though I don't know that they actually lived together but two of them. Two little ones. And he never stopped jumping in head first without looking. Usually jabbing at me about thinking too much the whole way." His arm tightened, drawing her up against his chest. He put one hand behind her head and held her there. His heart thumped beneath her ear, sure and solid.

He squeezed her closer, driving the breath from her lungs, as if he needed something to hang on to. So be it. Who needed to breathe?

"Damn it, I told him that stretch of the ice field didn't look safe. There could have been pockets anywhere. We were going to move slowly, not take any chances. He just couldn't wait to prove me wrong."

His voice shook. So slight, she doubted anyone but she would have noticed it.

"Jim? Why keep it a secret?"

He rubbed his chin across the crown of her head. "What good would it do? To have his family know that he'd not stopped for one minute to think of them and what would happen to them if he wasn't careful?"

And if the world believed Jim at fault, so be it, Kate thought. Oh, it would be so much easier if she didn't know he had this in him. It tugged at her emotions, making things far more complicated than she'd planned on. She knew the confines of this affair, and woe to her heart if it tried to ignore the boundaries.

"Jim?"

"Hmm?"

"Your money, the expedition funding, the book profits . . . you gave it to his family, didn't you?"

The time it took for him to answer told her more than he did. "We were partners. He'd earned it."

She tightened her arms around him.

"Don't make too much of it," he warned her. "I should have tried harder to stop him. I *knew* what he was like, and I let it happen anyway. It was stupid of me."

She turned her head so that she could press her open mouth against him, the abrasion of his shirt's fabric against her lips, the heat of him beneath, the thump of his heart vibrating against her mouth.

"There were *children*, Kate."

"Hmm." She rubbed her nose against him, breathing deeply, and then rose to her toes to taste his neck. He inhaled sharply.

"*Kate.*"

She loved the way he said her name, as if she'd driven it out of him. As if he was so filled up with *her* he couldn't hold it in. "Yes?" she murmured against his skin.

"Let's—" He grabbed her by the upper arms and thrust her away from him.

"What—" He pressed one finger to her mouth, shushing her, while he narrowed his eyes, staring over her shoulder.

She twisted but saw nothing except the trompe l'oeil windows and the lush folds of satin. And then he shoved her aside and pounced, yanking aside one of the drapes and dragging out a small figure swathed in white.

The Amir's son struggled against Jim's hold. His robes tangled around him, muting his efforts, but he twisted and turned, his booted foot shooting out, aiming for Jim's shins. Finally Jim simply lifted him up and dropped him into the nearest chair.

The boy kicked at the shroud of his robes, arms flapping, and made a move as if he meant to spring.

"I wouldn't," Jim advised him. "I'm bigger than you, and I'm faster than you, and even if by some miracle you managed to get past me, I'd find you. So if you're not prepared to bail overboard to get away from me, don't even bother."

The boy hunched over in the chair, the loose folds of his headgear hiding his face. Even under the enveloping robes, his shoulders were narrow. He looked small, and very young.

"Jim," Kate said, "he probably doesn't understand a word you say."

"Oh, I think he understands me just fine." Quick as a cobra strike, Jim snatched the robes back, baring the boy's head.

Thick chestnut brown hair, damp with sweat, lay smooth against his head where the robes had pressed it. He had the angular look of a boy who'd shot up too fast and not quite grown into his bones yet, long forehead and chin, cheekbones a hard slash. Eyes that, out of the shadows, now appeared shades lighter peered out from beneath thick brows set too low.

"Who are you?" Jim demanded.

The boy tried to summon a scowl and managed only to appear sulky. And more than a little scared.

Jim gave him three seconds. And then he reached out, grabbed fistfuls of robe at his neck, and hauled him out of the chair.

His feet, clad in black lace-up boots, so worn the leather was nearly white across the toes, the heels ground thin as a dime, dangled two inches from the floor. Not, Kate decided, the typical footwear of an Amir's son.

"*Who are you?*"

The boy tried to hold his gaze and failed miserably. He hung limply in Jim's grasp, his toes barely grazing the ground.

"You heard what I did to the major, didn't you?"

The boy's head snapped up, his eyes going big as dinner plates. "That'd be murder, way out here."

"Yes, it would," Jim agreed mildly. "Your English is excellent, by the way."

"Now stop that." Kate tugged at Jim's biceps, rock-solid, holding the boy easily. "You're scaring him."

"I should hope so."

"Oh, just put the child down. For now, at least."

Jim dropped him back into the chair. Kate placed herself in front of him, giving him a warning look over her shoulder, and addressed their reluctant captive. "Now, then."

The boy peeked at her from underneath his brows. He slumped back into his chair, looking more relaxed. "I'm not a boy."

"My apologies. How old are you?"

"Nineteen."

Kate merely lifted one brow and waited.

"Seventeen."

Kate beamed approvingly. His eyes glazed and red suffused his lean cheeks.

"Careful, Kate. Cooperative is one thing, but a full dose of you might strike him dumb."

"Oh, hush," she said over her shoulder before addressing the young man again. "While we're on a roll—what's your name?"

"I—" He pressed his lips together and shook his head unhappily.

Behind her, she felt Jim take a forward step. She put one hand behind her back and flapped her hand at him to get him to stay in place. Threatening the young man was only going to get his back up. She had much more efficient ways.

"My dear," she said. "Unless you are the result of several generations of captured European brides, you are obviously not the son of the Amir."

He shifted in his chair. "Didn't say I was."

Ah. New York, she thought; there was a telltale broadness to the vowels. She reached down and touched him gently on the knee. "Your name?" she prompted.

He gulped. "Johnny. Ah, Jonathan. Jonathan Duffy."

"Thank you, Jonathan. I'm very pleased to meet you." She extended a hand. Johnny stared at it for a moment, then started to stick out his own. He thought better of it and swiped it quickly down the front of his robes before he took her hand and pumped it with enthusiasm. "So. You stole the Amir's invitation so you could win the contest?"

"I—" He darted a worried glance at Jim.

"Oh, don't worry about it," she assured him. "We're not going to run to the *Sentinel*. And I rather preempted an invitation myself."

"Wasn't trying to win. I'm not stupid. I know I've got no chance against someone like him." He jerked his narrow chin toward Jim.

"What, then? Where'd you get the invitation?"

"I sold newspapers. I *knew* I could write, I just knew it. But they wouldn't give me a chance, no matter how many times I asked. Kept hiring all those college boys who looked good in their suits but who didn't know a thing about New York, not the way I know New York. And sure as hell—pardon ma'am—don't know a thing about wanting something so bad you'd be willing to do anything to get it. I tried to get them to read something, to give me a chance, any chance. But they just kept looking at me and seeing a newsie."

"I see." Sympathy welled. "Very few people can look beyond seeing what they expect to see."

"That's it." On surer ground, Johnny sat up straight. "I knew the only chance I had was to *show* them what I could do. Everybody at the paper was buzzing about the contest, about all the famous people who were going to participate, and how much the paper was putting into it and when the invitations were going out. I figured, why not? If I found a story nobody else did, I'd have a way in. And if not, so what? I wouldn't be any worse off than I was to start with." He shrugged. "I don't even know whose invitation I took. There was a whole pile of them in the mailroom. I arranged to send the articles to my sister so she could sneak them onto the editor's desk, took up this disguise, and here I am."

"You wrote the article," Jim said flatly.

Johnny eyed him warily. "Which article?"

"Mrs. Latimore."

Johnny winced. And then he lifted his chin, mustering his courage. "Nobody else got that story."

"You had no right," he said, danger threading low and sharp through his voice.

But this time Johnny held his ground—a little paler, but his shoulders were square, his gaze steady. "It's my job."

"Your job to spread people's private business out for the world to poke and prod and judge?"

"The people have a right to know."

"The people have a right to know things that are none of their goddamn business?"

Johnny surged out of the chair. "You mean the people who pay for your books, your lectures and swallow every word you tell them? Every word that you feed them through the newspapers you use to drum up interest in your expeditions? You mean *those* people?"

"There's a difference between news and plain old gossip."

"Lord Bennett, I—"

"Johnny," Kate said softly. "You can't write about what you just heard."

His expression turned glum. "I'm sorry to disappoint you, ma'am. You can't know how truly sorry I am, but—"

"You can't," she said again. She moved nearer and put her hand gently on his forearm. "You heard the entire story, didn't you? You *can't*."

"It's a good story, ma'am."

"People will get hurt."

He shook his head. "It's not the truth that hurts people. It's the lies."

"Johnny—"

"He's not going to write it." Jim moved between them, bumping her arm away, towering over the young reporter. His voice was pitched low, his posture a clear threat. "He's not going to write it, because he'd like to be able to write another story some day. Wouldn't you, Duffy?"

Johnny gulped but held his ground. "You're not going to kill me," he said, with only one tremor at "kill."

"I'm not? Are you sure? You did hear about the major, didn't you?"

Johnny managed a nod. "You weren't trying to kill him. He was only fifty feet from shore, there were dozens of boats around, and you threw him a life ring."

"You're very well informed. Planning on writing that one, too, were you?"

"I intend to be very good at my job, Lord Bennett."

"And you're so sure you're right about me? This wouldn't be about getting a story wrong. If you're mistaken, you're dead."

"You're not a murderer," Johnny said, growing more certain with every word. "I should have realized that right off, but you caught me by surprise."

"You're *sure*?" He edged closer. Johnny's nose was even with Jim's collar. His left eye twitched but he didn't back away.

"I'm sure," he squeaked.

Jim sighed deeply. "Oh, all right. You're right."

"I am?"

"I won't kill you." His eyes narrowed. "But I'm not opposed to making your life so very painful that you'd spend every second wishing I had just pitched you overboard and been done with it."

Kate stepped closer, ready to intervene if necessary. Not that seeing Jim so fierce and protective, so utterly sure of himself, didn't have her heart thumping like a schoolgirl's. Not that she didn't find him more appealing at that precise second than she ever had, and she'd found him quite outrageously appealing before.

Later, she promised herself. Later.

"This is not helpful," she said.

"Give it a chance," Jim said.

"No." She'd no doubt that he could instill fear-of-Jim quite effectively in Johnny. But all his threats would last about as long as the reporter was within fist's reach. It was too good a story to forget. As soon as they hit land, Johnny would put a few miles between himself and Jim and start writing. "Johnny, it's crucial that your sources can trust you and your word, isn't it? Otherwise no one would ever reveal anything important to you."

"Yes," Johnny agreed slowly.

"And so if you gave a promise," Kate continued, "you would be bound to keep it, wouldn't you? Otherwise your ability to do your job would be irretrievably compromised."

He had the look of a deer being drawn to a blind. As if he sensed there were danger ahead but couldn't quite see it. "Yes."

"Then perhaps you would be amenable to a trade. If I give you another story, one you could write freely without worry of retribution from Lord Bennett, you would have to promise to keep his quiet."

"Kate, shut up," Jim said.

"I would," Johnny said.

"Well, then." She extended her hand.

"Kate, *shut up!*"

"Hello, Mr. Duffy. I'm Kathryn Goodale."

"Kathryn Go—" His eyes widened, popping back and forth between the two of them. "Ohhhh." He took her hand but was too lost in thought to shake. Already forming sentences in his head, Kate decided.

"Damn it." Jim disengaged her hand and kept it in his, pulling her back. "If you write about her, Duffy, I wouldn't count on *'no retribution.'* I wouldn't count on it at all."

"He has nothing to say about it," Kate said briskly. "I'm giving you the story. You're welcome to it, as long as you keep Matt Wheeler and anything that happened on the Arctic expedition out of it."

Johnny eyed her speculatively. "You two seemed very friendly."

"Oh, we are. In fact—"

"For God's sake, Kate, if you don't shut up I'm throwing *you* overboard."

Johnny stepped back, a thoughtful look on his face. "There might be another possibility."

"Sure there is," Jim began. "I could—"

"Oh, be quiet," Kate said. "Nobody believes your threats anymore. Continue, Mr. Duffy."

Johnny tapped his hand against his thigh, then nodded, as if he'd made up his mind.

"There's a girl."

"Son," Jim said, "there's always a girl."

Chapter 20

❦

Half an hour later they strolled through the narrow passageway to Kate's cabin. Jim's hand was light at the small of her back, outwardly polite, but sensation radiated from his touch, a promise of what was to come.

Kate sighed, long and wistful.

"What was that for?"

"He's so in love."

"Kate, he's seventeen and he met her three days ago. Love's not what I'd call it."

"I know, but . . ." Their bodies brushed as they walked—a hint of contact, barely there, enough to make him want to throw her over his shoulder and sprint to her cabin. "It's sweet, isn't it?"

Something in her voice made him pause. Her eyes were hazy, her mouth soft. "Kate?"

"The way he looked when he spoke of her," she went on dreamily.

Of course, Jim thought in sudden realization. She'd spent her teens caring for her sisters, her twenties as Dr. Goodale's wife. "Wait in the cabin," he said.

"What?" she asked. "I thought we were . . ."

"I'll be back in half an hour."

"But—"

He bent, stamping her mouth with a quick, hard kiss. "Half an hour," he said, and sprinted away.

Twenty-five minutes later Jim stood in front of Kate's door. His palms were sweating. His heart couldn't figure out whether to beat too fast or too slow and so bounded uncomfortably between the two, unsettled and uneasy.

He stood in front of the door for a good long time, trying to steady his breath, his hands.

It shouldn't be this hard, he kept reminding himself. He knew Kate. Knew he could please her, knew how to touch her so she trembled and sighed. It was a simple affair, carefully bounded by the requirements of their lives and the frame of the contest. Mutual pleasure without complications.

But he wanted it to be right for her.

Maybe she'd have *right* again, with other men, other times. But he wanted to be the first to give her that. If she'd remembered fondly that evening in the gazebo, he wanted this time to burn its imprint irrevocably upon her soul. Because he knew for damn sure she'd already seared her image on his.

He lifted his hand to knock, letting it waver in the

air six inches from the door while he gathered his courage. And then the door yawned open.

"Oh, there you are," she said. She smiled slowly. "I was getting lonely."

His brain froze. He lost the power of speech, the ability to reason.

Kate.

Her hair tumbled down, a loose cloud of gold around her shoulders, begging a man to sink his hands in deep and hold her head steady for his kiss. Her skin gleamed—face, neck, shoulders—as if sprinkled by stardust.

She wore that confection of a nightgown she'd pulled out of her trunk that first night. It had been seductive enough in her hands, the thought of her in it devastating to his restraint.

No matter how much he'd imagined—and he'd imagined a lot—he'd come far short of the reality. She was a vision, a dream, the kind of beauty that spawned legends. If, over a campfire, someone had described her to him, he would have called them the worst kind of liar.

Glacier blue silk hugged her curves, the fabric so sheer he could see the indention of her navel. Except for straps so thin he could snap them with one finger, it bared her shoulders, dipping low across her breasts. Wide bands of loosely knitted lace wound diagonally around her, allowing glimpses of the skin beneath. The gown dipped low over her chest, the lace edging there, too, giving head-spinning glimpses of dark pink nipple.

"Aren't you coming in?" There was a note to her voice he'd never heard before. She'd been consciously seductive, certainly. But this note of open invitation . . . if she'd sounded like that, looked like this, that night in the gazebo, he never would have let her walk away from him, Doc Goodale be damned.

"Oh. Here." He thrust out the clutch of orchids he'd stolen from the greenhouse. They trembled in his hand, waxy white petals the color of her skin. His head whirling, he picked out the remnants of his plan. "Miss Bright, these are for you."

"Miss Bright?" She blinked in surprise, then quickly recovered. She glided toward him, hips moving with sinuous grace beneath the waterfall of silk. "For me? They're beautiful. But I've nothing to put them in."

"Here." From behind his back where he'd hidden it, he pulled out the slender silver vase he'd borrowed from the dining room.

"Don't you think of everything?"

"I try." He thought he had, planning out each detail to the very last. But he hadn't counted on *her*, the fact that he wasn't sure he could set foot in the same room with her and retain his sanity.

When she moved to the tap to fill up the vase, she turned away from him, giving him a view of her back. The blue silk flowed as she moved, clinging to curves, her lower back, the cleft that separated her buttocks. His gaze fastened there, clung as determinedly as the fabric.

What he had planned was going to be a thousand times harder than he thought. And he figured it to be pretty hard to begin with.

He ducked out of the cabin for an instant and shook his head, hoping to clear it. Two deep breaths, a quick reminder . . . yes, that was better. A little.

The little silver cart rattled as he rolled it in.

She turned at the sound, vase sprouting orchids in hand. "What this?"

"Dinner." He made a waiter's flourish, indicating the gleaming silver domes.

"Jim, it's barely noon."

"Pretend." He went to work, pulling a small table into the middle of the room and pairing it with two curvy, thin-legged chairs upholstered in cream. He snapped out a snowy tablecloth and lifted the cover of the first dish. "Oysters," he said. "I don't know if you like them, so . . ."

"I do," she murmured. She set the flowers down in the middle of the table and moved to him, very close, bare pink toes peeping between the glossy black leather of his shoes. With one finger she traced the lapel of his coat. "Nice clothes. Where'd you get them?"

He tugged at the stiff collar. The black long-tailed jacket pulled tight across the shoulders. The charcoal-striped pants hung on only with the help of three pins and ended an inch shy of his ankles. "When the major went overboard, his clothes stayed behind."

"Hmm." She rubbed the lapel between her fingers, as if testing the satin. "Where?"

"His cabin."

"Cabin? As in, there was a perfectly good empty cabin for you to stay in all this time, and you lied to me so you could stay here?"

"I—" Caught, he considered any number of half-truths. That he would have felt uncomfortable with her out of his sight, that even with the major off the boat he didn't want to risk a saboteur, that he had to be there to beat off the count or any of the other males who'd fallen under her spell.

Or that he simply couldn't stand to be that far away from her. "Yes."

Her palm flattened against him and his vision blotted. He took hold of her upper arms and set her away from him with as much gentleness as he could muster. "Miss Bright." He pulled out one of the chairs and sketched a bow. "If you'll allow me?"

Half puzzled, half intrigued, she slid into the chair.

He'd brought candles, six of them, which he clustered around the orchids and lit. And then the food, dish after dish on thin bone china, as many as he could fit on the small table, though there were a half dozen left on the cart.

"I didn't know what you liked . . ." he began.

"Jim," she said. "Beef tenderloin, poached turbot, endive salad. Not to mention a very lovely pudding. You've thought of everything."

"I tried." He found his own seat, his knees bumping the table, and spread a napkin in his lap. "Wait just a minute."

He dashed to the porthole and closed the thick blue velvet drapes, blocking all light but a thin strip before he returned to the tables. "There. That's better."

"Jim, it's all very lovely, but . . . what is this?"

"Miss Bright," he said, "I am so very pleased that you consented to dine with me."

Her brows drew together. And then, apparently deciding to play along, she said: "How could I not? When you asked so prettily?" She leaned forward and the fabric fell away, giving him a clear view of the inner curves of her breasts, the wide, bare expanse of her upper chest.

"I cannot help but be curious." He served her a portion of fish but left his own plate with but a token slice of beef. He wasn't going to be able to eat a thing, not unless he spent the rest of the meal with his eyes shut. "I know you have two sisters. What are they like?"

"Anthea's only a few years younger than I am. Emily is—well, suffice to say she is a far bit younger than me." She overlooked the fish and instead plucked a chocolate from a gold foil box. Her eyes sparkled at him as she ate, her lips wrapping around the sweet, a flash of teeth as she bit in. That mouth . . . sweat broke out on his temples.

He looked down at his plate, sawing away at the beef until his heartbeat settled down again. Now he could look at her, he judged, and not lunge across the table.

Wrong. Wrong, wrong, wrong.

She'd slid the straps off her shoulders, her nightdress down to her waist, leaving her breasts bare and beautiful. His mouth went dry; blood pounded in his temples.

"I—" He dove for the decanter and sloshed wine into his glass. "Wine?"

Twin lines appeared between her brows. "Thank you," she said, and lifted her glass for him to fill. Her breasts rose with her movement, a lush sway. The decanter clinked against the goblet, ringing a death knell for his good intentions. He tried to focus on the tabletop, the clutter of dishes and flatware and crystal swimming together.

"Jim?"

"Huh?"

"What is this?"

"This?"

"Yes, this." He heard the muffled thud as she set her glass back on the tabletop. "Jim, why won't you look at me?"

"I can't."

"You can't?" Silk swished. The chair scraped back. Footsteps padded around the table. "Jim, please," she said.

Still looking down, he moved his gaze a fraction. Toes peeped out from beneath her gown. And then— *swish*—blue silk puddled on the floor.

"Lord, Kate." He closed his eyes, his head falling back while he struggled to remain rooted in the chair, every muscle rigid. If he moved, if he breathed, he'd have her on that berth in an instant, plans be damned. "I should have known you couldn't just *cooperate*."

"It might be easier to cooperate, Jim, if I had the faintest idea what I was supposed to cooperate with." Her voice was soft, fluid, like a whisper of silk. The silk she was no longer wearing—oh, he was a dead man.

"I'm *trying* to court you."

"Court me? Isn't it a little late for that?"

He heard her move, a rasp—and then silk fell across his face, his mouth— soft, warm from her skin, smelling of her. It fluttered against him as he pulled it off, butterfly wings of sensation.

The gown slipped through his numbed fingers and fluttered to the floor. "I saw your face." He kept his eyes squeezed shut, because he knew if he looked at her the power of speech would leave him. "When you talked about Johnny and that girl. You wanted the romance you never had. The courting. So I'm going to give it to you."

She chuckled softly, champagne bubbles of laughter that frothed in his brain, muddling his plans. "Look at me, Jim."

He shook his head. "I told you, I can't."

"Look at me," she said, patient, waiting.

She had the advantage, because it was what he wanted, even if he knew it would only make it all the harder. And so he lifted his head.

Sights had taken his breath away before. Waterfalls, mountaintops, jeweled icons buried away for thousands of years. And all of those memories paled next to her.

She was all creamy skin and lavish femininity. Soft. Nothing angular, nothing abrupt, just big flowing curves, unstinting, generous. Her hair swung free, thick and golden, spilling down her back. Her breasts were lavish, rising and falling softly with each breath, the nipples tight, rose-tipped.

"I—" His mouth was dry. He swallowed and tried again. "Let me—"

"You know something, Jim?" She glided one hand over her torso, lightly, slowly—neck, breast, waist, belly—and his gaze followed. He couldn't have looked away if someone held a gun to his head. "I rarely indulge in regrets. Not useful, I've found. That does not mean that I am not sometimes, very seldom, slightly nostalgic for the things I missed." Slowly, drawing out his suffering with every fluid movement, she climbed into his lap, facing him, one leg on either side of his thigh, looping her arms around his neck.

"Kate—"

"Hush. I'm not finished." He could feel the damp heat of her against his thigh. He struggled to follow her words, hanging on to coherence by the merest thread. "But the truth is, given the same choice, I would have made the same one again. My sisters are well, healthy, grown. I was aware what I was sacrificing when I gave it up and it was worth it. An occasional passing twinge does not a regret make." She leaned forward, the tips of her breasts searing his chest. He gripped the seat of the chair, fingers biting in as if they could dent the wood. "Forget the courting. Forget the romance. Do you know what else I gave up, Jim? What I missed more than some silly adolescent wooing?"

Knowing speech was beyond him, he shook his head.

"This." She kissed him, full on, hard and deep. She burst upon him, the wonder of her—naked, passionate woman in his lap, his arms. Her hands tangled in his hair, pulling his mouth closer, her tongue plunging deep.

Somewhere back in his brain—dim, barely recognized—he knew he should go slow. Gentle, tender. But she was right there, exploding full upon his senses, and his blood was pumping hard and fast, too fast, but he didn't know how to slow them down.

He swept his hands down her back, his palms sliding through the textures, the springy, wavy silk of her hair, then the satin sweep of her back. Her waist narrowed abruptly and then flowed out again. Her buttocks, generous, soft, filled his hands, his fingertips slipping into the cleft that separated them.

She threw her head back on a moan, her hair spilling down, brushing the backs of his hands. He bent to put his mouth at her throat, her pulse beating against his lips, his tongue.

She tugged his hair to pull his head away. She was

flushed, color sweeping down her chest and neck to the full curves of her breasts. Her eyes burned, hot and blue, her lips parting with her ragged breathing. He tried to brand it into his brain, noting each detail, each shade, each line, for he knew that this picture was the one he'd choose to remain at the forefront of his memory, the one he'd want to call up on his deathbed to remember that yes, indeed, he had lived.

With one hand she lifted her breast, offering it to him, her thighs squeezing as she lifted herself. He dipped his head, drawing her breast deeply into his mouth.

Sweetness. So sweet, the plush softness of her skin, the nubbly texture of her nipple. The way she trembled and sighed when he flicked her with his tongue, when he drew it gently between his teeth. Her fingers threaded through his hair, an agitated motion, her body beginning to shift restlessly against his.

Gasping, he pulled back, trying to catch his breath and his sanity. But she couldn't pause, couldn't slow; she dove for his chest, ripping open his shirt, spreading it wide with a smile of triumph.

Her mouth, her hands, were fire-hot, moist, burning their imprint on him. He would have it no other way. If she left scars, tattoos of her possession on him, he would have welcomed them.

She bit his nipple gently and he reared up. And then she soothed the slight sting with her tongue, a slow swirl of pleasure.

Her hands were quick and graceful, gliding along his side and probing his ribs. He wanted to tell her to slow but she gave him no opening. Every time he opened his mouth to speak, she did something that left him gasping instead.

"What's this?" she murmured, tracing the four parallel lines that bisected his belly, pale stripes against darker skin.

"Tiger," he panted. "Nepal."

"Hmm." She bent and traced them with her tongue, too, soothing them as if the pain were fresh while his stomach muscles contracted and he nearly came off the chair.

"And here?" she asked, touching the small, wedged-shaped scar at his shoulder.

"Arrow. By Canelos. No poison. Lucky."

"Lucky?" She kissed this one, too, open-mouthed, so wet and hot that soon he would have welcomed another arrow as long as it gave her another spot to put that mouth.

"Any more scars?" she murmured against his skin.

"Lost two toes in the Arctic. Frostbite."

She laughed softly. "I think I'll wait on that."

And then she slid off his lap, as easily as the silk had slipped through his fingers, kneeling on the floor between his knees. Her fingers toyed with his waistband, dipping beneath and out again, teasing him, sending blood flooding through his veins.

"Kate—"

"Hush," she said. "My turn. You promised."

She went slower now, slipping each button from its hole with extreme care, as if to savor each second. His arousal pushed hard against the constriction of his trousers, a sweet-hot ache that veered toward pain, the sweetest kind, like throwing oneself into the sun.

She was not unsure. She lifted and moved his drawers away expertly—none of the awkward hooking men dread, no help necessary. And then, perched there between his knees, she smiled at him, naked and glorious, and he knew that every fantasy he'd ever conjured, every dream he'd ever owned, had never come close to this.

And then she touched him, wrapping her hand firmly around his cock, and he thought: I'm going to die. Right this minute, I'm going to be the first man on earth to die of pleasure.

He could not look away. The sight of her hand, slender, white, around him. The rapt concentration on her face. The glimmer of her hair in the soft light, the light sheen of perspiration on her skin.

She caressed him with her thumb, a slow arc right over the tip, and he nearly blacked out. "Kate!"

"Hush," she said again, intent. "You promised." Her thumb moved again, a light stroke that held more power than a blade. "I think there's a scar here."

"No, I—"

"You must have forgotten." She leaned forward. He could feel the softness of her breast press against his inner thigh, the silk of her hair pooling over his leg, his belly.

And then she licked him. One long delicate lap, base to head, a quick swirl at the top, and sound burst out of him. He grabbed her shoulders and dragged her up to face him, laying her against him, bare skin to nearly bare skin.

He kissed her, hard and long, drinking in the taste and feel of her, because he could kiss her and still think. Just barely, but he could.

"Later," he said, sounding as hoarse as if he'd spent days in a desert without water. "Later, as much as you want, however you want. I promise. But not now, not if you don't want this to end in two seconds."

"Hmm." She made a small, flirty moue of disappointment, her eyes dancing, bright as gems. "Two seconds would be a bit . . . abrupt."

"Yeah," he said. Now, he thought, now he could take over, slow it down, set a rhythm that they could savor. Court her in bed if not out of it, fill her up with the kind of pleasure that a woman would never forget.

But then she lifted herself up, slithering against him. She reached down and held him firm, positioning him right at her entrance.

Without a moment's hesitation she slid right down, as easily as if they'd done this a hundred times before. Perhaps they had—in his dreams, in hers. But oh, the pleasure of it. That was something entirely new, unimaginable, near unbearable. She was hot as the sun, slick and wet, closing around him as tightly as if she'd been made expressly to fit him.

Her head fell back, her mouth opening on a low moan, the sound vibrating in his belly, too. She lifted up, pushed back down. Pleasure surged through him, slapped at him, pushing him near the waterfall edge, threatening to sweep him over.

And again, while he pounded ever closer to the cliff.

"That's it," he said. He clamped one hand beneath her butt, another around her back, and stood. The movement drove him deeper inside her, making her gasp and wrap her ankles around his hips.

"I got the berth ready," she murmured in his ear, then nipped at the lobe for good measure.

"This'll do," he said, and lowered her to the floor before his knees gave out beneath him.

She lay back like a sultan's bride, back arched. He was still embedded in her and her thighs squeezed his hips. His clothes bunched around him; in the way, but he couldn't conceive of leaving her long enough to get rid of them. At least the important parts were uncovered.

Her hands started to wander, clutching at his butt, drawing him in. He reached back and captured her hands, anchoring them over her head, looping her wrists together with one hand.

"What's the matter, Jim?" she murmured, panting, seductive. "Don't like it when the woman sets the pace?"

"I love it when you set the pace," he said. "But if you keep that up, Kate, I'm not going to be able to withdraw in time. Not this first time."

"Withdraw? Why would you want to . . . oh." Shadows flickered through her eyes and he could have shot himself for bringing it up and putting that look there. And then she smiled until it chased away the shifting sadness. "You don't have to. I can't have children."

Tenderness washed him, deep and powerful as the passion. "Are you sorry about that?"

She swallowed. "Yes," she said. "I'm sorry about that."

"Then I'll be sorry, too." He dropped butterfly kisses over her face, touching her jawline, her eyebrow, the corner of her eye, anyplace he could reach, trying to press away any remnants of regret. "Later, I'll be as sorry as you want. But right now, Kate, I can't tell you how happy I am that I don't have to try and leave you at a critical moment."

Laughter bubbled up in her, a happy sound that brought her body closer, a jerky little movement with each chuckle.

He moved as slowly as he could, withdrawing by

increments, easing back in, not knowing how far behind him she was, how long he might last.

But she wasn't behind him at all. By the second thrust she was moaning, rotating her hips against him. Two more and she murmured "faster" between gasps, urging him on with the tilt of her pelvis, tugging him nearer with her legs wrapped around him.

He gave up any notion of control and surrendered to the passion. To *her*. They found the rhythm effortlessly—not hers, not his, but theirs.

It could have been a moment, it could have been a lifetime. And then Kate shattered beneath him, crying out, shaking, her inner muscles contracting around him, his name on her lips.

Yes, he thought in that extraordinary millisecond where he balanced at the edge, where the world, the future, the past, were all his.

This is it. It's Kate.

Chapter 21

The *Emperor* should steam into Le Havre tomorrow morning. Very early, Jim hoped; the less time allotted to search the ship, the better.

"Where *is* she?" Johnny whispered urgently. The three of them—Jim, dressed in basic black; Johnny, pale, so twitchy he hadn't been able to stand still for two consecutive seconds; and Ming Ho, who'd been recruited for the effort—lurked in a narrow passageway on the second-highest deck of the ship.

"These things take time," Jim replied.

"But—"

"It'll be worth it. Trust me."

Johnny edged up to the corner, peering around it until Jim yanked him back. "Do you want them to see you?"

"No. I just—" He bounced on his toes, cracking his

knuckles until Jim was tempted to crack them for him, permanently. "I still don't see why we had to wait until the last night. I mean, every night she's in there . . ."

"Is one less night the prince has to find her," Jim said, shaking his head at the thought. That Johnny Duffy, newsie, aspiring reporter, son of a tanner, had decided that the youngest and prettiest wife of a mysterious prince was his one true love still boggled his mind. It was outlandish and complicated enough that Jim would have backed right out, article be damned, except that Johnny's love was, of course, the sad young woman he'd seen escorted from the top deck, and that made it very hard to walk away.

So he and Kate had done a little research. Her husband was a prince, all right. He'd had the great good fortune to be absolute ruler of a tiny little island called Balthelay that floated, nearly unnoticed, off the coast of Ceylon. He'd had the even greater good fortune to, about fifteen years ago, discover that the earth beneath his insignificant island was utterly packed with very large, very high quality rubies.

"So," Jim said. "How many guards?"

The prince had taken over the entire corridor of rooms, laying out an amount that, it was rumored, was greater than the contest prize to displace the intended passengers.

"Eight, I think," Johnny said.

"One for each wife's room, two for his door," Jim murmured. "Well, Ming Ho, what do you think?"

He smiled in anticipation. "Not a problem."

"So you're just going to go knocking on every door until you find her?" Johnny asked.

"That's the general idea."

"But all those guards—"

"Let us worry about the guards, okay?" The kid was on the verge of working himself up into a nice frenzy of worry, Jim thought. As if they didn't have enough to concern themselves with as it was.

"But what if she's in the prince's room? How are you going to—"

"That's where Kate comes in."

"But why would he let her in if he's already with . . ." And then Johnny promptly forgot whatever he was about to say, his jaw dropping as he stared over Jim's shoulder.

Kate sashayed down the passageway toward them. She was clad in shimmering red that clung to every curve, the neckline exposing an amount of cleavage that bordered on illegal. She wore no jewelry, nothing to distract from the wide expanse of creamy skin, and her hair flowed down around her shoulders. In one hand she carried a bottle of champagne, two glinting crystal flutes in the other.

Jim waved his hand in front of Johnny's glazed eyes. "True love. Romantic rescue. Happily ever after. Remember?"

"Huh. Oh. Oh! Yeah." He swallowed. "Okay. I get it now."

"So," Kate said as she reached them. "Everybody ready?"

Jim took the bottle for a moment so he could kiss her hand. "Madame, you have truly outdone yourself."

She bobbed a curtsy before reclaiming the bottle. "Thank you, kind sir."

"Where'd you get the dress? That's truly . . . amazing," he said, though that didn't even come close to covering it.

"I have my ways."

"That you do," Jim said softly. "That you do."

They might have stood there all night, smiling at each other in intimate communication, if Ming Ho had not reminded them. "It's time."

"Yes," Jim said. "Just one more thing." He frowned at Kate, putting on what she thought of as his command expression. "Fifteen minutes," he told her sternly. "Or I'm coming after you. You need us earlier, just yell."

"I won't need," she said, supremely confident. "Not right now, anyway. Later . . ." He stopped her with a kiss, quick and hard. *Watch out, be careful, we'll finish this later.*

She whirled, her hair drifting and settling like spun gold. Hips swaying, she glided around the corner, going into battle in her own way.

"Fifteen minutes," he reminded her, loud as he dared. It would do no good to worry about her, he thought, even as his gut twisted. She was in familiar territory.

"All right," he said, turning to his troops. Ming Ho grinned at him.

"You and Miss Riley," he said. "You . . ." He nodded. "Good."

"Yes, me and Miss Riley." And yeah, it was good. Maybe too good. "Take the right side of the passageway. I'll take the left."

"What about me?" Johnny asked, so eager he might just choke on it.

"Stay out of the way."

The guards were even bigger up close. Surprising that a country as small as Balthelay managed to grow so many large specimens. They were all nearly as

wide as the doors they guarded, their heads all
turned toward Kate, strolling provocatively down the
hall, the luscious sway of her hips drawing their full
attention.

Guess they're not eunuchs after all, Jim thought,
slipping quietly up behind the first. He tapped him
on the shoulder, the giant turned, and he jabbed him
beneath the chin before the distracted guard registered his presence. He caught him as he dropped.

He glanced to see how Ming Ho was doing. He was
creeping up on the second man already, the first one
propped against the wall, jaw open, head sagging,
completely out. One quick clip of the side of Ming
Ho's hand against the guard's neck and this one, too,
was out cold.

Kate had nearly reached the end of the passageway.
She glanced over her shoulder, wiggling her fingers,
and the next guard took a step in her direction. That
was as far as he got.

The fellows might be good with their swords, Jim
thought, but they sure couldn't take a punch. Heavy,
though, Jim noted as he caught the full brunt of the
guard's weight, enough to make him stagger beneath
it, but he'd make too much noise if allowed to simply
crash to the floor.

He glanced quickly at Kate to check her progress.
She was right on schedule, smiling dazzlingly at the
two guards stationed in front of the door near the end
of the passageway before disappearing through it.

Damn. Just because it was the plan and Jim had
agreed to it didn't mean he had to like it.

But their luck didn't hold. Some noise, some sense,
had finally alerted the remaining guards. They turned
toward Jim, eyes rounding as if they couldn't believe

what they were seeing. Two rushed him, gorilla arms upraised, big feet pounding, while another headed for Ming Ho.

Balling his fists, Jim found his balance and waited. It had been a while—years, actually—since he'd thrown himself into a good barroom brawl. He hoped he hadn't lost his touch.

They were almost upon him, shoulder to shoulder, too close together in the tight confines of the passageway to mount a spread attack. He waited one beat, then crouched and sprang forward, driving upward with each fist.

They reeled back, clutching their bellies. A kick to the chest for one, an elbow to the chin for the other. A couple taps to the noggin with his fist and the two of them finally went down.

He stepped around the pile of their bodies.

Whoops. The last guard pounded toward him, legs pumping, face red. This one, though, had thought to draw his sword and held it in both fists, twisted back like a baseball player expecting an easy pitch.

Jim jumped back just as he swung, the blade whistling by an inch from his stomach. But he'd back jumped too far, forgetting about the two motionless guards right behind him, and he went down.

The guard with the sword had swung too hard, as if he'd planned to lop Jim in half with one blow. The force of the swing spun him halfway around, giving Jim clear aim at his broad backside. Jim kicked hard with both feet and the guard pitched forward, sword flying out of his grip.

Jim scrambled out of the tangle of thick limbs—he must have hit them good, they hadn't moved a muscle even when he fell on top of them—and went after the guard still—barely—on his feet. Without his sword, off balance, he wasn't much of a challenge. *The bigger they are, the slower they are . . .*

Chest heaving, blood pumping, the guard at his feet, Jim spun to give Ming Ho a hand. Ming Ho leaned comfortably against the opposite wall, arms crossed over his chest, slumbering guards lined up neatly beside him. "What took you so long?"

Jim dabbed at the blood across his knuckles with the corner of his shirt. "Thanks for the help."

"Wouldn't want to spoil your fun, would I?"

And it was fun. He'd almost forgotten what it was like to be forced to live in the moment, every sense, every thought, concentrated in the lone task of surviving for one more second.

Johnny dashed up to them, vibrating with excitement. "Oh, that was great!" He jabbed at the air with his fists. "Do you think you fellows could teach me—"

"No."

"Oh." His face fell briefly, brightened an instant later. Ah, the resiliency of youth. "I'm surprised no more guards showed up, once you all started making noise. Their room must be around here somewhere." He slashed at the air, hands flat, just like he'd seen Ming Ho chop at the guards. "I was ready for 'em, though."

"They're all sleeping," Jim said.

"Sleeping?"

"Like babies," Ming Ho put in, grinning. "Strange that men so big hold their brandy so poorly, isn't it?"

"But—"

"Come on." Jim grabbed Johnny by the shoulder and gave him a gentle shove toward the nearest door. "Start knocking."

"But there have to be more guards in the prince's room, don't you think?" The kid could clearly not take a hint. The image Jim had been fighting since Kate entered the cabin spread in his brain, corrosive as an acid spill: Kate, struggling with the prince, while impassive guards stood around them, swords at the ready.

"Probably never allowed to leave the prince's quarters while he's in residence," Ming Ho said, glancing sympathetically at Jim. "Now knock."

Jim started on the other side while Ming Ho took the far end. He rapped quickly. No answer. He pounded harder. Nothing.

The door wasn't locked. He poked his head inside. The cabin was twice the size of Kate's, in soft rose and yellow, packed with trunks nearly to the ceiling. No one. He closed the door and moved on.

At the next cabin a woman answered the door before he even finished knocking. Perhaps Jim's age, he guessed, though it was hard to tell with the turquoise robes that nearly covered her, and the brief glimpse he got before she gasped and slammed the door in his face.

He moved to the next without any better luck, until he stood before the door that Kate had entered minutes before. He glared at the wood as if that could help him see through into what was happening within, his insides twisting. *Careful, love.*

The knob turned and he sprang away, flattening himself against the wall, and his heart thumped. A guard? Or Kate?

Neither. A slight figure, enveloped in drifts of crimson, stepped out. She turned to stare at the door as it closed behind her, faint puzzlement on her face.

Mission accomplished. Right wife. Now to get her safely out of here before the guards woke up.

"Miss . . ." he began.

She turned her head toward him and gasped.

"No, no, it's okay," he said soothingly. "We've come to rescue you."

She backed away from him, shaking her head, panicked eyes darting from side to side.

"No, really. Don't worry."

She babbled something at him, completely unintelligible.

Oh, just wonderful. The girl didn't speak a word of English. Just how the hell did that brat reporter know she needed rescuing if he never so much as spoke to her? When he got his hands on him—

And then she stopped backing away, her gaze focused behind Jim. She straightened, a shimmer of moisture glazing her eyes, and smiled brilliantly.

Johnny came forward, hands outstretched. Without a second's hesitation, she placed hers in his.

"Ahh," Ming Ho said as he arrived from the far end of the passageway. "Young love. Isn't it sweet?"

"Yeah. Sweet." And stupid and impulsive and fragile. He'd take what he and Kate had now—whatever it was, and he was far from ready to name it—over what they'd had a dozen years ago any day. *Good luck, kids, you're going to need it.* "Let's get going."

They herded the young lovers around the corner to where Mrs. Latimore and Miss Dooley awaited them.

"*There* you are," Miss Dooley said. "I was having a terrible time keeping Anne from running to your assistance."

"I take it this is our young lady?" Mrs. Latimore stepped toward the young woman, who shrank away, huddling against Johnny's narrow chest.

"Johnny neglected to mention that she doesn't speak any English."

Mrs. Latimore's eyebrows rose to her hairline. "*None*?"

"We don't need any." Johnny looped his arms around the girl, two against the world.

"Is that right?" Mrs. Latimore asked coolly.

"I still don't understand why she can't stay with me tonight," Johnny said, the sulky droop of his mouth making him look years younger.

"Because the prince is unlikely to think of looking for her with Mrs. Latimore," Jim said, struggling to hold on to his patience. They'd been over this. And Kate was still in there. With *him*. "And Ming Ho has a plan to get her off the ship unseen. It's simply much safer this way, Johnny. It's been working so far. Let's just keep with the plan, okay?"

For a moment it looked like mutiny. Then Johnny sighed, an end-of-my-world sigh, and Jim almost felt sorry for the kid. He was so very lost on the girl. "All right." He led her over to Mrs. Latimore and carefully, as if she were spun of glass, put her hand in Mrs. Latimore's strong one. As Mrs. Latimore led her away, the prince's wayward bride looked longingly over her shoulder at Johnny. He nodded his reassurance.

"Might as well go to my room," he said thickly, blinking rapidly, when they'd turned out of sight.

"You do that," Jim said, patting him awkwardly on the shoulder. "It'll be all right."

And now he would make sure everything was all

right, Jim thought, heading for the prince's suite.

"You told her you'd give her fifteen minutes," Ming Ho reminded him.

"It has to have been at least twenty."

"No. Perhaps ten."

"Ten's more than enough." Once the guards were out of commission and he'd an instant to think, he'd spent every second of those ten minutes worrying what the prince could be doing with that time. And with Kate.

"She'll be fine."

Maybe she would. But *he* wouldn't, not if he had to endure one more second before assuring himself of her welfare.

But then she was there with him minus the champagne and glasses but—at least as far as Jim could see—*with* everything else, her hair smooth and shining, her dress unrumpled, a pleased smile on her face.

"There. You see?" Ming Ho said, and disappeared before either one noticed his absence. Jim just stood there stupidly, staring at her while his heart steadied and his fear eased.

He longed to reach for her, right there in the hallway. Strip off that garish dress and inspect her from head to toe and find out for himself that she was completely unharmed.

"So," he said around the clot in his throat, "any problems?"

"Not a one," she said serenely. "The girl who was in there— is she the one?"

"Yes."

Kate nodded. "Thought so."

"You had no trouble getting her out?"

"Oh, no. The prince was pleased to speak with me in private."

"Private?" He almost strangled on the word.

She laughed softly and looped her arm through his, leaning comfortably against him. "Well, as private as it can be with four guards there. Apparently they don't count."

"He speaks English?"

"Oh yes. Quite well, actually. Studied in England before inheriting the throne. A very worldly man."

Worldly. And unimaginably rich. And, from the pleasure in Kate's voice, perfectly charming. "He didn't want to . . ."

"Well, I suppose he did. In fact"— she paused— "don't you think we should head back to our cabin? Before some of those guards I saw strewn up and down the hallway begin to wake up? Or the prince decides to send for another wife and finds them?"

"I guess so." Though it was going to be hard to walk, considering how wobbly his knees were and were likely to remain until he heard every single detail of what happened in that room.

They strolled together as if nothing unusual had happened, simply a couple on a pleasant evening turn around the ship.

"Now, where was I?" Did she torture him on purpose? he wondered. Of course she did. "Oh yes. Did the prince wish to . . . get to know me better? I believe he did, but do you know, they have this interesting custom in Balthelay. It seems no one of royal blood can spend their . . . essence . . . on anyone but a wife. Wouldn't do for someone of regal blood to be born out of the royal line, apparently."

"Is that right?" Relief flooded him.

"Yes. And once he understood that I really was poorly suited to become his thirty-second wife, well, there was no reason for me to stay, was there?"

Jim froze in midstep. "He *proposed* to you?"

"Hmm. Although he was so businesslike about it, it hardly seemed much like a proposal."

"He wanted to *marry* you?" Vaguely he noted she was tugging at his arm, trying to get him to move, but his feet refused to budge.

"When you've so many wives to begin with, what's one more?" She shrugged. "Still flattering, of course, but not quite the same when you are asked to be one of so many. And since he apparently has no interest in giving up all the rest, well, we had little else to speak of, did we?"

"You asked him to give up the rest?" The thought lodged in his brain, big and brash, unwelcome, impossible to evict.

"It merely came up in the conversation." She laughed up at him, eyes glinting, and leaned against his arm, her breast soft and full against him until his brain fuzzed. "Can we go now? I'd like to get out of this dress." She trailed her fingers across her chest, where the assertive red barely covered her nipples. "It's really not my style."

Chapter 22

~~~~~~ᗧ◯ᗤ~~~~~~

The ship reached the French port ahead of schedule, as the sun barely lightened the sky to dove gray. The crossing back from New York, with the ship fully loaded, had taken twenty-eight hours longer than the inaugural voyage, but it was still faster than every other ship that sailed the Atlantic.

Despite the early hour, crowds thronged the docks, ready to welcome the *Emperor* home. On board, the regular passengers hung back, in no hurry to leave their floating palace, more than willing to allow the competitors to disembark first.

Kate and Jim stood near the back of the line. A few minutes at this point would make no difference, they decided, and the way the rest were jostling down the gangway someone was going to end up in the ocean.

Kate's clothes might have been borrowed from Mrs.

Latimore's closet: a plain white shirt, severe khaki skirt—she'd finally abandoned her bustle—her hair braided simply down her back. "You look nice," he said.

She squinted at him, as if she wasn't quite sure whether she believed him or not.

"No, you do." He tugged gently on her braid. "What'd you do with the red dress?"

Her lip curled. "Went back where it came from, and good riddance."

"I'm going to miss it."

"I'm sure you will."

The line began to move. Jim grabbed his pack and one of her cases while she lifted the other. "You want me to get that?" he asked her.

"It's fine," she said, a bit miffed that he'd offered. Oh, it was only polite, and men had been offering to carry things for her most of her life. But he should have known better.

The portmanteau bumped against her knee as she walked down the gangway, Jim right behind her. She should have been anxious to get on their way. More adventure, the next clue, and all that. But her heels rang hollowly on the planks, and she had to force her feet to move.

They stepped aside when they reached the docks, out of the stream of people.

"Well," she said. "To the Pyrénées, I suppose."

"So it seems." His hand rubbed lightly at the small of her back. They'd spent most of the past three days with his hands on her, and in far more intimate places. She should have been accustomed to it by now. But that was all it took, that slight, perfectly correct touch at her back, and her heart sped up, her mouth went dry. It seemed that the more he touched her, the more her body craved it, now that it knew the magic he could work.

"Hey," he said. "You're going to be fine."

"Of course I am," she said, completely unconvinced. Oh, she'd be in no danger. She knew that Jim would make sure of it. But she didn't *want* him to have to watch out for her. To spend his time taking care of her when it could be much better spent winning.

"You will," he said, touching her cheek, his fingers warm and familiar. "It's more rugged terrain than we've been in thus far, yes, but you've learned a lot."

Yes, she'd learned a lot. But she still knew her limitations, and clambering around rugged, remote mountains was one of them. It would only remind him, and her, of how different their lives were and how poorly she fit into his world.

But there was nothing she could do about it now. The map said the Pyrénées, so the Pyrénées it would be. "How are we getting there?"

"Train. For most of it, anyway."

She sighed. "Can we try and sneak onto a car that doesn't stink this time?"

"Oh, this time I think we'll spring for a ticket. One with a private compartment." He leered at her, so exaggerated she had to laugh.

"Lovely thought, Jim, but I doubt my funds will stretch that far."

"Yes, well . . ."

"Hmm." She set down her case and faced him squarely. "Now why, exactly, do you look so guilty?"

"Guilty? Me?" He reached for her case. "We'd best get started, don't you think?"

"Jim?"

"We can talk about this later."

"No, we can't." She grabbed the handle before he could and dragged her luggage out of reach.

"Kate . . ."

She looked at him expectantly.

"Oh, all right." He dropped his own load. "I'm not, perhaps, quite as . . . destitute as I allowed you to believe."

"Not destitute," she repeated flatly. "How *not destitute* are you?"

"Not too much," he assured her quickly. "Barely at all."

"Is that so."

"Yes," he said with absurd enthusiasm. "Really, I'm sure I would have run through what little I had in no time if I hadn't thrown in with you."

She glowered at him. "The horses. The food. All the other stuff that you kept magically finding. You bought them, didn't you?"

"I rented the mare."

"Rented. Oh, that's ever so much better, isn't it?" She shook her head. "I thought you were stealing things."

"*Stealing?*" He started laughing, hard enough that several disembarking passengers glanced worriedly his way.

"Jim." When he didn't answer, just laughed even more, she stood before him, perfectly straight, mouth sober. "Jim."

He finally quieted, pressing one hand to a belly that had started to hurt.

"Why did you agree to come with me, if you didn't need the money?"

And then his stomach really did ache, and not from

amusement this time. "I could use the money," he hedged. "I wasn't flat busted, but I didn't have enough to mount another expedition, nor enough to live on for much longer if I didn't go out again soon."

"Jim," she repeated, and waited for the truth.

He'd no idea how she was going to take it, Jim thought. He should have told her long ago, as soon as she became more than Dr. Goodale's wife to him. But things were going so well, he'd never believed in rocking the boat, it hadn't come up, and he'd really mostly forgotten about it.

And she'd see them all for the excuses they were.

"I promised the doc."

"*What?*" Shock sprang clear in her eyes, disbelief edged with suspicion.

He scrambled to find the right words. He never cared much how he put things, never had to pick and choose words to guard another's emotions. He was as out of his depth with her as she would be on a mountainside.

"Before . . . before we ever met. The first time, I mean. Maybe a year after Elaine died and he'd gone home to play father. He wrote me, right after he married you."

"What did he say about me?" she asked.

"I—" He hesitated.

"Jim, I'm not going to be offended. I'm just curious."

"Well, not much, to tell you the truth. That he'd married again, to someone who'd deal with the children. And that if something ever happened to him, he wanted me to make sure she was all right."

"That's it?" She shouldn't have been surprised. It

took a moment to sort through the mix of emotions, finding exactly where the source of her shock lay.

"I'm sorry," he murmured.

"Don't be." She tossed her braid over her shoulder and met his gaze fully. "Truth be told, the only thing surprising is that he thought even that much about my future."

"He should have," Jim said, sudden, unexpected anger surging. She'd been the doctor's *wife*. She'd watched over his children. He should have done more for her than a casually penned line to an old friend.

She shook her head. "Emily had a home and an education. He kept his end of the bargain." Her voice softened. "The only real question is why you felt bound by such a slight request."

He shrugged. "I had nothing when I left England. Nowhere to go. Signed on a freighter and ended up in Belém with no plans whatsoever. He allowed me to join his expedition. I can't even tell you how much I learned from him in the next five years. I . . . owed him," he said, shifting uncomfortably. Because while it was not a lie, it was only the slightest portion of the truth, a truth that Jim did not fully comprehend himself. There'd been guilt mixed in, guilt that he'd been able to continue to explore and experience while the doctor had been called so reluctantly home. A deeper reproach that he'd wanted the doctor's wife. Oh, that had begun unwittingly, but it hadn't ended there. He'd wanted her, all those years. Wanted her when she'd walked away from him, wanted her as he rambled the world and tried to forget her, wanted her when she'd drifted into his hotel room.

She was watching him carefully, one brow raised, waiting for him to elaborate. But he couldn't say it, not any of it. It was hard enough to admit to himself.

And then she lifted to her toes and kissed him, full on the mouth, brief but hard, and came away smiling.

"Ahh . . ." He glanced around at the milling crowds, the knowing smiles aimed their way.

"It's all right," she said. "We're in France. It's nothing they haven't seen before."

"Well, then . . ." He grinned and drew her closer. "How about we show them something they *haven't*—"

"Hello!"

They both groaned, turning reluctantly to face something that was not going to be nearly as much fun.

Johnny bounded up to them, eager as a young puppy anticipating a treat. "Where is she?"

"Um . . . ah . . ."

"She's gone," Kate said as kindly as she could.

"Gone?" He frowned, as if the word were unfamiliar to him. "What do you mean, gone?"

"I mean exactly that."

"But—" His voice rose in panic. "You mean he found her? Come on, Jim, we have to go steal her back!"

"Johnny," Kate said before he could go charging up the gangway, "it wasn't the prince." And truthfully, she didn't think the prince was likely to expend much energy looking for her. Oh, his pride—something he certainly owned in abundance—might be pricked a bit, but from their brief conversation she suspected he wasn't all that interested in his youngest bride. He'd married her as a favor to one of his nobles and, while he certainly understood his royal duties in the matter, thought of her more as a young cousin than a wife.

"But—"

"She's safe, I promise you that much."

Fists clenching, he spun on Jim. "What did you do with her?"

"Hey now, bud." Jim raised his hands, palm out. "I kept you from getting yourself skewered trying to rescue a girl you barely know, and that's *all* I did."

"Jim." Kate pursed her lips and shook her head slightly at him, hoping he'd get the message. A young man's heart was a delicate matter, one she was far better suited to handle.

"Now, Johnny." She took his hand in hers, bringing him around so he'd look at her. "She's safe, you must believe me. Mrs. Latimore knew of a place, with an old friend of hers, somewhere that the young woman can rest and think and decide about her future. She'll be well protected, far from the prince's reach."

"But—but—" His hand shook in hers. "I don't understand."

"You are very young. Both of you," she said carefully. Young people never wanted to believe it, never understood when wiser heads said such things. It didn't make it any less true. "We decided that—"

"*We?*" he shouted. "Who's *we?* Isn't *we* supposed to be *her* and *me?*"

"You barely know each other."

"What's that got to do with it?" He blinked rapidly and Kate's heart softened. They'd done the right thing and she knew it. But she still appreciated the young man's pain. "I love her!"

"Johnny," she said. He might not believe her now. But she still chose her words with extreme care because later perhaps he might remember them and understand. "I know you do, my dear. But she was in a difficult situation, one with few options. She wanted a way out."

He went rigid. "You think she *used* me?"

"Not quite that baldly, no. I am not insisting that she did, Johnny. Nor, if that *is* the case, may she have had any knowledge of her motives as she did so. I am saying that you cannot discount the possibility completely and it would be a grave mistake to make irreversible decisions based on such brief and dramatic events."

For a moment she was afraid he would burst into tears, at which point she was far too likely to spill it all. "It is not forever," she told him. "If it is truly love, it will not go away. And you can plan a future without any reservations whatsoever, knowing that it is love that holds you together and not merely circumstances."

He yanked his hand from hers and she sighed. A few weeks, a few months . . . they seemed like a lifetime when one was seventeen.

"Mrs. Latimore, you said?" he asked thoughtfully. "I saw them leave the ship a while ago. Mrs. Latimore and Miss Dooley and Ming Ho. I did not see . . ." He trailed off as he saw Ming Ho bound off the bottom of the ramp alone, waving cheerfully. "But . . ."

It had been so easy that Kate nearly hadn't believed it. In Ming Ho's dark baggy pants and tunic, and her hair stuffed up under a large straw hat, the slight young woman had strolled off the ship with the ladies without anyone giving them a second glance.

Comprehension dawned. And then came the anger, finally pushing ahead of the shock. Johnny grabbed Kate by her upper arms and hauled her up. *"Where is she?"*

"Hey, now, easy there." Jim deftly detached Johnny's grip and stepped between them. "No reason to be angry with the lady."

"Oh yeah?" He looked Jim up and down, worry leaking through his bravado. And then, squaring his shoulders, he put up his fists. "I don't care how much you hurt me," he said, then added honestly. "Much. But you're going to tell me where she is."

Arms crossed comfortably in front of his chest, Jim looked down at Johnny's bobbing fists, hiding his smile. "I thought you were supposed to be such a crack reporter," he said. "You want her that much?

"Then find her."

Chapter 23

R egular articles appeared on the front page of the *Daily Sentinel* during the next ten weeks.

ANNOUNCEMENT FROM THE EDITOR

We have received a number of inquiries as to the whereabouts of our anonymous reporter. At this time the management of this newspaper has made an editorial decision that we can no longer print articles without fully crediting their originators. However, we are certain that our faithful readers will continue to enjoy frequent reports from our intrepid reporter Charlie Hobson, who is closely shadowing the footsteps of the competitors as this goes to press . . .

COMPETITORS TANGLE NEAR ANDORRA

Many deemed Major Huddleston-Snell hopelessly out
of the race upon his unscheduled and very wet departure from the *Emperor* prior to her sailing. But
the major once again proved that he is not to be underestimated when he caught up with many of the
other competitors as they approached the mountains. Though this reporter did not personally ob-
serve the events hereafter described, numerous
witnesses attested to an ensuing physical confronta-
tion between the major and Lord James Bennett,
which was abruptly interrupted by Lord Bennett's
beautiful, ever-mysterious assistant and the arrival
of Mrs. Latimore's party before serious damage
could occur. It seems that countrymen do not com-
patriots make . . .

It is fortunate for Mr. Eiffel that he was not in residence at his apartment at the top of his brilliantly
engineered tower the third week in October. For
those seven days the elevator to the top, previously
perfectly reliable, suffered an inexplicable malfunc-
tion which took longer than expected to repair. Most
unfortunately for our competitors, that was precisely during the week that most of them arrived in
Paris in pursuit of their next clue. But a balky elevator could not daunt our intrepid contestants . . .

Three crushed toes, one broken forearm, and several
bruised lower regions were the unfortunate result of
several competitors' attempts to retrieve a clue
from the center of a bullring in Valencia. It no doubt
seemed a simple task until three furious bulls,
proudly bearing horns long and sharp as a duelist's
sword, unexpectedly broke into the ring . . .

The souks in Tangiers are colorful and chaotic places
at all times. But that is nothing compared to the bed-
lam that erupted this week when our competitors
arrived . . .

With only ten days remaining before the prize is
forfeit and uncounted miles behind them, only a day
separates the majority of the contestants. Now, as
winter threatens and the New Year approaches, our
now familiar group, weary but determined, turn toward England . . .

The small fishing vessel bucked through the chan-
nel. Two hours past sunset, two days after Christmas,
the temperature was dropping, damp, icy wind ripping across the water.

Kate shivered. Immediately Jim slipped his arm
around her, wrapping her in warmth, and she leaned
against him, sinking into the sensation, trying to imprint each scent, each touch.

Almost over. One way or another, they were reaching the end of this journey. Ahead of her the white
curve of the coast shimmered in the moonlight. The
land rose higher behind it, tiny flicks of light here and
there where houses roosted, a denser cluster by the
curve of the bay where a village nestled.

She peeked up at Jim. He had his collar pulled up
around his neck, his shoulders hunched against the
cold. His skin reddened, the sharp angles of his face
set impassively as he stared at the approaching shoreline, and the truth that she'd been assiduously ignoring for weeks hit her like the cold, a slap that couldn't
be avoided and bit deep, chilling to the bone.

Almost over, she thought again. Any excitement that

idea might once have sparked had died long ago. Win, lose . . . she'd be losing either way. Because this small, full, wonderful interlude in an otherwise pallid life would be over. It had to be.

For what were her choices? To follow Jim around the world? The idea tantalized her. As he had promised, he had kept her safe. Comfortable . . . well, not quite, she admitted honestly, although discomfort was a smaller price to pay than she might have thought to be with him. Yes, despite her worry, she'd held up all right in the mountains. She did not delude herself into believing that the Pyrénées were the Himalayas, nor that enduring a few weeks was anything like spending months, even years, on expedition.

The wind gusted, kicking spray into her face, stinging her eyes. She tasted brine, and regret.

For the truth of it was, as hard as she tried not to, she slowed him down. He worried over her. Went out of his way to court her along the way, to keep her warm and safe and dry. And they'd been in places far less remote than he typically chose to explore. She absolutely refused to be a handicap to him. Not to mention that she suspected his next trip would be back to the Arctic, taking another run at the North Pole. He was simply not the kind to allow a failure to rest. And to be out of touch with her sisters for months, perhaps even years on end? She could not imagine.

So where did that leave her? The woman who waited at home, worrying, praying, hoping for a few precious months of happiness before he left her again? Certain every second they were apart that this time might be the one he did not return from? She could not conceive of living a life that was primarily bound by loneliness and terror. And she knew herself. She would not be able to resist attempting to lure him into staying with her, trading on his emotion and hers, keeping him from his work a month longer, and then another, until it became more about duty than choice. Until they both blamed each other for not being something that they couldn't.

What, then? Perhaps she would marry again, she thought. Not for security this time, but for companionship and affection. Maybe there would even be a man with children again, younger ones this time, children who might not resent her as much as the doctor's had.

Depression pressed down on her, dark and thick as the clouds overhead.

"Almost there," she murmured. "If you're right about the clue."

"It's the right place," Jim said. *England*, he thought, trying to make the word sound anything but foreign in his head. *England*.

" 'The hawk's perch soars o'er sea and land, a folly meant to rule—' "?

" 'Failed in its purpose, except to view, but beneath it lies the jewel,' " she finished, wincing. "That's so awful."

"But easy," he said. "And that's good." After all these years of running from this place, forcing from his mind every memory and every thought until even he sometimes forgot where he'd come from, he was almost back.

He'd barely glanced at the clue before he knew where they were going. Out of all the places in the world, that they should send him here—it should have surprised him, a coincidence so large it bordered on absurd. And yet . . . he'd simply gone still inside, eerily calm. No matter how deeply he probed, there was nothing of the turbulent roil of emotion he might have expected. Nothing at all, in fact, but a vague amusement that Fate had finally taken him in hand and forced him back. As if he'd always known that this day would come eventually, that no matter how hard he ran he could never completely get away.

"How far is it?" she asked.

"Not far. Six or seven miles."

She shivered against him again. Poor thing, he thought, hugging her closer. He'd grown so accustomed to her there, tucked against him, the feel of her body against his in one way or another, that now it felt strange whenever she wasn't there. As if he'd lost part of himself, an empty pain like a phantom limb.

She would have lasted about five minutes in the Arctic if she found England cold. The sky spit a few flakes at them, melting so quickly on his face that he first took them to be spray. But he could see them in the light, icy little bits carried along on the wind, threatening to turn to sleet.

"Are we far behind, do you think?"

He shook his head. "They'll be taking the main shipping lanes, most likely, landing in Portsmouth or Brighton. I paid old Ned there to take us right into Shorehampton, and we can start from there."

"We can't land any closer?"

He'd been gone so long, one might have thought he'd forgotten what it looked like. The smell of the water, the way the low hills rolled back from the shore. But it all came back to him as if he'd left only days before. He remembered where the roads curved, where the land lifted and dipped. It was as if the places one saw as a child imprinted themselves upon one, carving a map in relief that could never be fully obliterated.

"No," he said. "That section of the coast is nasty. Abrupt shallows, shifting sand bars, cliffs, rip tides. This'll be safer. It won't take long to get there."

Jim was terribly wrong. He should have known, he thought. Once Fate had decided to take him in hand, she would not allow him to swing so close to Harrington and ignore it.

By the time they'd disembarked and located a small open carriage and horse for hire—and made their way unerringly through the town, Kate noted, no need for Jim to pause at corners to ponder the direction—the flurries turned to a torrent, thickly pelting down, piling against houses and hedgerows.

"Perhaps we should put up for the night," she suggested, glancing at the spill of large white flakes, glittering in lamplight, dropping out of the darkness, thinking fondly of comfortable inn beds, warm fires, and a naked Jim beside her.

"The farther we get today, the closer we are to the end," he said. "The road's not remote."

The end. It's not what he meant, Kate told herself, even as the chill settled into her stomach and lumped there, painful and heavy. "All right."

About a half-inch of snow coated the road. Jim had to coax the small, sturdy mare to set out on it but once they got going she went on well enough, hooves slicing neat half moons into the white that blurred and then filled smooth almost immediately.

They had to be near Jim's home, Kate reasoned. He

was too sure of the road, his gaze firmly fixed forward as if there was no point in looking around because he already knew what he'd see. Curious, she strained to peer through the snow until her vision fuzzed, unable to make out more than the occasional dark spear of a tree, the black bulk of a cottage with light blinking in its window, half of them, she was sure, as much her imagination as reality.

The world was hushed, as if the snow muted her hearing as much as her sight. The sea, Jim had told her when she asked, was no more than a half mile to her right. But she couldn't hear it at all, as if the storm absorbed its sound.

The snow grew thicker—in the air, on the ground, until the horse began to labor to pull them through.

She put her hand on Jim's arm to gain his attention. "Should we stop?"

This time he nodded. "The next place—we're almost there, I—"

They hit ice lurking invisibly under the snow. The world spun, a crazy whirl of white and dark flashing by. The wheels shrieked over the surface and, before Kate's mind truly registered what had happened, they were tilted at an odd angle, half buried in the ditch.

She pressed a hand to her chest where her heart beat a violent protest.

"Are you all right?" His hands were at her face, lifting it up to his: harsh lines, dark eyes, a backdrop of whirling white. "Damn it, Kate—"

"I'm absolutely fine," she said quickly, smiling, before he could apologize. "I always did like to spin."

"Are you sure?" He squeezed her shoulders, ran his hands down her arms as if to find out for himself if all her parts were well and whole.

"Completely." She nodded. "The horse?"

He leaped out of the curricle and ran around to the front, unhitching the mare before coming back to assist her down. The snow, heavy, cold, gave beneath her as he set her down; she sank to her shins.

"She's fine," he said. "But the carriage's done for."

"What's next?"

"We walk," he said. And they did, Jim in front, breaking a trail while she waded after him, leading the mare behind her.

"How far?"

"Only a few hundred steps," he answered over her shoulders while he plowed steadily on without hint of hesitation or fatigue.

They made an abrupt turn. Kate hurried behind him, expecting a cottage, perhaps a stables. Instead they passed between two stone pillars looming out of the snow, dark and malevolent guardians. Their path grew winding, veering to the right and left, a narrow trail between thick stands of trees that marched near, stretching overhead. Brush grew thick beneath them, dark tangles sifted with white.

She glimpsed a dark bulk over his shoulder, a huge shadow through the snow that she at first thought a hill, a small mountain. But then the indistinct form took shape, a rambling geometry pierced by chimneys. A house, more massive than she'd ever seen, dark stone that seemed windowless. But there were windows, she realized as they approached: empty rectangles—no glass, no light—carved gracelessly in the charcoal stone.

Jim stopped at the base of the front staircase, face uplifted while flakes melted on his cheeks, clung to his lashes. "Welcome to Harrington," he said. "Makes the Cuckoo's Nest look like a veritable palace, doesn't it?"

"Maybe it's not as bad as it looks," she said. Two urns had tumbled from their perches, blocking the door. One door, where there was meant to be two, the space yawning black like a gap-toothed smile. "I mean—"

"Oh, it's as bad as it looks," he said, starting up the stairs. "Be careful, half of them have crumbled."

"But the mare?"

"Bring her along inside," he said. "Doesn't make much difference at this point."

Harrington . . . What *is* this place, Kate wondered as they entered. She couldn't see far—a big, echoing room, the base of a broad staircase that swept up, dark passageways that she assumed led to other parts of the . . . what was it? A manor, a house, a castle? There was absolutely nothing in the place, not one chair, not a rug on the wet stone floor, not even a shred of drapery over the holes of the windows. Snow gusted through them, striping the floor, pooling in shadowy corners.

"This way," he said, and led her through a hallway, the ceiling soaring so far above her it was completely lost in shadows. He poked his head in doorways—not a single door remained—as they passed them, shaking his head before continuing on to the next. "Roof's mostly gone here. Not much more shelter than being outside." He quickly crossed the main foyer again with Kate, numb, wondering, in his wake, the mare's hooves echoing loudly on the stone behind her.

"Here," he said after quickly inspecting another

room. "Used to be the library. Seems in better shape than the rest. At least it's an interior room. No windows."

She followed him in. She could make out a little in the gloom—three walls of paneling, dull and scarred, and a blackened hearth taller than she.

"Do you mind waiting?" he asked. "I'll go put the horse in the ballroom." He smiled wryly. "She's better mannered than most of· the guests who've been invited here, anyway."

"Jim," she said, suspicion swirling with dread. "What is this place?"

"Can't you tell?" he asked, a bitter set to his mouth. "This is where I grew up."

And then he was gone, the *clomp-clomp* fading as they moved down the hallway, while Kate stood in the center of the room and tried to make sense of it all.

Once, it must have been grand. The proportions of the rooms, the endless scale of the place, the long, winding drive that led up to house, all hinted at past splendor. But it was beyond "past"—it was ruined, destroyed, utterly devastated.

She heard him returning, a soft scrape of footsteps on stone. She prepared herself to face him—smoothing her clothes, her expression, folding hands that trembled in front of her.

"My apologies," he said as he came in the doorway. "I expected it to be bad. But I didn't suspect it would be *this* bad, I—"

"This was your home?" she asked, unable to wonder a moment longer.

The question froze him, a half second of bared emotion, one foot in midstep. *Oh, Jim, I had no idea.*

"Home?" he said slowly, as if testing out the word.

"No, not that. Not for a long time." He shook his head slightly. "How long has it been since I thought of any place like that?"

Me too, she almost said. But it wasn't the truth, she thought with some surprise. Oh, she'd never had a specific *place*, four walls and a roof, that she'd considered hers, not for years. But wherever her family had been . . . that had been home. But Jim—Jim hadn't stayed in one place for more than a few weeks at a time as long as she'd known him. As for family . . . it bothered her that she didn't know. He never mentioned them, not at all, and sympathy welled, rich and deep.

"Oh, don't look at me like that."

He strode to her, wrapped her in his arms, enveloping her in the smell of snow and horse and Jim. "Yes," he said. "I grew up here. The primary seat of the earls of Harrington. A very long line of very, very bad, dissolute and debauched men, of which my father was the worst. Name a vice, he had it, though last I heard, a long time ago, my brother was doing his damnedest to pass him up. By the looks of this place, I assume he has by now."

She squeezed, the solid bulk of him that she'd found so easy to lean on. Familiar, yes, but never, not once, taken for granted because she knew from the first that she'd enjoy it only briefly.

"Well, hell, I would have told you this weeks ago if I'd have known it would get you all cuddled up against me like this," he said lightly.

"And the rest?" she murmured. His coat was wool—they'd bought it in France—itchy against her cheek.

"The rest?"

"The rest."

He sighed. "There's not much 'rest.' I took after my mother, not them, and, just like her, there wasn't a thing I could do to stop them, and I couldn't stand to stay around and watch them run it all to ruin. She couldn't either"— he paused, sucked in a breath— "though her way out was different than mine. But after she was gone, I couldn't leave fast enough. They didn't care. If I wasn't going to play, why would it matter whether I'm around?"

"Where are they?"

Wind whistled, blowing through a hole somewhere in the decrepit manse. "I didn't want to know a damn thing about them after I left. Got a letter from the solicitor once in a while when they could track me down, none of which I ever opened. I know my father died . . . must be four years ago or so now. They wrote that on the outside of the envelope." The sound of the wind grew sharper, harsher, a piercing keen. "My brother . . . I imagine he's in London. Never much cared for the country unless there was something here he could sell. Likely no one's been in residence since I left."

"Why didn't he sell your—" She broke off, unsure what to call it. Not home, never home. "This place?"

"Can't," he said, clipping out the words, shorter, briefer, as if to ensure no emotion could shadow them. "Entailed."

She shuddered.

"Oh, damn, you're still cold." He thrust her away and impatiently inspected the room. "I've got to get a fire started."

"Jim—"

He ignored her, stalking around as if the room

couldn't contain him, looking out in the hall, up at the ceiling, the staircase missing its banister. "Damn it, there's not even a picture frame left."

"I'm all right," she began.

But he didn't hear her. He swung around, focusing on the far wall. He strode across the room, gaining speed on the way, until she was afraid he would hurl himself right at the wall. At the last second he brought up his foot, ramming it furiously into the old carved panels. The wall shattered, a tremendous crash, his foot disappearing to the ankle.

"Jim!"

He yanked his foot out and bent, ripping off splinters of paneling, a foot-wide strip of what once must have been some precious, exotic wood. "There you go," he said, panting. "Firewood."

Chapter 24

I t snowed through the night and most of the next
day, until the drifts outside were hip deep in
places, the heavy kind of snow that held oceans of
water. Kate didn't mind a bit; for the first time in
months, the steady, nagging pressure to *hurry, hurry,
catch up* was absent. Mother Nature had imposed her
will upon the contest, and they could do nothing but
wait her out. And so all that was left to Kate was
twenty hours of ensuring that Jim had at least a few
lovely memories of this place to balance the rest.

When it stopped, the sky clearing abruptly, the inside of the house went light, as if a thousand candles
had suddenly sprung to life, the sun outside reflected
so brightly off all that pure, blinding snow.

"Looks worse in the light," Jim commented lightly,
as if he were talking about a place that had no connec-

tion to him whatsoever. The library was still dim, but enough light spilled through the open doorway to reveal the details hidden the night before. He lay on the floor in front of the fireplace, Kate sprawled on top of him, staring up at the ceiling. Cracks spread over the plaster like fine net, thick cobwebs shawling in the corners, a huge hole where a chandelier had once hung open clear to the upper floor.

He loved the weight of her. The feel of her hair tickling soft beneath his chin, the smell of her, even the rhythm of her breath—he could forget where he was, forget *anything* but her. The only flaw, he considered, was that they were rationing the wood and it was so damn cold they'd had to put their clothes back on.

"Do we have to go?" she murmured, sleepy-voiced, a sensual hum that thrummed in his bones, his blood.

No, never, he wanted to say. *We'll just stay right here, snowed in, and the world can go to hell.*

"Not yet," he said. "The roads will be slop. No point in even trying it."

She was silent for a moment. "How long?"

"Tomorrow. Maybe the next. Depends how quickly it warms up." His arm was around her waist, beneath her coat. He stroked her back, rubbed small circles low at her waist until she stretched into his touch like a cat. "I'll have to go out tomorrow, though. We'll need more food, wood. For the horse, if not for us."

"How far?" she asked.

"I don't know," he answered. "There are cottages not far away. Whether there's anyone there, any*thing* there, I don't know."

He kissed the top of her head, letting the feel of her drift through him, amazed that something so easy, so comfortable, could be so powerfully arousing at the same time. He wondered if there would have ever come a time, even if they had far more of it than they did—a lifetime of it—when she wouldn't have that effect on him.

Immediately she lifted up, sliding over him in a way that had his blood surging. "You can do better than that," she murmured, and lowered her mouth to his.

He let it simmer a bit, building slowly of its own accord, trying to savor. But there was no holding back where Kate was concerned—when had there ever been? Her tongue was sweet in his mouth, her weight glorious on him, her hands along his sides, slipping tantalizing farther down.

He yanked her blouse from her waistband, sliding his hands beneath. She hadn't put her shift back on, and her skin was warm, silky.

"Kate, I—" He stopped. *Kate, I* what? What had almost come out of his mouth? It hovered in his brain like a wisp of incense, more dangerous than opium. He knew what they had, knew even better what they couldn't.

And then she shifted her hips against him, circling, just tantalizingly short of a grind, and he forgot words. His hands slid higher, seeking—

"Hullo!" The shout startled them both, echoing— *hullo, hullo*—in the cavern of the foyer. They scrambled to their feet, checking buttons and tucks in a panicked flurry. It could be another competitor, a reporter.

"Who's here?"

"I'll go," Jim said quickly, heading for the foyer. "While you . . . repair."

Oh, well, Kate thought. Nothing important showing. And if she looked a bit—a lot—messy, who cared?

A man stood just inside the door—he should have been a big man, judging by the breadth of his shoulders, the size of his hands, his feet. But he was hollow-cheeked, hollow-eyed, a threadbare coat ridiculously insufficient for the weather pulled up around a long narrow neck, a fraying wool hat pulled low over his brows, so only a slice of his face showed, raw and red.

"Saw the smoke," he said, stamping snow from his boots. "I live"—he hooked a thumb over his shoulder—"thataway a bit. Figured some travelers mebbe got caught in the storm." He bobbed his head. "Guess I was right. Brought a few things, in case you—"

"Will?" Jim stepped forward, quietly alert.

"How'd you—" He broke off, squinting. "James?"

"Yes." Jim strode forward, an eagerness in his step Kate had not seen, one hand extended.

Will beamed, flashing a big, uneven smile and moved forward to greet him. At the last minute he pulled back, snatching his hat from his head, standing there while he crushed the wool in his work-battered hands. "Lord Harrington. Good to see you, m'lord."

"Come now, Will, no need to stand on . . ." *Lord*. He'd called him Lord Harrington, then his hand dropped to his side and hung there, open-palmed, limp. "Francis? . . ."

"They didn't find you?"

"No. They didn't find me."

"Oh." Will dropped his eyes, spun his hat around twice before continuing, clearly reluctant to deliver the news it shouldn't have been his responsibility to convey. "Your brother died. Three months ago, in London."

"How?"

"I—" He cut his eyes toward Kate, the red on his cheeks deepening. "I'm not sure. Not for certain."

"No matter," Jim said. What would be the point in probing more? Francis had obviously come to a bad end, nasty enough that Will didn't want to say it in front of Kate. No surprise there. A knife in a brothel, or some terrible disease he'd contracted there. A duel over cards, over a debt, over a woman. Pitching into the Thames too drunk to swim out. Maybe even in an opium den, wasting away to nothing.

My brother is dead, he thought experimentally, trying to make the words ring true, to discover if pain lurked beneath them. But it had been so long since he'd thought of himself as having a brother, a family . . . it seemed a tale of tragedy read in the newspaper or relayed over a drink. A vague pity, distant regret for another wasted life. Nothing more.

"There was no issue?"

Another quick, worried glance toward the woman present, and then he shook his head. "Ah . . . no. No heir."

"I see." So there could be—likely were—children. Maybe several of them. But none that the courts would recognize. Now he was James Bennett, Earl of Harrington.

It sounded false, patently unreal. He'd never thought it would come to him—for all the wild recklessness of the previous earls, they'd all managed to produce an heir or two, born and molded in their own image, before they stumbled into death.

His stomach went hollow, his head, light; he felt as dizzy and nauseous as when the Amazon fever gripped him most strongly.

Will was inspecting Kate with open speculation. Perhaps a little appreciation. He cocked an eyebrow at Jim, waiting.

"My apologies. This is . . ." He stumbled over the appropriate word to describe her. Fascinating, amazing, extraordinary. My lover, my friend, my . . . Kate. That's it, my Kate.

Gracefully she took the dilemma from him. "I'm Kate," she said simply, taking Will's hand and pumping it twice without a shred of discomfort while she smiled warmly at him. "I would tell you that Jim and I are old acquaintances, but I suspect you usurp me in that regard by a good many years."

"Will's father was . . . is?" Jim glanced at Will.

"Was."

"I'm very sorry."

Will nodded, accepting.

"Will's father was steward when I was young," Jim told her. "And as both our fathers were too occupied to keep too close an eye on us, we managed to get ourselves into and out of rather a lot of trouble together."

Will chuckled. "That we did."

"Really?" Kate said, surprised. She would have pegged Will at least ten, if not fifteen, years older than Jim.

"Yeah, well." He bobbed his head toward a small sack slumped by the door. "I brought a few things. Not much. A few boiled eggs, some bread. I know it's not what you're used to."

"It'll be a feast," Kate said, enough enthusiasm in her voice that he couldn't doubt her. "It's very kind of you. Doubly so that you didn't even know who was here."

"Oh." He flushed, ducking his head, embarrassed

as a schoolboy. "Times are hard round here. Have to help where you can." He backed away toward the door. "We've young ones at home. Promised the wife I'd be back soon."

"You've children?" she asked.

"Three of them." He beamed, a poor man suddenly transformed into a rich one.

"Girls or boys?"

"Girls, all of 'em. Pretty as their mother, sweet as sunshine."

"Congratulations," she said softly.

"I've a favor to ask you," Jim said.

Will straightened, nodded correctly as a servant. "Whatever you wish. If you'd rather not stay here . . . our place, it's not much, but you're welcome."

"No, we're well enough here, though the food is most appreciated. Please thank your wife for us."

Jim was frowning. Uncomfortable with being treated as a lord rather than a friend, Kate suspected.

"No, we've a mount and a lamentable lack of fodder. If you've supplies enough and could take her with you, I'd be most grateful."

"Where do you have her?" asked Will.

"I put her in the ballroom."

Will blinked twice before he started laughing. "That's very lordly of you, sir."

"And you'd do well to remember it," Jim returned, grinning.

Kate suspected that Will would do his best to maintain appropriate formality, but she thought the friendship was going to prove stronger than the gulf in their stations in no time.

By the time Will and the mare trudged down the drive, Kate had a mental list of two dozen questions.

She opened her mouth the instant he was out of earshot, and Jim laid a finger across it, stopping her, before the first word came out.

"Be warned," he told her. "For every question you shoot at me, I'll be asking one back. I'm not sure I've the answers you'll want, but I'll be expecting them back."

"But Jim . . ."

"I'm not sure I *know* the answers yet," he said quietly. "Let it settle and sort for a while and then you can ask."

"Then will you tell me?" she asked. He'd kept his own counsel for a long time. But she wanted as much of him as she could get in the time allowed, all the secrets he guarded, all the dark places he never allowed himself to stir around in.

He had to consider it. "I will." Deftly he pointed her toward the library and steered her that way.

"A bit early to go to bed, isn't it?"

"No." She smiled and leaned into him, her skin flushing with anticipation. One word, two little letters, and she was ready for him, instantly, completely, as if her body were more attuned to his will than hers.

It frightened her, how much she craved him, scared her even more to think about what she might do when he was gone. Perhaps she should begin to wean herself from the addiction. To hold off for a moment or two, not turning to him the instant he touched her. She searched for a delay, something that would distract them both for a little while—she had no hope it would last longer than that.

"So what did you want to ask *me*?" she said.

He paused just inside the doorway. Gently—oh, why did he have to be so gentle, so sweet? She would miss this as much as the passion, this warmth that glowed inside her, softer than the blaze, every bit as potent—he pushed a strand of hair from her face. Unsmiling, intent, as if he were as determined to memorize her face as she was his. "I don't remember."

She tsked, attempting lightness. "Always in such a hurry. What happened to anticipation? You made me wait when you kissed me in the cave, remember?"

"I was wrong. Anticipation's fine, but what comes after is better. *Much* better." He kneaded the back of her neck until her head fell back, eyes slumberous, her defenses down. "Does it always make you so sad, every time someone mentions a child?"

"Of course not," she snapped out, lifting her head. "I—" No, Kate thought. If she wanted honesty stripped bare from him, she must give him the same. "Not usually," she said. "I thought I'd come to terms with it long ago. Perhaps I just didn't allow myself to think about it, and now that Emily's grown it has lodged in the forefront again, demanding attention." She shrugged, having to consciously force her shoulders up, as if someone pressed down on them. "It'll pass," she said, determined that it would be true. What choice did she have?

"How fortunate for the doctor, since he couldn't have any more children, either, that he found you—"

She went rigid, brittle as thin glass. "Either?" She moved away from him, away from the distraction of his touch, needing to concentrate on every word, every nuance of expression.

"Yes, of course, I—" He frowned. "I assumed he'd told you."

"Told me what?" she asked, pronouncing each word with extreme care.

"He caught a fever once, when we were in the jungle. It settled into his, ah . . . settled lower. Ballocks swelled up the size of a melon. He said it was unlikely that he'd ever father another child. I thought you knew."

"He never told me." She flexed her hands—clench, extend, clench, extend, fingers stiff as if she'd aged a hundred years. "He never told me anything."

"I suppose it's not an easy thing for a man with the doc's pride to admit. And since it wasn't an issue . . ." Something in her expression warned him. He stepped back, his voice going flat. "Did he examine you? Was *he* the one who told you that you couldn't . . ."

"He told me *nothing*," she said, a savage edge to her voice. "No one did."

"Then how . . ."

"*I assumed. Me.*" The disappointment had been steady all those years ago, deep and horrible but never acute. A fresh welling every month, a constant shading of grief. This—this was huge, one quick, hard punch of it, concentrated, in her gut. "It had to be me, didn't it? It obviously wasn't him."

Rage gripped her, corrosive and hot, a kind she'd never known. "He *stole* that from me. Took my choice, my chance." It boiled within her, awful laughter edged with hysteria. "To think that I felt so guilty about *kissing* you, when all the time . . . I wish to God I'd slept with you then."

"God, Kate, I'm sorry, it never occurred to me or I'd have told you long ago. But maybe . . ." Maybe what? Jim wondered. What the hell did he almost suggest? Impulsive, irrevocable actions wouldn't correct the terrible wrong done to her. Words clogged his throat.

"It's too late now," she said, eyes a furious, fiery

blue, two bright flags of color burning high on her cheeks.

"Maybe not."

"No? And just how many times have we mated . . ." Her mind snagged on the word. *Mated.* "How many times have we been together? Dozens, more? If I still could, I would be. And I'm not. You know that."

"It's only been a few months," he said cautiously, while half his brain screamed, *No, stop. Think!*

"Oh, no, don't do this to me!" Grief thickened her voice. "I *won't* let you do this to me. I won't hope again, only to lose it. I *can't.*"

"But—"

"No!" She whirled, looking wildly around. "Damn it, there's not even anything left here to *break.* Stupid, useless ruin of a house!"

"So take it out on me."

"What?" She rounded on him.

"Take it out on me." He spread his coat, leaving his midsection, covered only by a thin layer of gray woven wool, exposed. "Pretend I'm the doc, pretend I'm fate, pretend I'm whatever or whoever wronged you."

"Don't be ridiculous."

"Too late." He *was* ridiculous, ridiculously lost in her, hurting for her, so much so that he'd rather she hurt him, if it would take some of it from her. "Hit me."

"Don't think I won't," she warned him, her eyes narrowing.

"Do it."

Though he'd urged her on, it still caught him by surprise. Her fist flew, dead square into his belly. He swallowed his grunt, forcing his face into impassive lines. If she saw any hint of hurt in his expression, she would quit and be sorry for the blow. "Is that all the harder you can hit? You're such a girl."

She filled her cheeks with air, blew it out in a torrid gust. This time she wound up, drawing her arm back and cocking it like an arrow before letting it fly. He tensed his stomach in preparation, absorbed the blow as he longed to absorb her pain. "Come on."

She thrust out her lip in concentration, drew her fist even farther back, and rammed it forward.

And froze an inch before impact, her small fist wavering in the air, her breath bellowing in and out. Then slowly, very slowly, she unfolded her fingers and spread them wide. And then she moved that last small inch, pressing her palm flat against his belly.

"I have a better idea." She rotated her hand, a slow stroke against him. "Make me forget."

Chapter 25

Men arrived throughout that evening, some-times alone, a few times in twos. Too-thin men, stoop-shouldered as if they carried an enor-mous burden—which Kate supposed they did—all dressed too lightly for the weather, their clothes thin and fraying, wet to the knee. They came in with their heads bowed, their faces raw-red with the cold, and their eyes lit with tentative hope. None came empty-handed. Their offerings were modest—a bit of cake, a small tart, a pot of jelly. Sometimes only a few sticks for the fireplace, but always something.

Kate stayed out of the way. They weren't the least bit interested in her, only the new earl. So she explored the ruin of the manor, poking her nose into endless, devastated rooms, trying and failing to imagine what it might have looked like in good repair. Trying

harder, and failing at that, too, to imagine what Jim
might have been like, young, headstrong, laughing,
running through the halls and tumbling into trouble.

Now and then she couldn't resist peeking in. Jim
seemed to be doing more listening than talking, his
head bent their way, nodding encouragement, his
face intent. She snatched a word here and there: *seed,
irrigation, breeding stock, repairs.*

Late in the day, as the sun slid rapidly down the
sky, the snow turning blue as twilight, she came down
the stairs to discover him standing in the foyer by the
tall, arched, broken-out window, unmindful of the
cold that gusted through, staring down the length of
the long driveway as yet another man trudged away.

"Jim?"

"Hmm?" he responded, automatic, distracted.

"How are the roads?" she asked as she came up beside him.

"A bloody mess." For the first time in weeks, he
didn't slip his arm around her as she stood near. So
she did it for him, resting against his side, sliding her
own arm around his waist. "We have to leave in the
morning, though, no matter what the condition.
We're running out of time."

"Yes." His arm came up, heavy across her shoulders, and he sighed. She could feel the stiffness ease
from him. *Good.* "We'll make it."

"We'd better," he said with a new fervency.

"Who were all those men?"

"Tenants." The cold seeped in, through her clothes,
beneath her skirts. She ignored it. "Can't believe there
are so many of them left, but I don't suppose they had
any choice. Better a slice of tired ground, a few lousy
walls, than none at all."

And now they'd all rushed here, hoping against hope, against hundreds of years of Harrington history, that they finally had a lord who wouldn't drain every last bloody scrap from the estate, leaving them with nothing.

"You're staying, aren't you?"

Jim had felt since the day they'd headed for England that Fate had suddenly, belatedly, decided to take his life in hand. What had surprised him was not the turn of events but how little he'd fought it. He should have been kicking and railing and running for the hills.

"Yes," he said calmly. Perhaps he'd wanted this all along, a chance to make it right. He'd roamed so far and run so hard because he'd never truly thought he'd have the opportunity. He hadn't been able to save his mother, but maybe he could repair some of the damage his family had done. She would have liked that.

Kate sighed and leaned against him, quietly accepting. Oh, what a gift she'd been to him, that this *time* had been.

"I don't know if I can do it," he said. "They all believe that I can save them. *Praying* that I can save them. But it might be too late. There's almost nothing left to work with."

"There's only one thing for it, then," she said. "We'll just have to win."

They started out early, both rising while it was still dark, silent, their nerves jittering. By unspoken accord, they left nearly everything there—minutes could make all the difference now. Time to travel light.

The temperature had climbed overnight, the snow melting into a thick icy stew of mud and rapidly shrinking drifts. It was slow, hard going, taking a good twenty minutes to wind their way through the narrow band of trees and across a field to Will's house.

Will's hut.

It seemed impossible to Kate that a growing family could be living in such a place. Perhaps after seeing her sister Emily's pitiful claim shack, such things should no longer surprise her. But there were *children* here, two quiet, shy girls with brown hair who hid behind their mother's skirts and a bald-headed baby who beamed indiscriminately from her mother's arms. Too thin, all of them, but friendly and polite, and all so proud of each other it shone from their faces every time they glanced each other's way.

"You're leaving?" Will frowned and opened his mouth to argue. Earl or no earl, if Jim needed a talking-to, Will wouldn't shrink from giving it.

"Only briefly," Jim said.

"Good." Will nodded. "That's good."

The two men tramped out to the stables—Kate had glimpsed it on the way in, a roughly built shed, nearly roofless—to bridle the mare.

Jane, Will's wife, stood uneasily near the tiny hearth, her babe on her hip. "Are you hungry?" she finally asked. "I could put on some tea."

"Goodness, no. We ate better last night than we have in weeks."

Jane smiled, tentative, hinting at the loveliness she might have carried as a young woman. "We were all pleased to welcome Lord Harrington home."

"Did you know him? When he was young?"

"Oh, we all knew him." She chuckled. "Hard not to.

He was a busy child, always here or there. Trying to get out of that house, most likely."

Oh, information! Other than the bits that Jim doled out. "Can we sit?"

"Of course." She rushed to pull out a chair by the small, scarred table.

"You too." At Jane's dubious look, Kate continued: "He may have a title, whether he wishes it or not, but I assure you I have none beyond *Mrs.* Please, join me."

She slid into a chair. "It's good to get off my feet," she admitted. Behind her, the little girls clattered pots together in a corner that served as the kitchen. The baby sat happily on her lap, stuffing her fist in her mouth.

"May I?" Kate asked, holding out her arms. She could either avoid it completely, or enjoy what she *could* have. She was going with the second option. Why not begin now?

Jane blinked in surprise. "Certainly."

The baby was light, swan's-down light, looking curiously up from her new perch. Her skin was perfect, her hair just a few tufts of near white.

"You do that well," Jane commented.

"I've nephews, a niece." From the robust appearance of her new brother-in-law, Emily would give her one or two more in the near future as well. And she would spend far more time with them all from now on, she vowed, pride be damned, and her sisters would just have to put up with her. "So what was Jim like as a child?"

Jane smiled knowingly. *Ah, so that's the way of it.* "Serious, for all that he seemed to be constantly bumping into trouble. *Kind.*"

Kate was being horribly obvious. She couldn't help it. "And his mother?"

"Ah, there was a quiet one. Sometimes you'd hardly know she was there for all she was a countess."

"His father? Did she love him?"

Jane frowned, her brow furrowing. "What's to say about that man? She had a fortune, he had a title, their fathers wanted the marriage. That's often the way of it, isn't it?"

Kate was no stranger to marriages that were more business transactions than bonds of the heart. So why did hearing it now bother her so much? But it did, coiling in her chest until she had to hug the babe to ease it.

"So she didn't love him."

"Who could? The man was—" She shook her head. "I shouldn't speak ill of the dead."

"Jane. Please," Kate said, making no attempt to hide the fact that there was far more than mere curiosity behind her probing.

Jane studied her carefully and then nodded. "All right then. Evil is not too strong a word for him—for the lot of them, really, all the earls up to this one. Have to say he got what he deserved, damn near blowing his own head off because he was too sotted to hold his hunting rifle the right way."

"And his mother's death?" she asked, almost afraid of the answer. Could his father have done something like that? It didn't seem beyond him, from what she was hearing about the man. If only she could call him back and take that rifle to him herself.

"Oh, now there was a sad one. I was young, you understand, but that didn't mean I couldn't hear what was whispered about it." Her expression pinched. "A sudden fever, it was. Over in a matter of days. But my mum always figured that the countess just couldn't bring herself to fight it any more than she'd ever been able to fight him."

"And his—"

The door slammed inward, startling them both, a quick squall of protest from the baby. Will charged in, Jim slung, belly-down, over his shoulder like a sack of grain.

"What happened?" Kate came to her feet in a rush, forgetting the baby in her arms who, startled, began to cry until her mother took her and shushed her.

"Got bit by a spider," Will said, dumping Jim on his bed below the window. Jim sprawled there, arms wide and limp, out cold.

"But . . ." She ran to his side, unable to catch enough air to form the words, her mouth opening, closing, without bringing in any air. "There aren't any poisonous spiders in England."

"Not for most people, no. But he never could be like most people," Will said. Jane took charge, handing the baby to her husband, bending over Jim, touching his brow, the side of his neck. "He always reacts like this—"

"Oh, hush, Will, you're scaring the girl." Jane straightened, hands on her hips, casting him a disapproving glance. "He'll be fine. His pulse is fast, his breath a bit labored. Stomach cramps, I'd wager, which I'll be giving him something for when he wakes up. A few hours rest and he'll be perking up. By tomorrow morning he'll be good as new, though I've not got high hopes about keeping him in bed that long."

"I . . ." Kate reached down and laid her own hand against his neck, needing to feel for herself. Just as Jane promised, his pulse was strong and steady, if quick, his throat warm, sturdily alive. But the way his chest pulled in and out . . . he coughed, hard enough to double him over, although he didn't wake. She bent a hard gaze on Jane, demanding the truth. "You're sure he's going to be all right?"

Jane nodded solemnly. "I promise."

Kate longed to plop right down on the edge of the bed and stand watch, measuring every breath Jim took. If something happened to him . . . her own heart nearly seized in her chest. She wouldn't consider it. She couldn't.

"Hmm." *A few hours, a few hours . . .* She glanced around the tiny cottage, more patches than wall, shredded blankets pinned over the windows. She thought of Harrington, the ruin they'd just left, and all those men who came to welcome him home. *A few hours.*

And she thought of Jim and what she knew he'd say if he could.

"Will," she said firmly. "Where's Jim's pack?"

The Hawk's Tower, Jim had told her, was built on the highest spot along the entire Sussex coast by the long-ago Marquess of Hawksbury, who liked to look down on all his neighbors. There was no other use for it, a slender column of stone perched on top of a cliff. It looked as if it might blow out to sea at any time, though it had stood for nearly three hundred years.

The small mare proved game, plodding steadily through the sloppy roads. Thank goodness they'd discussed their plans that morning. The tower was precisely where Jim had told her it would be, visible tall and sharp above the trees long before she reached it.

She was not the first one to arrive. A cluster of horses stomped to the right of the tower, a lone one tethered to a tree at the left. *Hurry, hurry.* She swung her leg over and slid off her mount, yanking off the coat that had felt good when she set out but had become far too heavy with the exertion and the sun.

Those who'd come before her had churned up the soft earth around the base. Kate skidded in the mud, nearly going down as she picked her way across the open ground, her heart beating faster, for no matter how much she hurried it didn't seem fast enough.

Up close, the tower seemed taller, forcing a painful bend in her neck as she looked up, and up. Thank heavens she wasn't going up there. *Beneath it lies the jewel . . .*

There was no one about as she hurriedly searched the ground at the base of the tower—oh, but her shoes were done for, the mud oozing in the seams. Had they found the clue already? Inside, too, the packed earth floor completely bare, no hint of anything buried beneath.

"Damn." It couldn't be easy, could it? Of course not.

She sidled up to the edge of the cliff—too much sea, too much sky. Too easy to sweep her right over it.

She took a deep breath—why was that supposed to help?—and looked down. *Way* down.

The chalky white cliffs fell away from her feet, the angle brutally sharp. Two ropes, looped around trees at the edge of the clearing, trailed over the edge. Far below curved a thin half-moon of beach, enclosed by two long arms of rock that ran out to sea.

People crawled over the beach, at least a half dozen. Off shore a boat headed in, carrying two figures who pulled hard on their oars. Even as she watched the current caught them, carrying them out to sea as they flailed wildly at the water with their oars.

A shout drifted up to her. Below her the people broke into a run, converging on a spot near the shoreline.

All right. They'd found it. That, at least, took any choice from her.

She briefly considered using one of the ropes already in place. They'd already held someone on the way down; they'd hold her. But their owners would soon be on the way up. If they pulled the ropes up while she was below she'd be stranded.

The trees looked too flexible to satisfy her, so she wound the rope from Jim's pack around the tower itself. Twice, because Jim had always told her that caution was not fear but wisdom. And then she worried over the knot he'd taught her until she heard distant hoofbeats on the road. She couldn't let anyone else get ahead of her, there were too many there already.

She didn't look down. Didn't look anywhere, except at her precious rope, her hands frozen around it.

The sun might have set as she inched her way down the cliff face, her feet planted against the wall as he'd taught her, her skirts rucked up around her thighs. It took forever. And yet she was surprised when she finally hit the bottom—on her rump, because she hadn't checked to see how close she was. She groaned and scrambled to her feet, her hands burning, the muscles of her arms trembling.

She spun and hit chest. A very solid one at that.

"Jim!" She blinked, wondering if fatigue could spur hallucinations of senses other than sight. He'd felt very real. "You're supposed to be in bed!"

He looked a little pale, a color reminiscent of the cliff beneath his tan, his hair clinging damply to his temples. But he stood steadily, smiling at her. "No fun without you," he said.

"Are you sure you're all right?"

"Good as new."

"Good. Remind me to tell you how stupid you are later, when we've time to do it properly." If she hadn't thought he might tip right over she'd have slugged him. "Did you just watch while I dangled there?"

"Well, part of the time I was climbing down, too." His smile widened. "You were doing just fine. Didn't want to interfere."

"Right past me?"

"Well . . . yes."

She tried to scowl at him. He deserved it. But try as she might, the frown kept turning the other way. "Don't we have a clue to find?"

He held up a curl of paper. "Done."

Had it taken her *that* long to crawl down that stupid cliff? "Where are we going?"

"London."

Thank God, she thought. No cliffs in London. "Where in London?"

"Big Ben."

"I don't think I can do it," she said moments later, her hand on the rope, the vast, sharp cliff rising above her. "My arms are still shaking."

"That's why I'll be right behind you."

"So we *both* can fall?"

"Oh, it'll hold us. I checked the knot on yours before I came down another rope. Good job, by the way."

"But—"

"Move it, Kate." He whacked her on the rump. "I didn't put up with you for all this time to lose."

Going up was easier than down. How could it not be, with Jim right behind her, murmuring encouragement, ready to catch her if she slipped. Gasping, she hauled herself over the edge and lay there for a minute until Jim stood over her and extended a hand to help her up.

"I'm not dead," she said, too tired to be more than vaguely surprised.

"Nope."

He pulled her to her feet.

"Who . . ." She started toward the figure she glimpsed kneeling near the ledge at the edge of the trees, breaking into a run when she saw who it was. "What the hell are you doing?"

Knife halfway through the rope, Hobson glanced up at her, then did a double take. "Miss Riley. You look . . . different."

She didn't care if she looked like Medusa. "*What* are you doing?"

His head jerked back at her tone. Then he shrugged. "There are two competitors still down there. Two ropes. With one less . . . it'll get more interesting. Oh, don't worry!" He held up a hand, all friendly innocence. "There's no one on there now. I checked."

"Well, wasn't that ever so thoughtful of you."

"The major," Jim said from behind her, "in France he insisted that not everything had been his fault. I didn't believe him at the time. But some of the sabotage was you, wasn't it?"

"Oh, no . . ." He saw their expressions and gave up, smiling tentatively. "I didn't do anything dangerous, I swear. Or anything to favor one competitor over another. None of the really bad stuff. That *was* all the major. I just . . . spiced things up a little bit. For the readers."

"Our boat?" Kate asked softly.

"Well, yeah." His careful smile turned into a leer, nasty and knowing. "But maybe you should thank me for that one, eh, Lord Bennett? I—"

She hit him. Square and sure on his nose. He howled, bringing his hands to his face, eyes screwed shut against the pain. Kate leaned forward to ensure he'd hear her. "Thank you," she whispered. Then she straightened, turning to Jim. "You got a horse?"

"Yup," Jim said carefully, battling a smile. Lord only knew what Kate might do if he smiled at her now. He pointed at the beautiful, long-legged roan.

"Where'd you—oh, never mind." She grabbed his arm, dragging him toward the horses. "Let's go find a clock."

Chapter 26

~~~~~~~~~~ ✎ ~~~~~~~~~~

They ran into trouble ten miles from London. The roads were still sloppy, slick with icy mud, but that apparently hadn't kept anyone home. Traffic clogged the roads—horses, people on foot, coaches with revelers hanging out the windows. Grand carriages pulled by matched teams, their drivers in glorious livery shouting for space ahead, had no more luck in parting the crowds than the gangs of laughing young men who'd obviously already tipped deeply into their flasks, starting the New Year's celebration a day early.

Kate and Jim picked their way along the edges of the crowds, swinging wide, until finally forced to a dead stop. Up ahead they could see a large carriage, side-tipped, people swarming around to see what had happened.

They'd been moving too slowly as it was, tense and impatient with every delay but unable to go any faster. It promised only to get worse the nearer they got to London.

"We have to go cross country," Jim said.

Twin hedgerows marched along the road, so thick nothing wider than a rabbit could push its way through, nearly as high as Kate's head. She eyed the leggy gelding Jim had managed to procure and his practiced management of it.

"Go ahead," she said. "We'll never make it over the first jump."

"I can't leave you here alone."

"Of course you can," she said, and waved her fist, showing the knuckles that had scraped against Hobson's face, her badge of victory. "Just let anyone try to accost me. I'm getting rather good at it, don't you think?"

"The best," he said, a note in his voice that had her looking at him closely, trying to read the expression in his eyes. He studied the mob in front of them, the limited paths around it. "Come up with me," he said. "I think the horse can manage."

"You'll be faster without me. Safer, too, and you know it."

She would never forget the way he looked right then. Bareheaded, hair tossed by the breeze, jacket and collar open. Sitting tall and correct on the horse, controlling it skillfully, his strong hands every bit as expert at other things. She had so many memories of him now, ones that made a youthful kiss under the moonlight pale. Stronger ones, *real* ones. Ones without a gauzy veil of innocence, ones with heat and grit and *hurt*, ones that lived in your heart and bones instead of your imagination.

"It doesn't seem right," he said, "to finish it without you."

"You're not finishing without me. You're *winning* it, for both of us."

He nodded, accepting. And leaned down to press his mouth against hers, the horses shifting so that their lips didn't fit quite right but he just kept kissing her anyway, making it work, hard and long, unbearably sweet. She felt the burn of it—her lips, her eyes, her heart, so that when he finally pulled back she had to bite her lip to keep the tears from gathering.

"Jim, I . . ."

"Yeah," he said softly. "Me too." He backed his gelding up a couple of steps and wheeled him around, aiming for a slight gap between the sweets vendor who'd set up at the side of the road and the ostensibly blind beggar who'd plopped down right there, tin cup at his side.

"The Queen's Arms Hotel, near Regent Street," he said. He tapped his heels against the horse's side, they sailed over the hedge, and were gone.

They'd won. Kate had read about it in the newspaper she'd bought from a vendor very early that morning, when she, unable to sleep, had stumbled out of her modest inn looking for tea.

There was no triumph in it and even less surprise. She'd known he would win.

Now, five minutes before midnight, Kate huddled on a narrow bench beside the Thames. Revelers crowded the walkways beside her, shifting crowds of happy people, chattering, laughing. Clusters of boats drifted on the Thames, oarsmen shouting cheerfully at each other as they jostled for a better view. Somewhere an orchestra played, the sound swelling and sliding, underlaid by a sprightly, military rhythm. Across the river someone had fashioned electric lights in the shape of an hourglass. Every few seconds another one blinked off from the upper cluster, lighting up on the bottom a second later. Lights, wavering, indistinct, reflected on the water.

She was cold. Far colder than the weather dictated.

Tomorrow, she thought. Tomorrow she would get on a ship and go . . . not home, where was that? But back to America, where she could begin the process of making one.

It had taken every ounce of self-control she could dredge up, and then some, not to sprint to the Queen's Arms. Once that afternoon, a light drizzle falling, the sky as dark and gray as her mood, she'd faltered, going to stand across from the inn and gaze hungrily at its façade. There, that window, where the light glowed cheerily . . . was that his room? Perhaps that one, dark, the curtains drawn, where he lay in bed and rested from the race, waiting for her.

It seemed such a small thing. What was one more night? She'd slept with him countless times; what harm could one more do? Except it would not be only one more, for she knew in her bones that she simply could not say good-bye to him again.

She'd no idea how long she'd stood there. It was only when a butcher, sturdy belly wrapped in a dark-stained apron, wandered from his shop to ask if she was all right that she moved on, shaking her head at the absurdity of it. She, Kathryn Bright Goodale, standing love-sick in the street drinking in the sight of where he might, *might*, be. Was it something that everyone must do at some point in their lives, be stupid in the name of love, and since she'd skipped it in her youth she was visited with it now, twice over? She'd hailed a cab and gone straight to the office to buy her ticket to America.

Across the river a spark shot skyward, whistling as it climbed, fizzling to almost nothing. And then it burst, a cluster of bright blue-green, cascading almost into the river. Proper appreciation from the crowd: *oooh, aaah.* The imprint of the fireworks remained in her retinas for a moment; she saw them streaking, sparkling, when she blinked.

The crowd fell silent, waiting, but the sky remained dark. Perhaps someone had made a mistake, firing one off prematurely. It was as if the world held its breath, waiting for the new century.

It was terribly unfair, Kate thought, that Fate had asked this of her. For in the same stroke that might have given Jim to her, the inheritance that finally tied him to one place, one home, had stripped him from her at the same time. It had laid out his future and responsibilities in front of him, undeniably clear: a wife who would supply a dowry that could restore the earldom and give him the sons that would carry it on, wisely and responsibly this time. She could do neither.

She closed her eyes. The vestiges of the single explosion still speared across the inside of her lids.

Something dropped into her lap. A package, medium-sized—smaller than a hatbox—but heavier, wrapped in plain paper, wound round and around with twine, tied with at least a dozen clumsy knots.

"You forgot something."

Don't look at him, she told herself. If she looked at him, she'd be lost. Lightly, she fingered the string.

He'd tied it not long ago, probably struggled with it and swore as he did so. "I didn't forget. Your tenants, all those repairs . . . they need the money more than I do. I don't want it."

"Try again."

"I don't want it much." One of the knots gave way, unraveling in her fingers. "I knew we'd work it out. That you'd insist on sending me something. But I couldn't take much. I *won't*. Consider it an investment in your business, if you must. You can pay me back."

"In about fifty or sixty years."

Oh, go away. Please, don't make me do this. I can't.
"Then there'll be plenty of interest, won't there?"

He sat down beside her. Too close, shoulders brushing, left hip pressed against her right one, so vibrantly aware of the contact she thought it must glow between them, white hot, visible to those who wandered by.

"That wasn't what I meant," he said. "What you forgot."

A whistle, a crimson spark arcing through the sky. This one was a dud, fizzling out before it bloomed.

"You forgot me."

Oh, God. "I didn't forget." *I'll never forget.*

"Kate." And again, a full minute later, when the crowds murmured restlessly and she hadn't moved: "Kate."

He was going to make her. Make her with his patient voice and the warmth of his body next to hers on the cold bench and his unignorable, beloved presence. She turned her head, a slow swivel she couldn't have halted any more than she could have willed her heart to stop beating.

He wore solid black, severe, ruthless. Bareheaded—

one would think a man who'd been to the Arctic would have learned the value of covering his head—hair mussed, as if he hadn't taken the time to comb it, eyes shadowed, nearly as dark as the sky.

More fireworks must have gone off. She didn't hear them, only saw the flicker of the lights across his face: red, blue, gold.

"I wasn't going to ask you," he said. "Told myself it was for the best. *Your* best."

The crowd roared. The sound came to her dimly, as if from very far away. Shut up, she wanted to shout at them. Shut up, because she had to hear, breathe in, every single word he spoke, each whisper, each nuance.

"And then I thought, who am I to decide that for you?" He smiled gently. "You'd break *my* nose if I presumed to do that."

A shower of sparks, dazzle-bright, violet as midnight, reflected in his eyes. "And so I'm asking you, Kate, what I should have asked a long time ago. On the boat, in Maine, the minute you walked in my door. I love you, Kate. Marry me."

"Jim—" Applause erupted, drowned out her answer.

"No, not yet. Don't answer me yet. You have to understand. The money we won is barely a start. There's so much to be done and the house has to come last. It *has* to, they've waited so long. It could be years before we even begin on the manor. Hell, it could be never. I'm going to be working, more like a farmer than a lord. You deserve better."

She almost turned it back on him. Spoke of titles and dowries, duty and babies. But he knew all that, knew it even better than she did. If he could trust her to know her own mind and heart, how could she do less for him?

"Do I?" she murmured. The world erupted in celebration around them, church bells clanging all over London, ringing in the New Year. People cheered, shouted, laughed, kissed. The last electric sand dropped through the lighted hourglass. Fireworks spangled the sky, a dozen explosions at once, two dozen, every color spearing into the next until they blazed and fell together, a million colored stars tumbling to earth. And all that wild celebration, a city, a *world* of welcome and joy, was nothing compared to the way she'd felt when Jim said "I love you."

"I want the best," she said. "I want you."

Chapter 27

Harrington had a chapel, built even before the current manor house, a small stone structure tucked beneath the boughs of an extraordinary chestnut tree at the far end of what had once been the gardens. It was in no better shape than the rest of the estate, the windows broken out, the pews and altar gone, half the roof slates missing. But there was an undeniable romance to the place, in its perfectly cut beige stones, the soaring roof, the vines that twined over the entrance.

Jim had suggested the village church. It was February, after all, and the chapel would likely be cold. But Kate insisted. If she were to be the new countess of Harrington—oh, how odd that sounded!—she would be married in Harrington's chapel.

Though it certainly did not seem the wedding of a

367

countess. Her first wedding had been quick and businesslike, in a judge's chambers, though her dress had been lovely, her jewelry expensive. She'd always assumed if she married again, it would be a grand affair, months in the planning, yards of silk and bouquets that speared toward the roof of a cathedral.

Instead this wedding seemed like it might have belonged to one of the estate's tenants rather than its lord.

Luckily the day was warm, soft for February, carrying hints of spring on a gentle breeze. So the guests—the tenants, dressed in their best, which no one but they would have known was so—made do with only light outergarments instead of the piles of blankets and coats that Jim had feared. They'd brought their own seats to the empty chapel, benches and chairs dragged from the nearest cottages, for the manor house itself was still barren of any furniture except the good bed its owner had insisted upon.

There were no flowers in the church. No frilly curls of ribbon, no trailing swags of silk, no glittering silver.

But there were candles, dozens of them, lumpy and homemade, some mere stubs, contributed by everyone. On every windowsill, flickering; lining the two stone steps that led up to the nave, a huge cluster of them glowing on the small wooden table that would serve as an altar. Their light filled the little church, a warm glow that turned the buff stone walls to gold.

All those candles gave the women no end of trouble as they tried to keep the children that squirmed and whispered and giggled and crawled all over the place out of the way of the flames, a happy chatter more festive than any organ chords.

There was no new gown for the bride. No jewels, no hair dressed in cascades of curls. Kate had spent nearly two weeks making over her dress—she'd had plenty of time, for Jim, true to his word, had been working so hard that she rarely saw him except late at night when he, bone tired, had tumbled into bed. That was fine with her; she understood the necessity of it, and besides, he always made it up to her when he did come home.

The orchid silk was stripped of lace, cut in perfectly severe, elegant lines. It barely clung to her shoulders, sweeping low over her bosom, adorned with nothing but glowing skin. Long sleeves, cut tight, ending in sharp points at the back of her hands; a bodice that hugged her curves; a luscious swoop of skirt that swept the ground in back. Her one indulgence had been a spool of silver thread and she'd put it to good use, embroidering sweeping swirls, great curving loops that glittered in the candlelight. She'd swept her hair straight back and pinned it in a simple twist that had taken all of three minutes to arrange.

Everyone said they'd never seen a more beautiful bride.

The groom would be wearing black and a sling, support for the shoulder injury he'd sustained two days before by sliding off the slick roof he'd been fixing on one of his tenant's cottages.

He was also late.

Jane leaned over to Kate, who was standing at the front of the church. "Do you want me to send Will after him?"

"Oh, he'll be here," Kate said serenely. He'd be here, and soon, or he'd be dealing with the consequences, something which Kate was sure the man understood.

And then he was there, charging down the makeshift aisle at an indecorous pace, a giant fistful of roses clutched in his good hand.

"Here," he said, panting, as he reached her, and thrust the bouquet at her. There were at least two dozen, wildly out of season, all colors—peach, pink, red, yellow—that should have clashed but instead looked utterly lovely together, their petals perfect, just opening, clouds of scent rising from them. The stems were uneven, stripped of their thorns, tied loosely—lopsided—together with a thin band of white ribbon.

"You shouldn't have—" She stopped, buried her nose in them to take in the smell. "Where did you . . . I know, I know you have your ways."

"That I do." And then he bent and kissed her, slow and sweet, as if they were the only two people in the room.

The vicar harrumphed and tapped Jim on the shoulder. "We haven't reached that part yet."

They broke apart, but only a bit, smiling into each other's eyes, the bouquet between them.

"We object!"

An instant later Kate shoved the flowers back at Jim and sprinted down the aisle, the pale purple silk floating behind her.

"We're not to that part yet, either," the clergyman said.

Kate hurled herself at the two women who'd just entered, squeezing one in each arm, hanging on for dear life. Jim bounded after her.

He would have pegged them as her sisters immediately, Jim decided, even if her reaction hadn't given it away. The brown-haired one had to be Anthea, a plain slip of a woman frowning at him over Kate's shoulder.

The other one was taller, slighter, the color of her hair somewhere between the others', younger and more conventionally pretty, though certainly no competition for Kate. Emily. Still, there was something in the set of their eyes, the curve of their mouths, that marked them as sisters.

The three finally disentangled themselves and faced him, clasping hands. Emily beamed at him, heart as open as her expression, while Anthea, free hand on her hip, regarded him like a schoolteacher might a rambunctious student.

"We object," she said, "because we refuse to have another Bright wedding without the rest of us there."

"That's right," Emily said. "Couldn't you have waited until we got here?"

"Ah, well . . ." Kate grinned at Jim, because she still couldn't believe it, though she'd been losing her breakfast for three weeks. "No, we really couldn't wait."

"Oh!" Emily squealed and launched herself at Jim, so hard he took a step back. He wrapped his arm around her automatically, the flowers drooping at her back, his shoulder pulling painfully. Over the top of her head he caught sight of Anthea, who he fully expected to be scowling at him with sisterly disapproval but who was smiling at him instead, a smile that transformed her face, her slight resemblance to Kate suddenly pronounced.

"We'd best get you married, then, musn't we?" she said, and herded them all back to the front. And so Kate said her vows with her sisters by her side. Emily sniffled. Anthea deftly rescued the roses when Kate's hands shook so hard that Jim had to take them in his to still them.

Halfway through the vows, Will and Jane's middle daughter, three-year-old Gwen, who'd taken a liking to Jim, decided to attach herself to his leg and remained there for the rest of the ceremony. And then the groom, who'd been so steady the entire time, stumbled over the last lines of the vows and had to ask the reverend to repeat them three times before he finally got them out. And if both the bride and groom cried a little—maybe more than a little—the guests all decided it would be better not to mention that small point. Especially since more than one of them were a bit misty themselves.

Everyone, including the new Earl and Countess of Harrington, agreed.

The wedding—and the marriage—was perfect.

Epilogue

In October, 1900, Wilcox & Sons, Publishers, New York City, printed the first edition of *The Jewel of Balthelay: Inside the Mysterious, Rich, and Unknown World of the Prince of Balthelay*, by Mahsi and Jonathan Duffy. It sold out in three weeks and went on to seven more printings.

Author's Note

Edward Whymper was the first man to scale the slopes of Mount Chimborazo in 1879, a feat the author borrowed to attribute to Baron von Hussman.

The island nation of Balthelay and the towns of Shorehampton and Hollingport are fictional.

Romance is always better with Avon Books . . . look for these crowd pleasers in November

THE PLEASURE OF HER KISS by Linda Needham
An Avon Romantic Treasure

The Earl of Hawkesly exchanged wedding vows with a woman he barely knew, then left her to play the spy for his country. Now two years later, he's ready to perform his much neglected husbandly duties . . . except Kate doesn't recognize him! He may have met his match in this spirited woman, and it will take a special seduction to win her heart.

A THOROUGHLY MODERN PRINCESS by Wendy Corsi Staub
An Avon Contemporary Romance

Her Highness, Emmaline of Verdunia, would have wed her suitable prince and be done with it—if she hadn't been swept off her feet by Granger Lockwood IV, "America's Sexiest Single Man." Now she's hurtling across the Atlantic in the private jet of the surprised playboy . . . and falling in love with the last man she could ever marry!

TO TEMPT A BRIDE by Edith Layton
An Avon Romance

From the moment she first saw tall, dashing Eric Ford, Camille's heart was lost. But Eric seems content to be no more than her unofficial protector, watching over the younger sister of his dear friend. When danger and betrayal threaten, will it destroy a secret love . . . or bind two hearts for all eternity?

WICKEDLY YOURS by Brenda Hiatt
An Avon Romance

The *ton* is abuzz over the arrival of Sarah Killian, a stunning stranger who shrouds her past in mystery. And no one is more intrigued than Lord Peter Northrup. The handsome rake wants to know *everything* about this beauty who has so enflamed his desire. But the enchantress guards her secrets well, even as she pulls him into a world of danger any self-respecting gentleman would be well advised to avoid.

REL 1003

Avon Romantic Treasures

*Unforgettable, enthralling love stories,
sparkling with passion and adventure
from Romance's bestselling authors*

WHEN IT'S PERFECT   *by Adele Ashworth*
0-380-81807-8/$5.99 US/$7.99 Can

THE IRRESISTIBLE MACRAE   *by Karen Ranney*
0-380-82105-2/$5.99 US/$7.99 Can

CAPTURED INNOCENCE   *by Susan Sizemore*
0-06-008289-5/$5.99 US/$7.99 Can

BORN IN SIN   *by Kinley MacGregor*
0-380-81790-X/$5.99 US/$7.99 Can

CONFESSIONS OF A SCOUNDREL   *by Karen Hawkins*
0-380-82080-3/$5.99 US/$7.99 Can

DANCE OF SEDUCTION   *by Sabrina Jeffries*
0-06-009213-0/$5.99 US/$7.99 Can

LONDON'S PERFECT SCOUNDREL *by Suzanne Enoch*
0-380-82083-8/$5.99 US/$7.99 Can

LOVE WITH A SCANDALOUS LORD *by Lorraine Heath*
0-380-81743-8/$5.99 US/$7.99 Can

STEALING THE BRIDE   *by Elizabeth Boyle*
0-380-82090-0/$5.99 US/$7.99 Can

TO LOVE A SCOTTISH LORD   *by Karen Ranney*
0-380-82106-0/$5.99 US/$7.99 Can

Available wherever books are sold or please call 1-800-331-376
to order.   RT 050

AVON TRADE... because every great bag
deserves a great book!

Elizabeth Jenns

A Girl's
Best Friend

Paperback $13.95
ISBN 0-06-056277-3

USA Today bestselling author of *I'm Better, For Worse*
CAROLE MATTHEWS

BARE
NECESSITY

"A FUN AND THOROUGHLY ENJOYABLE TALE"—*Marie Claire* (UK)

Paperback $13.95
ISBN 0-06-053214-9
Audio $18.95
ISBN 0-06-055710-9

The Accidental Virgin

Valerie Frankel

Paperback $13.95
($21.95 Can.)
ISBN 0-06-093841-2

does she or
doesn't she?
Alisa Kwitney

Paperback $13.95
($21.95 Can.)
ISBN 0-06-051237-7

Love and a
Bad Hair Day
A Novel

Annie Flannigan

Paperback $13.95
($21.95 Can.)
ISBN 0-380-81936-8

The Second
Coming of
Lucy Hatch

MARSHA MOYER

Paperback $13.95
($21.95 Can.)
ISBN 0-06-008166-X

Don't miss the next book by your favorite author.
Sign up for AuthorTracker by visiting *www.AuthorTracker.com*.

Available wherever books are sold, or call 1-800-331-3761 to order.

ATP 1003

Avon Romances—
the best in exceptional authors
and unforgettable novels!

A NECESSARY BRIDE   by Debra Mullins
0-380-81909-0/ $5.99 US/ $7.99 Can

TO WED A STRANGER   by Edith Layton
0-06-050217-7/ $5.99 US/ $7.99 Can

ONCE HE LOVES   by Sara Bennett
0-06-051970-3/ $5.99 US/ $7.99 Can

A SCANDALOUS LADY   by Rachelle Morgan
0-06-008470-7/ $5.99 US/ $7.99 Can

KISS ME QUICK   by Margaret Moore
0-06-052620-3/ $5.99 US/ $7.99 Can

CHEROKEE WARRIORS:
THE LONER   by Genell Dellin
0-06-000147-X/ $5.99 US/ $7.99 Can

THE CRIMSON LADY   by Mary Reed McCall
0-06-009770-1/ $5.99 US/ $7.99 Can

TO MARRY THE DUKE   by Julianne MacLean
0-06-052704-8/ $5.99 US/ $7.99 Can

SOARING EAGLE'S EMBRACE   by Karen Kay
0-380-82067-6/ $5.99 US/ $7.99 Can

THE PRINCESS AND HER PIRATE by Lois Greiman
0-06-050282-7/ $5.99 US/ $7.99 Can

ONCE A SCOUNDREL   by Candice Herns
0-06-050563-X/ $5.99 US/ $7.99 Can

ALL MEN ARE ROGUES   by Sari Robins
0-06-050354-8/ $5.99 US/ $7.99 Can

....

Available wherever books are sold or please call 1-800-331-3761
to order.   ROM 0603